A B A N D O N E D

ABANDONED

a novel

JENNIE
HANSEN

Covenant Communications, Inc.

Cover image from Eyewire Collection/Getty Images.

Cover design copyrighted 2002 by Covenant Communications, Inc.

Published by Covenant Communications, Inc.
American Fork, Utah

Printed in Canada
First Printing: August 2002

09 08 07 06 05 04 03   10 9 8 7 6 5 4 3 2

ISBN 1-59156-070-5

Dedication

This book is dedicated to the sisters I acquired by marriage: Carol, Patsy, ZoAnn, Mavis, Suzanne, LaRee, and Nancy. You're the best!

PROLOGUE

"If Pa catches you, he'll beat you."

"I know." She gave a fearful glance toward the door. Pa was gone; she'd seen him drive away. She turned back to her search of the boxes and cans littering the table. She picked up a Styrofoam cup, and when she tilted it toward her mouth, not a drop drained from it.

"Ain't nothin' there," Darren taunted her.

"Sometimes Josie . . ." The little girl's longing gaze moved without much hope around the cramped, dark kitchen. "Aren't you hungry?" she asked.

"Naw, Pa gave me some bread." His smug expression told her he was lying. Her eye caught a glint of purple in the overflowing trash can. It was a napkin from that place where Josie worked. Hope flared, then died. Pa hadn't given Darren anything. Josie had left a roll for each of them on the little purple napkins like she sometimes did when she came home really late, and Darren had eaten both of them!

Taking a furious swing at her brother, she felt the chair where she stood begin to topple. An involuntary scream left her throat while she clutched at the table for support, sending bottles and cans crashing to the floor. The cracked linoleum rose up to meet her in a burst of pain, and on some level she was aware of the chair landing noisily behind her. Holding her hands over her ears, she tried to shut out the sound of Darren's laughter.

"Shut up!" she screamed. The sound of a door opening with such force that it crashed against a wall brought his laughter to a sudden halt. Both children froze, then slowly turned their fearful eyes toward the door leading to the interior of the house. Momma stood framed in the doorway. The clingy, cotton shirt she wore hung off one shoulder, and her pale hair jutted out from her head in every direction. Her eyes were red and held a frightening wildness. Her slender frame trembled with fury, scaring both children into silence. When Momma ran out of her medicine she was scarier than Pa. Struggling to her feet, the girl swallowed a yelp of pain as her bare foot came down on a twisted piece of wire lying on the garbage-strewn floor.

Swiping one hand across the table, Momma sent more of the junk flying to the far corners of the room. Unintelligible words came in a screaming torrent from her mouth, then she raised her hand. It did no good to duck. Momma's hand smacked the girl across the side of her face before she ordered both children outside. They obeyed instantly, creeping out the back door while keeping a wary eye on their raging parent. At the last minute, the little girl grabbed a pink sweater off a chair and scuttled through the open door before her brother could slam it in her face.

She made her way to an old couch that rested, minus its cushions, in the far corner of the weedy yard behind a battered Oldsmobile with no doors or tires. She sat down carefully, mindful of her bruised bottom, and stared glumly at her feet. With one hand she touched the tender spot on her face. She shrugged, dismissing the slap. She'd had worse. After a moment she remembered her sweater and pulled it on.

"Ha! Yer stupid!" Darren taunted from on top of the Oldsmobile. "It ain't cold. It's summer."

She did her best to ignore him. Her stomach gave a loud growl, and she thought about how hungry she was and how she hadn't gotten any supper last night because Pa ate it all, and because Darren ate the rolls Josie brought this morning. Being hungry was about the worst thing, she thought.

"I know where there's some food." She raised her head at Darren's statement. She knew he was lying. Darren always told lies. "The Snoots had a party last night. They don't never eat all their food. They dump what's left in that can." His finger pointed to the adjoining backyard.

She knew Darren meant the people who lived in the house next door. Snoots wasn't really their name, he just called them that because they never spoke to him. She knew which can he meant. The Snoots had a shiny, silver garbage can, not a black, stinky barrel like the one that sat beside their own house. She wondered how Darren knew about the Snoots leaving food in the garbage can. He probably snooped she decided. She remembered one time she'd seen him sitting in the dirt behind the couch, eating cake. He'd given her a taste so she wouldn't tell.

"How we gonna get it?" she asked suspiciously. She'd like some cake, but she didn't trust Darren. He might be planning to get her in trouble.

"You could climb over the fence and grab some," Darren told her. "Wrap it up in that dumb sweater and throw it over the fence to our side."

"You do it!" she told him, eyeing the chain-link fence the neighbors had recently installed. It was pretty high.

"Can't! My feet are too big," he argued. "I'll be the lookout and warn you if somebody comes."

Her stomach growled again. Maybe Darren was telling the truth. Even if he had eaten both rolls he was probably still hungry, and he was lots bigger than she was. She stood up and stared at the fence. He couldn't climb it as easily as he used to slip between the broken boards of the old fence. *He doesn't care if you get any food; he just wants you to bring some back for him,* a voice whispered somewhere in her head. She wandered closer to the fence. Her stomach growled, and she thought about cake.

"Go ahead," her brother whispered. "Don't be chicken."

She placed a tentative hand on the wire. Her stomach cramped in hunger pains. She wiggled the toes of one foot into one of the wire squares. It was a little uncomfortable, but she could stand it. Grasping the wire with her other hand, she pulled herself up, then fitted her other foot a little higher than the first. She inched her way up, thinking about cake, or maybe pizza.

At the top she encountered the sharp ends of the wires. They'd been left poking up in sharp points, instead of being neatly folded down. With extreme care she lifted one foot over the wire and maneuvered her hands to avoid touching the closely spaced points. Her heart pounding, she avoided looking down as she slowly drew her other foot over the top. She made it!

"All right!" Darren whispered encouragement from his perch atop the Oldsmobile.

She clung to the fence, breathing in and out, reminding herself she was closer to her goal. If Darren hadn't lied to her, she'd soon find something to eat.

She looked back at her yard. The weeds, the old car, even Darren shimmered in the summer heat with little wavy lines. It was hot today, and she hadn't had anything to eat since Josie gave her a roll yesterday morning. Darren motioned for her to keep going. She bent her head toward the wire and lowered one foot. A wave of dizziness made her tremble, and she thought she might throw up, only she didn't think she could throw up when she hadn't eaten anything for such a long time.

Blinking her eyes to chase away the dizziness, she prepared to lower herself a little farther. A strange sound came from beneath her, and she glanced down, straight into the gaping jaws of a huge black dog. Fear shot adrenalin to every limb of her body and sent her scrambling back over the top. Her dress caught on the wire points, ensnaring her mere inches from the snarling dog. In terror she frantically tugged at her dress until the fabric ripped, sending her plunging to the hard dirt, where she lay unable to move. Only the wire fence separated her from the dog's fearsome teeth. She could feel the animal's breath on her face as it snarled and lunged at the thin barrier separating them. Two hands grasped her arms and dragged her toward the old couch.

Slowly she regained the ability to breathe. Sitting up, she promptly leaned back against the back side of the broken piece of furniture. She felt awful, all hot and dizzy. And hungry. She could hear an awful sound like someone being sick and crying at the same time.

"Quiet!" Darren growled at her. "You got that dog all stirred up, and if he wakes Momma 'fore Pa gets back with her stuff, she'll near kill us!"

"Wasn't my fault . . ." she wheezed. "You didn't tell me 'bout the dog."

"Didn't see him till it was too late," Darren defended himself. "You shoulda hurried. You could've been back with something to eat before he came." His voice told her he mourned the loss of the meal they might have had as much as she did, and he blamed her for that loss.

"Yore dress is all tore." Darren looked at her critically.

She looked at her dress in despair. It was little more than a rag. Several pink streamers of yarn dangled from her sweater, and blood oozed from a long gash on her leg and numerous smaller scratches on her arms.

"You better get rid of that dress," Darren told her. "If Pa sees what ya done, he'll whip ya."

"Ain't got another one," she responded.

A sly look appeared on her brother's face. "I seen some big pins in Pa's toolbox."

She glanced toward the sagging structure where Pa parked his truck. It was so full of junk she wasn't sure how he got his truck in it. She never went in there. Pa said she and Darren weren't allowed in there, and she knew better than to disobey Pa, but Darren sneaked in sometimes. It wasn't fair. Darren did lots of things he was told not to, and he never got caught, but if she did one little thing bad somebody punished her.

She stood up. She was going to get punished no matter what, so she might as well get the pins. If she pinned her dress, she might get to eat before Pa found out. She marched resolutely toward the garage. Kneeling on the rotted floor, she flipped open the metal chest that held Pa's tools. Her eyes felt like they might pop out of her head and a sharp cramp in her stomach nearly doubled her over. The pins were right where Darren had said they would be, and lying beside them was a candy bar, a great big one in a yellow-and-blue wrapper, the kind that was two, short chocolate-and-peanut-butter candy bars on one long piece of stiff brown paper. Pa would kill her if she took his candy bar. He might not miss a few pins, but he'd know somebody took the candy.

She couldn't help it; she reached for the candy, then hesitated. Darren would tell on her. If she shared, he might not. Her hand shot out, and clutching the candy and a fistful of pins, she dashed to the back of the yard to hide behind the couch. Darren was already there.

Settling in the dirt beside her brother, she handed him one of the pieces of candy. Without saying a word he popped the whole thing into his mouth. When she caught him eyeing the remaining piece in her hand, she thrust it into her mouth, nearly choking for her effort, but at least he couldn't snatch it from her. She chewed, savoring the soft, melting chocolate and peanut butter, unmindful of the trickle that found its way down her chin. At last she ran her tongue around her mouth, seeking the last smidgeon of candy.

Spotting the pins lying in the dirt where she'd dropped them, she picked one up and stuck it through the worn fabric of her dress. After closing the pin, she stared critically at what she'd done. The pin showed, plain as could be. Pa would notice. With a sigh she pulled off her sweater, then her dress. She'd have to stick the pins in the back side so they wouldn't show. Catching her lower lip between her teeth, she went to work.

She'd almost finished closing the holes in her dress with safety pins when Darren swooped over the top of the couch and snatched the dress from her hands. Waving the ragged blue cloth in the air like a flag, he raced around the yard.

"Give that back!" she shouted as she charged after him, waving her sweater as though it were a weapon. He laughed and ran faster.

He stopped beneath a large tree and grinned. "Want this?" he taunted waving the dress in front of him. She lunged for it just as he tossed it into the air where it caught on a twig, high above her head. She stared at the dress in dismay.

If Darren jumped, he might . . . She turned in time to see her brother dart inside the house. The unmistakable sound of the rusty dead bolt sliding into place sounded loud in the hot summer air.

She jumped and jumped, but she couldn't reach her dress. She tried climbing the tree and only succeeded in breaking open the gash in her leg so that it bled again. At last she sat in the dirt, waiting for Darren to get tired of his game and come back outside. Even under the tree it was hot, and she fell asleep curled on her side, her head resting on the pink sweater.

"Git up!" a voice roared from nearby. Her eyes flew open and she found herself looking straight into Pa's rage-mottled face. Pa was shouting something about finding the candy bar wrapper and the evidence being all over her face as he dragged her inside the house. He said a lot of bad words about her stealing from him.

She tried to tell him how hungry she'd been, but the words wouldn't come out. Terrible pain streaked through her leg when he popped his belt across the wound on it.

"Pa, don't hurt me, please love me," she screamed, as he continued to hit her. Pain exploded inside her head. Darkness approached, but through the fog of pain she saw Darren coming.

His small fists rained blows against Pa's side. Out of his mouth came frenzied words. "Don't kill her, Pa. Fathers ain't s'posed to hurt their little girls."

Pa turned to shove Darren aside. His scream sounded in her ears, then subsided to distant whimpering. She was crying too. Momma appeared in the doorway and yelled at her to be quiet. "If you can't mind, you deserve to be whipped," her mother said before staggering back to her bed.

A quiet voice whispered inside her head, telling her to lie still, not to resist or cry, then she didn't remember anymore until Darren knelt beside her in a now dark, silent house.

"I'm sorry," he mumbled through tears, and she felt him cover her still body with the pink sweater. She didn't know how long he knelt on the cracked linoleum beside her, but he was gone when Josie bent over her, whispering for her to be quiet. "Shh! I'm home now. I'll take care of you, but we mustn't wake your pa." She could feel Josie tugging her dress on over her aching body, smoothing the sweater over the pain in her back, then lifting her in her arms.

Coolness brushed her face, and she was aware that night had come. She tensed when she heard a male voice, but Josie said something soothing, and she fell asleep again.

"What are you going to do with the kid?" A deep voice reached through the fog. She'd become aware some time ago that she was on the backseat of a car that was going fast, but it had been too much effort to call out. "I'm not doing time for kidnapping," the voice continued.

"I'll think of something," Josie's voice reached her ears. "I couldn't leave her there. That big goon nearly killed her."

"What about your sister?" the deep voice asked.

"She's nothing but a stoned-out zombie. If she ever sobers up, she'll sell the kid for her next fix." Josie's voice was flat.

"We don't need no kid holding us back. You'll have to get rid of her." The deep voice was adamant.

"I know." Josie's answer came with a sigh that sounded like regret.

"Now!" The hard voice snarled, and the car lurched to a stop. "The kid will be a dead giveaway. If we had more time we could find someone who would pay good money for a blond little girl."

"Okay! Okay! I just thought she'd help us look like a family taking a vacation or something." Josie defended her decision to bring her sister's child with them.

"You let me do the thinking," the man's voice warned Josie. His words were accompanied by the sound of a door opening.

"You don't mean to leave her out here?" Josie sounded scared.

"There's no time for anything else." Through the fog that seemed to surround her, the little girl felt herself being lifted from the car. A few moments later she was lying on the ground. Beside her she could see strands of wire.

"Look, baby," Josie knelt beside her and spoke in a whisper. "Hang onto this fence and you'll be all right. When we're through with this job, I'll come back for you. Don't wander off, or I won't be able to find you." She heard the rattle of paper. "I got you a hamburger and a milkshake, fries too, last time we stopped for gas. I'll leave them here beside you."

"Come on, Josie!" The man's voice was impatient. "Get in the car, or I'll leave you too."

"You won't leave me!" Josie shouted back. "Your scheme won't work without me and you know it!"

A car door slammed and an engine roared. Slowly the girl sat up. Wire like the Snootses' fence was at her back, but this wasn't her yard. This was nobody's backyard. There weren't any houses or lights anywhere. She leaned back against the fence and grasped it, with both hands close to the ground. She lifted her face to the night and was surprised to see there were lights in the sky. Sometimes when she couldn't sleep, she looked out the window and looked at the stars, but she'd never seen so many, nor had they been so close.

She wondered where she was. Maybe she was on another planet. Once in a while, when Darren wasn't being mean, they pretended the Oldsmobile was a spaceship, and they traveled to other planets. But she hadn't come in a spaceship. It had been a car, just an ordinary car with a tear in the backseat where her head had been. Maybe there were two cars; the first one didn't have a hole in the seat.

Two bright eyes came out of the darkness. Faster and faster they came. They were round and angry, making her heart beat faster. She tightened her hold and shut her eyes. Wire cut into her fingers, but she didn't let go even though she wanted to clap her hands over her ears to shut out the terrible roar. The monster's breath sucked at her clothes, pulled on her fingers, and rattled the paper bag at her feet. Then it was gone, and she was safe, she could sleep—until the next one came.

A deep shudder wracked her thin body and she was glad she had on her pink sweater even though Darren laughed at her whenever she put it on. Darren was always mean to her; not as mean as Pa, but really mean. The sweater was the nicest thing she owned, and it hid some of the holes in her dress. Josie had given her the sweater. Josie was the nicest person she knew. She slept all day most days, then put on a pretty dress to go to work at night. She smelled nice and sometimes she gave her things. Josie didn't say mean things to her, or hit her like Momma did, and sometimes she told Darren and Pa to "leave the poor kid alone." She wished Josie would come back.

She didn't like being alone, especially at night. There were strange sounds, and she couldn't tell if a monster was sneaking up behind her. She should eat the food Josie gave her; she wanted to, but she was afraid to let go of the fence. If she let go, she might fall down where the big monsters rushed past. Perhaps if she was really careful. With one hand clutching the wire, she groped with the other for the paper bag. It was gone! Darren . . . no Darren wasn't here. A monster took it! What if a monster took her?

She shouldn't sleep anymore; she didn't dare for fear something awful might come. The night grew cold, and she shivered in her pink sweater. Her leg smarted and her hands ached from clutching the wire fence. Her head hurt something fierce too. Something moved in the bushes, and she heard footsteps. She tried to make herself smaller so the monsters wouldn't see her. She didn't care about food anymore, but she needed something to drink. Even the nasty brown stuff she sometimes found in the bottom of Pa's cup would be better than this dryness in her mouth. She wished Josie would come back to get her, but after a while she knew Josie wasn't coming.

CHAPTER 1

"Not again!" Peter groaned aloud. "I really thought this time . . ."

"I did too," Tisa agreed glumly. "But . . ."

"I know. I know." Peter ran his long fingers through his thick black hair as he turned to look at her. "The closer the date got, the more uncertain you became. Mark's flaws became impossible. You're not ready to settle down. You don't think you really love him. His expectations are too high. Tell me, little sister, how is Mark taking this?"

His voice was slightly mocking, and he made her sound like someone who was impossible to please. Maybe he was right, but maybe marriage just wasn't for her. Peter had every right to think her capricious, even callous. She knew he really liked, even approved of Mark, and that he was disappointed in her. She was disappointed in herself. She'd hurt Mark and there was nothing she could do to make amends.

"Not too well," she mumbled in answer to his question, remembering the stricken look on her former fiancé's face. She couldn't tell even Peter how Mark had pleaded for her to keep his ring and think about it more before making a decision. But she didn't need to think about it anymore. She already knew. Next to Peter, Mark was the nicest man in the world, but she didn't love him enough to marry him. She couldn't marry him, and all the thinking in the world wouldn't change her mind. She'd give almost anything not to have hurt him, though. He was a good man and he didn't deserve what she had done to him.

How could she explain that one day she had looked at her fiancé and knew she couldn't face seeing him across the breakfast table every morning for the next fifty years, and certainly not for all eternity. She didn't feel the same way about Mark as he felt about her, and all the wishing in the world wouldn't change that. She sank lower in the armchair across from Peter's desk. She'd messed up again. There wasn't anything wrong with Mark; she was the problem.

Peter stood and walked around the desk to stop in front of her. He reached for her, and she flung herself into his arms. He held her as her body shook with the force of the intense emotions that filled her heart.

"Sorry," she said between sniffs. After what seemed a long time, she released herself and gave him a shaky smile. He looked at her with eyes full of sympathy.

"Want to talk about it?" he asked. He kept his voice low and motioned for her to sit back down.

"What's to talk about?" She shrugged her shoulders in a small gesture of defeat as she sat in the chair. "I messed up again, and this time I hurt a truly fine man."

"Any chance you'll get back together?" Peter asked.

She shook her head without verbalizing an answer, but it was just as definite as if she'd spoken.

"You can't go on like this," Peter reminded her.

"I know." There was a touch of self-directed bitterness in her tone. "Everyone has to grow up sometime. Let me see—five universities, four majors, at least a dozen different apartments and as many changes of hair color, nine jobs, who knows how many causes I've been involved with, and let's not forget six fiancés!"

Peter shook his head and his mouth quirked up at one corner. "I wasn't going to lecture."

"No, but you were going to say a few things about commitment and maturity, then suggest, oh so nicely, that I should see a shrink." She glanced up at him with a hint of her old impudence and he chuckled.

"Got me!" he conceded.

"Oh, Peter, why do I care so much so quickly, then panic when anything or anyone starts to look permanent?" Her big brother was the only permanent factor she'd allowed in her life since their father had died when she was twenty-two, and her mom had followed six months later.

"That kind of question is for a shrink to answer," he responded with a wry smile.

"You know I'm not going to let anyone mess with my head." She grimaced, remembering the psychiatrist she'd seen weekly for two years when she'd been a child. She'd detested the man. Even now her hands felt clammy and her head ached when she thought of those sessions. She'd always suspected he knew something she didn't, and if she was not careful enough, she'd have to go back. Only she didn't know where back was, nor why she didn't want to go there. Those sessions had always been followed by a food orgy and a nightmare where some huge monster with round yellow eyes and gaping jaws pursued her.

"Actually I was going to suggest you talk to your bishop." He held up his hand to stop her when she started to protest. "I know you don't go to church anymore, but hear me out. I think you have some unresolved questions concerning the gospel. As a girl, the Church was important to you, and you never missed a meeting. Then when you came to live with Lara and me you stopped going. I thought it was only the anger that accompanies the grieving process and I didn't pressure you, but now I suspect it's something deeper, and you won't be happy until you deal with it."

"You're a better cop than shrink." She laughed, then added quietly, "For your information, I have been going to church lately—with Mark. Mark isn't right for me, but I've discovered I want to feel the way I once did about the Church. I don't know if I'm looking for the warmth and security our parents gave us . . . and because the Church was so much a part of them, I feel closer to them at church, or if I'm really drawn toward God and looking for spiritual answers of my own, but going to church with Mark has made me feel things I haven't felt for a long time." Without giving him an opportunity to comment she stood and stepped toward him. He opened his arms and simply hugged her, but she didn't miss the sad expression on his face.

"I'd better be on my way," she told him, standing on her toes to kiss his cheek. He gripped her tightly to give her another hug, just as the door to his office flew open. Peter's arms tightened around her, and he instinctively turned his body, as though shielding her.

"Got it!" a man's voice announced, and from the corner of her eye Tisa caught the movement of a sheaf of papers being waved triumphantly by a large man standing in the doorway.

Peter's arms dropped from around her, and he practically pushed her toward the door. The severe expression on his face told her he was no longer her gentle, loving, older brother, but Lieutenant Peter Lewis, head of the city narcotics division. She didn't argue. She'd always respected the single-minded drive that allowed him to shut out all else and focus on the job at hand. She knew about his near obsession with eliminating drug trade and use. It didn't mean he cared any less about her; it was just something he had to do. He'd been nine years old when he'd been rescued from an exploding meth lab by a firefighter, and his parents had relinquished all rights to him when they'd gone to prison. She understood his hatred of drugs and any reminder of his abusive early childhood.

She expected the man standing in the doorway to step aside, allowing her to pass. When he didn't, she was forced to take a better look at him. He was tall, but at five-foot-zero most men looked tall to her. He was probably no more than six feet. His hair was plain old brown and just a little long for a cop, which probably meant he did undercover work. Tight jeans and a faded T-shirt showed off his physique. He either did hard physical labor or spent a lot of time at the gym. Her gaze traveled to his face where she received a rude shock. Deep blue eyes dominated a seemingly ordinary face, making his appearance anything but ordinary, and those eyes were sending her an unmistakable message. He didn't like her. She'd never even met the man, but the contempt in his eyes was unmistakable. She saw or imagined something else, too, something that sent a shiver that wasn't altogether unpleasant down her spine.

Instantly her defenses went up. Forcing a neutral expression to her face and an icy element to her voice, she continued walking toward him. "Excuse me." She made her voice cold and imperial as she brushed past him, and at the last possible second, he shifted position enough to allow her access to the door.

Her heels tapped a sharp staccato as she moved swiftly down the hall. The eerie feeling that she was being watched followed her, but her steps never faltered. Only as she reached the corner did she cast a quick glance behind her. The door to Peter's office was closed. The stranger was gone, presumably inside her brother's office.

Slowing her steps, she crossed the lobby with a cheerful wave and a smile for several officers she recognized as Peter's friends. It wasn't until she reached her car and climbed inside that she relaxed her guard. Her shoulders slumped, and if she'd been any other woman she would have given in to tears. Telling Peter about her broken engagement had been every bit as difficult as she'd expected. Breaking her engagement hadn't been easy either. She'd known for weeks that she couldn't marry Mark, but she hadn't wanted to hurt him. She hadn't wanted to disappoint Peter either. Her brother wanted her to be happy, and to him that meant marriage.

Her thoughts turned with sadness to her former fiancé; Mark had been a good friend, and she would miss him. He hadn't been anything like her five earlier fiancés. They'd been little more than immature boys, nothing like Mark. Mark hadn't been only handsome and fun, but there was a depth to him that had made Tisa want to be better. Something about his faith in God had caused her to want to be the kind of woman who could satisfy his desire to marry in the temple. But she couldn't satisfy that desire, not at this point in her life. Mark deserved a wife who was good and sweet, one who shared his beliefs and values. He didn't deserve a chameleon who could only make herself look like the woman he wanted, but who had only emptiness and darkness at her center—where it really counted.

That man, the one in Peter's office, had seen the emptiness and the darkness. There had been contempt for her in his eyes—desire too, though it was overlaid with dislike. Even so, something inside her had responded. Somehow he knew the secrets she herself could only guess at, but knew she must keep hidden.

Now she was being fanciful, she admonished herself. That man didn't know anything at all about her. He wasn't like Peter, who had always known about the monsters. She had been living as a foster child in Norm and Dixie Lewises' home when the lady from social services brought an angry little boy to their farmhouse in southern Utah twenty-two years ago. She and Peter had looked in each other's eyes, and they'd both seen what no one else could see. At that moment a bond had been forged between the two children. The

Lewises adopted them both and Norm had turned Peter's rage into a determination to fight the drugs and abuse that had nearly taken his life, but no one, not even Peter, had been able to wipe away the black hole in Tisa's soul.

She straightened her slumped shoulders, telling herself she was being maudlin, then, reaching for the gearshift, she started her car and shifted into reverse. She'd be home soon, back in her new apartment. She would likely never see that man again. If he was a friend of Peter's she would have met him before, and if he was new to Peter's department, Peter would have introduced them. *Not if he were an undercover agent she shouldn't have seen*, the voice of reason reminded her. Annoyed with herself for giving the man a second thought, she shifted into first gear, looked both ways, then pressed a little too hard on the gas pedal, sending her bright red Jaguar shooting into traffic with a squeal of its tires.

* * *

McCabe Evans—or "Cabe" as he was usually called—watched the blond until she'd almost reached the end of the hall. There was something about her . . . He shook his head, denying what that something might be. She was a looker, and he could almost forgive Lewis. No! He wasn't here to judge his unwilling partner. Peter Lewis was one of the best in his field; he got results and his arrests led to solid convictions. Lewis's personal life was none of his business. Shutting down the Dempsky crime syndicate was the only business that mattered. He turned to see the other man watching him. Peter's slightly narrowed eyes revealed a hint of animosity.

Cabe knew he should have knocked, but the last thing he'd expected was to find the lieutenant with a blond babe in his arms who definitely wasn't his wife. Cabe had seen a picture of Lara Lewis, and the blond bombshell who had been locked in Peter's arms definitely wasn't Lara. In the picture Cabe had seen, Lewis's wife had the look of old Spanish nobility that looked right with the sharp, lean features of her husband, whose bearing and coloring hinted of a few Native American genes in his family tree. He wished he'd knocked and waited to be properly invited into the lieutenant's office.

Catching Lewis in a compromising situation certainly wouldn't help to ease the resentment Lewis felt by being forced to work with him.

Holding out the papers Lewis had insisted on, Cabe approached the other man. "Your chief okayed everything."

Peter's frown as he took the papers from Cabe spoke volumes about his displeasure at being coerced into sharing his investigation. Cabe watched as the other man studied the papers, and he could almost feel sympathy for him. When he'd been with the Los Angeles police force, Cabe wouldn't have been pleased to have a federal investigator honing in on one of his cases either. He, too, preferred to work alone, but this case was too big. He'd requested Lewis for a partner instead of a fellow FBI agent because Lewis was the best. It went beyond Lewis being a former Drug Enforcement Administration officer; the lieutenant had an uncanny knack for sniffing out drugs. It was almost an obsession with the Salt Lake City cop.

Lewis didn't share his enthusiasm for working together and had resisted the partnership when he'd first been approached, but Cabe had felt justified in going over his head. The papers Cabe had just handed Peter had been from Peter's chief, assigning him to work with Cabe. The Dempskys had to be stopped, and he'd use whatever tactics were necessary to bring them down.

"When you first arrived you said your objective was to stop Artel and Reuben Dempsky." There was a coldness in Lewis's voice. "I don't know anything about Artel's operation. My case is against Jorge Ortega. There are indications he's connected to Reuben, but as far as I know, neither of the Dempsky brothers has ever set foot in Utah. Ortega's behind the flood of drugs reaching my city through a rash of illegal aliens. They bring it in; he parcels it out all over the area. I've got a solid investigation, and I'm getting close to an arrest. I don't want any federal hunt messing up my case."

"You won't stop the drugs without getting Artel and Reuben," Cabe spoke flatly. "I suspect Reuben's son is in it up to his ears too."

Lewis didn't argue. He merely turned his attention back to the papers in his hand. After a few minutes of silence he lifted his head. "You left one thing out," Lewis met his eyes with a challenging stare. "You're posing as a PI, and I understand you even have a real client. I want to know who your client is and what that client has to do with my case."

"I have an informant, not a client. Your chief agreed that you only need to know my informant's motive, not the name," Cabe answered, his voice remaining smooth and controlled. He'd expected Lewis to challenge him on this point, but it was imperative that his informant's identity be kept secret. Not that he didn't trust Lewis, but one hint of who gave him the information that might finally lead to an arrest in the Annie Langtry murder could destroy his informant's career, and cost her life. In the interest of lowering Lewis's antagonism, he would tell what he could.

"My informant's daughter and the girl's friend started out sneaking into Artel Dempsky's club to dance when they were underage." Cabe launched into as much of his informant's background as he considered necessary. "Artel Dempsky himself caught them and promised not to tell their parents if they would make a few deliveries for him. They agreed and soon became well-paid couriers—mules. They thought it was fun and gradually started experimenting with the drugs Dempsky's lieutenant made available to them. After a while the drugs were no longer free. From there it was a short step to becoming high-priced call girls. At seventeen they disappeared from their homes for good. The friend surfaced in a Los Angeles morgue two years later, dead from a presumably accidental overdose. My informant's daughter wandered into an American embassy in a South American city requesting asylum a year later. She made a call home, and a private jet was sent for her. When the plane arrived the pilot and a bodyguard collected a dead body with a bullet hole in her temple. That was three years ago."

Cabe left out more than he shared. The young girl's name had been Annie. Lewis didn't need to know the details that haunted Cabe night and day. He didn't need to know that Cabe had been the bodyguard and detective hired by Annie's mother, who had arrived too late. It was no one's business but his that he'd had a school-boy crush on Annie for years, and that his mother's friendship with Annie's mother had been a welcome excuse to see her frequently without giving away his interest in the younger girl. And Lewis certainly didn't need to know that Cabe still saw Annie's white face with a narrow trail of blood seeping into her long, pale hair in his dreams at night.

"The girl's father had ties to Dempsky's playmates-for-hire which had been a factor in her parents' divorce, which in turn was one of the catalysts that fueled her rebellion. Her mother's career was also a factor. The mother is famous and went to great lengths to keep her daughter out of the spotlight, which ironically the daughter resented, and the father capitalized on," Cabe continued. "Now the woman blames herself for her daughter's death. She believes that if she had come forward with what she knows about her ex-husband and Dempsky, her daughter would still be alive. I want to find her daughter's killer."

"Prostitution is a small portion of the Dempsky empire. Drugs are their big money game." Peter's caustic remark confirmed in Cabe's mind that Lewis knew more than he was willing to admit at this point about the Dempsky crime family.

"That's why I need you," Cabe leveled with Lewis. "You have a feel for drugs like no one else on this side of the law. I know you've been collecting info on the Dempskys' drug empire for years, and that you're just as aware as I am that shutting down Ortega isn't the answer. You send Ortega to prison, and Artel and Reuben will simply replace him with someone new. My investigation leads me to believe there's something in this Utah operation that is the key to bringing down the Dempskys' entire operation. You want to close a major drug distribution program, and I want a murder conviction. I think my informant's information can close some of the gaps in your research, and giving me access to your investigation will lead to the Dempskys' conviction."

Cabe knew the moment Lewis accepted the inevitable. Only someone trained as Cabe was to observe the smallest changes in someone else's demeanor would have noticed the way Lewis tucked away his personal feelings in a hidden compartment of his mind, or the way he switched gears to focus fully on the case. Cabe had known that when Lewis finally capitulated—and Lewis was too much the professional not to—he would put away his personal reservations entirely to devote himself to the case, and to working with Cabe.

Cabe liked Lewis, even if his respect for him had dipped some-what on catching him with the blond. He'd admired and looked forward to working with the Salt Lake lieutenant from the time he'd first been handed a profile of the man. Lewis was committed and thorough. He hadn't allowed his years of pursuing some of the worst scum on earth to dent his own high standards. He had a squeaky-clean reputation, which was almost an anomaly for an officer who had devoted as many years to drug enforcement as Lewis had, first with the Rangers, then the DEA, and now in his home state.

Cabe pushed aside the one area of disappointment. His usual cynical view of his fellowmen should have prepared him; warned him somehow that Peter Lewis's reputation was too good to take at face value, but for some reason he had wanted to believe the lieutenant was all he appeared to be. Cabe was a member of The Church of Jesus Christ of Latter-day Saints, and he knew Peter Lewis was a member as well. Cabe had wanted to believe that made him different. His own father's infidelity and casual dismissal of his temple vows, along with his obsession for his lucrative, Hollywood legal career, had destroyed his family and left Cabe with no patience for men who cheated on their wives. Little Annie's wasted young life was directly attributable to her father's infidelity as well, and had served to solidify Cabe's attitude toward men who cheated on their wives.

He'd had occasion more than once to be disappointed when a friend or colleague didn't live up to the standards he espoused, but somehow it always hurt a little more when he spotted a fellow member's feet of clay. Seeing Lewis with the blond femme fatale in his arms disturbed him far more than it should and required real effort to put it out of his mind.

"All right." Lewis got down to business, and Cabe welcomed the interruption of his thoughts. "Space is at a premium around here, so you'll have to share my office. I'll have a desk, a telephone, and a computer moved in here for you. Until they arrive, there's a table over there," he pointed to a table piled high with charts and maps. "You can use it. I'll have a key made for you for the small file cabinet behind my desk and move all of the files except those pertaining to the Dempsky case out of it. I'll expect immediate access to your records as well."

"Fine with me," Cabe agreed to Lewis's offer. "I have duplicates of all my files in my office back in Los Angeles, and I brought two sets of disks with me. I assumed you'd want one." He set a thin disk carrier on Lewis's desk. "The other set is in the safe at the hotel where I'm staying."

Lewis opened a desk drawer and withdrew a thick manilla folder. "I would prefer this doesn't leave this room," he said, handing the folder to Cabe. He walked on past Cabe to the table he'd offered as an interim desk. He began rolling the charts and maps scattered across its surface into tight cylinders. As Lewis worked, Cabe flipped open the folder and began to read. He hid a smile. Lewis had known all along he would have to cooperate and was prepared. When the lieutenant finished tidying up, he waved to the table.

"It's all yours, Evans," he announced, none too graciously, before seating himself behind his own desk, popping the disk into his computer, and scowling at the screen.

After an hour interrupted only by shuffling papers in Cabe's hands, an occasional squeak from Lewis's chair, and a couple of phone calls which Lewis dispatched abruptly, Lewis clicked off his computer and rose to his feet.

"Since I don't have the luxury of dealing with only one case at a time like you do, I've got a few appointments to take care of," he announced. Cabe sensed a lessening of the earlier chill in his voice, but there was also a definite warning that the lieutenant had no intention of becoming the junior partner in their newly formed team. That was fine with him; he looked forward to an equal give-and-take with Lewis. He took Lewis's slight softening as an indication that Lewis had found the information on the disk promising.

Lewis walked toward the door, but before opening it, he turned back to say, "Stay as long as you like, Evans; I'll meet you back here at eight in the morning. I think an in-depth discussion will be due by then."

Cabe nodded an acknowledgment, then added, just as the lieutenant reached for the door, "I'm impressed with what I'm seeing here. Good work, Lieutenant."

Peter Lewis paused and almost cracked a smile. "Seems to me, if we're going to be practically living in each other's pockets for the next few months, we might be a little less formal. Call me Peter."

"Thank you, Peter." Cabe smiled, partly in relief that Peter was ending the cold war, and partly in genuine appreciation for the giant leap forward his case was about to take with the addition of the careful data Peter had accumulated. "My name is McCabe, usually shortened to Cabe."

CHAPTER 2

Watching her own reflection in the mirror, Tisa fastened small gold hoops in her ears, and appraised herself critically. She liked the new hairstyle. Really short suited her well. Peter would frown when he saw the neon pink streak in her platinum-blond hair. He'd grumble about the new shorter length too. Poor Peter! He was so conservative, and though she'd never doubted his love for her, she knew he'd never quite understood her need for change, and frankly she'd always gotten a kick out of shocking him a bit.

Mark was a lot like Peter she mused. Before their breakup she'd begun to wonder if his similarity to Peter was what had drawn her to him in the first place. He was solid and steady, kind to children, dogs, and little old ladies. He never split a check, waded in the lake in his best shoes, or cooked breakfast on the pedestrian walkways over the highway. In short, he was a tad boring. Still, for Mark she'd let her hair grow, worn dresses, and even gone to church. She'd almost traded her Jaguar XK8 Coupe for a Buick because the little sports car made him uncomfortable. Thank goodness she hadn't gone quite that far! She freely admitted she missed Mark, but not enough to regret breaking their engagement. Marrying Mark would have been like marrying her brother, and though she adored Peter, a daily dose of Mr. Solid Citizen would have bored her to tears.

Through the mirror she caught sight of the glittering gold-and-black waist-skimmer blouse hanging on the outside of the closet door. Peter would hate it! Lara would laugh and threaten to buy one just like it. She wouldn't really do it, which was too bad. Peter could stand a little shaking up once in a while.

She hummed as she slipped into the black hip-hugger capri pants that complemented her blouse and fastened the discreetly hidden zipper. Next she wiggled her toes into a matching pair of gold stiletto sandals that showed off a tiny gold toe ring. The shoes looked great, but wearing them was a risk. If she stepped off the patio onto the grass, the slender heels would sink into the soft ground and she might fall. She didn't mind, in fact she generally enjoyed creating a little excitement, but she didn't want to be the center of attention that way. Kicking off the shoes, she reached for a pair of black, chunky platform sandals. She seldom wore any shoes that failed to add a smidgeon of height to her diminutive stature.

She was looking forward to dinner with Peter and Lara. The day after telling Peter of her broken engagement Tisa had flown to Houston, Texas. She'd been gone for almost two weeks and this would be their first get-together since her return. She only regretted that they wouldn't be having a quiet dinner, just the three of them with plenty of interruptions from four-year-old Jamie and two-year-old Peter, Jr.

Peter's cookouts, Tisa acknowledged with a wide grin, verged on ordinary as a rule, or at least they would if she and Lara didn't spice them up. She loved to shock his guests a little bit by wearing something outlandish, while Lara quite literally spiced up the food. Lara considered Peter's sauces a little bland and usually succeeded in adding some of her own Tex-Mex flavoring to any sauce he left unattended for more than two seconds!

Giving herself one last appraisal in the mirror, she picked up the tiny gold purse that matched her outfit and draped its long, slender chain over one shoulder. She was ready.

Smiling in satisfaction, she closed her apartment door behind her. While waiting for the elevator, her thoughts turned once more to her former fiancé. Mark hadn't wanted her to invest so much money in an apartment. He'd let her know he planned to buy his parents' ranch-style house when they retired to a new home in Arizona next year. They wouldn't need two homes, but something about the condo had appealed to her from the first moment she'd seen it, and frankly, she had no burning desire to live in Mark's parents' house. From the dark interior colors Mark considered warm and soothing, to the tightly fenced Xeriscaped yard he lauded as energy efficient, the house gave her the creeps.

She'd loved at first sight the large, airy rooms and the recessed angles of the condo that added private little nooks to the various living spaces. Of course it had changed a great deal, as had all of the units in the trendy, upscale buildings located at the south end of the Salt Lake valley. She'd been hired to take over the decorating when the previous decorator had taken an emergency bed-rest maternity leave, and the first thing she'd done was add the bright colors and crisp cottons of early morning. Young executive buyers had snapped up the units immediately, liking her use of quality furniture and fabrics without the old, exhausted look of musty antiques or the space-age phoniness of chrome and plastics. She had purchased one of the apartments for herself and loved it just as much as she'd thought she would.

Of all the jobs she'd held, she liked this one best, decorating expensive homes, hotels, and condos, though her stint as a magazine layout designer had come close. Her trip to Houston had been a combined vacation and conference where she'd won a top design award for a hotel in Park City where she'd blended soft pastels with rich, warm woods, and brilliant splashes of vibrant color to create a mood of relaxed comfort with a hint of dazzling excitement. She had a feeling she'd found a niche she could finally stay with.

The elevator arrived and she rode it down to the parking garage, where she climbed in her car and drove quickly to the barbeque. When she reached the street where Peter and Lara lived, she found parking spaces at a premium. Lara loved entertaining, and even her backyard barbeques had a way of escalating to epic proportions. Peter would grumble and complain, but Tisa knew he actually took a great deal of pride in his dark-haired Texas bride's entertaining skills. Tisa used to worry about her big brother's reluctance to make friends or interact socially with other people. His early years had seemed to leave him with an insurmountable suspicion of people, and he hadn't formed many close attachments outside of their small family—until Lara entered his life.

Tisa smiled thinking of Lara. Lara was easily the best female friend she'd ever had, though she'd been prepared to dislike her from the first moment she'd heard Peter was bringing a woman home with him from Texas, where he'd spent three months working on a case that involved both the INS and the DEA. She hadn't been able to imagine what her brother could find appealing about a Houston socialite, and when they had met, Lara seemed to be just what Tisa had expected: an expensive designer dress, perfect hair, and a single-strand pearl necklace at her throat, gracious ladylike manners, and an annoyingly sweet southern drawl. Tisa had spotted the redeeming silver-trimmed red cowboy boots about the same time the other girl had thrown her arms around her and, half laughing, half crying, vowed Tisa was the exact little sister she'd always wanted. Their friendship had only gotten better from that day on. Peter's decision—influenced by Lara—to resign from the DEA, take a job with the Salt Lake City Police Department, and buy a home, had also endeared Lara to Tisa.

Following the path that led to the rear of the house, Tisa took a deep breath before stepping through the gate that had been propped open. The party was in full swing, but she didn't see Peter. He was usually near one of the large, gas grills, but this time his next-door neighbor and one of the sergeants from the department were doing the honors.

"Tisa!" a familiar voice called, and she turned to see Bob White, a grin splitting his freckled face in cheery welcome. Seconds later he wrapped her in a welcoming embrace. She hugged him back. She'd known Bob since elementary school. He'd been in her parents' ward and had lived on a neighboring farm. He'd become a rural sheriff's deputy, then, shortly after Peter joined the Salt Lake City Police Department, he too had joined the force. They had dated casually in those early group-dating years before they'd both moved on to more serious relationships, and had remained friends ever since. A few times she'd suspected he might still have a small crush on her, but since he never acted on it, she'd decided it was just her vanity speaking.

"Haven't seen you for ages." There was cheerful enthusiasm in his voice. He might have said more, but they were interrupted by two more officers Tisa knew. She spoke with them for a few moments before making her way, greeting other officers and friends of her brother and his family en route, to the table where Lara sat trying to coax Jamie to eat something other than potato chips.

"Hi, Jamie!" She flashed a smile at her niece as she sat down across from her.

"Hi, Aunt Tisa." The child smiled back, her dark eyes, so like her mother's, sparkling with excitement.

"Where's Petey?" Tisa looked around, but didn't see the energetic two-year-old.

"My parents arrived today," Lara said. "They're a little tired from the trip and wanted an early night. They offered to watch both of the kids and put them to bed, but you know Jamie. There's no way she'd miss a party!" Both women laughed.

"Takes after her mother," Tisa said as she winked at Jamie, who was paying more attention to a couple of neighborhood kids that had stopped to urge her to join their game than she was to the adults' conversation.

"More like her aunt." Lara sighed, and Tisa knew she was refer-ring to Tisa's broken engagements, and to the fact that both children talking to her daughter were little boys.

"Not me," Tisa laughed. "If she were more like me, she'd tell both of those guys to go play so she could concentrate on that plate of food."

"I believe that's my cue." Bob slid a plate piled high with salads and ribs in front of her, then commandeered a seat beside her.

"You always did know the way to my heart," Tisa told him with a burst of laughter while reaching for the fork Bob had helpfully supplied along with the heaping plate of food. The odd expression on Bob's face made her pause. Surely Bob didn't feel *that* way about her. No, that couldn't be. Bob had always been a dear friend, almost another brother, but he knew her too well to think there could ever be anything more between them. She was just letting her imagination get carried away. Bob was one of the few people, besides her brother and Lara, she could relax with, and not worry that he might want more from her than she could give.

* * *

As Cabe and Peter pulled up to the curb, Cabe let his eyes roam over the two-story home shaded by large oaks in an obviously comfortable Salt Lake City neighborhood. The house didn't shout affluence, but it was definitely a cut above average. Cabe had been reluctant to attend the party at Peter's house, but Peter had persuaded him that since he had to eat anyway, and they weren't scheduled to relieve the detectives at the warehouse until eleven, he might as well drop in on the party. As well as their relationship was progressing, Cabe had thought it wise to accept the invitation.

He and Peter were late. They'd spent more time than expected debriefing the two men who had been assigned to watch a warehouse Peter was certain belonged to the Dempskys, though a check of records showed a tangled trail of blind corporations as owners. Carmichael and Jones, the two undercover officers assigned to keep tabs on the warehouse, had reported an unusual amount of activity in the past twenty-four hours, and he and Peter had decided to take the next watch themselves. Cabe felt a wave of excitement. Something was about to happen and this time he'd be there.

Cabe followed Peter along a stone path that led around the house to the backyard. He spotted the blond the moment he and Peter joined the party, which was already well underway. Her hair was shorter than it had been when he'd seen her in Peter's office, and he'd swear the bright pink streak hadn't been in it before. She was sitting at the same table as Peter's wife and daughter, but she was flirting with some character that looked like a young Andy Rooney. He watched as she leaned her forehead against the man's shoulder for a moment then raised her head; Cabe could see she was laughing. He felt vaguely annoyed, and he didn't know whether it was because the woman had the nerve to attend the party or because she was flirting with another man right in front of Peter, a man who was quickly becoming a good friend in spite of his initial reluctance to work with an outsider.

"Grab a plate," Peter invited. "With Carreras doing the cooking, the ribs won't be quite up to my usual standard, but they'll still be good. That is, if he's managed to keep Lara away from the barbeque sauce!"

"Hey, don't knock the chef!" the big sergeant, sporting a bushy, black mustache and standing behind the grill, chided with a good-natured grin. He piled spicy meat onto their plates. "Me and that wife of yours make a great team!"

"Oh, no," Peter groaned, reaching for a full pitcher of lemonade. Turning back to Cabe he whispered in a falsely subtle voice, "We'll need at least a gallon of liquid to put out the fire. Don't ever trust your stomach to a Texan and some guy that swam the river."

"Hey, it's you gringos that are weak-stomached!" Carreras retorted with a deep chuckle. Shaking his head, Peter walked away, and Cabe followed. Carreras's laughter followed them.

A wave of uneasiness swept over Cabe as he and Peter made their way to the table where Peter's wife and the blond both sat surrounded by a cadre of men, many of whom were police officers he recognized. He expected Peter would make a public show of sitting with his wife. In an LDS community, husbands and wives generally sat together at social functions of any type, and it would look odd if Peter sat elsewhere. The blond had probably chosen to sit near Lara Lewis, knowing that would be where Peter would sit. He had to hand it to Peter; he was certainly cool enough about the situation. Peter slid his plate onto the table next to his wife's plate then leaned over to give her a quick kiss. Straightening, he indicated Cabe should sit across from him, next to the other woman. The young man occupying the chair obligingly moved over.

He had little choice, short of creating a scene, but to make his way to the indicated seat. He schooled his face not to give away any hint of recognizing the woman. If Peter chose to pretend that scene in his office had never occurred, Cabe could do the same. As he settled into his chair his arm brushed the blond's shoulder, sending a tingle of awareness through him. His arm burned where they had touched. His own reaction to the casual contact startled him. It had been a long time, at least since before that trip to South America, since he had reacted so strongly to a woman. At first he had been too involved in trying to find Annie's killer to pay more than superficial attention to the women he met. Then he'd accepted an offer to train at Quantico and become a federal agent. Three years had passed and there had been little time for a social life, but it was worth it. He was finally on the Dempskys' trail.

It was several seconds before he realized Peter was making introductions.

"This is Lara," Peter placed a hand on the shoulder of the vivacious, dark-eyed brunette, sitting on the chair Peter had stopped behind. Cabe had already recognized her from her photograph. "She's the one you can thank for the heartburn those ribs are about to send your way." Cabe was surprised by the gentle teasing and the adoring look that passed between Peter and Lara.

"Peter!" Lara protested, then gestured for Cabe to stay seated as he attempted to stand to acknowledge the introduction. Peter was already continuing, "My daughter, Jamie." He winked at the little girl who was, yet again, paying more attention to a group of children clustered around her chair than to the adult her father had brought to their table.

Then Peter reached across the table and took the blond's hand, holding it with obvious tenderness, and turned to speak to Cabe once more. The affectionate gesture startled Cabe and he wondered how his new friend would explain the woman.

"This is my sister, Patricia, usually shortened to Tisa. A couple of weeks ago you almost met in my office, perhaps *collided* might be a better way to put it." Peter went on. "Tisa, this is Cabe Evans, a private investigator from Los Angeles who will be working with me for a few months."

The woman extended her hand, and Cabe automatically reached for it, feeling small shock waves as their fingers touched. She was even more sensational than he had remembered. But Peter's sister? Cabe's eyes went from the woman to Peter and back. Of all the scenarios he'd considered to explain the clinch he'd interrupted, that they were siblings had never occurred to him. He'd swear the woman was a natural blond, and her pale skin was a dozen shades lighter than Peter's. She could more easily pass as the sister of the red-haired officer sitting next to her than as any relative of Peter's. A burst of laughter made him aware that he was staring.

"Er . . . hello! Peter didn't tell me he had a sister," he offered in a lame attempt to cover his confusion.

The Rooney look-alike and several other men laughed. He recognized many of them as officers from Peter Lewis's division. He'd seen quite a bit of Stone Aldredge and Marco Vasquez. They'd been friendly enough around the office, but they weren't smiling now. He recognized a decidedly unwelcoming demeanor on both their faces. With a jolt he realized they were eyeing him as competition. Quite clearly they were letting him know they each had a personal interest in Tisa Lewis.

"Meeting Tisa is a pleasant shock to most men, but finding out old Lewis has a sister who looks like Tisa is the real shocker!" someone made a friendly dig at Peter. Cabe glanced quickly toward Peter, wondering if he was the victim of some weird "get-the-new-guy" razzing—there was just no way Peter and the woman could be siblings . . . unless one of them had been adopted. He hadn't considered that possibility.

"I hope you're married with six kids," Stone said. "Tisa doesn't date married men."

"No wife or kiddies." Cabe decided to play along.

"She doesn't date cops, either," Marco chimed in, his own disappointment evident before he addressed his next remark to Tisa. "Remember, PIs are just hired cops."

"Hmm, a rent-a-cop. That's something I haven't tried." She let her eyes travel slowly from his head to his feet, then back. While Cabe squirmed, she laughed a warm, low chuckle that sent shivers down his spine, then as if she knew the effect she was having on him, she burst into full-scale laughter.

Cabe couldn't quite decide whether they were teasing him or still joking about the implausibility of Tisa being Peter's sister. Seeing his confusion, the redhead volunteered his own explanation, "You should have known their dad. What a character! He always claimed he found them under different sagebrush bushes."

Cabe was sitting close enough to Tisa to feel her stiffen and knew she didn't find the explanation as hilarious as did the group of men gathered near her.

Seeing his continued puzzlement, Lara leaned closer and quietly whispered, "They were both adopted at a young age, but are closer than many birth siblings."

"Gang way! Out of my way!" Carreras brought a sudden end to the teasing and introductions as he pushed his way through the crowd to set a huge platter of barbequed ribs and chicken on the table. "Can't have my best girl going hungry." He winked broadly at Tisa as he used a pair of tongs to refill her plate.

"Ahh Manuel, my one true love," Tisa exclaimed dramatically, clasping her hands together over her heart. "If only I weren't so afraid of Angelica, we could run away and live happily ever after!"

"Till the food ran out," Bob snorted, and everyone laughed before he turned the attention back to Cabe. "Only a rich man can afford this one," he whispered in a loud aside behind Tisa's back. "That's why she doesn't date cops. Any of us would go broke trying to keep her fed on what the city pays us."

"You're hurting my feelings," Tisa sniffed in mock offense, but Cabe noticed she wasn't really offended, and that Bob's words didn't slow down her attack on her plate. Taking a bite of the food on his own plate, he hastily reached for his glass. A whoop of laughter greeted his action.

"Come on, guys. Let him eat his dinner," Tisa implored even as she joined their laughter. Cabe could tell she was enjoying both the banter and his discomfort.

"You mean let you eat *your* dinner," Lara teased.

"Well, that too." Tisa laughed as she lifted a huge rib, dripping with sauce, to her mouth.

Cabe watched her with a kind of awe. Taking dainty nibbles, she stripped the bone and licked a drop of sauce from the corner of her mouth in obvious enjoyment. He wondered how she could do that—that sauce was sheer fire! But it didn't seem to faze Tisa at all. From the rapidly escalating pile of rib bones on her plate, he was equally amazed at the quantity she consumed. If she ate like that all of the time, how did she manage to stay so slim? Dakota Langtry, poor Annie's mother, was a legendary Hollywood beauty he'd known for years, but he couldn't remember a time she hadn't been dieting. She'd cheerfully hand over her entire fortune for this woman's metabolism!

Once his taste buds adjusted to the spicy food, Cabe found the dinner delicious, and as his tablemates and Tisa's entourage of admirers went on to other topics, he began to enjoy himself. A soft brush, followed by a firmer bump against his pant leg startled him. He glanced at the woman next to him. *No way!* She was completely absorbed in the food and conversation. Feeling a stronger thump against his leg, he eased back to glance under the table. He wasn't conceited enough to believe Tisa was engaging in some under-the-table flirting, but someone or something was definitely playing some kind of game under the table.

Two round yellow eyes stared back at him. A huge yellow, pug-faced cat gave his pant leg one more rub before the animal bared its teeth and gave him a menacing glare.

"That's Snuffy. He likes barbeque," Jamie whispered across the table.

From the expression on the cat's face, it appeared that feeding him might be the wisest choice. Picking up a small chunk of the fiery meat, Cabe lowered his hand, intending to toss the morsel under the table. Like lightening, Snuffy snatched the offering before Cabe could drop it, nearly taking his fingers with it.

Jerking backward, he swallowed the exclamation that nearly escaped his mouth, and his eyes met the amused eyes of Peter's sister.

"That's a good way to lose a few fingers," she whispered. "Snuffy isn't known for his table manners."

"That's some cat." He watched the dog-sized feline wolf down the chunk of meat, completely undisturbed by the Tex-Mex flavoring, then proceed to stroke the pant leg of the next guest.

"He'll leave you alone now," Tisa continued to speak in a low voice. "Snuffy goes down the line and demands tribute from each person just once." She laughed, delighting him with the bright sound.

"What if someone refuses to be coerced?" he teased, watching the cat's progress.

"Oh, that would be unwise," Tisa said with mock seriousness. "Snuffy would have to teach him a lesson, and it wouldn't be pretty."

His awareness of the woman seated next to him seemed to heighten his senses, making him more conscious of the setting sun's brilliant colors, the smoky odor of grilling food, and children's laughter. Peter asked Cabe a question, and as the two men conversed, Cabe experienced an enhanced warmth toward the man. Knowing Peter wasn't the cheat he'd thought him to be earlier, seemed to strengthen the relationship he'd been forming with the man. And it had been a long time since he'd enjoyed the company of a woman as much as he was enjoying sitting beside Tisa. He found himself almost relaxing. He was glad he'd come, and in a few hours he might even get a glimpse of the younger Dempsky, Reuben's son, an illusive figure without a blemish on his record, but who was the most likely suspect in Annie's murder. With a little luck, he might gain a piece of the puzzle that would put the man who had killed Annie behind bars for the rest of his life!

"Is this your first trip to Utah?" Cabe realized Tisa was speaking to him.

"No, I came here to Salt Lake with a group of friends when I was sixteen, then returned several times with my mother to Park City. She's an avid skier, and I enjoy the sport too," he explained.

"I didn't get to ski much last winter," Tisa told him. "Something seemed to come up every time I had a day off."

From there, conversation seemed to flow easily to the recent Olympics and other forms of recreation they each enjoyed, followed by a discussion of books they'd both read. At some point she managed to persuade most of the young men hanging around their table to fill plates and find places at other tables. Cabe was impressed with the easy way she dismissed her admirers without offending them. He found her warm and funny, and as they talked he wondered why he had earlier categorized her as vain and arrogant. Was it his first impression of her as a home-wrecker, or was it simply because she was tiny, blond, and beautiful? He hoped he wasn't guilty of falling for that stereotype.

He looked into her eyes as she explained a concept she used in her work, and he suddenly knew the answer: she was an incredible actress. He'd seen her just the way she'd wanted him to see her— proud and tough. Now, for some reason, she wanted him to see a different woman. Contrary to being cold and uncaring, she was warm, funny, and very bright. She easily rivaled Dakota Langtry in being able to project whatever personality she chose.

"Peter!" An older man hurried from the house and practically ran to their table. He held a portable phone in his hand. Peter reached for it and everyone at their table watched silently as he held it to his ear. After listening for several seconds, he spoke abruptly, "I'll be right there!"

After returning the phone to the man Cabe guessed was Peter's father-in-law, Peter rose to his feet and spoke tersely, "It's Jones! The warehouse is on fire!"

Cabe stood. He didn't have to ask which warehouse Peter referred to. It was the one he and Peter had planned to stake out later that night. A dozen men left the party to sprint toward parked cars. He and Peter were among them.

CHAPTER 3

The young officer glanced at Peter's ID and waved his car past the yellow tape. A network of hoses snaked across the weedy parking lot, and revolving red and blue lights lent an air of unreality to the smoldering ruins that were all that was left of the old wooden warehouse. Firemen in their heavy gear were still shooting streams of water across the blackened debris left by the fire, but their usual keen edge of urgency was gone. Containment had been reached, no lives or property were considered in imminent danger, and the sagging old building had been slated for demolition in the near future anyway. The firefighters were ready to call it a wrap and head back to their stations.

Cabe and Peter went through the motions too. They talked to the fire captain and heard just what they'd expected. They'd have to wait until the fire investigator made his report to determine whether or not the fire had been deliberately set. They listened as the captain brushed perspiration from his face, then told them, "It was probably transients. They get in these old, abandoned buildings and light fires to cook or keep warm. Sometimes they fall asleep or pass out smoking. Everyone in the department will be glad when these warehouses are demolished for the new park. The fire could be arson, but most arson fires have multiple acceleration points and this one didn't. I doubt it was insured for enough to entice anyone to insurance fraud." He turned to shout an order to a firefighter, and Peter and Cabe stepped back to leave the path clear for rewinding hoses. They paused to speak with the two uniformed cops who had first responded to the call. They had nothing out of the ordinary to report and in minutes left to resume their patrol.

"What do you think?" Peter asked as they stood side by side, breathing the acrid air, and watching the firefighters gather their hoses and prepare to leave the fire scene. A sense of desolation swept over Cabe as he looked at the burned-out building that had been reduced to a pile of rubble. Peter and his staff had spent months gathering intelligence on Jorge Ortega's operations. The Salt Lake warehouse had been a major distribution hub for the western region. And Peter had been within a day of obtaining a warrant to search the place.

"I don't believe in coincidences." Cabe struggled not to vent his frustration. "And I don't buy the transient theory. This fire was just a little too convenient."

"Yeah," Peter sighed. "Transients accidently setting fires isn't generally a problem in the summer, but it's not unheard of. I suspect the Dempskys spotted our stake and ordered Ortega to cover his tracks before we could get any closer."

"Speaking of Carmichael and Jones, where are they?" Cabe asked, looking around. "I thought they were going to meet us here."

"I told them to stay out of sight, keep watch until the fire was under control, and then meet us at the station," Peter told him. "We better get back there and see what they can tell us. The fire inspector won't start his investigation before morning."

The two men moved briskly toward Peter's Blazer. Peter slid behind the wheel and backed up before turning toward the exit, only to find the exit blocked by a hook-and-ladder truck. Impatiently Peter drummed his fingers against the steering wheel, then, when it looked as though they would be waiting for some time, he cranked the wheel, and turned toward the far end of the parking lot. The low cement curb around the lot offered little obstacle to the Blazer. The SUV easily crawled over the barrier to the neighboring weed patch. From there it was a short spin of the wheels to the road.

"Wait a minute!" Cabe yelled as the Blazer bounced from the weed-choked ground to the street. He'd caught a glimpse of something that didn't belong in the patch of weeds. It was probably nothing, but . . .

Peter slammed on the brakes, and Cabe felt the restraining strap of his seat belt tighten across his chest as his body was thrust forward.

He had the belt off and the door opened, before Peter could ask what he'd seen. He took off running, then stopped to check his bearings. For a moment he thought he might have been mistaken, then he caught sight of an indentation in the weeds. It looked as though something heavy had been dragged through them. Following the path of bent and twisted foliage with his eyes, he squinted, seeking a better look, then he saw a pale gleam at the end of the trail.

Cabe searched automatically for the .9mm he usually carried beneath his jacket, then he remembered he'd left his weapon in Peter's Blazer before joining the party at the lieutenant's house earlier. But he didn't run back to get it; he hurried on. He was kneeling beside a body, checking for a pulse, when Peter caught up to him.

"I'll call for an ambulance." Cabe turned to see Peter return his gun to a holster beneath his jacket and reach for the small radio on his belt that looked like a cell phone.

"Too late for that," Cabe muttered.

"Are you sure?" Peter knelt beside him, and Cabe could read the look of dread on his colleague's face as he viewed the man lying face-down with an unmistakable bullet wound behind his right ear. Together they turned over the body, which was still warm. Jack Carmichael stared back at them with empty eyes. Peter swallowed, then looked back at the broken path behind the body. Gently he reached forward to touch the man's neck just as Cabe had done earlier. After a few seconds he dropped his hand and his shoulders slumped.

Peter cleared his throat before speaking. "It looks as though he crawled here from over that way. He and Jones were staked out the other side of that old service station over there." He pointed to a boarded-up building on the other side of the lot from where they now stood. "We'd better check on Jones," he added with little inflection in his voice. His lack of expression told Cabe he didn't expect to find Carmichael's partner alive.

"You think the Dempskys are behind this as well as the fire?" Peter asked.

"Probably Reuben, Artel's in California, according to the people who are supposed to be keeping an eye on him," Cabe answered and saw Peter's jaw clench. Peter had only wanted Reuben Dempsky for drug trafficking; now his incentive to catch the man had just doubled.

Peter radioed for backup and Cabe returned to the Blazer for his weapon before the two men began their cautious approach to the service station.

* * *

After Peter and Cabe left the party, a subdued air hovered over the Lewises' backyard; guests made their excuses and left early. Lara fussed over storing leftovers and straightening the deserted patio. Tisa stayed to help, and though several of Tisa's admirers offered to assist them, the two women accepted only Manuel and Angelica's offer to clean up and put away the grills.

Neither woman spoke beyond practical necessity as they worked. Tisa usually managed to put Peter's dangerous profession out of her mind, but she knew it was harder for Lara, who lived with him and was more acutely aware of times when he was called out unexpectedly or arrived home late.

Lara's mother took Jamie inside and put her to bed, while her father silently accepted the bowls and platters Lara and Tisa carried to the back door of the house. When the patio and lawn were back to their usual pristine order, Tisa followed Lara inside. Surreptitiously she peeked at the wall clock hanging in the kitchen and calculated that two hours had passed since her brother received the call that had sent him and Cabe Evans scrambling for Peter's Blazer. Hurriedly she opened the refrigerator and began stacking plastic containers until she ran out of them.

There was really no reason to stay once all of the food was stored; still Tisa found herself puttering around the kitchen, rinsing dishes, and generally trying not to look at the clock. She watched Lara pick up a broom and begin sweeping nonexistent crumbs.

"I don't know how you stand it," Tisa suddenly exploded. Lara didn't pretend that she didn't understand, or that she wasn't inventing work to keep herself from worrying about Peter.

"Most of the time I just picture him in his office seated at that big desk, and I tell myself he's so busy organizing his unit and doing paperwork that he doesn't have time to be out in the field where it's dangerous. Tonight I know he isn't sitting at that desk." She finished by bursting into tears, and Tisa found her arms going around her sister-in-law in an awkward attempt to comfort her.

As Lara sobbed, Tisa wished she could weep out her own fears, but instead of tears she felt herself slipping into the dark hole inside herself. Tisa always went there whenever she felt intense negative emotions. She'd been in about the fifth grade when she'd first realized there was something terribly wrong with her. It wasn't just that she couldn't cry; it was the monster that lurked somewhere in her mind, waiting to get her. Other children cried; they screamed and yelled, and sometimes they even struck out at each other. They never, ever disappeared into a dark place where no one could see or hear them, where monsters would eat them if they made a sound.

Tisa had no memory of before she came to live with Norm and Dixie Lewis. The psychiatrist she'd despised had said that, though she'd been only about four when she'd been abandoned, the reason she couldn't remember her previous life was because she didn't want to remember it. He'd also said that, in time, she really would forget it in the way most people forget their early years. Not even the social worker who brought her to the Lewises' house knew who she was or where she'd come from. It had been explained to her that she'd been found by a truck driver along a lonely stretch of freeway in southern Utah, and that Norm and Dixie Lewis had wanted a little girl of their own for such a long time that a judge had said she could be their little girl.

Dixie had been the most wonderful mother a little girl could have, and she'd done everything possible to answer Tisa's questions and comfort her. Her adoptive mother had assured her that her parents hadn't abandoned her because of something she'd done. Over and over she'd told Tisa that Heavenly Father loved her, and that a child as young as she had been when abandoned was incapable of committing any sin worthy of so terrible a punishment. But somewhere deep in her mind she knew her parents really had abandoned her because she was bad. She had done something terrible, so terrible they didn't care if the monsters got her. Whatever she had done, or whatever was missing inside her, made her so unlovable that not even her parents had wanted her. She'd tried to explain this to Lara after her third or fourth engagement ended, but Lara had scoffed at her, saying her problem wasn't that no one could love her, but that *everyone* fell in love with her, especially men.

Norm and Dixie had loved her she knew, and she'd never doubted their love because they were exceptional people who loved everyone, but they hadn't understood about the black, dark hole; only Peter knew and understood. He had his own black place; only, he knew all about his monster. It even had a name. Drugs. His parents had loved drugs more than they had loved him. They'd neglected him, drugged him to keep him quiet, forced him to steal for them, and at least once had tried to sell him for money to buy drugs. He would have died in a meth lab explosion if a firefighter hadn't heard his cries and risked his own life to save the child. He'd suffered unspeakable pain as his body had healed from massive burns and the torture of withdrawal. When he was released from the hospital, and after other foster parents had given up, he too had been taken in by Norm and Dixie. The bond between the two children, who were usually slow to trust, had been almost instantaneous.

As Tisa struggled not to slip into that dark place, she gripped her hands until her nails cut into the heels of her palms. She willed herself to cry, but she could not. With physical pain, she let her mind go blank—distracting her from her uncontrollable emotions. If she didn't feel anything, the horrible monsters couldn't drag her into that endless hole where the pain went on forever. Even when she'd gotten too old to believe in monsters, she'd thought it was insanity that waited just beyond the edge of that dark place in her mind. Now as an adult, she felt reasonably certain she wasn't insane, but she also knew she wasn't quite like other people.

Only Peter knew how to draw her back from that black pit. Frantically she tried to replace her fear with thoughts of Peter, but it was Cabe's face that materialized in her mind. That frightened her too, and she struggled to banish the man from her thoughts.

"Tisa! Tisa, are you all right?" Lara's mother's voice reached her and she gradually became aware that Lara was no longer crying in her arms. Lara was standing beside her father and they were all three looking at her with great compassion. Tisa willed her hands to relax and took deep breaths to calm herself.

"I'm fine." She gulped and forced a smile to her lips. "Between being really tired and my overactive imagination, I think I got a little carried away." She attempted to laugh. "I think it's time I run along home and get some sleep."

"If you're sure . . ." Lara spoke hesitantly, the worry still shimmering in her eyes.

"You two are worried about Peter," Lara's father spoke up, his voice filled with sympathy. "Why don't we step into the living room and kneel for a word of prayer before you leave, Tisa? We'll all sleep better knowing he's being watched over."

Lara reached for her father's hand and nodded her head, her gratitude for his suggestion apparent. Tisa said nothing, but followed the other three into the next room. She wasn't sure praying would help. She couldn't honestly say prayer actually helped anyone, though sometimes it made those doing the praying feel like they were contributing something. If praying would sooth Lara's fears, Tisa certainly wouldn't object, but she didn't expect it to bring any calm to her own fears.

Kneeling in front of the sofa she went through all the familiar motions, clasping her hands together and closing her eyes. She held herself still as she listened to Raymond Aguilera's softly spoken words. The arrogant aura of his powerful Spanish forebears seemed to disappear, leaving only the humble demeanor of the Indian maid who had been his grandmother. It was hard to equate the Houston corporate executive with the concerned father who held his daughter's hand as he pleaded for Heavenly Father to protect her husband and bring peace to Lara's and Tisa's hearts. He prayed like no one she'd ever heard before. A feeling permeated her heart, telling her he knew the Being he addressed. Tempted to open her eyes to see if someone actually stood before him, she instead squeezed her eyes more tightly shut.

As Lara's father continued to pray, a quiet peace crept inside Tisa's mind, and a soft warmth stilled her trembling hands. When he stopped speaking, Tisa remained motionless for what seemed a long time, afraid to move for fear the fragile serenity would shatter.

At last she stood, hugged her sister-in-law, and quietly bade Lara's parents good night. Feeling as though she had barely missed falling through a fragile layer of ice, she opened the door to step outside into the darkness of a warm summer night.

Long after Tisa drove away, leaving her sister-in-law with a reminder to call as soon as she heard from Peter, she felt a lingering calm. *What happened?* she asked herself as she undressed for bed in her own apartment. Something was different this time. She'd prayed before, and she'd listened as countless others prayed. She'd believed she was doing something right and good when she said bedtime prayers before jumping into her bed as she grew up. Her parents, Norm and Dixie, were firm believers in the power of prayer. Dixie had told her many times that she, Tisa, was the answer to Dixie's prayers. From the day she'd gone to live in the Lewis household she'd participated in family prayers, said her prayers as she'd been taught each night, and took her turn asking for a blessing on the food; then there were all those church and seminary prayers. She'd felt good about those prayers, but never before had she felt what she felt tonight. It wasn't the burning in her bosom she'd heard about so much, but there had been something. It had been more soft than burning, a peace so fragile it was like the gentle flutter of snowflakes.

Had her time with Mark prepared her in some way to have a spiritual experience, or had she imagined those feelings because tonight she needed assurance that Peter and Cabe were safe? And why did Cabe's welfare loom as large in her mind as that of her brother? Slowly she undressed, tossing her clothes on a chair, and reached for the first sleep-shirt that came to hand. As she stood before the bathroom mirror, brushing her teeth, she caught a glimpse of herself and nearly choked. Here she was standing in a Tasmanian Devil nightshirt that showed gaping toothy jaws stretching almost from her neck to her knees, wondering if what she'd just experienced was the most intense spiritual moment of her life!

Going to her closet, she pulled out a lightweight robe and pulled it over the shirt. She looked at her bed, but knew she couldn't sleep. Instead she wandered into the kitchen. After staring around blankly for several minutes, she picked up a package of cookies and a can of juice before returning to the front room. Flipping on the television, she saw that the news was already over and realized she really didn't want to watch anything anyway. Turning the TV off again, she paced to the windows. The view was spectacular as usual, but tonight there was something bleak and lonely about the long vista of lights spread across the valley. At last she picked up a book and curled up at one end of the sofa. She opened the book, but didn't read. Instead her thoughts wandered to the man she'd met tonight at Peter and Lara's home. McCabe Evans, that's what some guys had called him. Peter had called him Cabe; she liked the shortened version. Was he the reason her concern for Peter was so intense tonight? Peter was good at his job, and he was good at taking care of himself, but never before had he or the department allowed a private investigator to work with him. Did that somehow make this case different, more dangerous?

The first time she'd seen Cabe something about him had disturbed her greatly, and when he'd arrived with her brother earlier tonight she'd at first resented his intrusion into the party. She'd enjoyed his confusion when Bob and the others had teased him, then something had gradually shifted, and she'd found herself enjoying sitting beside him. She'd talked with him in a way she never talked to men, without pretense, without any thought for the impression she was making. Something about him both frightened and exhilarated her. As she'd knelt with Lara and her parents, she'd found herself thinking of Cabe right along with her brother as Raymond Aguilera prayed for their safety. That was when the incredible peace had lifted and warmed her.

Suddenly it hit her what was different about the prayer Lara's father had offered. It hadn't only been the unwavering faith of the man who uttered the prayer. Her parents, Peter, and even Mark had that kind of faith too. She had witnessed and desired that kind of faith as a young girl, had prayed for it, and longed to have it wipe away the black hole inside herself, but it hadn't happened, and she had been left feeling empty. The difference about this prayer was that she hadn't expected to feel anything tonight. She hadn't once thought of the prayer as a means of bringing peace to herself, only to Lara. She'd been totally focused on Peter and Cabe and their safety; she'd repeated in her heart and her mind the plea for their protection, never once thinking of her own needs.

Norm had told her something long ago about the necessity of losing one's self in order to find one's self. Surely she wasn't so self-centered that she'd thought only of herself and her wants each time she'd prayed in the past! Still, she didn't remember ever being so focused on others during a prayer before.

Jumping to her feet, she paced to the window again. Honesty compelled her to remember the times she'd prayed for the emptiness to go away; for first Norm, then Dixie to get well so she would not be left alone; and to know which college or career would bring her happiness. Her parents had taught her she should seek the Lord's help in all phases of her life, so those prayers had not been wrong. But had they been enough?

* * *

Cabe flattened himself against one side of the abandoned service station and his fingers tightened against the Glock he gripped with his right hand. After calling for backup and notifying Homicide, the two men had picked their way through the weed- and debris-infested lot to the area where Peter's men had set up their stakeout. With Carmichael dead and no response to the silent signal sent to Jones's radio, they felt an urgency to check on him.

"Stay here," Peter whispered before slipping from the shelter of the building. Cabe slid forward, keeping watch as Peter, crouching low, ran toward the older-model Ford half-hidden in the weeds. The passenger-side door hung open, and the car appeared to be just another derelict vehicle abandoned in a vacant lot.

Peter paused beside the open car door, then hurried to the other side. With one hand he motioned for Cabe to join him. When Cabe reached Peter's side he saw by the beam of Peter's mag light the other stakeout officer, Jones, lying sprawled across the seat with his head resting in a darker shadow. He had been shot in the temple from close range. Cabe had seen victims of violence many times, but this one struck him hard. He'd talked to this young man just hours ago and there was something about the temple wound that reminded him in a sickening way of Annie. Like her, this young man wore an expression on his face that indicated surprise at the suddenness of death.

Taking care not to touch anything, both men backed a short distance away. Peter canceled backup and asked instead for the crime scene unit. While they waited, Cabe forced himself to look around, memorizing the details of the moon-flooded area. He saw what he thought was a trail of bent and broken weeds leading from the back of an abandoned building that faced the street a short distance away. Had the killer waited out of sight around the end of the building for the two officers? There was ample space to park a car there. The angle of the trail suggested the gunman had been in sight of the car as he walked toward it. Had Carmichael and Jones been so intent on the warehouse fire on the other side of their hiding place that they hadn't seen the killer approach?

"As soon as it's light, I think we should check behind that building for tire prints, cigarette butts, whatever." Peter's thoughts followed his own. A siren sounded, and both men turned their attention to securing the crime scene.

It was nearly midnight when they returned to the station. Peter declined Cabe's offer to accompany him to the Carmichael home to break the news to the man's wife. Instead he requested that Bob White go with him and sent Aldredge and Vasquez to break the news to Jones's parents.

Cabe was too keyed up to return to his hotel immediately. It would be some time before he could put the faces of the two men who died tonight in the back of his mind. And their deaths had brought fresh reminders of Annie. He needed to work for a while.

Making his way to the office he shared with Peter, he sat down at his makeshift desk and clicked on his computer. Peter would be writing an official report, but he felt a need to jot down his own impressions. Even without the aid of official findings, which wouldn't be in for several days, he strongly believed the warehouse had been torched. The transient theory was too coincidental. But if drugs had been hidden there, then moved, what was the point in burning the place?

Those two officers had been murdered; that was a given, but why? Artel and Reuben Dempsky usually took pains to steer clear of any obvious attack on law enforcement. The deliberate attack on the two officers—who were not making a direct threat—seemed out of character. But maybe it wasn't out of character for Reuben. The man had a vicious streak a mile wide, and he didn't work alone. Any of his hired thugs may have been responsible. It was also possible Reuben's son was in charge of the Utah operation. He never left witnesses.

Both officers had been alive when they'd called in the fire, then spoken with Peter. Jones had been excited, anxious to tell Peter something. Had someone overheard Jones speaking to Peter and acted to keep him from telling whatever he had discovered? He didn't doubt Ballistics would verify the gun was mere inches from Jones's head when it was fired.

Every indication pointed to one person approaching the stakeout openly, then firing at close range, killing Jones. A quick second shot had grazed Carmichael, who then fled from the car. The third shot had struck him somewhere between the car and the spot where he had collapsed. That would indicate Carmichael hadn't drawn his weapon until after he left the vehicle. If that scenario was correct, then how did the shooter get so close to his quarry without being seen? Or was he seen, but thought to be a friend? Cabe finished his notes, printed a copy for himself which he tucked in his pocket, then forwarded a copy to Dave Woods, Special Agent in Charge of the FBI's Salt Lake field office. Last of all, he pressed Delete.

CHAPTER 4

It seemed only minutes after she had finally dozed off that Lara's call awakened Tisa, instantly bringing her to full alertness. She started to reach toward the table, then remembered she'd been holding the small portable phone in her lap when she'd fallen asleep. She clicked it on.

"Hello!" she practically shouted into the phone.

"It's okay, he's safe," Lara assured her at once. Something about her sister-in-law's voice wasn't quite as reassuring as it should have been.

"Something's wrong. Was he injured? What about Cabe?" She gripped the phone tightly as she waited for Lara to speak.

"Peter's fine! Really he is, and Cabe too." Lara spoke carefully as though Tisa's questions had sidetracked her thoughts rather than continuing their focus. After a moment's pause, she went on. "Peter called from the station to let me know they were back and all of the men who had been at our party were accounted for and safe, but two undercover officers were killed tonight. He didn't want me to hear that on the radio or television and worry needlessly, so he called. He also wanted me to know he was going to the two men's homes to speak with their families, so it will be late when he returns."

"Poor Peter. He blames himself every time anything happens to one of his people. He'll take this hard." In her mind, Tisa could see the somber hurt in her brother's eyes.

"Yes," Lara agreed. "He feels responsible even when he's taken every possible precaution."

"I'm glad you called, Lara," Tisa thanked her sister-in-law. "Peter looked so remote when he left; he does that when he's upset, so I couldn't help worrying."

"The police wives will get together tomorrow to try to do something for the families of the two men who were killed. If you'd like to go with me . . ." Lara let her voice trail off.

"No, but if you need me to babysit . . ."

"Mom and Dad will be here for a couple of weeks, so I won't need a sitter." Lara hesitated before she asked, "Are you interested in that PI from California? The two of you seemed pretty absorbed in whatever you were talking about . . . and you asked about him as though you were concerned."

Uh-oh, I shouldn't have asked about Cabe, she thought. Aloud, Tisa made her voice noncommittal. "He seemed lonely and a long way from home, that's all. Thanks again for calling, and try to get some sleep now. Bye."

After an infinitesimal pause, Lara echoed the single-word farewell, "Bye."

Tisa settled the phone back on its stand, picked up a cookie and nibbled on it as she made her way to her bedroom. She lay down, and pulled the covers to her chin, but she didn't immediately fall asleep. At first she relished a tremendous sense of relief that Peter was safe. And yes, she was glad Cabe was safe too. The man had made an impression on her, but she wasn't sure what it meant. There was no denying he was physically attractive; he was intelligent and easy to talk to, too, but there was something about him that made her uncomfortable. Mark was the only man she'd ever dated more than once who hadn't been an outgoing extrovert. Cabe Evans really wasn't an introvert, and he was nothing like Mark either. He also lacked that quick wit and zany humor she usually found herself attracted to, and . . . *attracted* to? Was she attracted to Cabe? No. *Attracted* wasn't the right word. She wasn't interested in romance; she wasn't sure she was really cut out for a romantic twosome. But something about Cabe definitely interested her. Flipping her pillow over, she pounded it a couple of times. She was tired, and now that she knew Peter was safe, she should be sleeping. Cabe had no business intruding on her thoughts and keeping her awake.

* * *

It had been late when Cabe returned to his hotel room the night before, but he was up shortly after sunup. He showered, shaved, then made his way to the hotel coffee shop for breakfast. Nothing on the breakfast buffet held tremendous appeal for him, but he filled his plate, knowing he needed to eat to retain his strength. A picture of Peter's sister flashed through his mind. He'd never seen anyone enjoy eating more than she had the previous evening. He'd learned she'd just come back from some kind of business trip a few hours before the party. He smiled. Obviously the airline peanuts hadn't been too filling! He smiled again, then ate quickly.

When he reached the station, he discovered a subdued atmosphere and a hint of anger in the air. He'd witnessed the phenomenon before. Almost every cop he'd ever known exhibited a kind of cocky self-confidence at times; telling the world that if someone was going to die, it wouldn't be him. They based their calmness on superior training and skills. Sometimes an absolute commitment to justice or honor made them feel invincible. So when a fellow officer died in the line of duty, his brother cops suffered a glimpse of their own mortality that left them angry because their protective shield had been cracked. Their anger at glimpsing their own vulnerability was compounded by the sorrow they felt at their friends' deaths.

He'd barely seated himself at the computer when Peter walked in. He too had showered and shaved, but judging by the dark circles under his eyes, he hadn't gotten much sleep.

"Morning," Cabe greeted the other man.

"Short night," Peter grunted as he sat down and turned his own computer on. Silence filled the room for a quarter of an hour before Peter swivelled his chair to face Cabe. "Reports aren't in yet, but from where I'm sitting, something smells."

Cabe breathed a sigh of relief. Peter wanted to talk about it. He turned his chair so he was facing Peter. "I didn't want to be the one to bring it up, but I'd swear those two men knew their attacker," Cabe said.

"Yeah. They were both killed by .9 mm slugs from a Glock 17. They're standard issue around here, though most of the guys in this unit have gone to 19s. A few carry them off duty." Peter's face revealed how much it pained him that a fellow cop might be involved in the two men's deaths.

"Plenty of perpetrators carry the same guns we do," Cabe pointed out the obvious.

"Yeah, perps do, but who but another cop could have openly approached the two men on stakeout?" Peter refuted Cabe's statement with a question. "The only other option is that Carmichael and Jones were involved with the drug runners and their contact double-crossed them."

"You don't believe that, do you?" Cabe asked.

"No, I don't. Much as it pains me to believe it, I have to accept that we've got a rogue cop, but I don't believe Carmichael or Jones was involved. Carmichael was one of the best. I've known him for eleven years and never had reason to doubt his integrity on or off the job. Jones was newer, but Carmichael thought highly of him. His previous supervisor gave him the highest recommendation when he transferred to my unit."

"So what do we do now?" Cabe asked, but went on without waiting for an answer. "Someone is going to file an insurance claim on that building, and I've set in place some electronic tracking to see who cashes the check. The registered companies are obviously a false front to hide the real owners. I've already started some computer tracing that will hopefully unsnarl the ownership. I'm also looking for other property owned by those same 'blind' companies."

"That's a good start," Peter approved Cabe's plans. "Undoubtedly we're going to be stumbling over Internal Affairs for the rest of the investigation as well."

"I suppose that's a given." Cabe sighed as Peter's intercom sounded.

"Lieutenant Lewis, Captain Jacoby from the fire department is here, and Ballistics just dropped by the report you were expecting," an efficient voice announced. "Should I send the captain in?"

"Certainly," Peter affirmed.

Minutes later both men stood to greet the uniformed fire captain who entered the room. He was tall and held himself as erect as any military officer. He was easily thirty years older than the lieutenant, Cabe observed. He sported closely cropped white hair and a short, neat mustache. He was also clutching a thick accordion file folder. Peter shook hands with the fire captain then introduced Cabe.

"Nice to meet you, Captain." Cabe extended his hand. The captain shook it with a quick, firm grip, then turned back to Peter.

"The investigation isn't complete, but since you said it was critical that you receive a preliminary report as soon as possible, I decided to drop it by myself. Your suspicions were right on! Chemical accelerant. The lab hasn't identified the chemical yet, but they will. Not gasoline or kerosene. Wasn't splashed around. Unusual, but the lab will figure it out. It burned hot, too hot, in the acceleration area, which was lucky for us." The captain looked proud of himself.

"What do you mean, 'lucky for us'?" Peter indicated that he was as confused as Cabe from the terse report.

"Ever see a forest fire? No?" The captain launched into his explanation with obvious enjoyment. "Sometimes when a forest fire is really hot, and there's a high wind, the flames skim across the tops of trees, moving so fast they don't touch ground. Animals and plants on the forest floor get scorched, but they don't burn. Happened like that. The blaze at the warehouse started with some kind of fast, hot explosion that threw the flames upward and outward from the ignition point, which was in a large metal wastebasket. The material on top blew out and burned quickly, but the tightly packed items in the bottom of the basket didn't burn."

Peter and Cabe leaned toward their visitor with bated breath. When the captain continued to beam, but said nothing further, Cabe felt an urge to shake the exasperating man.

"Well, what did the unburned material tell you?" Peter finally asked.

"Oh!" Captain Jacoby looked startled, then quickly thrust the folder toward Peter. "It's all in here. The chief said to turn it over to you since it had nothing to do with starting the fire, but might be the reason it was set. It's possible the arsonist may have only intended to burn the things in the wastebasket, used too much accelerant, and accidently burned the building too."

Slowly Peter opened the folder and slid its contents onto the desktop. Cabe stared incredulously as a cascade of papers and four computer disks slid across the smooth surface. He had a hunch Peter's months of investigative work hadn't been wasted after all.

* * *

Tisa juggled a fast-food breakfast sandwich as she drove. It wasn't nearly as good as the television commercials led one to believe, and she regretted she hadn't taken time for a bowl of cereal or even a frozen waffle before leaving her apartment. Once she'd finally fallen asleep, she'd slept so soundly that she hadn't heard her alarm go off. Now she was going to be late, and she was meeting a new client today!

A car horn blared as she whipped onto Foothill Boulevard, and she wished she could apologize. Undoubtedly she'd cut someone off. Late or not, she needed to slow down and pay more attention. Norm had always told her "dead on time doesn't count."

A quick glance at her watch as she pulled into the parking lot behind Kurt's Interiors told her she was only ten minutes late. That would only get her a mild frown from Phillip Kurt, not the full glare that came with being a half hour behind schedule, but she really had wanted to be punctual this morning. She wanted to make a good impression on the new client, Mr. Bronson. He represented a large corporation that was adding four resorts to its western holdings and wanted each resort to be uniquely decorated in keeping with the varied settings.

Slipping in the back door, she made it to her office without encountering her boss, but she barely had time to stash her bag in her desk drawer and freshen her lipstick before Gloria DeMott's voice summoned her to the presentation room. A hasty glimpse of herself in the full-length mirror behind a closet door assured Tisa she looked more poised than she felt. No after-effects from her night of worrying about her brother showed on her face, and her short dress covered with tiny bright flowers looked both dramatic and professional. Gathering up a notebook filled with sketches, she hurried down the hall, passing Gloria DeMott, the company receptionist, and Howard Harmon, one of the company's top designers, on her way to the meeting. They both wore forced smiles. Tisa knew the two of them believed that Howard, with his years of experience, should have been the decorator given a chance at this plum of an assignment. She couldn't explain, and she wouldn't apologize for Phillip's choice.

The door to the presentation room stood open, and she paused there a moment. Her gaze flew right by Phillip to the man who stood at his side. He wasn't particularly tall, probably five-foot-nine or -ten, but he was well built, deeply tanned, and exuded confidence that bordered on arrogance. His professionally styled hair was a pale, almost white blond, lighter than her own. But it was his eyes that captured hers, sending a slight shiver down her spine. She felt, as much as saw, an answering reaction in the silvery-gray eyes staring back at her.

"Patricia, this is Daman Bronson. Daman, Patricia Lewis." Phillip was the only person of her acquaintance who never shortened her name, which was fine with her. She rather liked the way it distinguished her professional life from her personal one.

Gathering poise around her like a protective cloak, she offered her hand as Phillip made the introductions. Just as smoothly, the man she'd guessed was Daman Bronson, even before Phillip's introduction, greeted her warmly. "I'm staying at the Skye in Park City," he told her with a congenial smile, holding her hand a bit longer than necessary. "I've been told my beautiful, relaxing room was decorated by the talented Patricia Lewis. It's a pleasure to discover the woman behind the name is as lovely as her designs."

As he pressed the hand she offered, she was surprised that his touch felt slightly repugnant. No, *repugnant* wasn't the right word. She didn't know what the right word was, but *disappointment* might describe her feelings. After the electric moment when their eyes met as she'd entered the room, she'd expected his touch to be more . . . more . . . something. Perhaps more like the tingling awareness, the vibrant aliveness she'd experienced last night when Cabe brushed against her as he sat down. It was strange that she should meet two fascinating men in such a short period of time.

Whoa! She wasn't going there! It was time to concentrate on selling her design plans. Plastering a megawatt smile on her face, she reached for her portfolio. In seconds all three heads bent their attention toward the sketches and swatches of color spread across the conference table.

"People visiting resorts generally choose a hotel because of an interest in a particular activity or feature of the area near the resort," Tisa pointed out. "I doubt many people pick a hotel first, then look around to see what the area offers. That's why I prefer to bring the feature that enticed the visitors to the area right inside their rooms."

"I'm not sure that will work," Daman chuckled. "Snow brings well-heeled ski enthusiasts to Park City, but not too many of them want to sleep in a snowdrift."

Tisa's laughter joined Daman's. "You're right, but I meant the peripheral features, not the main attraction. Thick, puffy feather comforters and mounds of pillows in stark whites; sweeping white paint with hints of deep pine-green swirls on the walls; sheer, airy curtains backed by practical hunter-green, room-darkening blinds for those who wish to shut out the stars; plenty of rich natural woods; lamps, rugs, statuary, and vases in the colorful shades of ski togs; stone fireplaces with easy-to-switch-on gas logs; and bubbling jetted tubs—big enough for two—will remind visitors not only of the snow adventure, but will add a taste of those winter-vacation peripherals."

"Many of the existing hotels already rely heavily on early mining days and wildlife motifs," Phillip added. "A hint of *those* attractions could be used if care is taken not to overwhelm the senses by creating an atmosphere of the historical hardships or frontier businesses."

"A hotel room should be restful, comforting even, but never boring. It should be a continuation of the adventure," Tisa spoke softly, coaxingly, as she pointed to a sketch of a young couple cuddling in front of a floor-to-ceiling stone fireplace in one of the rooms she'd envisioned, their bright, colorful ski jackets tossed on the arm of the settee where they snuggled.

Daman's hand skimmed across the back of hers as he reached to touch the sketch. It took a conscious effort not to jerk her hand back. He held the picture a moment, then set it down before picking up another one.

"What did you have in mind for Island Park?" he asked as he set the drawing in front of her. This time his fingers just grazed her forearm, and she read a hint of challenge in his voice. Choosing to interpret the challenge as pertaining to her work, she launched into an explanation of the colors of mountains, streams, and flower-strewn meadows.

Four hours later the preferred sketches, mounted on display boards, circled the room; pizza boxes and soft-drink cans cluttered the tabletop, and a signed conditional contract sat before Phillip Kurt.

"I'll expect work to begin immediately," Bronson said as he closed his briefcase and rose to his feet. "My attorney will deliver the formal contract tomorrow along with the retainer fee. Perhaps you would both join me then for dinner, to celebrate the beginning of what I expect to be a profitable relationship for us." He spoke to both of them, but his gaze lingered on Tisa.

"Of course, should we say six o'clock?" Phillip responded, smoothly accepting the invitation for both of them.

As the door closed behind their new client, Tisa turned to Phillip with a broad grin. Simultaneously they raised their right hands and smacked them together in a high-five salute.

"I'm not sure whether it was our designs or you that clinched the deal." Phillip teased. "The guy couldn't take his eyes off you; I think you've made a conquest!"

"Was that a sexist insult?" Tisa growled in mock outrage. Deftly she hid the fluttering sensation in the area of her heart. Later she'd examine just what there was about the new client that both excited and disturbed her.

"I meant it as a compliment," Phillip hastened to assure her. "I know very well you never flirt nor imply any personal relationship in your presentations. Your ideas, coupled with my knowledge of the business, are an unbeatable combination, if I do say so myself. But sometimes a client, such as Daman Bronson, is helped along a bit by a pretty face."

Phillip's words disturbed Tisa more than soothed her. She liked being found attractive, and she was realistic enough to know that personality and appearance were often large factors in sales, but she still wanted her ideas to stand on their own merits. Also the attraction Mr. Bronson seemed to feel for her, and that he made no attempt to disguise, made her uneasy. The man was undeniably attractive, wealthy, and exhibited the kind of self-confidence she generally found appealing, but there was something about him that almost frightened her.

Gathering up her portfolio, she made her way toward the door. Side by side she and Phillip left the room. At the receptionist's desk, where Gloria and two of the other three decorators had gathered, he reached for her arm to bring her to a stop before her co-workers.

"Good news!" Phillip announced, waving the contract in the air. "This job calls for fast work, so I will be handling the Las Vegas hotel and casino personally, while Patricia will be undertaking the three smaller resort hotels in Park City, Island Park, and Lake Tahoe."

A smatter of applause greeted his announcement. "How soon can you finish up your current projects?" Phillip turned to question Tisa.

"I just finished the Moab project and can be finished with Dr. Caswell's home by the end of the week. That leaves three smaller office projects on the boards, and a proposal for a ski lodge to prepare," Tisa ran through her pending projects. She'd be working around the clock to juggle projects.

"Okay, finish the Caswell job, turn the offices over to Stacy. Eileen and Howard can both prepare proposals for the ski lodge." Phillip turned to Howard, "I think you should take over the new seniors' condominiums on Wasatch I've been working on too."

As Phillip spoke to Howard, Tisa took advantage of the absence of attention to slip into her office. After stowing her drawings in a cupboard, she sank into the deep chair behind her desk and reached for her phone. She wanted to share her news with Peter. He'd be happy for her, and proud of her landing the largest contract of her career. He might even begin to see that she was at last settling into a career she really cared about. She could hardly wait to start detailed sketches, but first, Peter. Even though Lara had assured her he was fine, she still needed to hear his voice and offer her sympathy for the two men he'd lost.

"Lieutenant Lewis's office," a deep voice rumbled in her ear. She nearly apologized for misdialing and set the phone back down before she recognized Cabe Evans's voice.

"Is Peter there? This is Tisa." She narrowly avoided stammering. Cabe Evans's voice set off slight tingles along her spine.

"No, he stepped out for a few minutes," Cabe's warm voice informed her. "If you'd like to leave a message, I'll make sure he gets it," he went on to offer.

"Oh, it's not really important," she said, then feeling reluctant to end the call, added, "I just thought a little good news might cheer him up; I suspect he's taking the deaths of those two officers pretty hard."

"It's hard for everyone in the department," Cabe concurred. "Even me, and I barely knew them." He hesitated as though concerned he might appear too forward. "I could use a little good news."

"I wanted to tell Peter I just landed a really big contract, one that will take at least six months to a year to fill." She laughed in a slightly self-conscious way before continuing. "I've changed jobs quite a few times, and I thought that learning I've committed myself to a long-term contract would please Peter."

"I don't know about Peter," Cabe said, a smile in his voice, "but it certainly pleases me, and it sounds like a cause for celebration. How about having dinner with me tonight and allowing me to help you celebrate?"

"Okay!" Her prompt acceptance surprised her. She hadn't dated since Mark, and she wasn't sure she was ready yet to plunge back into the dating scene. She almost retracted her acceptance, but something in Cabe's voice made her hesitate. He was probably lonely. He'd been in Utah such a short time, he probably didn't know anyone other than a few police officers, and she knew what it was like to be stuck in a strange city alone. Her job required enough traveling for her to know that spending nights alone in a motel room could become terribly boring. She wondered if he ordered all his meals through room service so he wouldn't have to eat alone in a restaurant the way she did when traveling.

Peter didn't have time to entertain Cabe all of the time. She'd be doing her brother a favor as well as being kind to Cabe. She couldn't quite bring herself to admit she was rationalizing doing precisely what she wanted to do, which was to celebrate with Cabe.

CHAPTER 5

"It's hopeless." Cabe rolled his chair back and tossed the disk he'd been attempting to read on the stack beside his computer. "The disks are too damaged. I can't do anything with them. We'll have to pass them on to the Bureau to see if their experts can salvage anything. That could take weeks."

Peter didn't look up from the papers he was examining. His voice was flat and his shoulders slumped. "I've a hunch I'll lose control of the case once the Bureau gets its hands on these disks."

Cabe pushed his chair back and stretched his long legs beneath the table. He hated to admit what was becoming increasingly obvious. "There are too many fingers in this particular pie. I've already been contacted by the CIA, and your chief passed on a message from your internal affairs people demanding we immediately forward any evidence we've collected to them. My boss at the Bureau is sending someone here from the Justice Department for a complete briefing on everything we've got."

"Are we going to be stuck wasting time on a jurisdiction fight then?" Peter practically snarled.

"No, the murders were in your jurisdiction. No one can stop your investigation there. Same for the arson. I can't force the other federal people to share information, but I don't have a problem giving you or them access to what I've gathered. The question is, how much are you willing to share?" Cabe looked sideways at him.

"No more than I have to; I won't take a backseat on this case. My men already think it's odd that I'm working with a private investigator," Peter growled. "Once they discover how much attention we're getting from Washington, they'll know you're not who you claim to be. If they know, and if we have a bad cop, the Dempskys will also know. There will be a lot of talk, too, about your so-called California client."

"Won't they figure the client was just part of my cover story?"

"I don't think so, and what if the wrong person figures out who your client is and why she wants Artel and Reuben Dempsky?" Peter asked, never taking his eyes from Cabe's face. "Just as I did."

Cabe felt shock settle through him, followed by resignation. He should have known Peter would do his own checking, and that he would find answers. What Peter had discovered, so might the Dempsky spies. *If Artel and Reuben Dempsky learn Dakota is talking and is willing to testify, she'll disappear before the case can even come to trial.* He had to make certain that didn't happen.

"You know who my informant is?" The question was rhetorical. Of course Peter knew. Cabe reeled from the possible ramifications if word leaked out that Dakota Langtry had any connection with the Dempsky crime syndicate.

"It wasn't too hard to figure out that your informant is Dakota Langtry, the actress who married that obscure rock-band drummer Wallace Delray in the late seventies. She gave birth to a daughter most of her fans don't even know existed, and asked for, and got, a court order sealing all of the divorce proceedings when she booted Delray out. The daughter, Annie, died three years ago in Bolivia, shortly before you gave up a short stint as a private investigator to go to work for the government. It wasn't too hard to discover the identity of the American girl who died near the Dempskys' South American supplier's territory three years ago, or the fact that your name appears on the documents releasing the body for return to the United States." Peter's eyes narrowed. "Do the federal boys know you have a personal interest that might border on revenge in this case?"

"My boss knows, and he thinks that gives me an inside edge. As for revenge, I suppose there is an element of that. But the same could be said for you. Isn't there more than a little personal vengeance in your pursuit of drug criminals?"

Peter stared at his clasped hands for several minutes before nodding affirmatively. "I have to remind myself each time I go after some piece of slime who's out there putting drugs on the streets that God claims the sole right to vengeance. I tell myself I'm driven to keep drugs from destroying children's lives because of my love for children, and that's true, but it's not all of it. Each time I look in my children's faces I know I love them too much to let anyone do to them what my parents and the greedy people who fed their habits did to me. Sometimes I take an honest look at my motives, and I admit that under it all there's still anger and a thirst for revenge. Those feelings play a large part in my pursuit of the Dempsky family. I wanted Ortega; I still do. I've got enough to take him down now, but you were right when you said I couldn't shut down Ortega's pipeline without stopping the Dempskys. The Dempsky name has come up in over half the drug operations I've closed in the past four years, and sending Reuben and Artel Dempsky to prison has come close to being an obsession with me."

Cabe voiced the questions he sometimes asked himself. "How do you justify those feelings? You hold the priesthood and you're an active member of the Church. Don't the feelings you've just expressed constitute hate, and doesn't hatred require you to seek forgiveness?"

"Seeking forgiveness is still an issue for me. I adhere strictly to the law and follow correct procedures always. Above all, I pray for daily help to deal with my feelings." Peter lifted his head and faced Cabe straight on waiting for the next question.

"But is that enough? I rely on God to grant me the ability to stop the crime without resorting to revenge too. And He has never failed me." Cabe matched Peter's statement of faith, then went on a little more hesitantly. "But, I admit that this case worries me. Sometimes I wonder if I can be objective where any of the Dempskys are concerned. I can't help wondering if I can truly hate the crime without hating the criminal." The men looked at each other in silence, their respect and understanding of each other grown. Then Peter redirected the conversation to the case itself.

"It's been three years. Why did Ms. Langtry approach you now?" Peter asked.

"The Dempskys destroyed her family, but there's more to it than that." Cabe began the fuller explanation he hadn't shared earlier. "Recently she learned she has cancer and has been forced into retirement.

In the emptiness of her huge house, she's begun to look at her illustrious career and feels she paid too high a price for fame. Facing the possibility that her own demise may not be far off, guilt has surfaced. She's convinced that her silence contributed to the Dempskys becoming the powerful crime family it is today. She believes, too, that her daughter would still be alive if she had spoken up sooner, and that it's up to her to stop them now."

"I found no trace of any connection between Dakota and either Reuben or Artel Dempsky," Peter pointed out.

"It goes back a long way." Cabe picked up a bottle of water sitting on his desk and took a long swallow before he began the story. "Dakota's husband was the connection. Wallace Delray played in the Dempskys' Starlight Room during the seventies. Artel was a two-bit hustler then, with a backroom bookie business and drugs for sale on the side, but he had big dreams. His brother Reuben worked behind the scenes in the business as well. Reuben was the muscle. He has a record for involvement in fights and protection schemes that stretches clear back into juvenile court. And most people don't even know that Artel had another brother named Stefan. Stefan disappeared several years ago and is presumed to be dead. He was the youngest and probably the smartest. If he were alive, he'd probably be the boss of the organization by now. He was a suspect, though no one ever proved anything, in several casino heists and a couple of strong-arm robberies.

"Anyway, Delray supplemented his music income by running errands for the Dempskys, but he somehow managed to get a bit part in one of Dakota's movies and put on the performance of his life—for her, if not for the camera. They were married while on location in Mexico. She knew nothing of the Dempskys' illegal activities at that time.

"I think she knew from the start the marriage was a mistake, and that was why she never allowed a hint of it to escape to the press. She learned early on that her husband was using, and she soon learned where he got his drugs. She didn't like it, but she dismissed it as something a lot of Hollywood people were doing.

"There were two sisters who sang in Delray's band—Loretta and Josie. Loretta was married to Reuben. Delray was gone a lot and eventually Dakota began to suspect he was having an affair with one of the sisters, but she didn't know which one. So she decided to sneak backstage to see if she could catch them. She found both of the singers and her husband with Artel and Reuben. Reuben was threatening to rearrange Delray's face if he didn't stay away from his wife. Dakota could hear him shouting from halfway down the hall and thought she might learn more by staying out of sight and listening than by confronting her husband. She hid herself in an adjoining dressing room where she had a perfect view of everything that was going on.

"Loretta denied she was having an affair and counterthreatened to go to the police with information about the brothers' illegal activities if Reuben didn't leave her alone. The shouting match ended with Artel holding her down while Reuben drove a needle into her arm. Delray did nothing to protect the woman he was allegedly seeing behind his wife's back. Stefan arrived in time to grab the other sister and hold her so she couldn't interfere. Loretta suffered terrible convulsions before she passed out. Dakota thought the woman was dead, and has never forgiven herself for tiptoeing away without reporting what she saw. The publicity could have destroyed her career back then, but she couldn't stop thinking about what she'd seen, and shortly after she filed for divorce."

"That was about the time she became something of a recluse," Peter mused.

"Yes, she became almost paranoid about publicity that didn't concern her movies. She holed up in that big old Malibu house overlooking the ocean, and saw almost no one other than the five families who shared the same stretch of beach. She also tried to distance her daughter from her father," Cabe said. "At first she seemed quite successful and Annie led a pretty normal life. Thanks to California's community property law, my mother bought the house next door, and Annie and I became good friends. Later, when I was hired to look for Annie, I was shocked to learn that without her mother's knowledge the girl had contacted her father, and that she had frequently sneaked away to spend time with him and his friends. It was one of Delray's girlfriends who introduced her and her friend to the Starlight, which had become a slick, topless bar. There they met the Dempskys, who were rapidly expanding their operation with the help of Reuben's son."

"What do you know about Reuben's son?" Peter cut in. "I found little on the disks you brought other than his name."

"He's pretty illusive and has managed to keep a clean record as far as arrests and convictions go. A snitch claims he was the hit man who shot Annie. He was in South America at the time, but the local authorities didn't make any real effort to determine who the shooter was. He doesn't use the Dempsky name anymore, but instead uses several aliases. We suspect he handles most of the legitimate businesses through which the family's drug money is laundered. He's smart and he doesn't generally get his hands dirty, though he is the number-one suspect in Wallace Delray's disappearance." Cabe shook his head. "Nothing has ever been proven, and there's no body, but there was some kind of grudge between the two that went way back to when his mother, Loretta, was alive. She didn't die as Dakota Langtry believed. She lived another ten years, though from all I've been able to learn, she was a hopeless heroin addict."

"The boy couldn't have been very old when his mother died," Peter stated.

"Sixteen, but he was being groomed even then to take his uncle Stefan's place in the business, and everyone knew there was no love lost between him and Delray, the man he blamed for his mother's addiction and her sister's disappearance," Cabe pointed out. He didn't add that there was no love lost between himself and Reuben's son either, a man so adept at hiding from the law that Cabe didn't even own a good picture of Annie's suspected killer.

"Another disappearance?" Peter raised his eyebrows.

"That family is good at making people disappear," Cabe said. He stood and paced the small space between his and Peter's desks. "It wasn't only Loretta's sister and Delray who disappeared without a trace; Stefan dropped out of sight too, and there's a rumor Reuben and Loretta had another child, a daughter. There isn't any trace of her."

"All right, I think it's time we come up with a new plan," Peter indicated. It was time to get down to serious business. "I'm not turning this stuff over to the Bureau until I get a good look at it, say, until tomorrow. That should give my department a twenty-four-hour head start. The warehouse was a key component in my case, and losing it hurts. I'm still tracing who actually owned it. I'd like to give a friend of mine—Howie Jacobs, who sometimes does a few jobs for the department—a crack at those four disks before we send them on to your boss. Most of the papers Captain Jacoby gave us are worthless, but I found a few names on a couple of them, four to be exact, that I think we should follow up on."

"All right," Cabe said looking at the slip of paper Peter handed him. He read the four names: ROSS AVENDALE, TRACY ROBERTS, JEB, and BRO, then reached for the phone on his desk. "If you're through with the papers, I'll send them on. I can stall my people on the disks until tomorrow."

"Good. While you research the names, I'll run and give these disks to Howie."

Finding background information on the first two names took little time. The other two names presented more of a challenge since they seemed to be a first name and then an incomplete name which could be either a first or last name. When Peter returned, Cabe showed him what he had found.

"*BRO* could even be a nickname," Peter suggested. "It's a common enough designation between brothers."

"You're thinking of Artel and Reuben."

"Yes," Peter verified, "but I think this is a partial name because of the context it appeared in on the charred paper."

"I agree," Cabe said, closing the file he'd been searching on the Internet. "We can't pull up anything significant with such a brief partial, but I've got addresses for the two complete names. They're local. Let's go check them out."

Peter left word with Dispatch where they could be reached and followed Cabe out the door. Minutes later they were on their way to a garage on the west side of town to talk to Ross Avendale, an ex-con who had served four years at the Point of the Mountain for his part in a burglary. He'd been released six years ago and had seemingly gone straight since then.

A dog barked somewhere in the distance, and the sound of children playing could be heard as the two men stepped out of Peter's car in one of the older, tree-lined neighborhoods west of the main business district. Businesses seemed to be almost evenly dispersed among the small, single-family frame houses, many of which were in need of paint and repairs. The slight breeze carried the faint aroma of frying chicken, and Cabe remembered they'd passed "The Colonel's" half a block back.

"This area was all residential a few years ago," Peter remarked as they walked up the sloping cement drive toward the open bay of a run-down mechanics garage. A late eighties Ford pickup was hoisted off the floor, and the blare of a radio came from the pit beneath it. They stopped at the edge of the pit to observe a man in coveralls with a baseball cap, reversed and pulled tight against his scalp, tinkering with the truck. He looked to be in his mid-thirties and fit the description they'd found for Avendale. Their shadows blocked the light, and Avendale looked up with an easy smile that slowly changed to a scowl.

"Boss is in the office." He indicated a door with a jerk of his head.

"I think you're the man we're looking for," Peter spoke evenly. "That is, if you're Ross Avendale?"

"What's this about?" Avendale looked at them with a great deal of suspicion in his eyes and seemed about to turn back to his tinkering.

"We'd just like you to answer a few questions," Peter went on. "Why don't you come up here where we can talk." He opened his wallet and showed the man his badge.

"I can talk from down here just fine." Avendale's words were defiant, but he reached for a rag to wipe his hands and climbed the pit steps until he was standing even with Peter and Cabe. "Now what's this all about?" He stood with his legs braced apart and his elbows bent.

"Maybe nothing," Cabe spoke for the first time. "We'd just like you to tell us what you know about a warehouse on the west side of the tracks near Eleventh South."

"Warehouse? I don't know nothing about any warehouse." The man seemed genuinely puzzled.

"That's not what we heard," Peter interjected, and this time there was a hardness behind his words.

"I tell you, I've never been to no warehouse anywhere near the tracks or anyplace else. Whatever happened there, I had nothing to do with it. I'm clean, and you cops ain't going to pin nothing on me!" The man's eyes narrowed as he glared back at them.

"We're not accusing you of anything," Cabe spoke reasonably. "We'd just like you to help us out. The place burned down last night and we're looking for the owner. Someone said you knew him."

"What are you guys trying to pull?" The man's tone turned to suspicion. "I don't know no guy that owns a warehouse."

"Maybe you did a little work on his car or one of his big rigs," Cabe suggested.

"I ain't no diesel mechanic, and I don't have time for a fishing trip." He turned away as though heading back into the grease pit.

"What about a new, white, four-door Lexus?" Peter suggested the latest and most expensive model vehicle Carmichael and Jones had reported seeing while staking out the warehouse. Cabe already knew, as did Peter, that the car was unregistered, and the plates were off a wrecked Taurus. Peter had run a check on every license plate his men had seen near the warehouse and had come up dry. They all belonged to junked cars or to dummy companies.

Avendale's facial muscles registered no change, but Cabe couldn't help feeling they'd made a hit. There was something, perhaps a stepped-up alertness in Avendale's eyes. The man knew something about the car.

"This ain't exactly the kind of shop a rich dude would pick to have his oil changed in," the mechanic sneered. "I don't have time to listen to any more of your questions. If you're going to charge me with something, do it. If not, get out of here. I've got work to do."

Cabe could see Peter's frustration. They had nothing with which to charge the man, which left them with no choice but to leave.

"All right," Peter agreed. "But if you suddenly remember seeing that white Lexus, I'd advise you to give us a call." He set his business card on an open tool case before walking away.

Back at the car, Cabe turned back to view the garage as Peter unlocked the doors. A movement caught his attention. A figure darted behind the garage and dived into the shrubs bordering the alley—a figure wearing coveralls and an inverted baseball cap!

Leaping into the car, he pointed toward the alley. Peter hit the gas without waiting for an explanation.

"Here!" Cabe yelled, and Peter screeched to a stop. Cabe tore toward the bushes, but when he parted them he saw nothing but a weed-infested yard littered with trash. He checked the adjoining yards and an alley, but didn't catch a glimpse of Avendale.

He returned to the car and explained to Peter what he'd seen. For the next half hour they slowly patrolled the nearby streets and alleys, finally conceding that if the figure Cabe had seen was Avendale, he could be holed up in any of the houses or small businesses in the area, and even if they did spot him, they couldn't justify detaining him.

Checking out Tracy Roberts proved even more unrewarding. There were two people with that name in the Salt Lake valley and another half dozen throughout the state. They decided to visit the two with local addresses. One turned out to be a college student, a shy freshman from New Hampshire living in a dorm on the Westminster campus, and the other a Sandy housewife who was expecting her fourth baby and was busy supervising eight Cub Scouts when they pulled into her driveway.

It was nearly five when they returned to their office. Peter called the records department to see what they'd found on the two partial names and hung up the phone feeling discouraged.

"No luck on the other names," he reported to Cabe. "Both partials are too common."

"I'll call my office and start a search of known Dempsky associates," Cabe offered. "But I think our best bet is Avendale. I feel certain he knows something."

"He does," Peter agreed. "I can have patrol cars swing by his house and the garage more frequently, but we don't have enough to warrant a close watch."

Cabe lowered himself to his desk chair and reached for the telephone. "I'll call my office and get that name-search started."

"I think I'll stop on my way home and see if Howie has been able to get into those disks," Peter said with a sigh. "Will you be here if there's anything to report?"

"No, I'm leaving too, as soon as I make that call." His hand hovered over the phone while he debated telling Peter about his date with Tisa. Feeling awkward, like a kid meeting his girlfriend's father for the first time, he added. "I'm taking your sister to dinner tonight."

"Tisa?" Peter sounded startled and not altogether approving.

"You have more than one sister?" Cabe found himself grinning at the expression on Peter's face. It seemed to be a mixture of worry and pleasure.

"No, of course not." Peter continued to sound taken aback. "It's just that Tisa doesn't generally date law enforcement people."

"She thinks I'm a PI." Cabe wondered if that made a difference and if he should tell Tisa the truth. There was no reason he decided. A single dinner date didn't warrant risking his cover, though remaining quiet seemed a little dishonest.

"I don't think she has anything against cops," Peter hurried to clarify. "She just doesn't want to cause me or the people I work with any awkwardness. I'm only surprised because she recently ended an engagement, and the last I heard, she said she wasn't ready to start dating again."

"Well," Cabe said, "when she called earlier for you, I took the call and she told me about her big contract." Cabe wasn't sure why he was explaining to Peter how he'd come to ask Tisa out. "She sounded like she'd like to celebrate."

"She told me about it too, when I returned her call." Peter checked his desk for any new messages. "She sounded pretty excited that a representative from a major hotel chain specifically chose her designs over those of more experienced decorators."

"It sounded like a big deal to her, so when she told me, I offered to take her to any restaurant she wished to celebrate at, and she agreed," Cabe told him.

"That's what did it," Peter snorted. "I hope you're prepared to pay for the biggest, most expensive meal in town!"

"That bad, huh?" Cabe grinned. "I noticed she enjoyed eating last night."

"She eats nonstop! I've never figured out how she can always be so hungry. Mom used to take her to doctors to see if she had a tapeworm or something." Peter shook his head. "Dad said she was a skinny, malnourished little thing, and covered with welts from a severe beating when they got her, and he figured she'd been darn near starved to death by whoever her first parents were, and that something in her head equates food with security. He always said when she felt secure enough, she wouldn't need to eat so much."

"Your parents must have been pretty special people," Cabe said.

"They were," Peter agreed. "There aren't many people who would take a ten-year-old addict who had already been tossed out of three foster homes and add him to a home with a frightened five-year-old whose background they knew nothing about."

"They adopted Tisa first?"

"Yes, she'd been with them about a year before they took me in. It took longer to clear her for adoption than it did me. My parents were happy to sign relinquishment papers, but there were a lot of hoops to jump through before a judge okayed Tisa's adoption. Then, because I was over eight, it took a while longer for me to decide I wanted to be baptized and to be sealed to them in the temple. Actually that worked out all right, too, because Tisa and I were able to be sealed to our parents at the same time."

"The two of you are close." It was more statement than question.

"From the moment I walked into the Lewises' house I felt a connection with that little girl that I can't explain. Perhaps it was some similarity in our backgrounds we instinctively recognized in each other. Lara is more romantic. She thinks we made a pact before we were ever born to help each other." He neither seconded nor scoffed at his wife's theory, but left the possibility hanging in the air while he gathered up a portfolio of papers to take with him. At the door he paused to make one last statement, "Have a good time, but be careful. She has a bad habit of breaking hearts." He closed the door softly behind himself.

Cabe stared at the closed door for several minutes. He'd half expected a warning from Peter against hurting Tisa. The oblique warning that he might be the one to be hurt lingered in his mind, distracting him as he picked up the phone to call his office.

* * *

Tisa glanced at her watch. There wasn't time to return home and change before meeting Cabe. She'd worked longer than she'd intended on the outline of her plans for the Island Park Hotel. She jumped to her feet and hurried to the mirror behind the closet door. She checked her appearance and smoothed the silky dress she wore against her slim hips. It was one of her favorite outfits and dressy enough to wear almost anywhere. Her hands paused and she stared at her reflection in the glass. Her cheeks were flushed and her hands were making fluttery movements. She was nervous! She hadn't been nervous about a date for years! Was it Cabe? Granted, he wasn't like any other man she knew, but he was *just* a man.

Annoyed with herself, she snatched up her purse and marched to the door, pausing only to give the lock a twist before stepping into the hall, allowing the door to lock behind her as it closed. The lights had been dimmed and the doors that stood open most of the day were closed, giving the building a quiet, deserted feel. She should have been watching the time better; now she'd have to set the burglar alarm. She hated setting the alarm; no matter how carefully she went through the procedure, she always climbed in her car feeling like she'd forgotten something or done something wrong. She was almost to the receptionist's desk when a soft metallic click caught her attention. Her head came up. She wasn't alone after all. Someone else was working late.

She rounded a corner and saw Howard Harmon kneeling in front of a file cabinet behind the receptionist's desk with a sheaf of papers spread before him. Thank goodness! She wouldn't have to set the alarm.

"Good night, Howard," she called and watched in amusement as his head jerked up. She hadn't been the only one who thought herself the last one to leave. From his startled expression she guessed he hadn't heard her approach.

"Oh! Patricia." He stood in a jerky movement, and his eyes seemed to search the darkness behind her. His eyes changed from wariness to anger, which he hastily concealed. She noticed the way his foot nervously edged a sheet of paper under the desk. She started to move past him, but hesitated when he spoke, "I'd like to talk to you about the Bronson account."

"Can't now," she told him. "I'm meeting someone, and I'm already late. I'll see you tomorrow." She waved and hurried toward the exit. She was in no mood to listen to Howard moan about the unfairness of the deal. Just because he'd been with the firm the longest, that didn't entitle him to pick and choose his assignments, or give him the right to make her feel guilty because she'd been given an assignment he wanted. She didn't want to soothe his ego; she wanted to celebrate.

* * *

Glints of light reflected in Tisa's eyes, and the magenta streak in her pale hair gleamed from the flickering candlelight. Cabe watched her face and enjoyed the obvious delight she took in her dinner. She ate fettuccine with shrimp marinara sauce with the same enthusiasm she'd eaten the barbequed spareribs the night before. She looked up to catch him watching her. A faint ridge of pink highlighted her cheekbones.

"I know, it's not too ladylike to eat so much."

"I didn't say that." He smiled. "I've never liked sitting down to dinner with a woman who nibbles on lettuce leaves while I'm trying to eat a real meal."

She lowered her eyes to the table, then lifted them back to his face. A smile reached her eyes, telling him his empty plate went a long way toward assuring her that her healthy appetite really didn't bother him. It also told him it was an issue that had hurt and embarrassed her in the past. Reaching for her hand, he cradled it between his palms while his eyes searched her face. He read appreciation for his understanding in her eyes.

"I like a woman who enjoys what she does, whether its food or anything else," Encouraged, Cabe told her, "Last night at your brother's home you looked happy, laughing with friends, watching your small niece, and even while talking to me. In my line of work I see too many people who don't know how to enjoy what they have or to take pleasure in small things." He paused, then deliberately changed the subject. "On the phone earlier today you sounded happy and excited over your new account. I want to hear all about it."

She seemed to welcome the shift in topic. "It's a terrific opportunity," she told him. "There are four vacation hotels in the deal. They're all located on choice pieces of property with exciting natural backdrops, and I've been given the go-ahead to use themes and color schemes that will flow smoothly into the outdoor charm of the various areas."

"Four hotels? With all the new hotels built for the Olympics, can the area support that many more?" Cabe asked.

"They won't be in Salt Lake," Tisa told him.

"You're leaving?" He felt a stab of disappointment.

"No," she smiled, looking pleased that he cared. "I'll do much of the work right here in my office, though I will have to make frequent on-site visits once the construction is nearly complete. I'll be decorating the three smaller hotels: Park City, Island Park, and Lake Tahoe. Phillip Kurt will do the larger one in Las Vegas. None of them are terribly far away."

"No, not too far," he agreed, somehow feeling better, especially at the mention of Lake Tahoe. That wasn't too great a distance from his home. *Slow down,* he reminded himself. *This is only one date and I'm just beginning to get acquainted with Tisa. It's much too soon to be thinking of ways to continue seeing her once I return to California.*

"These hotels will be different from most hotels," Tisa went on, her voice sparkling with excitement. "I decorated a hotel in Park City a short time ago. It was fun, but there were definite limits to what I could do because the owners already had concepts they wanted carried out, and there had to be a certain amount of uniformity to the rooms. These hotels will be composed of small, intimate luxury suites, and the owner says he prefers that each one be individually decorated."

"Sounds like a lot of work." Cabe sounded appreciative of the effort she would be putting into the project.

Tisa smiled, and gestured toward his strawberry meringue. "Are you going to eat that?"

He looked down at the dessert and shook his head before pushing it across the table. "If you can eat it, it's yours." He smiled as he offered it to her. He'd only ordered it because it sounded light, and he was already full, but hadn't wanted Tisa to hesitate over ordering dessert.

"Thanks." She smiled back, and he watched as she speared a strawberry, soaked in chocolate syrup, and daintily thrust it between her teeth. He was in trouble here. This woman was getting to him in a way no other woman ever had, not even Annie, and he wasn't sure that was a good thing. He hadn't come to Salt Lake expecting to find a woman who fascinated him so much he felt an edge of excitement just watching her eat! He'd come to catch a killer, not to fall for a pint-sized human food processor.

CHAPTER 6

Cabe had been at work for nearly an hour when Peter came striding into the office with a broad grin on his face. "Look at this!" He set two disks on Cabe's desk. "Howie came through for us."

"He found something on the disks?" Cabe couldn't believe they had lucked out. "Is it usable?"

"When I stopped at Howie's place last night, he said he was making progress, but he hadn't salvaged anything yet." Peter's grin grew wider. "He also said one of the disks was so severely heat damaged he could do nothing with it, another one was debatable, but he thought with time he could read the other two. This morning he called to say he'd gotten into the disks and found they contained data stored in code, but it wasn't a complicated code, so he translated it for us."

"You're kidding, right?" Cabe touched one of the disks with the tip of his finger as though he couldn't quite believe it was real.

"No. By the time I got there, he'd copied everything from the two better disks onto these two new disks. He said the Bureau might be able to pull something up from the one partially destroyed disk, but the other disk is useless."

"Anything we can use on the ones he copied?" Cabe queried with anticipation in his voice.

"I haven't looked at them yet," Peter answered, but Cabe recognized an edge of triumph behind his words. "Howie seemed to think they might be important. He said they're mostly numbers, probably an extensive profit-and-loss statement."

"I assume you have the originals too. My office will send a secure courier for them."

Peter set the disks Captain Jacoby had turned over to them on the table beside the new disks. Cabe reached for one of the disks copied by Howie, but before he could slide it into his computer the sound of footsteps approaching the open door caught his attention.

"Lieutenant Lewis?" Bob White stood in the doorway. "Wesley in Vice asked that you sit in on the interrogation of one of the ladies he picked up last night. He said she's pretty desperate to get out, and he thinks it's more than needing a fix. She's willing to cut a deal by giving us information on a dealer."

Peter turned anxious eyes toward the disks, then back to the plainclothes officer standing in the doorway. He clearly wanted to know what was on the two reclaimed disks, yet he couldn't pass up a chance to question a defendant who was willing to talk about a supplier.

"I'll call for the secure courier to come and get the originals after I take a look at the copies," Cabe assured him. "I'll give you a rundown as soon as you get back, then you can scan the files yourself whenever you have time."

"Tell him I'll be right there," Peter told Bob, then, with one last lingering glance at the disks on Cabe's desk, followed the Vice officer out the door.

Cabe dropped the originals in his coat pocket. He'd turn them over to the evidence room to hold until the Bureau picked them up. Booting up his computer, he inserted the first disk Howie had prepared for them. He didn't dare hope for much, but as figures began to fill his screen he couldn't restrain a whoop of joy. Page after page of transactions scrolled before him complete with headings. Here was a detailed list of prices paid for imported cocaine, expenses paid, and profits derived from the transactions. A name caught his attention. JEB. JEB was a corporation, not a partial name of a person! That information could aid in untangling the warehouse ownership issue. He could hardly wait to show the disk's contents to Peter.

Half a dozen different abbreviated names, several of which were familiar to him, appeared in the shippers column, confirming the link between the drugs being distributed through the warehouse and the Dempsky organization. This was the link Peter needed to connect Ortega to the Dempsky organization. Jotting the names on a yellow pad of paper brought deep satisfaction. The disk was a gold mine of information that would keep dozens of prosecutors busy for a long time.

The Justice Department would have a field day when they got their hands on the disk. It alone was almost enough to get a warrant for the Dempskys' arrests. Pressing the scroll button, he moved through the pages of figures, pausing only when words replaced numbers on the screen. There weren't many of those; they only appeared to head columns and to identify switches in consignments or carriers. He had a hunch INS would be interested in a list of the carriers' names. Too bad addresses weren't included.

When he finished with the disk, he began preparing a synopsis of the information. At the sound of the opening office door, Cabe turned to see Peter's jaunty step and a smile lurking at the corners of his mouth.

"This woman just might be the break we're looking for!" Peter lost no time outlining the information gained in the session with the prostitute. "She has family in Mexico, and she hasn't been here long. Someone by the name of Munez arranged for her to slip across the border with a package. She claims she doesn't know what the package contained; her only interest was in getting here so she could make money to send back to her family."

"I don't suppose she knows this Munez's full name?" Cabe narrowed his eyes.

"She says no, but here's the good part; one of the vehicles Carmichael and Jones documented as arriving regularly at the warehouse belongs to one Raul Munez. They got long-range photos of Munez and Ortega together."

"That should convince a jury there's a link between the two."

Peter continued, "The woman said her delivery point for the package was a warehouse two blocks from the one that burned." A look of smug satisfaction crossed the lieutenant's face. He had the address he needed to continue pursuing the operation.

"Yes!" Cabe shared Peter's euphoria with a one punch in the air. "Why do you think they burned the first warehouse only to move such a short distance?"

"The warehouse that burned was old and hard to secure. The whole block is scheduled for demolition, and I think they wanted out before their presence invited too much attention. Once they discovered our stakeout, they lost no time leaving and covering their tracks." The pained look on Peter's face as he finished explaining told Cabe he was thinking of the two men he'd lost.

"I have good news too." Cabe attempted to divert Peter's thoughts from the painful loss. "The disks are a bonanza. They're a definite link to the Dempsky organization. It'll be a race to convict them for their drug operations before the IRS puts them away for tax evasion!"

Peter reached for the notes Cabe handed him. He silently perused them for several minutes before releasing a long, slow whistle. "This is fantastic! Nailing down the numbers for even one part of the Dempsky operation is a tremendous break. This should put Reuben and Artel behind bars for the rest of their lives."

"I want Reuben's son, too." Cabe spoke with determination. "If the Justice Department moves too swiftly on this, they'll close down Reuben's arm of the organization, but only temporarily. It won't take long for Artel to find someone to take his brother's place. Maybe even his nephew. Justice is so antsy to close the drug ring they'll settle for Reuben, and we'll miss our chance at the other two."

"That means we move quickly before the Justice Department starts making raids and before the Dempsky organization learns we have those disks," Peter said. "I have a feeling they'll be watching more closely now for surveillance at the new warehouse, which will make snooping more difficult."

Cabe rose to his feet and paced to Peter's desk and back. "What are your plans for the new warehouse?"

"I've already sent two men to check on an apartment half a block away. It has a good view of the loading dock and back door of the building. With heavier traffic and great visual from the third-floor apartment, carriers may be easier to watch. Besides, the Dempskys won't be expecting us to have discovered their new warehouse this quickly." Peter turned his attention back to the papers he held in his hand. "These numbers are great, but I was hoping the disks would provide us with more names. I'll have Marco get in touch with INS and see if he can track down any of the illegals. Alldredge and White can follow up with DEA to see what they have on the suppliers."

"I've already contacted my office," Cabe reported. "A dozen agents are on standby if we need them."

Peter checked his watch. "I've got court this afternoon, but there's time to grab a sandwich first. We can plan our next move while we eat."

"Sounds good to me." Cabe reached for his jacket. "I have an appointment at the federal building in an hour, then I'd like to come back here and take a look at that second disk."

Peter was almost to the door. He stopped to look back at Cabe. "You got all that from just one of those disks?" He waved toward Cabe's computer where Cabe was locking the disks and the yellow notepad in a drawer.

"Yes, I expect the second disk will be more of the same, but I'm anxious to take a look at it anyway."

"Maybe we should just order in sandwiches." Peter now seemed reluctant to leave his office.

"There isn't time, if you're going to make it to court by two." Cabe checked his watch.

"Judge Davis will just get everyone assembled," Peter said. "The defense will ask for a delay. Davis will grant it, and we'll all be out of there with nothing to show for our time but a couple of wasted hours." His voice revealed the familiar cynicism of a cop frustrated, but resigned, to the idiosyncrasies of the judicial system.

Seated across from each other a quarter of an hour later, Peter took a large bite of his burger, chewing slowly for several minutes, then asked the question Cabe had been expecting all morning.

"How'd your date go last night?"

"Fine." Cabe held a straight face and offered no further information.

"Are you going to see her again?" Peter persisted.

"I might." Cabe kept his answer brief.

"Tisa isn't like other women." Peter set his sandwich down and stirred the catsup and mayonnaise mixture before him with a long french fry.

"Is this a big brother warning?" Cabe lifted his own sandwich to his mouth to hide his amusement. Tisa was twenty-six years old, certainly old enough to pick her own male friends.

"Maybe," Peter conceded. "I've watched a lot of men fall hard for my little sister and then get hurt."

"Hey!" Cabe's eyebrows shot up. "Are you warning me off because I might get hurt? I thought big brothers' warnings were all about protecting their little sisters!"

"I might forget I'm a cop and do a little taking the law into my own hands if some guy hurts Tisa in that way." Peter's glare lent credence to his words. "But with Tisa, I've discovered she's quite capable of taking care of herself unless some guy springs out of the bushes with assault on his mind. Even then, she can handle herself better than most."

Peter looked around as though he felt uncomfortable discussing his sister with Cabe, yet seemed to feel it was his duty to warn him. "You're a man who cares deeply, and that's where you could regret tangling with Tisa. Emotionally, she doesn't let many people get close. There's a part of her she hides from even me, and we're as close as a brother and sister can get. I've never been certain whether she was too young to remember her life before our parents adopted her, or if she somehow chose to forget her previous life, but something from that time continues to have a hold over her. If you're interested in more than casual friendship with her, sit her down and insist she tell you about her former fiancés."

"Fiancés? That's plural?" Cabe raised an eyebrow.

"That's right." Peter gathered up the tray and headed for the nearest trash receptacle. Cabe followed, though his mind lingered on Peter's warning. He'd expected a little good-natured teasing from the lieutenant, even a veiled threat or two if he didn't treat Tisa right, but he hadn't expected Peter to imply that Tisa might be a heartbreaker, or that *he* might be the one to get hurt.

"I'll see you back at the office about four," Peter said by way of farewell. "If the second disk is more of the same stuff you found on the first, make copies for us and send both the original and the trans-lated copies on. I don't want to give your boss the impression I'm holding back. We might have time when I get back to drive by that new warehouse before calling it a day."

Cabe continued to think about Peter's unusual warning during his visit to the federal building. After a quick visit there, he returned to the office he and Peter shared. For long minutes he stared into space and thought about Tisa. He hardly knew her, yet he couldn't deny the pull he felt toward her. Last night, sitting across the table from her had been like coming home. It had been a new experience for him. He'd dated beautiful women before, but he'd never experienced the sensation of completeness he'd felt last night with Tisa.

Before getting down to work, he pulled up all the case records and newspaper stories he could find on the Internet and law enforcement files concerning the little girl who had been abandoned alongside a highway twenty years ago. There wasn't much. The most recent story had been written ten years ago and had appeared in a women's magazine. It was about children who had been found abandoned in shopping malls, service stations, or in unmarked, lonely graves. Tisa's story was one the journalist had shared, speculating that she might have been born at home, her birth unrecorded, and been abused until the day the mother decided she'd had enough and tossed her from her car for some minor childish offense.

Several couples whose daughters had been kidnapped or whose children had disappeared at early ages had inquired about her, hoping she was their missing child, but she had never matched any known missing child. The truck driver found her alongside I-15 just north of St. George, Utah. He reported she'd spoken to him, told him her name was Tisa, and mumbled a few words when he stopped at a truck stop to eat and call the highway patrol to report finding her. He hadn't taken the child inside the café, but had ordered two sandwiches to go.

Tisa had eaten both sandwiches and a double order of fries while the truck driver had been on the phone with the highway patrol. The officer he'd spoken to had warned him about an oil spill that had caused multiple collisions ahead, tying up every patrol car for hundreds of miles. He'd told the driver to take the child to Fillmore, Utah, and turn her over to the sheriff there.

They'd been forced to stop at the accident scene, where the driver had volunteered to help clear the road so traffic could proceed once the accident victims had been removed from the wreckage of their cars. When he'd climbed back inside the cab, the little girl had been curled in a ball on the passenger's seat with her eyes wide and staring.

She'd looked terrified and didn't speak another word for several months. Neither the deputy who took charge of her in Fillmore, nor the social workers who attempted to discover clues to her identity, had been able to find a connection between any of the accident victims and the little girl. A psychiatrist the reporter consulted had speculated that the child had been traumatized by the blood and gore she'd witnessed from the high vantage point of the truck cab. Under the loving care of Norm and Dixie Lewis, she'd resumed speaking, but she'd never talked of the past.

Cabe stared in frustration at his computer screen. He had work to do, and here he was wasting precious time chasing links that might tell him more about Tisa. Was it the mystery of who she was and where she'd come from that fascinated him? Or was it the woman herself? He'd known many beautiful and talented women in his life, but none had captured his attention the way Tisa had, and he wasn't sure that was a good thing. He'd always pictured himself settling down someday with a wife and children. He liked women who were tall, athletic, impeccably groomed, and capable; the kind of women who could manage a household, be Primary president, work in the PTA, chauffeur kids to ball games and dance lessons, and still be fresh and lovely on his arm at one of his mother's charity functions. His thought brought a chuckle. His mother wouldn't hesitate to tell him what he could do with his "dream wife," and she'd be right.

A vision of Tisa in a purple miniskirt and thigh-high red boots with four-inch platform soles sprang into his mind. The skirt would be topped with a bright yellow blouse sporting silver bangles. He could see the multi-shades of hair on her head leaning toward one of his mother's elegant buffets and the food disappearing as if by magic. He grinned, enjoying the fantasy. It might be fun. Even with the tallest shoes she could find, Tisa would never be tall, but he suspected she could manage the rest of his fantasy. And she'd do it with a flair and style that just might shake up the staid world he knew.

"All right, Cabe," he spoke aloud to himself. "Stop the daydreaming and get to work. Admit you've got it bad for a woman you just met; and even though you've been warned she's trouble, in all your arrogance, you've no intention of backing off. So work now, and call her tonight to see if she's interested in getting better acquainted."

He shoved the waiting disk into drive A and remembered she was having dinner tonight with the guy who had just signed a mammoth contract with her design company. That thought brought a twinge of jealousy that he studiously attempted to ignore.

* * *

Tisa smiled as she merged from I-215 onto I-80. The sun was shining, and her Jaguar jumped at the increased pressure on the accelerator. She'd be in Park City in plenty of time to deliver the two small sculptures she'd ordered for the manager's office of the Skye Hotel. The bronzes had captured the man's fancy when she'd first shown him samples of the Heber artist's work when she'd begun decorating the hotel, but it had taken longer than expected for the sculptor to cast the special editions and ship them. Because of their tardy arrival she felt obliged to deliver them personally.

She didn't mind the extra trip. It was a perfect day to drive up the canyon, and since she had a dinner date with Daman Bronson anyway, she'd called before leaving her office suggesting she meet him at the hotel. He'd been out when she called, but she'd left a message and her cell phone number with instructions to call her if he'd prefer to meet somewhere else.

Moving to the inside lane to pass the trucks and RVs moving slowly up the outside lane, she breathed in the pine-scented air and thought about the man she would soon be meeting. He both fascinated and frightened her. Perhaps *frightened* wasn't the right word she amended, but just thinking about him gave her goose bumps. It was more than his looks, and she'd be the first to admit he had more than his fair share of that commodity.

A persistent ringing interrupted her thoughts, and she fished with one hand in her bag for her phone, then watched for a lookout point where she could pull off the road. Driving up Parley's Canyon wasn't an ideal situation for talking on the phone. She found a scenic overlook just as she flipped the button on her phone to take the call.

"Just a moment," she spoke into the tiny instrument, then dropped it into her lap as she brought her car to a stop in the narrow space. "Hi!" She put a lot of enthusiasm into her greeting. "I had to pull off the road to talk," she explained.

"That's okay," a deep voice rumbled in her ear, then almost disappeared behind the whoosh of traffic. "This is Daman. I just wanted to let you know meeting at the hotel is fine with me, but I'll be a little later than six. It'll probably be closer to seven before I get there."

"That's fine. I'm meeting with the hotel manager and that may take a while. If I get through early, there's a craft shop I've been meaning to check out. I'll plan on meeting you at seven."

"Great!" Daman expressed his agreement, and after mutual farewells Tisa dropped her phone into the space between the bucket seats and began watching traffic for an opening.

It didn't take long to deliver the bronzes, and seeing that she had more than an hour left before meeting Daman, she left her car in the hotel parking lot and began a slow trek down Park City's busy Main Street toward the craft shop. The picturesque former mining town had received a lot of attention during the recent winter Olympics, which had resulted in an increased number of tourists. She paused to window-shop, and when a pair of hiking boots with green-and-lavender laces caught her eye, she stepped inside the small store to try them on.

Emerging from the store ten minutes later with a bright shopping bag in one hand, she was surprised to see Daman disappearing around the side of a nearby building. Hurrying after him, she arrived at the alley in time to see him step through a door opening onto the alley from the building next door. She started to call out to him, then hesitated. She was either overly imaginative or there had been something secretive about the way he'd opened that door and slipped inside. At any rate he was gone, and she'd feel uncomfortable following him into some shop's back room. It was possible the man she'd seen wasn't even Daman; she'd only caught a quick glimpse before he was out of sight. And anyway, she wanted to visit the craft shop.

Pulling a slip of paper from her pocket, she checked the address. The craft shop had to be close. It took only a moment to realize she was standing practically in front of it. It was one of several shops facing a narrow street that looked like it had stepped out of the pages of a history book. While most of the shops looked freshly painted and inviting, the craft shop appeared to be in need of some serious renovation, as did the rest of the long, two-story building with *FOR SALE* signs in almost every window.

Giving the building a dubious look, she stepped closer. Now she could see the entryway was split with one door leading into the craft shop and the other into a different shop. A bell tinkled as she pushed open the door. No one came to greet her, so after a moment's hesitation she began wandering around the narrow, cluttered space. She made note of a couple of nice watercolors and a small wood carving of an old man, but was disappointed overall. Most of the items on display had the look of mass productions meant for unwary tourists. Deciding the trip had been for nothing, she left without leaving her card for the owner.

Catching sight of a clock prominently displayed on a bank across the street, she began to walk faster. After waiting an hour for Daman, she didn't want to be late. Besides, she was famished. She couldn't help turning her eyes toward the door Daman, or someone who looked a lot like him, had disappeared through earlier. As she did, she noticed the building was the same building that housed the craft shop she'd just left.

No lights highlighted the large display windows of the other shop, and no sign proclaimed the name of a business. Puzzled, she stepped closer to the large, empty window before her. Through the glass she could see a bare room, a long counter running at a right angle from the front door, and rows of empty shelves lining the walls. At the back of the room she could see a closed door, doubtless leading to the same back room Daman had so recently entered. She wondered if the two shops shared a back room and if the person running the craft shop had been talking with Daman, which would explain why no one was in the showroom.

A slight shiver ran down her spine, and her imagination began to crank out dramatic scenarios explaining Daman's mysterious connection to the old building, until a small sign in one corner of the window caught her attention. *FOR SALE.* A giggle tickled its way to the surface. Daman was a businessman. He was no doubt checking out the building as a business investment.

In moments she was striding across the bright Skye Hotel foyer toward Daman, who waited for her beside a massive urn filled with exotic plants.

"Hello, pretty lady." He greeted her with a wide, appreciative smile.

She smiled back as he tucked her hand into the crook of his elbow and led the way to his car. It was a short drive to the restaurant where he had reservations. They could have easily walked, but she suspected he'd chosen to drive in order to impress her with his luxurious Lexus.

The restaurant, built to resemble a French chateau, was charming and tasteful, and with just the slightest flourish, the maitre d' showed them to a table overlooking breathtaking mountain scenery. The decor contributed to the ambiance, providing a touch of European grandeur.

"Would you care to see the wine list, monsieur, madame?" The man asked with an accent that sounded convincing enough to Tisa. She'd never been to France nor studied the French language, so she didn't know if the waiter was an authentic Frenchman, but she thought the accent was a nice touch, real or not.

She shook her head at the same time Daman nodded his assent. The waiter took his cue from Daman and set an elegant wine list on the table in front of him. He made his selection and the waiter left to return a few minutes later with stemmed glasses and a thin bottle resting in a bucket of ice. Both Daman and the waiter looked puzzled when Tisa refused the wine he'd selected for them.

"You go ahead." She smiled at him before picking up the menu. "I don't drink, and I'll be happy to drive if you want more than one. I've never driven a Lexus."

He laughed easily. "Two with dinner, and I'm well within the legal limit. You won't get to practice on my car."

"Darn!" She faked disappointment with a brief impudent pout before opening the elaborate menu to discover it was in French. Her face must have shown her dismay.

"Would you like me to order for you?" Daman asked, a smile playing at the corner of his lips, filling her with an unpleasant suspicion. He'd picked this restaurant to make himself appear superior. Well, she had a surprise for him. She didn't read or understand the French language, but she knew about food, and she liked it all— except escargot. If she didn't recognize the French names of dishes she enjoyed, she'd simply point at something, make sure it didn't contain the word *escargot*, and order it.

"No, I can order for myself," she told him.

When the waiter returned, she pointed to the fourth item on the menu.

"Are you sure?" Daman asked, and she felt he was being a mite condescending, so she quickly reaffirmed her order. He shrugged his shoulders and placed his own order.

They chatted agreeably about plans for the hotels until their orders arrived. Just as she expected, Daman's order consisted of a plate full of snails swimming in butter with a small serving of uncut green beans. When her order was placed before her, she felt like clasping her hands in the air and shouting, "Yes!" A whole stuffed bird of some kind, bigger than a game hen, but smaller than a chicken, rested in the place of honor. It was accompanied by an endive salad.

"I've instructed the architect to rush blueprints to you." Daman wiped his mouth and reached for his glass. "They should be in your hands by Monday."

"Good." Tisa lifted her fork to her lips and her answer was as much in appreciation of the stuffed capon as for Daman's plans. "Which hotel will be completed first? Should I plan on ordering materials in a particular order?"

"Island Park is almost complete. It will be ready for carpet in two weeks." He shook his head as the wine steward approached their table, and Tisa was glad he was sticking to his promise of two glasses of wine. Even so, she couldn't avoid a vague sense of disappointment that he was drinking wine at all.

"I'll need to visit the site right away then." Tisa sat up straighter, feeling a surge of excitement for the project. "I like to see the surrounding area and familiarize myself with the layout before I begin ordering. This doesn't allow time for custom-designed carpet, but there are so many choices available, I'm sure I'll be able to find the right pattern."

"I'll be going there Tuesday, perhaps you'd like to accompany me?" Daman offered.

"I'd really like to go sooner than that," Tisa hesitated. "If I drive up Monday night, would I have access on Tuesday?"

"I'll arrange it and give you directions," Daman promised, "on one condition." When Tisa met his eyes with a question in her own, he smiled and added, "If you'll have lunch with me Tuesday."

"I seldom turn down an offer for a meal." She turned her attention back to her dinner and quickly polished off her entrée. Daman watched her, but said nothing. She reached for a roll from the elegant little basket the waiter had set before them and discovered it was empty. She didn't remember eating more than a couple of the dainty puffs of bread.

"I can ask the waiter for more," Daman offered.

"No, I'm fine," she assured him. For some reason she felt reluctant to have Daman discover the extent of her appetite. Lowering her eyes to the table, she discovered Daman had eaten every one of the snails on his plate, and there wasn't a sliver of the beans left.

"Dessert?" he asked.

"Oh, yes," she murmured, glad he was hungry too.

When the dessert cart arrived she selected a mouthwatering puff pastry and regretted not taking two when she saw the two large slices of rich fudge cake the waiter set before Daman. She checked the smile that yearned to break free. Could it be possible she'd found a kindred spirit? The first bite of the pastry was heavenly, and she closed her eyes to savor the rich, fruity taste. When she opened them it was to see Daman scarfing the cake down so quickly he couldn't possibly taste it. Nausea rose in her stomach and panic made her head spin. Before her a young boy sat in the dirt stuffing chocolate cake in his mouth with both hands. Her head reeled, and she set her fork back on her plate.

"If you're too full to eat that, I'll finish it for you." Daman reached across the table to take her plate. She blinked in confusion and the nausea left as quickly as it had arrived.

Stunned, she watched her pastry disappear. She didn't know whether to laugh or cry. It was the first time she could remember anyone finishing her dessert for her; she was the one who generally eyed her date's dessert and jumped at the chance to finish it for him!

CHAPTER 7

Cabe scrolled to the bottom of the last column. Like the first disk, the second disk held extensive financial records. He'd spent all afternoon collecting and sorting the data from the disk. There was just one file left to be opened, and he wondered if he should leave it until tomorrow. It was after seven and Peter hadn't returned as he'd promised. He hadn't gone home either; Lara had called a short time ago to see how soon she might expect her husband. Cabe decided he would work a little longer, then go to dinner. Peter must have gotten tied up with some other case.

Thinking of dinner brought Tisa to mind. He'd enjoyed the previous night's meal with her across the table from him. He wished he were the one sharing her table tonight instead of some hotel tycoon. Shaking off thoughts of Tisa, he watched the last file open on his screen.

"Pay dirt!" He stared in awe, unable to fathom the extent of the information unfolding on the small screen. Names. Dates. Amounts. "This is it!" he breathed the words as softly as a benediction.

"This is what?" The voice behind him caused him to jump, his hand automatically going to the drawer where he'd left his weapon before his mind processed a face to go with the voice.

"Peter!" A broad smile spread across his face, and he turned to face the lieutenant. "Look at this!" He couldn't wait to share his discovery.

Soon both men were peering at the screen with only an occasional whistle or reading of a name interrupting the silence in the room. The first screen depicted a large company called AR, which apparently made huge profits from several smaller subsidiary companies.

Most were companies Cabe recognized as businesses long suspected of a crime connection, and some were names of individuals well known in law enforcement circles for their involvement in various vice operations. The Dempsky brothers' names were prominent as controlling officers of every company under the larger AR umbrella.

"*AR* is quite obviously for *Artel* and *Reuben*," Peter said, examining a scanned document showing profits from Artel's Starlight Lounge, with the man's signature clearly in place.

"There's enough here to indict them for tax fraud, money laundering, and large-scale drug importation. And, we can finally verify Reuben's connection to several violent crimes," Cabe's voice was jubilant.

"I recognize some of the company names from the search for the owner of the warehouse that burned. I suspect this is going to untangle that trail," Peter said with great satisfaction.

Leaning forward, both men continued to stare at the monitor. A few screens later another large operation took shape. This one had the code name TBD. Cabe moved slowly through what appeared to be the controlling board of the company. None of the names were repeated from the previous company, and only one name stood out—that of Tracy Roberts. A Sacramento, California, address was listed, and it appeared Roberts was the CEO of a well-known chain of retail stores.

"This explains why we couldn't find a connection between the warehouse and any of the local Tracy Roberts we checked out. I'll run a check on this Roberts, but there's nothing here that would link him to any illegal activity." Peter sounded both puzzled and disappointed.

"Reuben's son runs a number of legitimate businesses. Whether he uses them to launder drug money or not has never been proven." Cabe turned his attention back to the screen. "Roberts could be a genuine CEO with no idea that his business has any connection to a crime family. TBD might be the umbrella organization for the family's legitimate companies. They probably avoid using the Dempsky name."

"TBD could be a code name for the new warehouse," Peter speculated as Cabe eased the scroll bar down the side of the screen. Minutes later Peter shook his head. "TBD isn't the warehouse, but it could be a property holding company."

"I think you've hit on it," Cabe agreed. "The company seems to own or manage tracts of land ranging from city lots to hundreds of acres in most of the western states, including a number of fairly large businesses."

"Wait." Peter stretched a hand toward the screen. Cabe paused on a page similar to the TBD page. Letters identified this group of names as LAB, and the board members were different from those for TBD. Instead of Tracy Roberts as CEO, Jorge Ortega was named. Peter's smile turned wolfish, and it wasn't hard for Cabe to recognize the lieutenant's eagerness to put Ortega behind bars. Peter pointed to the initials *LAB*. "Do you suppose this means they are operating a laboratory somewhere?"

"I doubt the letters stand for *laboratory*," Cabe theorized. "But drugs are definitely involved." Each succeeding page designated a smaller group or unit, followed by individual names with amounts delivered, a list of dates when payments were supposedly made to the individual, and the amounts of products obtained. One of the larger subgroups under LAB was designated as SD and controlled a number of gambling operations.

The last page showed two-thirds of the profits from LAB, with the exception of the gambling profits from SD, being forwarded to a column entitled AR. The other third was shifted to TBD's profit column, and from there was distributed to foreign accounts bearing numbers instead of names. The profits from what appeared to be legitimate businesses were divided among their respective boards and stockholders with nothing going to AR. Cabe made a note to find out who the major stockholders of those companies might be.

SD profits, which were considerable, were renamed JEB and funneled back into development for the legitimate businesses under the names of various lending companies. It appeared to be the only visible link between the two types of companies.

"If AR is Artel and Reuben, then that might be the key to the other initials. It appears AR is the parent company with TBD a shadow company used to hide assets." Peter seemed to be thinking out loud as he tried to make sense of the confusing numbers and initials.

"I'm not sure TBD is a true subsidiary," Cabe said. "It looks to me like someone is running a parallel organization that is skimming from AR and growing both faster and more profitably than the original company. Let's print some of this out. I think better when I'm looking at paper than at a screen." He pressed Print. "Who or what do you think the other initials represent?" he returned to Peter's speculation concerning the initials representing companies.

"It's just a theory, but since the Dempskys run a crime family organization, *SD* could stand for *Stefan Dempsky*, the brother who dropped out of sight. Reuben's wife was Loretta and her sister, Josie." Peter pointed to JEB and LAB.

"Okay, that theory might work, but what about TBD?" Cabe gave consideration to Peter's theory. "That's the biggest company, and it looks to me like it's set up so that if the other companies fold—or their owners go to jail—it can survive as an independent, legitimate business portfolio. Convenient—if someone wanted to cut himself loose from the family and have a tidy little fortune of his own."

"Might be *her* own," Peter suggested. He moved closer and ran his finger down the list of company names Cabe had compiled. "If our theory holds up that the initials representing the various Dempsky holdings represent members of the family, most of whom are presumed dead, except for Artel, Reuben, and his son, then TBD might represent Reuben and Loretta's daughter—that is if the rumors are true that they had a daughter."

"It might be interesting to discover who controls the businesses should all those dead people fail to show up to claim their bank accounts and company stock," Cabe observed.

"I don't know." Peter picked up one of the pages Cabe had printed. "It sounds like you're thinking Reuben's son might be preparing an escape plan or to double-cross his father and uncle."

"I think it's possible. He heads up a chain of fancy resorts in southern California, Hawaii, and the Bahamas. They appear to be legitimate businesses. He's very cunning, though. He's used his mother's maiden name for years, which is Bronson. Each time he's been associated with his father and uncle it has been under a different assumed name, while the Bronson name has never been connected to crime. You'll notice his hotels aren't listed anywhere on this disk, and much as I'd like to, I haven't been able to prove Bronson Enterprises has any connection to Daman Bronson's unsavory family."

"Daman Bronson!" Peter's chair fell over backward as he surged to his feet. His face turned pale and his hands visibly shook. "Daman Bronson is Tisa's new client. She's having dinner with him tonight."

Cabe spun his chair around to face Peter. He couldn't have heard him right. Tisa wouldn't go anywhere with a Dempsky. She wasn't some infatuated teenager, glamorizing crime to make her feel daring and important. Slowly he rose to his feet with a sick feeling in his midsection.

"I've got to find her!" Peter stormed toward the door, kicking his chair out of the way.

"Wait!" Cabe sprang after him, catching his arm before he could fling the door open. "Bronson isn't going to hurt Tisa. Theirs is a legitimate business deal." Silently he prayed he was right. "Unless you've discussed this case with her, she's probably never even heard of the Dempsky crime family. Chances are Bronson knows nothing more about her than her professional credentials reveal. Coincidence brought them together, that's all."

"I've never placed much credence in coincidences," Peter's voice was an angry growl.

"All right, worst-case scenario, Bronson knows Tisa is your sister and is deliberately establishing a relationship with her to get at you. He knows your position with the city police, and he's also aware of your affiliation with the statewide drug enforcement board, so he wants to neutralize you. He isn't crude like his father, and he's not going to physically hurt Tisa. He'll attempt to build trust with her, then pump her for information. Call her in the morning, and warn her to avoid seeing him again. She respects your opinion, so that's probably all it will take." Cabe was finding it hard to be rational himself. He felt sick to his stomach thinking of Tisa with Daman Bronson, but he also knew he and Peter couldn't rush in like the cavalry to rescue her and in the process destroy their case. "Besides she told me her boss was making it a threesome," Cabe added for good measure.

"Yeah, and she told me Kurt bowed out, discovered his wife had other plans, and that Tisa would have to represent the firm for both of them." Peter took up pacing the floor, but at least he was no longer contemplating storming out of the room to place an all-points bulletin for his sister and Bronson. Much as Cabe struggled with the same impulse, he knew confronting Bronson now would be a mistake.

"She carries a cell phone. At least I can call, make sure she's all right." Peter picked up the phone and punched in the number. By the increasingly cold glitter in the lieutenant's eyes, Cabe knew he wasn't the only one thinking Tisa was taking much too long to answer. When Peter finally set the phone back down, the grim expression on his face told him Peter was set to explode with fear and worry.

"She probably turned it off," Cabe reasoned. "She might consider the distraction rude."

Peter resumed his pacing and Cabe stared after him, feeling his own tension escalate.

"Try her apartment," Cabe suggested, hoping she'd ended her date early and returned home.

"She wouldn't take Bronson to her apartment; she's not like that." Peter dismissed the suggestion with a defensive snarl.

"I didn't mean Bronson might be there with her," Cabe explained. "But it's after ten; she may have had dinner, said good night, and gone on home."

Peter snatched up the phone and began dialing. He paused at the sound of running footsteps in the hall.

"Peter, it's Tisa!" Stone Aldredge crashed into the room. His partner Marco Vasquez was a step behind him.

"What about Tisa?" Peter dropped the phone and turned to the two detectives.

"There's been an accident." Aldredge choked on the words. "We heard Dispatch call for an ambulance and ask for an ID on her plates."

"Which hospital?" Cabe snatched up the disks, and shoved them and the papers they had printed into his desk drawer and turned the key. He grabbed his jacket and pocketed the key; his fingers brushed the original disks he'd dropped there earlier. With his attention focused on his computer screen all day he'd forgotten to call for a courier or to turn the disks in to the evidence room for safekeeping. Now there wasn't time.

"University," Vasquez responded. "Want us to drive you?"

"No, I can drive," Peter spoke through clenched teeth from the hall.

"Have a black and white meet us out front," Cabe called over his shoulder while running to catch up to Peter. Peter was too upset to drive no matter what he thought. He'd drive Peter's Blazer himself if Peter wouldn't wait for the patrol car, but from the way his heart was pounding and the rubbery sensation in his legs, Cabe wasn't sure he should be driving either. He just prayed a patrol car would be waiting outside by the time they reached the front door.

Cabe's prayer seemed to be answered when he and Peter burst through the front door to see Bob White holding open the door of a police cruiser parked at the curb. A uniformed officer was at the wheel. Peter didn't argue; he jumped into the backseat and Cabe piled in behind him. White jumped into a 1957 Chevy, driven by Aldredge, that waited behind the police car.

Cabe and Peter didn't speak as the car rushed through traffic, which was fortunately light. One look at Peter's face told Cabe he was praying for Tisa. Cabe closed his eyes and did the same. From somewhere deep within him came the conviction that if Tisa didn't survive, something irreplaceable would be lost from his own life.

It took less than ten minutes to reach the hospital. Cabe and Peter had their doors open and were sprinting across the entry before the cruiser came to a full stop. The automatic doors slid open and they slowed to a walk, albeit a fast one. Peter knew where to go and Cabe followed to find a desk where they could demand information.

A nurse directed them to a room down a short hall. Tisa's voice reached them before they spotted her lying on a gurney with two figures in green surgical scrubs leaning over her. One held a syringe.

"No anesthesia! No pain killers! Just fix it!" Tisa came close to shouting.

"Look, miss, I don't think you understand how painful sutures without anesthesia will be."

"I don't care," Tisa's voice sounded petulant. "Anesthesia makes me sick to my stomach."

"Not for long," one green-garbed figure attempted to soothe the distraught patient. "In a few hours the queasiness will pass and by tomorrow night, you'll be eating dinner like nothing happened."

"See! That's what I mean. I'll have to go a whole day without eating."

"Unless you have a drug allergy you haven't told us about, it won't be that long," the doctor attempted to reassure her.

"Just use tape." Tisa attempted to sit up. The nurse pushed her back down.

"I'm okay." Tisa swung her legs over the side of the gurney. "I need a phone. I have to make arrangements to get my car repaired. That guy better have insurance because it's going to cost a fortune to fix my Jag. Do you have any idea what a Jaguar XK8 costs?"

"Oh, about 70,000 big ones." The doctor's voice betrayed his growing exasperation with his uncooperative patient.

"Need a little help?" Peter approached the doctor, pointedly ignoring Tisa. Cabe couldn't resist a quick scan of Tisa's injuries. She appeared too active and flexible to have sustained any broken bones or internal injuries. Her argument with the doctor might be the result of a head injury, though her head looked fine even if her hair was mussed and her makeup gone. A knot in his stomach tightened when he considered her lipstick might have disappeared before she started the drive down Parley's Canyon. His inspection continued until he noticed a deep abrasion on her left arm, undoubtedly the object of Tisa and the doctor's argument.

"Stitch it," Peter told the doctor. The nurse lifted the syringe in a tentative gesture. Peter looked right at her and said, "Do it."

"I don't want . . ." Tisa objected.

"A local anesthetic isn't going to cause you to starve to death." Peter brushed aside her protest. The nurse quickly jabbed Tisa's arm. Tisa flinched, then glared at the nurse.

"Now, how did this happen?" Peter demanded Tisa's attention. Cabe hid a smile. For a man who was on the verge of a panic attack ten minutes ago, Peter was being pretty calm now. He gave every indication of having gotten his sister out of more than one scrape in the past.

"It wasn't my fault," Tisa defended herself. Peter looked as though he'd heard that defense before and wasn't buying it.

"I slowed down for a truck that looked like it might be headed for the runaway lane and somebody rear-ended me. My airbag popped out, nearly choking me to death in dust. The impact broke my side window and a chunk of flying glass cut my arm." Peter scowled and Tisa hurried on. "I'm fine, really I am, but my poor car. I don't know if I'll be able to drive it again."

"It's insured, isn't it?" Peter asked.

"Yes, of course, but I need it next week. I don't have time to wait for repairs. I'm supposed to meet a client next Tuesday."

"You'll just have to reschedule for a later date."

"There! All done." The doctor interrupted to point out the completion of a neat row of stitches. Tisa looked down, then made a lunge for the small plastic tray on the stand beside the gurney. Her fingers fell short and Cabe thrust the bowl in front of her. Her shoulders shook and he placed an arm around her as she retched. When her body stilled, he laid her carefully back against the padded gurney and took her hand. The nurse moved closer with a damp cloth.

"I knew I'd be sick," Tisa said, treating the doctor to a baleful glare.

"Would you like a blessing?" Peter asked, stepping forward. Tisa looked thoughtful for a moment, then nodded her head

Peter stood opposite Cabe and handed him a tiny vial of oil he took from his wallet, and Cabe, taking great care not to spill any, placed a drop on Tisa's head before settling his hands beside Peter's. A quiet assurance that Tisa would be fine filled him as Peter asked God to bless his sister that she would heal.

"You'll be fine now," Peter whispered after he finished the blessing. Cabe nodded in agreement when Tisa said nothing, but instead glanced around the room as if she were puzzled by her surroundings.

The nurse stepped forward, but Peter elbowed her aside to wrap an arm around his sister. "Come on, I'll take you home, then you'll feel much better tomorrow."

"What about my car?"

"I'll check on it and see what can be done," Cabe promised.

"You are going to release her, aren't you?" Peter turned to the doctor.

"Yes, she isn't concussed and nothing's broken, but she's going to be stiff tomorrow. She may suffer some pain from that laceration on her arm. I suspect it would be useless to offer her a prescription for a painkiller, but I'll give you one anyway. If she'll take it, give her aspirin or Tylenol. Even though there's no head injury, it would be best if she isn't alone tonight. Is one of you gentlemen her husband?"

"I'm her brother. She can stay at my house tonight." Peter didn't seem to see the doctor's skeptical look. He was too busy scooping Tisa off the gurney and into his arms. Cabe noticed the way she snuggled her cheek against Peter's chest and wished he hadn't wasted time looking around for a wheelchair for her. He should have just picked her up the way Peter had. The doctor wisely didn't comment when Peter bypassed the orderly who hurried forward with the customary mode of transportation for patients.

"My sketches!" Tisa's head popped up, and she turned to the nurse who was trailing behind them.

"They're right here." The nurse lifted Tisa's sketch case high enough for her to see. "She insisted it accompany her right into the examination room when she was brought in," the nurse grumbled to Cabe.

"Thank you. We appreciate your help." Cabe smiled at the woman who looked suddenly flustered. She tugged at the hem of her scrub shirt and smiled back coyly. Tisa glared at the nurse before settling back against her brother's chest. Cabe reached for the portfolio, and the nurse handed him Tisa's handbag as well. It may have been his imagination but her hand seemed to linger on his in the transaction. From the corner of his eye he saw Tisa frown. He hoped the frown was the result of a tinge of jealousy, and not pain.

Suddenly, just around the corner, they heard several excited voices calling out Tisa's name.

"Are you all right?"

"How badly is she hurt?" Half a dozen police officers hurried toward them, their questions overlapping.

"I'm fine." Tisa smiled at each of the men.

"She's going straight home to bed." Peter frowned at the group. "Aren't some of you supposed to be working?"

"Well, yeah," Vasquez stammered.

"We were just making certain Tisa was okay," Aldredge attempted to justify their presence at the hospital.

"Let's go, guys." Bob White winked at Tisa, then made motions as though shooing the men toward the door.

When they were all gone, Tisa turned to Peter, "Do you think we could stop at Burger King on the way home?" He shook his head and Cabe hid a grin. The emergency room doors swished open, allowing them to leave the hospital.

CHAPTER 8

Cabe was up early Monday morning. He was finally able to reach the garage where Tisa's insurance company had sent her car. He hadn't been able to learn anything about the car's condition over the weekend, but now he learned the insurance investigator considered it totaled. He thought of calling Tisa with the information, but gave into an urge to tell her in person. He grabbed his keys off the bedside table and started toward the door. He stopped, wondering if he might need his jacket if something should come up requiring more formal attire. If Tisa was feeling better he might ask her to meet him for lunch. Snatching up the jacket from where he'd tossed it the night before, he slipped it on and headed for the hotel parking garage.

Lara answered the door when he arrived at the Lewis home, and before he'd taken two steps he could hear Peter and Tisa arguing. They stopped when he entered the room, but he'd heard enough to know Tisa was determined to return to her apartment to pack for her trip to Idaho, and Peter was equally determined that she remain in his home for a few more days. Peter appeared almost triumphant when Cabe delivered the bad news about her car.

"I still want to go to my apartment," Tisa informed her brother.

"There's plenty of room here," Peter protested. "Lara will keep you company, and she and the kids will love having you."

"I know, but her parents are here, and I don't want to spoil their plans. I need a change of clothes, and besides, if I have to delay my trip, I can do a little preliminary sketching at my place."

"That's what I'm afraid of. If I let you go home, you'll start working and wear yourself out."

Cabe knew immediately that Peter had made a tactical error. He never should have said "let."

"I'm going home." Tisa thrust out her chin and stood glaring at her brother. "If you won't take me I'll call a cab."

"Can't you wait until this afternoon? I've got court this morning and Judge Reardon doesn't tolerate tardiness." Peter made one last effort to stall Tisa's departure.

"Cabe can take me." Tisa turned to appeal to him. Her big gray eyes didn't give him any choice. He'd visited her a couple of times at her brother's home over the weekend, and the more he saw of her the more he was drawn to her.

"Sure, I can drop her off at her place and make certain she's settled." Cabe turned to Peter. "I don't have an appointment until ten, so I have plenty of time."

"I just need to get my bag." Tisa flashed Cabe a grateful smile before hurrying from the room. When she was out of sight, Peter warned Cabe not to let Tisa talk him into stopping at her office.

"I won't," Cabe promised, then asked, "Did you get a chance to warn her about Bronson?"

"No, I'll stop by this evening to check on her. I'll tell her then," Peter said. "She's trying to be brave about an injury that has to hurt plenty, and she's upset about her car. When our parents died they left us each a tidy sum. I invested my share in this house, but Tisa wanted a sports car. She bought the Jag and later her condo. In a way, I think losing her car is a raw reminder of losing Mom and Dad. Perhaps returning to the condo will help. I know she thinks my reluctance to take her is because I don't think she can take care of herself, so I'm glad you agreed to do it."

"My pleasure. There is plenty of time before my meeting with Dave Woods, and I . . ." Cabe's voice trailed off as he caught sight of Tisa hurrying down the stairs toward them.

"I'm ready!" She whirled into the room.

Peter bent to kiss her cheek and give her a strict warning, "Straight home."

"Yes, sir!" She gave him a mock salute. Cabe thought the gesture was added for Peter's benefit to make him feel good about her leaving, but he suspected she was hurting both emotionally and physically more than she wanted him to know. They both turned when Lara entered the room carrying the portfolio that had been rescued from Tisa's car and a plastic bag, presumably holding the clothes Tisa had been wearing when she was taken to the hospital. Peter reached for the items, set them on the floor, then hugged his wife. After a lingering kiss, he picked up the portfolio and bag of clothing again. Tisa hugged Lara, too, and Peter kissed his sister's cheek before hurrying out the door.

Cabe placed the heavy case in the back of the vehicle while Peter saw Tisa settled in the passenger seat. Cabe rounded the front of his rented Lincoln Navigator to climb behind the wheel. As he started the engine, Tisa waved to her sister-in-law who was still standing in the doorway. Peter was already striding toward his Blazer.

"All set?" Cabe smiled at his passenger. Tisa nodded her head and he noticed the way her hand stroked the leather seat. She looked sad and he assumed she was thinking of her Jag. They'd traveled several blocks before she spoke again.

"I never realized how much more you can see from one of these things." She was peering through the windshield at oncoming traffic.

"It's great," he agreed. "I'm thinking of trading in my Audi when I get back home for one like this. They're a lot safer on the highway than small cars are."

"It's not yours?"

"No, it's a rental. I flew in, but discovered I needed a vehicle after I got here. Where do I turn?" He finished with a question.

"Two more lights, then turn left," Tisa told him. Her voice seemed to have regained its customary sparkle. He was glad he'd agreed to take her home. In a few minutes they were turning up a steep lane to a row of condominiums set on a hill overlooking the valley. The buildings jutted like massive granite cliffs on the edge of a shrub-filled ravine.

"You can park right here." Tisa directed him to a visitors' parking area. A wide sloping lawn extended from the concrete pad to disappear into the trees along the edge of the ravine. Cabe pulled into a parking spot, then looked questioningly toward the buildings before climbing out and retrieving Tisa's artist case. He then circled the SUV to the passenger side, opened the door, and extended his hand.

"Wow!" was all he said as he looked around after helping Tisa out of the car. He felt like an eagle perched on the top of a cliff. The city looked both huge and far away. The sun beat down with a fierceness that had him removing his jacket and placing it on top of Tisa's sketch case.

Tisa chuckled. "We could have parked in the underground parking area where it's cool, but I wanted you to see the view from here. By the way, I saw that look you gave the parking area when I told you to park here, but you don't need to worry. Peter checked out the security before I moved in."

"Pretty impressive." Tucking the portfolio and his jacket under one arm, he offered Tisa his other arm and together they strolled toward her building. A short ride later in a keyed elevator brought them to Tisa's apartment. Tisa unlocked the door, and he whistled appreciatively when he saw the deep maroon leather sofas and the bold prints contrasting with bright white walls and a huge river-rock fireplace.

Mica flecks glittered from the granite surface of a square coffee table situated in the center of the three sofas forming a conversation area in front of the fireplace. Pewter pieces depicting various kinds of wildlife were scattered about the room, and bright dreamscape paintings were placed strategically. Floor-to-ceiling, west-facing windows looked out over the valley. Bright cotton pillows and throw rugs added a lighter touch to the room.

"Would you mind carrying my portfolio into my studio?" Tisa asked.

"No problem. Lead the way." Cabe draped his jacket over the back of a chair and reached for the heavy case he'd set on the floor.

Following Tisa down the hall to the north-facing bedroom she'd turned into a studio, he noticed her careful movements and the way she protected her injured arm from movement. His guess had been correct; she wasn't as healed as she'd like others to think. As soon as he could set down her case, he would insist she rest before attempting to work on her sketches.

He stepped into the studio and looked around. There was little furniture in the room beyond a row of shelves, a table cluttered with art supplies, and a stool. An easel stood before tall windows, and he recognized at once that Tisa was the artist who had painted the vivid paintings he'd noticed in her living room. Several more paintings lined the walls and a partially completed sketch sat on an easel.

"Set the case on the table," Tisa instructed. Cabe did so, then wandered to the windows, where he stood for long minutes looking west toward the Oquirrh Mountains and north toward the city's high rises. After a moment he was able to pick out both the Jordan River and Salt Lake Temples. It gave him a little thrill to see both of them gleaming in the summer sun from one window.

"Well?" Tisa finally asked. He looked down to see that she'd come to stand beside him.

"Unbelievable," he murmured. "I didn't think anything could match the view of the ocean from my mother's home, but this is incredible. I like your apartment, and not only the view. I think it's partly the way you've decorated it. The rock and metal should give a heavy somberness to the room. Instead it feels solid and comfortable. Most apartments have a temporary feel about them, but this one feels like it's part of the mountain and will last through all kinds of storm."

The smile that lit Tisa's face told him he'd said the right thing, but he truly meant what he'd said. The main room had communicated to him both solid security and breezy coolness. The views from that room and again from the studio were simply icing on the cake. They stood side by side for some time without speaking, then Cabe turned to study Tisa's paintings more closely; he recognized the view from the window, Peter's children, a sumptuous feast, children playing, but though the colors were bold and exciting and the subjects identifiable, there was something not quite real about the paintings. They were painted as though the artist saw them in a dream or as an outsider looking in. Cabe felt a deeper communication than if she had shared her life story with him.

Looking down at the tiny woman beside him, he felt an urge to hold and comfort her, to give her all those things her heart longed for. He saw the fatigue and pain in her eyes and placed an arm around her. He wasn't an impulsive man; still his arms went out to her, and he swept her off her feet, causing Tisa to laugh in surprise. Cradling her as her brother had done the night of the accident, he carried her back down the hall, to the room he'd glimpsed earlier and had guessed was her bedroom.

Settling her in the middle of the queen-sized bed, he reached for a soft throw he found, draped over the back of a chair, to cover her. After tucking her in as though she were a child, he straightened and asked if she would like some aspirin. She shook her head and he didn't persist. She looked so small and sad lying in the middle of the large bed, that he felt a longing to sit beside her until she fell asleep. He considered settling in the chair and remaining with her to make certain she rested, but he had an appointment to keep and an important case that needed his attention.

"I'd better be going," he said in an attempt to overcome his reluctance to leave. He was gratified to see a flash of disappointment on Tisa's face.

"All right," she said as though understanding in some subtle way that he was asking permission. "Thank you for bringing me home."

"As I told Peter, it's my pleasure." He meant it. "Don't work too hard," he added with an understanding smile. She returned an impish grin that made him hesitate. Could she be up to something? No, he was just looking for an excuse not to leave her. Once he left she would sleep and give her body a chance to begin healing. She would be fine, and he really did need to keep his ten o'clock appointment.

For a moment he wondered if he should warn her about Bronson. Deciding that would be overstepping Peter's decision to tell her tonight, he dismissed the urge as another delay tactic. Bronson hadn't hurt her, and she wasn't likely to see him before Peter checked on her this evening. Moving slowly toward the door he told her good-bye and promised to call later to see if she needed anything.

He whistled as he merged onto the freeway a few minutes later. With the recent completion of the I-15 project it would only take a few minutes to get downtown. Taking Tisa to her condo had delayed the early start he'd planned for the day, but he certainly had no regrets. He'd enjoyed being with her and hoped to spend more time getting to know her better before he returned to California. He smiled just thinking about her. Unfortunately, he was spending too much time thinking about her. He had a case to build and a major arrest to make. After all this time he was almost ready to crush the Dempsky crime organization and put the people responsible for killing Annie in prison for the rest of their lives. He changed lanes and headed for the exit ramp. In a few minutes he was pulling into the police parking area.

Leaving his car, Cabe hurried inside the building where he put thoughts of Tisa aside. He greeted several men from Peter's unit as he walked down the hall. A glance at his watch told him Peter wouldn't be back yet, and he still had a half hour before his ten o'clock meeting with Dave Woods, FBI Special Agent in Charge.

The door to Peter's office seemed to stick as he pushed on it. Looking down he saw a photo frame lying wedged beneath the door. Alarms started going off in his mind. He bent down to retrieve the picture and the door swung open. From long practice, his eyes scanned the room, finding a trail of papers leading to both his and Peter's desks.

His muscles tensed, and he slowly straightened with the picture frame in his hand. Taking care not to disturb anything, he approached his desk to stare down at the broken lock on the open drawer. He knew before he looked inside, but he had to look. The disks, printed files, and the notes he had written were gone. Raising his eyes to his desktop, he found a gaping hole in the back of his PC unit. Someone had decided to take no chances that there might be something on his hard drive. What couldn't be removed was smashed.

A quick survey of Peter's desk showed it was undamaged. The drawers hung open, but his computer appeared intact. Papers were scattered across the desk's surface and spilled across the floor. The desk had been ransacked, but it looked like whoever had vandalized the room had known how to get what he wanted from Peter's side of the room without breaking anything. The framed portrait of Lara and the children was missing from its usual place on top of the file cabinet, but the cabinet itself didn't look damaged. A glance at the picture frame he held in his hand told him what had happened to the framed photograph. Had the thief ripped the picture from the frame, then dropped the frame once he had the photograph? Reasons why the thief might want a picture of Peter's family brought frightening thoughts to his mind.

Peter arrived while Cabe was on the phone canceling his appointment with Dave Woods. He let out a low whistle and repeated Cabe's survey of the office. Without moving from the doorway, he visually cataloged the damage.

"What happened?" he asked as Cabe hung up the phone. He listened to Cabe's explanation then picked up the phone himself to order a dusting for prints on and around both desks and anything else the intruder might have touched.

"It takes a pretty brash thief to break into a police station," Peter complained, stomping across the room to take a closer look at his desk drawer while he waited for an evidence team to arrive.

"He didn't break into the station or even into your office," Cabe pointed out. "Whoever did this used a key to access your office and only *broke* into my computer and desk. It appears he had a key to your desk, too, and knew how to access your computer files. I didn't examine your file cabinet too closely, but it doesn't show signs of tampering, so if anything is missing the perp had a key to that too. The guy who did this destroyed my computer, but not yours, though he turned it on."

"Have you discovered what the thief was after?" Peter asked.

"The only things missing are the disks I left in that drawer last night, my notes, and the printouts I ran from the disks." Cabe ran his fingers through his hair and shook his head. "I think our intruder was someone who knew we had those disks, and he was specifically looking for the evidence Captain Jacoby gave us from the warehouse fire. He found what he was looking for in my drawer. When he couldn't get into my computer to see if I'd copied the disks onto my hard drive, he destroyed it."

"You're saying it was someone on the force who did this?" Peter worded his conclusion as a question. Cabe nodded his head in silent confirmation. Peter pulled out his keys and began unlocking his metal file cabinet. Turning his head, he asked, "Who? I still can't believe any man in this unit might be working for the Dempskys." Though Peter denied the possibility, Cabe knew Peter was too experienced to not know that even in the best of law enforcement units, crooked cops existed. Damage from within tended to be worse than what any outside force could inflict.

Cabe didn't say anything, but merely watched Peter flip through the files in the upright cabinet until he reached the Dempsky file. With great care, he thumbed through the thick file, pausing occasionally to frown at something.

"Nothing seems to be missing," Peter finally spoke. "But someone may have gone through this. I can't be sure, but my gut instinct tells me someone took a good look at what's in here. Nearly all of my people have used my keys at one time or another to access the office and the files. I suppose one of them could have made copies of the keys. I'll have to talk to Internal Affairs, find out if someone is living beyond his salary or gambling. By the time they're through walking all over our investigation, we'll be lucky to have a case to take to court." Peter paused. "I suppose our case is dead anyway. Without those disks we don't have enough evidence for a conviction."

"How many people knew about the copies your friend Howie made?" Cabe asked.

"Most of the men in the drug unit knew the fire department recovered some disks. Not many knew about the copies Howie made."

"Aldredge and Vasquez both saw me lock Howie's copies in my desk drawer before we left for the hospital last night," Cabe remembered. "They may not have been aware of the significance of those particular disks, but if they could have put two and two together and made an intelligent guess, that would make them both suspects."

Peter shook his head. "They're a couple of the finest officers I've ever worked with. Besides Aldredge and Carmichael were cousins. He's taking Carmichael's death pretty hard."

All the more reason Carmichael and Jones wouldn't have suspected a thing if Aldredge was the person who approached their stakeout car. Cabe didn't voice his thoughts aloud, but he could see Peter was sickened by the same thought.

"Bob White was in here earlier too, as were a number of others," Peter said. "Several men have asked me about the disks. They heard Jacoby tell the desk sergeant the fire investigator had rescued some disks from the warehouse fire. That makes for a lengthy list of suspects."

"But they didn't all have access to your keys," Cabe reminded him just as a knock sounded on the door.

"Come in," Peter called, but from the defeated tone of his voice, Cabe knew he didn't expect any worthwhile results from the evidence crew. Every suspect they had would have had a legitimate reason to have left fingerprints in Peter's office at some time.

Peter greeted the officer who stepped inside his office and waved toward Cabe's desk.

"I don't think you'll find anything, but go to it," he told the officer who waited awkwardly in the doorway. "We'll find someplace to go for a few hours." He picked up the briefcase he'd set on the floor minutes earlier.

"Let's go," he spoke to Cabe.

Cabe reached to the back of his chair, then paused, momentarily puzzled. He remembered he'd had a jacket when he left his hotel room. Then he remembered. He'd left it hanging on the back of a chair at Tisa's apartment. Had his subconscious mind forgotten the jacket to give him an excuse to go back there? He didn't need an excuse. He'd intended all along to drive back out to Tisa's apartment when he got off work.

Peter was halfway down the hall by the time Cabe caught up to him. "I'll head back to my room and write down everything I can remember from those disks," Cabe said. "It won't hold up in court, but it will be a starting place to continue the investigation."

"I should have turned those disks over to the Bureau immediately." Peter faulted himself. "But that reminds me . . ." He reached into his pocket and withdrew a folded sheet of paper which he handed to Cabe. "This was faxed to me earlier." Cabe paused to look at a grainy copy of a newspaper photo of Tracy Roberts. It appeared to have been shot from a distance, then enlarged, losing any quality it might have once had.

"Any of my men who were that careless with evidence would be facing disciplinary action," Peter continued, still berating himself for not turning over the evidence to the federal law enforcement group as soon as he received it.

"Don't blame yourself, I was the one who was careless." Cabe took the blame. "I'm the one who tossed Howie's disks in that drawer. I didn't have time to check the originals into the evidence room when we left for the hospital." He took another step, then paused.

"Peter!" He reached to halt the other man's step. Peter turned his head just as a broad grin spread across Cabe's face. "The thief got the copies, but I still have the originals. I put them in my jacket pocket, planning to call a courier, but I didn't do it."

"You have them?" Peter's voice mirrored the incredulous look on his face.

"Not on me. I never removed them from my pocket."

"Then let's head for your hotel." The light was back on in Peter's eyes.

"My jacket isn't at the hotel." Cabe spoke slowly, piecing together his own actions. "I almost didn't wear a jacket this morning, then at the last minute I picked up the one I'd left on the back of a chair in my room last night. I remember putting it on before driving to your house."

"You're not wearing a jacket now." Peter looked at him pointedly, then suddenly seemed to become aware of his surroundings. Cabe, too, realized the hall where they stood was a little too public for their discussion.

Cabe dropped his voice to a whisper. "It's at Tisa's condo. I was carrying it when she asked me to move her sketch case to her studio. I hung my jacket over a chair before picking up the case again."

"All right, let's go." Peter's gaze swept the nearby doors and Cabe felt a sense of urgency.

"Perhaps we should call, warn her to be careful," Cabe suggested as they left the building to begin hurrying toward Peter's car. Peter nodded his head and Cabe reached for his cell phone as he slid behind the wheel. By tacit agreement neither one considered using the official car phone sitting on Peter's dashboard.

Peter rattled off Tisa's phone number and Cabe turned from fastening his seat belt to punch in the number. He clutched the armrest as Peter dug out from the parking lot. The monotonous buzz of the busy tone sounded in his ear. "Line's busy," he informed Peter. "I'll try again in a few minutes."

CHAPTER 9

Tisa hung up the phone and moved gingerly to her bedroom. She'd been careful to hide her stiffness from Peter and Cabe. If Peter had any idea how bruised she really was, he would have been adamant about her staying at his home and doing nothing while she healed. She didn't want to be babied. The soreness would go away in a few days, probably much more quickly if she was busy than if she sat around. Besides, she had work to do. No way would she let the Bronson account slip through her fingers. *Howard Harmon would love that,* she thought as she tugged her suitcase from the closet. *He'd like nothing better than to step in and take over my project!*

By the time her buzzer sounded, alerting her that the car she'd ordered had arrived, she was packed and ready to go. Taking a last look around, she noticed Cabe's jacket hanging on the back of a chair. She let her fingers trail across the fabric and she smiled, thinking of the man who seemed to be occupying her thoughts a great deal lately. The buzzer sounded again and she hurried to her door, accepting the keys a young man from the rental agency held out to her along with a clipboard holding papers for her to sign. She signed with a flourish and pocketed the copy of the rental agreement he handed back to her.

Minutes later, with her sketches packed in a light traveling case and carrying a small suitcase, she closed her apartment door and hurried toward the elevator. The doors swished open, and she paused. She heart the faint ring of a telephone coming from her apartment. She hesitated, then boarded the elevator that would take her directly to the lobby. *It was probably just a telemarketer anyway,* she dismissed the call.

In the lobby she glanced toward the office. Ms. Edwards, the building manager, could nearly always be seen at her desk, but there was no sign of her. Tisa stopped long enough to drop an envelope on the manager's desk, then hurried out the door. She saw a florist's van pull away from the curb, then her attention focused on two vehicles parked farther along the drive leading to the parking garage. One followed the florist's van, and she held the keys to the other.

As she settled behind the wheel of the Bronco the delivery man had left for her, she whispered an almost silent thank you to Cabe. She had a hunch he wouldn't be too pleased if he knew his rented vehicle had given her the idea of arranging for a rental of her own, but she was glad he'd put the idea in her mind.

After driving her Jag for almost two years, it felt strange to sit so high above the road, but it took only a few minutes to decide she liked the greater visibility. She didn't suppose she would need the four-wheel drive on the trip to Idaho Falls, but it might come in handy when she visited the construction site in Island Park tomorrow. The man at the agency she'd spoken with said it was easy to use and that there would be a book in the glove box that would explain all about it. She made a mental note to take the manual to her motel room that night.

Pulling onto I-15 she concentrated on watching the traffic. A stab of conscience reminded her she should have let Peter know she was leaving town. Peter wouldn't consider the note she'd left for Ms. Edwards good enough. She'd call him she decided, as soon as she passed Salt Lake and she could find a spot to pull off. She didn't like to talk on her phone while driving, and the traffic through the Salt Lake valley was always heavy and fast. Besides, her arm was too tender to manage holding her phone and driving.

If she called, Peter would be angry and order her to turn around. Guiltily she acknowledged that was the real reason she hadn't called his office. He'd insist she needed to stay home to recuperate from the accident. She sighed in exasperation. She loved her brother, she really did, but she doubted he would ever admit she was an adult and that she could make her own decisions.

Slowing for a truck that should have moved to the outside lane for slower traffic, she focused on driving for several minutes before her thoughts returned to leaving word with Peter she'd be out of town for a few days. She could call Cabe and ask him to give Peter a message. No, that wasn't a good idea, though she'd like to talk to Cabe. If she could be sure she would catch him alone—but he was sharing her brother's office. He'd hand the phone to Peter, and she really didn't want to talk to him just yet. An idea came to her and she grinned.

She'd call his house and leave a message on his answering machine. Lara had gone somewhere with her parents, so she'd have several hours before Peter would even learn she'd left her condo. He wouldn't worry until this evening when he planned to check up on her. She smiled and pressed a little harder on the gas. She'd be in Tremonton in less than two hours. That would be as good a place as any to call from.

* * *

"There's no answer," Cabe muttered as he clicked off the small phone in his hand.

"She has to be there!" Peter thumped the steering wheel. "It hasn't been much more than two hours since you left her there."

"Do you think she might have gone somewhere for snacks or groceries? The way she likes to eat I should have checked to see if she needed anything before I left," Cabe berated himself.

"There's a grocery store where the road starts to wind up the hill," Peter said, sounding relieved that Cabe had found a plausible reason for Tisa not answering her telephone. "She shops there, so that could be the answer, but without a car I don't think she'd walk that far. Of course she might have persuaded a neighbor to take her. Try calling her on her cell phone. She takes that everywhere with her." He gave Cabe the number.

"Out of service," he reported after a few moments.

"She couldn't have gone that far!"

"She might have turned it off for some reason." Cabe fiddled with the phone and pushed Redial, only to receive the same message.

"I guess that's possible," Peter acknowledged, but didn't sound convinced. "She would have had to turn it off at the hospital and she could have forgotten to turn it back on."

"Or it might have been damaged," Cabe suggested.

"Or someone overheard us talking and knows those disks are in Tisa's apartment." Peter pressed on the gas and in minutes he was parking as close to Tisa's condo as he could get. Peter's urgency spread to Cabe, and they found themselves practically sprinting as they entered the building. Peter picked up the guest phone and dialed Tisa's number. When there was no response, he tried again.

"She has to be there, she doesn't have a car, and bus service is pretty sketchy out here." Peter punched in the number more forcefully.

"She didn't seem ill when I left her." Guilt started to bother Cabe. He shouldn't have agreed to take her home. She should have stayed at her brother's house. The least he could have done was listen to the prompting he'd felt to stay with her.

"She's not answering." Cabe whirled around to face two men he hadn't noticed as he and Peter entered the lobby.

"Aldredge. Vasquez. What are you two doing out here? Aren't you out of your jurisdiction?" Peter didn't sound happy to see two of his detectives in the lobby of his sister's condo.

"We just got off. Marco, here, is looking for an apartment, and since we were out this way, we thought we'd stop here first to see how Tisa is doing." Stone Aldredge appeared oblivious to Peter's scowling face.

"Good morning, Lieutenant." All four men turned abruptly to see an attractive woman in her mid-thirties standing a few feet away. She was holding a huge arrangement of pale peach roses. "I was just taking these up to your sister's room," the woman said to Peter, indicating the bouquet with a nod of her head. "The florist delivered them half an hour ago."

"Would it be all right if we went up with you?" Peter asked. "Tisa was in a slight accident Friday night, and she's not answering her phone. I'm sure she's all right, but I'd like to check on her."

"Of course." The woman smiled and led the way to the elevator. She cast Cabe an appreciative glance over her shoulder as she pushed the button for the fourth floor. Inside, she maneuvered to stand so close the flowers she held tickled his nose and her arm brushed his. She was an attractive woman who was making it clear she was interested, but he felt nothing. His entire being seemed focused on Tisa, and his stomach churned as his mind invented one reason after another to explain why she wasn't answering her telephone.

"Wait for me!" a voice called, and Cabe instinctively held his arm out to stop the closing elevator door.

"Bob! What are you doing here?" Peter asked as the youthful-looking detective joined them in the elevator.

He grinned sheepishly. "I was worried about Tisa and thought I'd stop by to see how she's doing. I brought her a little something to cheer her up." He lifted a five-pound box of chocolates so they could see it. Stone and Marco lifted similar boxes, indicating they'd had the same thought.

Peter chuckled, but Cabe wasn't amused. Was it just a coincidence that the three detectives had arrived almost as quickly as he and Peter? Had they, or even just one of them, overheard his and Peter's conversation and knew the computer disks were at Tisa's apartment? Or were his suspicions founded in jealousy? Bob had been a childhood friend to the woman Cabe was finding increasingly important to him. He remembered their closeness the night of Peter's backyard barbeque and wondered if their relationship was closer than he'd assumed that night. The other two men were obviously interested in Tisa, but she hadn't shown any indication that she considered them more than friends.

When Tisa didn't answer her door buzzer, Ms. Edwards, the building manager, reached in her pocket for a key. "Tisa often receives flowers or deliveries while she's at work or out of town," she explained. "She asked me to take anything that comes for her to her apartment so they don't clutter up my office. I'm sure she won't mind me letting you in to check on her."

Cabe glanced at the flowers the manager was still holding and wondered who had sent them. That slight hesitation placed him a step behind Bob, who followed on Peter's heels into the apartment. As he turned to close the door behind him, the click of a softly closing door across the hall caught his ear. Sometimes a nosy neighbor is as much of a security asset as a watchdog, he thought before turning his attention to the room where he had stood little more than an hour ago.

Stone was already in the kitchen as though he expected to find Tisa there. Marco had his back to him and seemed interested in something on the other side of the room near the dining room table. At once Cabe's eyes fell on his jacket still hanging on the back of one of the gracefully carved maple chairs surrounding the table. Bob stood inches away from it, his hand suspiciously close to the side pocket where Cabe had placed the disks.

"Excuse me." Cabe reached past the other men to retrieve his sport coat. He slipped it on, and his hands, in the guise of straightening the jacket, felt for the disks in the pocket. They were there. His eyes met Peter's, and he gave an almost infinitesimal nod of his head and saw the answering glint of satisfaction in Peter's eyes.

"Tisa?" the woman called.

"Tisa!" Peter's voice echoed, before he turned to the hallway leading to his sister's bedroom and studio. He returned a few minutes later to report she wasn't in either room.

"She might be visiting a neighbor," Bob suggested. Deep furrows creased his forehead as he walked toward the large window. "Or she might have gone outside to take a walk."

"It's hot today. I don't think she'd go for a walk in this heat," Peter responded to Bob's speculation. "But we'd better not overlook any possibility. You and Stone check the grounds. Cabe and Marco can knock on doors to see if any of the neighbors have seen her. I'll stay here and see if I can find anything that might give us a lead to her whereabouts." He whirled about and headed back down the hall.

Cabe followed Bob and Stone out the door, and as Tisa's childhood friend punched the button for the elevator, Cabe knocked on the door he'd seen closing earlier. The rap of Marco's knuckles on the next door over echoed down the hall.

A quavering voice invited Cabe in, and he heard the sound of a security chain being released. In moments, a much-too-trusting elderly woman pulled the door open.

"I'm McCabe Evans, a friend of Ms. Lewis," he told the gray-haired lady who stood clutching her robe and smiling a hesitant smile. "We were going to meet for lunch. Did you happen to see her leave?"

"I know who you are." The woman's smile widened. "You brought her home this morning. You must be Miss Lewis's new boyfriend. Has she been with you all this time? I worried when she was gone all weekend, but I'm glad she has a new boyfriend. That Mr.

Sanborn was really nice, but he just didn't seem lively enough for Miss Lewis."

"Uh, did you see her leave?" Cabe reminded the woman of his earlier question.

"Not exactly." The woman shook her head regretfully. "She was just getting in the elevator by the time I got to the door. I did see she had one of those portfolio cases she carries around with her. I'm afraid she was late for work again."

After listening to the woman ramble a few minutes more, he thanked her for her time, then hurried back to Tisa's apartment. Ms. Edwards met him at the door. "I was just thinking," she said before Cabe could make his way to Peter. "Tisa is quite friendly with two young men on the second floor, but I saw them both leave for work at their usual time this morning. That was before you brought her home. She has several friends in the next building, but if she'd gone there I would have seen her get off the elevator."

"Did she have any visitors after I left?" Cabe asked.

"The florist delivery came, but the delivery boy didn't go up to her apartment. He just set the flowers on my desk and left. There was a young man in coveralls too. She buzzed him right up."

"Did you recognize him?"

"No, but he didn't stay long. He left almost immediately."

"You're sure he left alone?"

"Tisa didn't leave with him if that's what you mean, but he wasn't alone. He left with another man who pulled his truck up almost to the front door to wait for him. I saw him cross the lobby alone and walk toward the truck. That's when I took the flowers back to my office," Ms. Edwards informed him, a touch of irritation in her voice warning him he'd let his questioning become an interrogation. He also realized belatedly that the woman was interested in him, and was offended by his single-minded determination to track down another woman.

Lowering his voice and attempting to appear more relaxed, he asked in an almost conversational voice, "You were in the lobby— except for the few minutes you stepped into your office with the flowers—the whole time after I left until I returned a few minutes ago?" Cabe wanted to be certain the lobby and elevators hadn't been left unattended. According to the neighbor he'd talked with, Tisa had gotten on the elevator, but Ms. Edwards denied she'd seen her exit the elevator any time that morning.

It was possible Tisa had merely walked the man in coveralls back to the elevator and hadn't actually gotten on herself. But he also knew there was a human tendency for most people to think they're more aware than they really are, and it would be common for Ms. Edwards to discount trips to the bathroom or short errands to another room.

"The only time I haven't been in the front office all morning, where I have a view of the entire lobby, was right after the roses arrived. I wasn't gone long, I just had to speak to the plumber who came to work on Miss Morgan's leaky sink and let him in to her apartment. It didn't take more than five minutes." Ms. Edwards folded her arms and tapped her foot.

Uh-oh, she's becoming defensive. Cabe warned himself to relax further and keep the conversation nonthreatening.

"So you saw the delivery man leave before the plumber left?" He acted impressed at her nod, then added the simple compliment, "You're highly observant—and have an eye for detail. You didn't happen to recognize the name of the florist, did you?"

"Oh, yes. It was the same young man who used to stop by once a week with flowers from Mr. Sanborn when he and Tisa were engaged. I must say he never sent anything quite this nice." She ran a fingertip across a velvety petal while lifting her eyebrows as though asking a pointed question.

"Uh, no, they're not from me," he responded, catching on to her silent question. She smiled and moved a step closer. Struggling not to offend her by stepping back, he stood his ground and added, "I don't know who sent them, but I intend to find out." He reached for the card. He didn't like what he read.

"Peter," he bellowed and ignored Ms. Edwards's startled look. Charging down the hall, he stopped at the door to Tisa's studio where Peter was straightening from examining the heavy portfolio case Cabe had put on the table earlier for Tisa. Now it lay spread across the floor and it was empty.

"Read this!" Stepping over the case, Cabe thrust the note in front of Peter. Peter blanched as he read the message. *Until I see you tomorrow.* It was signed, *Daman.*

Peter brushed the portfolio case aside with his foot before charging down the hall with Cabe right behind him.

"We've got to get back to the office. Lock up and don't let anyone in before my sister returns!" Peter took Ms. Edwards's arm and hustled her toward the door.

"But . . ." Ms. Edwards made a sputtering sound. After she locked the door, Peter hurried her toward the elevator. Marco emerged from an apartment farther down the hall. Peter told him to go after the other men. "Tisa has gone back to work." He gave a half-hearted explanation. "Against doctor's orders!" he added for good measure.

Back in the lobby, Ms. Edwards glared at Cabe, as if to tell him she was no longer interested, before stalking to her desk. The two men were almost to the front door when she stopped them.

"Lieutenant, I found this on my desk." Both men turned, and Cabe saw the woman holding out a scrap of paper toward Peter as if it might bite her. Peter retraced his steps to snatch the note from her hand. The note read, *Lucy, I'll be out of town until Friday*. It was signed, *Tisa*.

CHAPTER 10

"You can't report her missing," Cabe reminded Peter as they left Phillip Kurt's office. "She's an adult, free to come and go as she pleases. Just because her boss doesn't know where she's planning to meet Daman is no reason to suspect foul play."

"I know that, but I don't like it," Peter grumbled. "The man's dirt. She wouldn't meet him on a personal basis; it has to be business. I feel certain she's heading for one of the locations where he's planning to build a hotel. We'd better get back to the office, call for a courier, and get those disks locked up, then decide what to do about Tisa."

"I've been thinking about that." Cabe tapped the fingers of one hand against the dashboard in a restless fashion, revealing his reluctance to express his concern. "If there's a cop involved with the Dempskys and he was responsible for the theft of the copies, the originals probably won't be safe in the evidence room. It might be best if we deliver them directly to the Bureau ourselves."

"You're right." Peter's thundercloud expression deepened. Suddenly he slammed on his brakes and flipped on his turn signal. In response to Cabe's questioning look, he explained a bit defensively, "I thought it might be a good idea to swing by Howie's place first to get new copies for us."

The car wound down a narrow lane with thick shrubbery on either side and came to a stop in front of a small house in dire need of a paint job. A rusty Datsun, more than two decades old, sat hunched against the side of the sagging porch. Two large growling dogs rushed the car, but quickly backed off when Peter ordered them to lie down.

"Great watch dogs," Cabe commented while watching the two animals slink around the side of the house.

"Useless and Hopeless," Peter said, taking the porch steps two at a time.

"What?"

"Useless and Hopeless. That's their names. They're both dropouts from a police dog training program." Peter pounded on the door. "Howie rescued them and brought them home."

"They suit me," a voice came from behind a sagging screen door. "I bailed out of the police academy a few weeks after starting too. All that discipline wasn't for me either." A wiry young man in need of both a haircut and a shave opened the door. Peter introduced him as Howie Jacobs.

"Come on in," Howie invited, and Cabe followed Peter into a room originally intended to be a living room, but now filled from one end to the other with state-of-the-art computer equipment. No less than four screens were lit up.

Peter explained why they had come and Howie scratched his head as he listened.

"All right, I can make a copy," he said. "But it will take a couple of hours to decode it again. The equipment I need is in use right now, and I can't interrupt the project I'm working on without losing a lot of data."

"We need to turn these disks over to the FBI right away." Cabe removed the disks from his pocket.

"Tell you what," Howie said. "I can copy them onto the hard drive of another unit in a couple of minutes. Then you can keep the disks and I'll work from the copy." They agreed and ten minutes later they were once more in Peter's vehicle with the original disks safely back in Cabe's pocket.

"Come in, Twenty-seven," dispatch called as Peter negotiated the rutted lane on their way back to the street. Peter picked up the dashboard phone to hear the dispatcher say, "Lewis, your wife wants you to call her. She says it's important."

"Maybe she's heard from Tisa," Peter said, smiling. "Mind if I use your phone? I can't make a personal call on the department's phone."

"Go ahead." Cabe offered Peter his cell phone, and Peter pulled his car to the side of the lane before accepting it. Peter's home phone was picked up on the first ring.

"What's the problem, honey?" Peter asked. He was quiet for several minutes, but Cabe watched the other man's knuckles tighten on the small phone and his face take on the stony expression of extreme anger. Some instinct warned him this was more serious than Tisa leaving on a business trip without word of where she might be reached. Her appointment with Daman Bronson wasn't until tomorrow, so there was still time to locate her before she would be in any kind of danger from him, Cabe reminded himself in an attempt to quell his growing uneasiness.

"All right, pack a few things for you and the kids. I'll be right there." He thrust the phone back toward Cabe, and, throwing the car in gear, dug out. He barely paused before pulling onto the street at the end of Howie's lane.

"Has something happened to Tisa?" Cabe asked, feeling his heart beating at an alarming rate.

"No, not Tisa. Lara found a threatening call on the answering machine when she and her parents returned to the house. Some jerk said that if I don't turn the disks that survived the warehouse fire over to him, my family will disappear." Peter spoke through gritted teeth. He hunched forward over the steering wheel like a race car driver.

Cabe felt fear slam into his chest and he thought of Tisa. Was she included in the threat?

"There's no question of it being a prank?" Cabe asked, calling on his years of training and experience to keep his voice calm, but instinct had already told him the call wasn't a prank.

"I wouldn't take that risk even if I thought there was a chance the threat was someone's idea of a joke," Peter said, taking a curve at high speed.

"Careful," Cabe cautioned. "You'll be no use to Lara if you kill yourself speeding."

"You're right." Peter reduced his speed a barely noticeable amount.

"What are you going to do? With the strong possibility there's an officer involved, can you risk assigning anyone from your department to watch them? I could get them into a federal safe house," Cabe offered.

"No, Lara's dad wants to take them back to Texas with him. He lives in an old walled hacienda with all the latest security gizmos and a staff that is fiercely loyal to the señor and his family. I think that would be best. Lara doesn't want to go, but she agrees it would be best for the children. I intend to make certain she goes." He swung the wheel, and the car turned into the tree-lined street where his house sat.

"What about Tisa?" Cabe asked.

"She's going too. Just as soon as we find her." Peter slammed on the brakes, stopping inches from the garage. He flung open his car door and raced up the front steps.

"Peter!" Lara met him at the door. Instead of giving her the reassuring hug she expected, Peter launched into a lecture. "You shouldn't come to the door or answer the phone. You shouldn't even stand in front of a window. I didn't install dead bolts and an alarm system for nothing, but if you don't use them they're worthless."

Lara's face fell and her bottom lip quivered. "Oh, Lara," Peter swept her into his arms. "I'm sorry. I'm just so worried about you. What about the kids? Where are they?"

"Mom took them upstairs. She said she'd read to them until they fall asleep."

"You're packed?"

"I don't want to be away from you," Lara attempted to protest.

"You can't be with me every minute, and I've got work to do. I'd be useless worrying about you if you stayed here. You're going with your dad, whether you want to or not." He looked so severe, Cabe felt sympathy for Lara.

"She's packed," Raymond Aguilera spoke up. The severe expression on his face matched that of his son-in-law. "I've been in touch with one of my company pilots who was in Casper, Wyoming. He should be setting down at Airport #2 in forty-five minutes. He has instructions not to turn his back on the plane for two seconds. We'll be airborne in less than an hour."

"Let's go then. My car's in the driveway," Peter said.

"I think it would be better if we traveled to the airport in the car I rented at the main airport when we arrived. It's in the garage and our luggage is already loaded in it," Aguilera pointed out.

Cabe couldn't help admiring the older man's efficiency. He obviously wasn't the CEO of a major corporation simply because he'd inherited the company. He was wise to avoid a commercial flight, and his rental would be far less likely to be recognized than Peter's SUV or Lara's minivan if anyone was watching.

"You're right." Peter ran his fingers through his hair and looked around, appearing almost helpless for a second or two, then his features tightened and he turned to his wife. "I'll get the kids." He paused on the stairs to turn back toward Lara, "Have you heard from Tisa?"

"Oh, Peter. Yes, I'm sorry. She left a message on the answering machine too. I listened to it first. Then when I heard the second message, I forgot all about Tisa's message." Lara looked like she might burst into tears again. "You don't think? . . . Was that man threatening Tisa too? I should have thought . . ." Now she did burst into tears.

"It's okay, Lara. Don't worry." Peter quickly descended back down the stairs and placed his arms around his wife.

Cabe spotted the answering machine next to a phone he could see in the entry. In two steps he was beside it, and without waiting for permission he pushed Play.

Hi! I'm on my way to Island Park to look at the hotel my client is building. I'll be gone for a week. I would have called sooner, but my cell phone was broken in that little accident I had, so I had to find a phone booth and there aren't many of those anymore. I'm fine, so don't worry. I'll call when I get back.

"Island Park! Where's Island Park?" The words almost exploded from him, making him realize how concerned he was for a young woman he'd only dated once.

"It's near . . ." Peter began, then stopped when the second message started. Cabe strained to hear each muffled word of the threat. Something in the voice sent a shiver down his spine, and he remembered the broken picture frame in Peter's office. The photograph of Peter's family should have been in that frame and wasn't. Had someone taken it to provide an assassin with a means of recognizing Peter's family? If he hadn't already been convinced that Lara and the children, and most likely Tisa too, were in danger, the message on the machine left no doubt in his mind.

No one moved or said anything for several seconds after the message ended, then Peter said, "I'll have it analyzed. Would you take it out of the machine, Cabe?" He turned around to resume his trek up the stairs to get the children. He returned moments later with Jamie jumping from step to step beside him and Peter, Jr. soundly sleeping in his arms. A pale-skinned, dark-haired woman dressed in a designer traveling suit trailed behind them. Cabe recognized her immediately as Lara's mother. Lara was a beautiful woman, he thought, but he doubted she would ever be quite the polished, classic beauty her mother was.

"Come," Raymond motioned toward his wife and she moved toward him. "There's only a moment to ask God's blessing, then we must be on our way."

"I want to stay with Daddy." Jamie stuck out a petulant lip.

"Mommy needs your help." Peter scooped her up in one arm, still holding his sleeping son in the other. Lara joined him with one arm going around his waist while leaning her head against his shoulder. Peter's eyes met those of his father-in-law and he gave a slight nod. At once the older man bowed his head and began to ask the Lord's blessings on the trip the family was about to undertake. He also asked for protection for Peter. When he finished speaking there was only a moment's silence, then the older couple reached for the children and Lara went into her husband's arms, and stayed there for several minutes.

In all the confusion of settling the family in the car and saying good-bye, formal introductions were forgotten, and Cabe offered to move Peter's SUV from the driveway to give the family a moment's privacy to say their farewells.

"I'll call when we get there," he heard Lara promise Peter.

"Don't call here," Peter answered, and Cabe winced at the gruff sternness of Peter's voice. He was glad to see Lara didn't appear hurt by her husband's strict refusal of her promise. Cabe knew Peter well enough by now to know the other man would arrange a secure means of communicating with his wife, and he was glad Lara seemed to understand that too. If he'd known Peter as well six weeks ago, he would never have assumed Tisa was an extramarital girlfriend.

Thinking of Tisa brought a rush of mixed emotions. He hadn't felt this churning dread in his stomach since he'd headed for South America to pick up Annie. In spite of Tisa's cheerful voice on the answering machine, he couldn't help feeling she was heading into some kind of danger. He had to find a way of contacting her. Better yet, as soon as he found out where Island Park was, he'd go get her and make certain she was safe.

* * *

Tisa considered stopping in Pocatello for the night, but drove right past the exits, deciding she could make it as far as Idaho Falls even if she was tired and her shoulder ached. She didn't want her first glimpse of Island Park to be in the half-light of dusk, so she would definitely stop in Idaho Falls. She reached a hand into the bag of chips on her lap and winced. Her arm was becoming increasingly painful, but she didn't want to take a painkiller since they made her ill. All she needed was a good night's sleep.

She yawned and reached for the radio. Perhaps if she turned up the volume she wouldn't feel so tired. Letting out a cry, she pulled her hand back. The pain reminded her that the doctor had said something about ice packs at frequent intervals. She probably should have put off the trip for another day, but once the idea of renting a car had come to her, she hadn't thought beyond keeping her appointment—and thwarting her big brother who seemed to forget that she was an adult and perfectly capable of making her own decisions.

He meant well, she reminded herself. She would have been more upset if he hadn't cared enough to be a little bossy. A surge of guilt swept through her. She should have called him and told him of her plans sooner. Actually, she would have called him from the first rest stop, but that was where she discovered her phone didn't work, so she'd had to drive on to Tremonton to find a pay phone. Her poor cell phone looked as though someone might have stepped on it after the accident. Several other items in her handbag also looked as though her purse had been sadly abused.

She should have called Peter's office before she left her condo. It was an act of childish defiance not to have done so. Cabe might have answered, and to be perfectly honest, she would have enjoyed chatting with him. She smiled, thinking of the handsome PI.

She sighed. Why was she even daydreaming about him? What was there about Cabe Evans that made her think he was any different from the other men she'd been attracted to? Was it just that he made her feel different? She'd felt that shivery little frisson of excitement before when she'd met an attractive man, but with Cabe there was an edge of awareness and a sense of peace. She laughed. She doubted many men would want to be described as peaceful, and *peaceful* really wasn't quite the right word. Strangely, the closest thing she could come up with was the relaxed calm she'd felt listening to Raymond Aguilera pray. Perhaps *rightness* was the word she searched for.

Just thinking about Cabe brought a strange longing. She'd never felt that before either. She'd loved every minute she'd spent with Mark, but when she was away from him she hadn't particularly missed him. So what was she almost saying? Did she have feelings for Cabe? She didn't consider herself a coward, but she didn't want to answer that.

* * *

Cabe and Peter sat in Peter's SUV a mile west of Airport #2 and watched the Aguilera plane lift off. When it was just a small speck against the sky, Peter hunched his shoulders as though relaxing them after a burden had been lifted.

"Let's go," he said, reaching for the ignition key. They didn't talk about Lara and the children's departure as they drove back toward the city, but Cabe knew it was a constant presence in the back of Peter's mind. Because he couldn't stop thinking about Peter's sister, and to distract Peter, he asked about Island Park.

"Island Park is a recreation area in Idaho, north of Idaho Falls and about half an hour from Yellowstone Park. It's sandwiched between two state parks, Harriman and Henry's Lake. It's a large area with several resorts and camping areas," Peter told him. "I think it's safe to assume Tisa won't be camping, so she must be planning to stay at one of the resorts."

"She doesn't like camping?" Cabe asked.

"Not really," Peter answered. "She loves the outdoors in the daytime, but it frightens her at night. She'd rather do her camping in a cabin or motel than in a tent."

"I guess I can't blame her after being abandoned outdoors in the middle of the night," Cabe mused. "Any idea where she might stay?"

"No. Mack's Inn is the most prominent resort in the area. When we get back to the office, I suggest we start calling there." He pounded his fist against the steering wheel. "She can't have reached Island Park yet. We know from the message on the answering machine that she's driving, but even driving fast, there hasn't been enough time for her to get there. If we had an idea of what kind of car she's driving I could ask the Idaho Highway Patrol to watch for her."

"If she's driving, we can assume she's driving a rented or borrowed car." Cabe was thinking out loud. "We can check with the various resorts in Island Park to see if she has reservations, but I have a feeling her departure today was rather impulsive and it might be better to trace the vehicle she's driving. Do you know who might loan her a car?"

"No." Peter shook his head. "Once we get back to the office we can check the various rental companies."

"What about the disks?" Cabe patted his pocket.

"I won't be blackmailed. Let's swing back past Howie's place, pick up the new copies, and then drop all of them off at the Bureau," Peter spoke with steely determination, but Cabe understood how hard it would be for him to give up the bargaining chip they held.

For the second time that day they bumped down the rutted lane leading to Howie's small house. An almost ominous silence filled the narrow opening in the trees.

"Well, that's a first," Peter said as the Blazer jolted across the area that might have once been a lawn.

"What?" Cabe felt confused.

"The dogs! They usually start barking before I clear the trees." Peter glanced toward the house and Cabe's gaze followed. He noticed at once that the front door to the shacklike structure stood open. The open door didn't strike him as unusual at first because the day was hot and the house was old, then remembering the sophisticated computer equipment in the house, he knew there would be an equally sophisticated cooling system protecting it. Someone like Howie might ignore his own comfort, but he wouldn't expose his equipment to the ravages of heat. Peter reached for his radio, but Cabe was out of the car and moving swiftly toward the building before Peter finished calling in.

Avoiding the direct approach to the open door, he circled the sagging porch. From the corner of his eye he saw Peter draw his weapon and disappear around the side of the house. Reaching the open front door, he flattened himself against the wall, fingering his own gun. He paused, giving Peter time to get in position at the back door, before swiftly stepping around the door frame into the room where he'd stood with Peter and Howie a couple hours earlier.

His heart lurched at the sight that met his eyes. Every computer in the room had been savaged as though someone had swung a sledgehammer with wild abandon. Plastic and twisted metal mingled with shards of glass and a mass of wires on the floor. Tables were tipped over and the boxes that had held Howie's disks were conspicuously absent.

"Howie?" Peter stood framed in the arch separating the room from the short hall that led to the back door. A moan came from a pile of debris near an upended table, and both men thrust aside mangled machines and broken furniture to make their way toward the sound. Cabe found Useless first. The old dog was lying in a pool of blood, half hidden under an overturned chair. Cabe knelt to press a chunk of stuffing from a shredded sofa cushion to the wound in the poor animal's chest. With one hand he stroked the dog's head and was rewarded with a small thump of Useless's tail.

"Hopeless is near the back step. It's too late for him." Peter remained standing and his eyes continued to probe the room. "I've already called for backup. I'll request a vet to pick up Useless." Peter wasn't as unaffected by old Hopeless's death and Useless's condition as his brisk, professional tone seemed to imply.

"Howie?" Cabe lifted his head, meeting the other man's bleak eyes.

"We'll keep looking. Here." Peter handed Cabe one of Howie's shirts that lay in the debris littering the floor. Cabe took a moment to secure it to Useless's wound, then stood. Peter was already opening the door to what he assumed was Howie's bedroom.

Picking his way through the ruined machines, Cabe made his way to the room Peter had disappeared inside. This room, too, had been trashed. Seeing Peter struggling to lift a mattress, wedged between a bed and the wall, he hurried to help, stepping on clothes and bedding on his way. Bits of glass and plastic crunched beneath his shoes. At last he could see one sandal-clad foot protruding from beneath the heavy mattress.

The wail of sirens somewhere in the distance broke the quiet as Peter and Cabe shoved the mattress toward the bed and knelt beside Howie.

"He's breathing." Peter's voice shook.

"He's been beaten pretty badly." Cabe began a meticulous, though gentle search of the unconscious man's body, drawing on the emergency technician training he'd taken early in his law enforcement career. "There are no knife or bullet wounds. The only bleeding seems to be from a blow to his nose. He's probably concussed, and from the looks of that lump on his head, I'd say he was hit hard by something heavy. Both arms are broken, several fingers, and I suspect he has a few broken ribs. His lungs sound clear, but he'll have to be moved with care."

"Is he going to make it?" Peter's voice was filled with concern.

"It's too soon to say. I've had EMT training, but I'm not a doctor."

Peter spoke into his phone, then turned to say, "There's an ambulance on the way." He continued to hold his weapon, and his gaze moved rapidly across the ransacked room. "They were looking for the disks." He spoke with conviction and Cabe felt suddenly conscious of the flat objects in his pocket. The Dempskys' men would stop at nothing to get those disks. Without them, a clever attorney could convince a jury they never existed, even accuse Peter and Cabe of inventing the facts they'd gleaned from the disks.

"Take my car." Peter handed Cabe the keys to his Blazer. Peter's thoughts were evidently following the same train as his own. "Get those disks to the Bureau. I'll stay with Howie and accompany him to the hospital."

A small scraping sound came from the doorway. Startled, Cabe lifted his eyes to see old Useless dragging his way toward Howie. Stepping toward the dog, Peter lifted him in his arms then gently placed him beside his master. The dog's tongue licked the inert man's hand, then he lowered his muzzle and closed his eyes.

The wail of the siren they'd heard moments earlier came to a halt as a police cruiser stopped outside, and Cabe hesitated. It might be best not to leave Peter alone just yet. He'd stay with him and Howie until the ambulance arrived. As anxious as he felt to transfer responsibility for the disks to his supervisor, and go after Tisa, he felt reluctant to leave Peter or the helpless Howie until they were safely on their way to the hospital.

He didn't recognize any of the uniformed officers who arrived and went about their business of securing the crime scene. He walked beside Peter to the ambulance and watched him duck his head to climb in beside his unconscious friend. Cabe watched as the flashing lights raced back down the rutted lane before he stepped inside Peter's SUV.

Cabe patted his pocket several times as he drove toward the federal building. Wondering if he'd become paranoid, he checked his mirror repeatedly to see if he was being followed. If he had a tail, the guy knew what he was doing and never gave away his position once. Moments after entering the underground parking garage he was in the office of Special Agent in Charge Dave Woods.

"Evans!" Dave Woods stood to shake Cabe's hand. "It's about time you came to see me."

"Yeah, well, I've been pretty busy," Cabe responded, knowing he'd been negligent in his visits. Woods had been Cabe's senior partner on one of the first sensitive cases he had been assigned. The older man had left field work shortly after that case and had moved into management in a different area.

Cabe explained about the disks and handed them to the other man. "If I was followed, the Dempskys' people may conclude I'm here for Lewis, so my cover is probably not blown."

"Might," Dave Woods conceded. "But it's more likely they'll run a check on you, then disappear for a time. We'd better not take chances. If these disks contain all you claim, we should have warrants for Reuben and Artel in forty-eight hours." Reaching for his phone he added, "I'll start the procedure now to have them picked up and tell our computer geeks to rush on the disks."

"What about Bronson? Can you have him picked up too? Lewis's sister is supposed to meet him in Idaho sometime tomorrow."

Woods hesitated, then set the phone back down. "You know, and I know, Daman Bronson is up to his eyeballs in the family business, but unless these disks can prove that, we can't touch him. Are you saying we finally have that proof?"

Cabe took his time answering. "I don't know. One section that Peter Lewis's friend was able to recover deals with disbursement of funds. At a glance it appears that someone is redirecting large portions of the Dempskys' illegal gains to hidden accounts. Whether our people in Accounting can prove that *someone* is Bronson, is questionable. Finding those accounts will take time."

"We don't have time. If Reuben and Artel even suspect we have these disks, they'll leave the country. Our agents in California have a good case, though much of it is circumstantial. If these disks contain all you claim," he picked up a disk and held it almost reverently, "we've got to act now or risk losing years of investigation."

"You're right," Cabe conceded with a weary sigh, "but I can't help feeling Bronson is the greater threat. Removing his father and uncle might be the biggest favor we could do him. If the theory Lewis and I pieced together—of a second organization using the assets from the Dempsky crime family to build a quasi-legitimate empire—is correct, Bronson will take over the family business and become harder to topple than those two."

Woods stared at the disks for several minutes, lost in thought. Cabe waited. Finally the older man raised his head. "All right, I'll get someone right on the disks and have both of the Dempskys placed on close watch. If they spot their shadows or even look like they might bolt, I'll have them pulled in. At best, that might give you a week to go after Bronson, but if he's as clever as he's been in the past, it won't be enough."

"It has to be," Cabe spoke with a determined set to his mouth. His mind conjured up a picture of Tisa and an overwhelming sense of impending disaster filled him. He had to find her. After the threat to Peter's family, she had to be found before she made contact with Bronson.

CHAPTER 11

Tisa was exhausted by the time she pulled into a national chain motel parking lot. It wasn't the fanciest motel she'd ever visited, but it had a reputation for being clean.

She should have been here an hour ago, but she'd pulled off the freeway in Blackfoot for gas and lunch. With her poor sense of direction and a major headache, she had been almost to Arco before she discovered she'd turned the wrong way when she tried to return to the freeway. Then it had taken what seemed like forever to find an exit where she could turn around.

As she parked the Bronco, she noticed that the motel had a great view of the river and the Idaho Falls Temple. Tomorrow she'd explore the enticing park across the street that bordered the falls. There would be time before her appointment with Daman. Right now all she wanted was sleep—and something to eat. She laughed. She was almost too tired to eat, and for her that was *tired!*

After checking in and finding her room, she carried her bag and portfolio inside, then searched out an ice machine. Back in her room, she used a plastic bag to fashion an ice pack for her arm. She eyed the bed longingly. It was the usual queen-sized motel-room bed, but somehow the neutral-toned, machine-quilted spread looked more inviting than usual. She sat on the edge and slipped off her shoes. Leaning back against the pillows, she draped the bag of ice over her arm. The cool ice was welcome after the long, hot drive. She'd rest a few minutes with the ice soothing her throbbing arm, then find a restaurant. First dinner, then bed, she decided. She should call Peter, too, to let him know she'd arrived safely. She would—as soon as she rested a few minutes.

It was dark when she awoke, and not just in her room; she could see through a crack where the curtains didn't quite meet that sunset was long past and that the only light coming into the room came from a row of pole lights at the edge of the parking lot. She lay still, debating whether to undress and crawl between the sheets or see if she could find a restaurant. Then her stomach growled, making up her mind for her.

Sliding off the bed, she slipped her toes into her shoes and picked up her purse. She knew she must look a fright after sleeping in her clothes, but she wouldn't go far. Surely she could find a fast-food place where she wouldn't even have to leave her car.

At the end of a long hall she rounded a corner and approached the outside door. Headlights from a lone car swept across the parking lot, bringing a shiver to her slender body. Something, almost a memory tugged at her mind. The parking lot was full, and she had a sinking feeling it was far later than she'd originally thought. Like her cell phone, her watch had suffered from her accident. She hadn't even bothered to wear it today.

A sense of apprehension filled her as she looked through the glass door at the parking lot. She'd always hated going outside at night. If she hadn't missed dinner . . . if being hungry didn't make her feel panicky . . . Her eyes caught sight of a row of vending machines in a nearby alcove. She needn't go out. She could . . . no, she was giving into the childish fears that had plagued her as long as she could remember. She was an adult and she was hungry. She needed a meal, not chips and candy bars.

Taking a deep breath, she pushed open the door that led to the parking lot. She'd parked near the door, and it only took seconds to reach the Bronco she'd rented in Salt Lake. Quick pressure on the security pad attached to her key released the door lock and she tugged on the door, nearly collapsing inside as she pulled the door closed behind her and stabbed at the lock button. For several minutes she sat still, breathing deeply.

"I'm fine, really I am," she told herself over and over until she started to believe it and her pulse rate slowed to a more normal rate. She was a grown woman, she reminded herself, much too old to be afraid of the dark. Headlights from the street flashed across the parking lot and she shuddered, wanting to curl into a ball too small for the monster to find.

"Stop this!" she ordered herself, making an effort to straighten and reach for the ignition. Her fingers fumbled, failing to find the slot where she could insert the key. It took several attempts before the key finally fit in the ignition. With a sigh of relief she turned the key. At first nothing happened. She tried again. By her third attempt, she was shaking so badly, she could barely hang on to the key, but to her immense relief the engine sputtered, seemed about to die, then roared to life.

Her fingers trembled as she shifted gears and backed out of the parking space. When she reached the street she wondered which way to go. Idaho Falls had felt like a busy, bustling town when she'd arrived, but it seemed awfully quiet now. She couldn't remember whether she had passed any restaurants between the freeway and the motel, but if she headed back toward the freeway she'd be sure to find an all-night truck stop. The food was good at truck stops, but something caused her to hesitate. For some reason she never felt really comfortable at the café/service stations that catered to truckers, nor around the big rigs themselves.

A sign across the street caught her eye. It pointed toward the airport, and she let out a sigh of relief. She'd go there. There were usually all-night restaurants at or near an airport.

Traffic increased slightly as she neared the airport and a glance at the dashboard clock brought a smile. No wonder she was hungry. It was almost five o'clock in the morning! It wasn't the middle of the night, after all. Instead of dinner she'd be ordering breakfast. The thought of pancakes and eggs, or maybe hashbrowns and an omelet, chased away the edginess she'd been experiencing. She pressed the accelerator a little harder, and in less than a minute she was pulling into a well-lit parking spot.

Her car made a strange sputtering sound when she turned it off, and she wondered if she'd have trouble starting it again. Deciding to worry about that after she'd eaten, she pushed the button to lock the vehicle and started walking toward the terminal.

Tisa sighed in anticipation when the waitress set a plate heaped with pancakes, eggs, and sausages before her, along with a side order of shredded potatoes. Although famished, she ate slowly, savoring each bite, and pitied those around her who gulped their food and ran, or nibbled a few bites, then pushed away their plates. When she finished she paid for her meal and stocked up on a supply of snacks before starting back toward her rented SUV.

Just as she'd feared, the Bronco wouldn't start. After repeated attempts, she removed the rental papers from the glove box and trudged back to the terminal where she'd noticed a branch of the car rental company that had delivered the Bronco to her in Salt Lake. She made arrangements for the car to be towed by the Idaho Falls branch of the leasing company, and took delivery of a new Lincoln Navigator.

When she finally settled behind the wheel of the Navigator, she smiled remembering Cabe's Navigator. They were just alike, right down to the deep blue paint on the outside and the glove-soft gray leather interiors. After adjusting the seat and mirrors to accommodate her short stature, she started back toward the motel. As she passed the parking lot, she noticed a tow truck stopped in front of the Bronco. She was just glad it hadn't died on her before she got to Idaho Falls. It might have been even worse if the car had waited to malfunction until she reached the mountains of Island Park.

Thinking of Island Park, she decided to return to her room for her things, check out, then take that walk she'd promised herself. She had plenty of time to reach the site where Daman's hotel was and have a look around before she met him for lunch.

* * *

Peter set down the phone with barely suppressed excitement. "I think this is it!"

Cabe turned toward him expectantly. They were in Peter's office pouring over directories, searching for a clue to Tisa's destination.

"Enterprise's Sandy office rented a Bronco to Tisa yesterday morning. It was delivered to her door." He slapped a piece of paper with a scribbled license-plate number on the desk in front of Cabe, then reached once more for the telephone.

After a call to the Idaho State Police, explaining he wanted the driver of the car located, but not apprehended, he and Cabe turned to face each other.

"The Idaho police should spot her quickly enough, but I can't stop worrying," Peter said. His eyes were dark and shadowed. Cabe suspected he'd gotten no sleep at all between worrying about his family and the leak in his department. He'd also spent much of the night at the hospital with his friend Howie, who still hadn't regained consciousness.

"I'll get a flight to Idaho Falls and go after her," Cabe offered. "I've already checked with the airline and there's a flight leaving a little after ten."

"She's my sister, I'll go," Peter said.

"You know you can't." Cabe kept his voice mild and reasonable. He wasn't ready to share the fact of his growing attachment to the lieutenant's sister. "You're needed here. You can't turn your back on the surveillance operation at the new warehouse. There's something wrong there and you know it. The traffic moving in and out is much too innocent, which tells us someone tipped them off. You have to find that leak. Howie needs you too. And you have to be within reach should Lara need you. I can explain the situation to Tisa and bring her back. At the same time I can get a look at Bronson's new venture."

"You're right, but you don't understand about Tisa. I'm the only person she really trusts. She came to Norm and Dixie in a highly traumatized state. A psychiatrist treated her for years and never found the root of her fears. Oh, he figured she'd been physically abused before she was abandoned, that much was obvious, as was the severe malnutrition, but there was something else he could never get her to divulge. Once in a while something frightens her and she freezes—totally unable to move. She told me when we were children that she was afraid the monster would get her. I could never get her to explain who or what the monster is, but it's just as real to her today as it was when she was four."

Cabe felt sick. Was Tisa mentally ill? Had the nightmare she'd endured as a child stolen something vital from her mind? But instead of deterring him, he felt a greater certainty that he should be the one to go after her. Perhaps he was being egotistical, but he had a strong feeling inside that she needed him.

"Peter, I think she does trust me enough to believe me when I tell her of the risk she's facing. But more than that, I trust that the Spirit is telling me I should go." Cabe didn't elaborate, but prayed Peter would accept and understand that he, too, shared not only Peter's concern for Tisa, but some elusive bond with her.

Peter walked across the room and stood with his back to Cabe for several minutes. When he turned, he spoke in a quiet voice, "Go. Call as soon as you reach Idaho Falls, and I'll fill you in on whatever I find out on this end. I have your cell-phone number, but once you reach the mountains in Island Park, the reception could be spotty."

Cabe wanted to share his concern with Peter, so he offered what he'd done to find Tisa. "I've called every resort and realtor in Island Park without luck, so I'm guessing she stayed last night at one of the motels along the way. I've got someone from the Bureau checking every motel near the freeway between Pocatello and Island Park. I've also got someone calling Island Park's planning and zoning board to find possible locations of Bronson's resort." He looked for Peter's reaction, and was glad to see there was no resentment that he had involved his own agency without okaying it with Peter first. "I'm going to swing by that place she works on the way to the airport," Cabe continued. "Her boss must have an address, a map, or something that will tell me where this new hotel is being built." Cabe outlined the plan he'd come up with during his own sleepless hours spent in his hotel room.

"All right." Peter nodded his head. "Call as soon as you land. The Idaho Highway Patrol might have something." Cabe started toward the door without telling Peter he'd packed a bag hours ago when some silent prompting began urging him to go after Tisa—whether he had Peter's approval or not.

A pretty, slightly plump receptionist greeted Cabe when he entered Kurt's Interiors, and he was pleasantly surprised when she ushered him straight into Phillip Kurt's office, a large rectangular space with numerous tables, chairs, and sofas, all covered with sketches, swatches of fabric, and mounds of carpet, wood, and stone samples. She left the room, but didn't close the door behind her. Cabe took in the room with a glance, when a thin, wiry man in his late forties jumped to his feet and rushed across the room with an extended hand.

"Patricia's brother called to say you were coming," he said by way of greeting. "I've searched everywhere, but I can't find a description of the property where she's working. I thought a map was included in the material Mr. Bronson gave us, but when I checked a few minutes ago, there wasn't one. Patricia usually leaves her itinerary with Gloria, but she didn't this time, probably because she expected to be here today before leaving for her appointment. But the accident—"

"I'd like to talk to the other employees, see if any of them know her travel plans," Cabe interrupted. He had to make this stop fast. He was well aware that airports no longer permitted late arrivals to rush through the boarding procedure.

"We don't have a lot of employees," Kurt responded. "Stacy and Eileen are both out on jobs. They're two of the four decorators I employ. Right after Peter Lewis called I took the liberty of calling both of them to see what they knew. They both said Patricia didn't discuss her plans with either of them. Howard Harman is our other decorator, but I wasn't able to speak to him. He's on vacation, and I have no idea where to reach him."

A flicker of movement caught Cabe's eyes, and he noticed the receptionist hadn't returned to her desk, but was watering a tropical tree of some sort just outside her boss's office. Was she eavesdropping he wondered, then dismissed the thought. He sometimes let his work make him a bit paranoid. Nevertheless, after thanking Kurt for his time, he didn't leave the building immediately, but stopped to talk to the receptionist.

"Gloria?" He remembered Kurt's reference to his receptionist's name.

She smiled back at him with a hint of flirtation, and he decided to play along. Giving her what an old girlfriend had called his "90-watt smile," he asked how long she'd worked for Phillip Kurt.

"Oh, not long." Her long lashes flickered. "I started last January."

"Oh, about the same time as Ms. Lewis." Cabe noticed that at the mention of Tisa, Gloria's smile dimmed.

"Are you two good friends?" he went on as though he hadn't noticed Gloria's reaction.

"We all work closely here," the woman hedged.

"What is Miss Lewis like?" Cabe moved a step closer to Gloria and lowered his voice, inviting an illusion of intimacy. "I've heard she's pretty assertive—and she has a big appetite."

"She has a big appetite all right, and not just for food." The woman clamped her mouth shut as though she feared she'd said too much.

Cabe went on as though he hadn't noticed the bitter element in the woman's voice. "A little man-crazy, is she? Do you think she's gone off with some boyfriend, maybe Mr. Harman, who happens to be on vacation this week?"

"She's not with How . . . Mr. Harman." Gloria caught herself, but Cabe wondered why she was even attempting to keep her references to her co-workers on a formal footing. As she went on, Cabe could detect both spite and jealousy in her words. "Mr. Harman doesn't like her at all. When she first started he invited her to lunch several times just to be friendly, but she was quite rude to him. Since then she's stolen several really good accounts from him. The Bronson account should be his, but she's Mr. Kurt's little pet, and he wanted her to get the assignment so badly he didn't even allow Mr. Harman to make a presentation. If you ask me, there's something going on between the two of *them*."

Cabe had a pretty good idea that Gloria and her vacationing co-worker were a lot closer than the woman wanted him to believe. He wondered, too, if her jealousy might have led her to withhold Tisa's itinerary. A glance at his watch told him he didn't have time to question Gloria further, but asking Peter to take a look at Howard Harman's vacation plans might be warranted. He could only hope that when he reached Idaho Falls, either an agent from the Bureau or Peter would have more information for him. Surely the Idaho Highway Patrol would have located Tisa by then.

* * *

Tisa pulled up beside the parkway and locked her newly rented Navigator. At ten o'clock in the morning the temperature was already well on its way to setting a record, but under the trees there was a refreshing breeze coming off the water. She watched the thundering mass of water plunge over the giant steps of the falls, feeling a shiver of awe at the tremendous power exhibited before her. Sunlight seemed to electrify the cascading water before it fell into dark swirling pools that were flecked with foam that hinted at an unseen power. Mist rose from the falls, caught on a slight breeze, and billowed toward the shore. She took a step backward, then felt foolish. She'd never been afraid of water, yet there was something about the wild, untamed force before her that both humbled and frightened her until she lifted her head and gazed across the river to the gleaming spire of the temple.

This temple reminded her in some way of the temple she could see from her condo; it seemed to offer peace, but she doubted that promise, just as she had shied away from the quiet promise she'd sensed from the stately spire across the valley each evening as the setting sun turned the Jordan River Temple's spire to gold.

Finding a bench she seated herself. That few feet of distance from the surging water drove away the ominous mood of moments before. Now she could see a grand beauty in the river and the falls, with the temple sitting serenely on the opposite shore. A duck squawked from somewhere nearby, and she looked down to see a muddy-brown creature watching her with eyes that reminded her of a dog begging for a handout. She laughed and reached for her purse. She certainly understood the need for an occasional snack!

The duck waited, with what she suspected was feigned patience, as she searched the voluminous bag for a granola bar. She didn't know whether or not a duck should eat granola, but this bar was made of oats and honey, so it should be safe, she reasoned, before breaking off a piece and tossing it to the waiting moocher. The duck grabbed it in midair. She laughed, then shared another bit. Without quite knowing how it happened, she was soon surrounded by quarreling birds begging for a morning handout. She noticed they disappeared just as quickly as they'd arrived once the last crumb of the granola bar had been dispensed.

Once again she was alone, enjoying the roar of the water and the sun that filtered through the canopy of trees. She was alone, but she didn't feel alone quite the same way as she usually did. She felt as though something was shifting, changing inside her. Over the past few days her mind had returned at frequent intervals to the night Lara's father had prayed for Peter and Cabe. She didn't understand why that prayer was different; she only knew it was. And something inside *her* had become different that night.

In the distance she watched a bird, perhaps the same brown duck who had mooched granola crumbs, drift out from the shore. The water appeared placid and calm, requiring little effort on the bird's part. Seeing how close the duck was to reaching the place just above the roaring falls and swirling pools—where the river seemed to gather its forces and build speed before rushing over the fortresslike wall of rock—she felt her muscles tighten. She wanted to shout a warning, even leap forward to save the small creature. She stood, and without conscious thought took a step toward the river. Out on the water the duck flapped its wings and took to the air. She heaved a sigh of relief, then wondered why she hadn't known the bird could save itself, that it would fly away when the tug of the current became threatening.

A picture of the little duck stayed in her mind as she continued walking slowly along the path, and she wondered if she shared that same survival instinct. Was it a sense of survival that had caused her to break her engagement to Mark? It was strange that she continued to think about him as much as she did. After ending her other engagements she'd quickly put those other fiancés out of her mind, and had experienced no lingering regret over ending the relationships.

Pausing where the trees ended, and a small cove provided a shallow beach populated by a flock of ducks, her eyes drifted across the water to the temple spire. A single thought entered her mind, giving her a small gleam of light and knowledge. She now recognized that when she thought of her former fiancé it wasn't because she missed him. It was because she had associated Mark with the Church. She'd thought the feelings of warmth and homecoming she'd experienced while with Mark were evidence of her love for him, while in fact, those feelings were the faint stirrings of her soul urging her to return to the faith that had once given her hope. Further, had she broken her engagement because she didn't truly love Mark, and because she had known unconsciously that she had the power within her to lift herself out of dangerous waters?

I should pray. Not sure why the longing to pray was tugging at her mind, she looked around, and saw that the little park was nearly empty. She was alone at this end except for the ducks. *I don't know how to pray like Lara's father,* she argued, even as she noticed a large boulder near the water's edge and she started walking toward it. Overhanging shrubs partially hid the spot from the tree-lined path, and she slipped past them to seat herself on the rock. Her eyes closed, and with pounding heart she began to pray.

A floodgate opened and she found herself pouring out her need to know that her Father in Heaven existed and cared about her. She voiced the old childhood questions: *Where were you? Did You care when I was abandoned? Why wasn't I wanted?* She told Him of her longing to know where she came from and her need to know what terrible thing she'd done that even her parents couldn't love her. She spoke of her love for Dixie and Norm Lewis and how much she missed them, then admitted how afraid she'd always been that she would displease them and they wouldn't love her anymore. An ache filled her heart, knowing that she'd always withheld some part of herself from her adoptive parents—out of fear that if she loved them too much, she wouldn't survive if they ever abandoned her too.

Her whispered words caught in her throat as she told Him of her many failed engagements and of her longing to be loved. *Most of all, Father, I need to know, who am I?*

After whispering an "amen" she continued to sit on the rock. Several hopeful ducks gathered at her feet, but she hardly noticed them. When she paid them no attention they finally waddled away. She didn't feel any burning acknowledgment from God that her prayer had been heard. She didn't even feel that wonderful peace and calm that had followed Raymond Aguilera's humble prayer. Instead her head was filled with thoughts and memories so sharp and clear that they were like that spire across the river, glistening in the brilliant morning light.

She had thought the prayer Lara's father had expressed heralded some kind of turning point in her life, but now she could see that it hadn't been the beginning of the change she sensed within herself. The groundwork for this change had been laid when she'd reluctantly started attending church with Mark. Gentle, kind Mark had answered her questions and led her back to the point where she recognized a spiritual need in her life. It seemed so unfair to think of him as merely the means God used to tell her it was time to return. Mark had been hurt by their breakup, yet something whispered to her heart that he'd be happy that she was continuing to go to church and asking the questions she'd previously run from.

Now that the relationship was over, she was seeing it more clearly. The gospel meant so much to Mark, and for her to someday share his love for it, in retrospect, seemed the greatest basis for his love for her—he saw her potential, and he'd grown stronger too as he helped her catch that vision. An understanding of his feelings for her took shape in her mind, and she understood that he had loved her, but not in the way he would someday love another woman. His easygoing nature had made it simple for him to passively allow his mother and previous girlfriends to dominate him; but with her he had grown as he'd taken charge of their relationship and played the role of teacher and missionary in her life. She suspected she'd left him more ready for marriage—to neither dominate nor be dominated. Theirs had been a true friendship, and they had met each other's needs for that time in their lives. Tisa's heart lightened with new understanding.

She wondered if the thoughts flooding her mind and the understanding filling her heart were an answer to her prayer. She'd grown up with daily prayer, but she didn't really know much about it. However, she seemed to remember Norm telling her that sometimes the answers to prayer come in different ways, and that one of those ways was an opening of the mind, enabling a person to think and reason on a heightened plane.

Into her mind came the memory of another recent prayer. She'd avoided thinking too much about the night Cabe and her brother had placed their hands on her head in the hospital. But she couldn't deny that she'd felt a tingling sensation start from their hands and move steadily down her body to her heart. She hadn't been hurt seriously that night, and it hadn't been the gash on her arm or the sight of her own blood that had upset her. It was just something about the atmosphere; the dark night, the cars lined up for miles with their headlights glowing in the dark, and the flashing emergency lights that had overwhelmed her with fear and allowed her mind to drift away into darkness. The touch of Peter's and Cabe's hands on her head had soothed away the confusion and fear, allowing her to draw back from the blackness she'd felt creeping over her. She'd never been able to halt that encroaching blackness before.

She'd felt something else that night. There had been an almost physical sensation that had seemed to touch her, coming from Peter's and Cabe's hands, easing the pain, and giving her the expectant feeling that she was about to reach some momentous breakthrough in her life. It had been like hovering on the edge of forgotten memories. Had it simply been the religious training of her youth she'd almost remembered? Was it the similarity to a childhood incident when Peter had held her and soothed her fears one night when they'd stayed too long at a playmate's house? She remembered that night now with sharp clarity. She could feel her tennis shoe rubbing against her heel where one sock had slipped down too far. Peter's hand holding hers was warm and slightly damp. He steadied her when she tripped over a small indentation in the ground. The clouds above the western mountains brought night with unexpected suddenness. Their denim jeans made a whispering sound as they walked beside the road, and she felt safe beside Peter until she heard the mechanical roar of a truck coming toward them, growling as the driver changed gears. Headlights cut through the darkness like a malevolent pair of eyes. Screaming, she lunged toward the fence, clinging with all her might. She couldn't breathe. The monster was coming!

Tisa felt the world tilt and darken as she was overwhelmed by the memories of that dark night. She staggered, then eased her way to one of the benches that lined the path. That long-ago night Peter had held her until his soothing voice chased away her terror. Peter wasn't here now, but she knew who she could turn to. "Father, help me," she whispered.

It wasn't instantaneous, but the darkness faded gradually as it was replaced by more light and knowledge. There had never been a monster with malevolent yellow eyes; the monster's eyes had been the headlights of a truck rushing past her as she had walked with Peter, and the night of her accident they had been the lights of a speeding truck cutting across traffic to reach the runaway lane . . . An older memory began forming, and she remembered being frightened and alone, with wire cutting into her fingers, while the eyes of monsters glowed ominously close. But the monster's eyes had always only been headlights in the dark.

Feeling something on her face, she lifted a hand to brush it away and felt moisture. Staring at the dampness on her fingers in awe, she realized her face was wet with tears. She was crying. For the first time in memory she was crying. Her shoulders shook, and she sobbed for the frightened little girl who had seen the monsters coming to get her, for the young girl growing up uncertain of her own identity, and for the woman she'd become who wanted to believe she was worthy of love, but wasn't certain she had the courage to leave her fears behind. She cried for her, for the Tisa who still needed to know who she was.

At last she fished dark glasses from her purse to hide her swollen eyes and tugged the brim of her baseball cap lower. It was time to leave the parkway. She'd told Daman she would meet him at one o'clock, so it was time to be on her way.

CHAPTER 12

Cabe hurried through the airport terminal with his one piece of luggage slung over his shoulder. At the rental counter he picked up keys for an Isuzu Rodeo. It only took minutes to toss his luggage inside and climb behind the wheel. Pausing in the parking lot, he put through a call to Peter.

"The Idaho troopers haven't found her yet," Peter reported, frustration apparent in his voice. "They have both a description of the Bronco she's driving and the plate number. They should have found her by now."

"How about the motels?" Cabe asked.

"Nothing so far. With her injured arm, I doubt she drove all the way to Island Park yesterday. Besides, she doesn't like to drive at night. I feel certain she stopped somewhere along the way and the highway patrol should spot her soon."

"Has Howie regained consciousness?" Cabe thought to ask, though his mind was busy churning over possible means of locating Tisa.

"He's holding his own, but he hasn't fully come to yet," Peter said. "And before you ask, Lara and the children are safe. I talked to her a few minutes ago—and to my father-in-law. There's been no sign of trouble, and I have complete confidence in Raymond's ability to protect them. She asked me to stop by the house to feed Jamie's cat. In their hurry to leave no one thought of Snuffy, so I think I'll drive over to the vet's to check on old Useless, then head home to feed Snuffy."

After each promised to call the other if he had any news, Cabe ended the call and dropped the cell phone into the cup tray between the bucket seats. He sat still, wondering where to begin his search. Tisa could be right here in Idaho Falls or she could have pulled off last night in Blackfoot or any of a dozen other small towns. Rather than aimlessly driving around, he would head for Island Park, which he knew was her ultimate destination. By the time he arrived there he hoped someone would have spotted her car.

Putting the car in motion once more he exited the parking lot. After a moment's hesitation, he turned left from Skyline Drive toward the freeway.

His phone rang before he could change lanes to enter the freeway ramp. With one hand he fished it out of the cup holder and pressed it to his ear. Half of his mind registered that he'd missed the on-ramp as he began looking for a place to pull over.

"Cabe?" Dave Woods's voice asked. "I think we've located Lewis's sister. A Patricia Lewis registered at the Best Western motel along River Parkway last night. She paid in advance for one night."

"I can see the river just ahead. Do you have an address?"

Dave read Cabe the address, then before ending the call promised to continue searching the Island Park area for a possible reservation.

In minutes, Cabe pulled onto Lindsay Boulevard with the Snake River on his left and discovered the long narrow parkway following the river. The motel appeared on his right. No blue Bronco could be seen in his quick scan of the parking lot, so making a sharp turn he halted in front of the door marked *Office* and hurried inside. Minutes later he returned to his vehicle feeling let down. Tisa had been there, but had checked out early.

Instead of opening his car door he stood staring across the street. Some force seemed to draw him toward the river. On an impulse he crossed to the park and found his way to the path that led along the riverbank. As he walked along he experienced a sensation of being close to Tisa, almost as though he could reach out and take her hand. He scanned the path, seeing some tourist groups and several solitary walkers, but no one who remotely resembled Tisa.

A break in the trees provided a spectacular view of the water, plunging in a foaming mass over the falls. In the distance he could see a large white building; he recognized it from pictures as the Idaho Falls Temple. Someday he'd like to come back, he thought, and enter that temple with Tisa at his side. The thought didn't surprise him as much as it might have. He could be letting the excitement of the situation they were in dramatize his feelings, but he didn't think so. He'd known when his arm brushed her shoulder at Peter's barbeque that Tisa had an effect on him no other woman ever had, and she would play an important role in his life. He'd begun to wonder if she might be the woman he'd choose to spend eternity with.

He couldn't spend eternity with her if he didn't find her soon though. Instead of acting like a tourist, he needed to go after her. If Bronson knew her relationship to Peter she could be in grave danger. He snapped his attention back to the job at hand, practically running back to his vehicle, where he started the engine and began making his way to the freeway.

* * *

From a quarter mile away Tisa saw the black-and-white cruiser at the side of the road. A quick glance at the speedometer told her she had nothing to worry about. She was aware of her tendency to speed, but she was being meticulously careful today. The accident played a role, of course, in her strict compliance with the posted speed limits, but the fact that she'd passed three different highway patrol cars since leaving Idaho Falls was a convincing factor on its own.

Once past Ashton, she turned off the air-conditioning and opened her window, letting the scent of pine fill the car. Breathing deeply, she congratulated herself on her decision to go ahead with this trip. The contract with Daman Bronson didn't allow a lot of time for preparing a detailed plan, and seeing the structure and its natural environment was essential to the way she worked—and a week in the mountains would almost be a vacation.

She didn't remember a time before when she'd felt such a need for a vacation. A lack of energy had never been a problem for her. She liked to work early in the morning when the world seemed bright and new, and she often sketched late at night, safe in the sheltering warmth of her condo. Few days went past without a long walk, a quick run, or a session of swimming laps in the condo pool. Her small stature had never kept her from being a fierce competitor in any sport, and she'd once seriously considered becoming a professional dancer. But today she felt the weariness of a much-too-short night, too many hours driving with a sore shoulder, and a haunting sense of uneasiness as though she'd forgotten to do something or done something wrong, but she didn't know what that something was.

Mentally she reviewed her departure from Salt Lake. That was probably why she was feeling guilty. She knew she hadn't forgotten to turn off a stove burner or lock her door, but she had been deliberately evasive with Peter, and she knew that wasn't fair. He wasn't really controlling or manipulative, but this time his concern for her had felt like a burden. Her strange mood was more than that. Cabe and Daman were part of the problem too. Her reactions to the two new men in her life were different from the way she'd responded to any of the numerous men she'd known up until now.

There had been instant awareness the first time she'd seen Cabe, and when they'd finally met, she'd felt an empathetic bonding that canceled out any desire to play the games she'd previously played with men. With Cabe she could be honest and direct. She found herself thinking of him at odd moments and wondering when she would see him again. If she hadn't been quite so anxious to call the rental place and keep her appointment with Daman, she would have encouraged Cabe to stay longer yesterday morning.

Daman intrigued her too, but in a different way. When she'd walked into Phillip Kurt's boardroom she'd experienced a sense of recognition, and she'd sensed he felt it too. There was an almost familiar tension between them. When he spoke she had the uncanny feeling that she knew what he was going to say before he said it. But she didn't approve of his casual attitude toward drinking or his arrogance. The night she'd met him for dinner, she thought he was showing off for her benefit, which instead of flattering her had made her question his maturity. And another thing, he wasn't a member of the Church. Six months ago it wouldn't have been that important, but since Mark, she'd discovered it did matter. She wasn't interested romantically in Daman she assured herself, but if her interest wasn't romantic, why did she feel such a strong connection to him?

With a longer list of negatives than positives on Daman's side, she wondered why her heart accelerated and she felt a heightened excitement as she drove up the winding mountain road. She wouldn't be fooling anyone, least of all herself, if she didn't admit she was anxious to see him again. She could tell herself it was the professional challenge of decorating his hotels she was looking forward to, but she knew that would be a lie. There was something about Daman that was a challenge she couldn't resist.

She passed Harriman State Park and began looking for the private road leading to the cabin where Daman had arranged for her to stay. He'd told her that the property he'd purchased had formerly belonged to a small tourist operation that rented luxury summer cabins, and that he'd decided not to tear the cabins down until the hotel was ready for occupancy. He'd retained a local couple to keep them ready for any of his key people who might need accommodations during the construction phase.

The road wasn't well marked, but Daman had given her detailed driving directions and she was soon turning onto a dirt road that was sadly in need of being paved. He'd told her he employed a security guard to keep vandals away from the property, so it didn't surprise her when she passed a man relaxing beneath a tree in a small, four-wheel, all-terrain vehicle; but his military fatigues and the rifle he held did surprise her.

A half mile farther down the road she found the first cabin. When she reached the fourth cabin she turned onto a short side lane and parked in front of the low, log structure. The log walls glistened and a large covered porch, sporting several deeply cushioned chairs and a porch swing, suggested pleasant summer evenings. Mountain air and sunshine poured in the car window relaxing her, and the ache in her arm seemed to diminish. This trip was just what she needed. She hoped Daman had some place in mind for lunch where the food was really good.

* * *

Cabe saw the sign for Mack's Inn on his right and decided to pull over. It would be as good a place as any to get a room. He needed a base from which to search for Tisa. Stepping from the car, he looked around, taking in the tree-covered mountains and the sound of water flowing under the highway bridge. Weathered cabins sloped up the hill, disappearing into the trees, and a larger structure, more like a motel than an inn, stood at the water's edge. Farther up the hill he could see a new log building. This was the kind of place he'd like to return to someday with a family, he thought, as he looked around at a group of teenagers splashing in the river, a family group floating slowly on a rubber raft, and three little girls emerging from the small store with ice-cream treats clutched in their hands.

His thoughts turned wistful. Growing up without a father or siblings, he'd often imagined what it would be like to stay in a fishing cabin with a father and a couple of brothers, maybe even a sister he could tease. He'd imagined himself making certain his siblings didn't fall in the water and helping them bait their fishhooks.

Stretching to get the travel kinks out of his back, he looked around, noticing a cabin under construction across the road and tucked back in the trees. He found the sight encouraging. Island Park was only twenty-two miles from end to end and someone building a resort or lodge would surely want it close enough to the highway— which served as the park's main street—that it would be easy for tourists to find.

It didn't take long to get checked into the motel and place a call to Dave Woods. "I don't understand why no one has spotted her car," he complained to the special agent. "I checked out the motel where she stayed last night. I looked at her registration card and saw that she listed the plate number we're searching for."

"There's a possibility she's driving a different vehicle now," Dave suggested. "I have someone checking into that. The dealer here said he'd been notified that one of his cars was experiencing mechanical difficulty and had been turned in at the Idaho Falls airport."

"Check it out," Cabe said. "And if it was the Bronco Tisa rented, see if you can get the new vehicle's plate number." Had they been that close to each other and he'd missed her? Cabe wondered. He'd had the expectant feeling she was close and he only needed to round a corner to find her.

"There are several lodges being built in Island Park at the present time," Dave continued. "Island Park is actually an incorporated city, and I've talked with someone at their city office who is checking building permits. Their planning and zoning department should have something for you within the hour." He gave Cabe directions to the city offices, located three miles farther up the highway.

After concluding the call to Dave Woods, Cabe dialed Peter's private office line. When there was no answer, he tried Dispatch. When he reached Dispatch and identified himself, he was told Peter was responding to an emergency and was unavailable. He left word for Peter to call him as soon as possible.

Hanging up the phone, Cabe stared out the window without seeing the river or mountains. Peter dealt with emergencies all day long, he thought, why should he assume this emergency was of a more personal nature? Had something happened to Lara, one of the children, or Tisa? Had Howie awakened—or died?

Without bothering to unpack his small duffle, he pulled a pair of jeans and his Nikes from the bag and quickly changed. Then pausing only to get a drink of water before leaving his room, he hurried back to his car. When he started the engine he saw the gas gauge read less than half a tank, so he pulled into a nearby service station. Wherever the search took him, he didn't want to run out of gas. As he waited to pay for his purchase, he noticed a stack of insulated backpacks, the kind used to carry soft-drink cans or water bottles while hiking. He decided to purchase one and drinks to fill it. Impulsively he picked up a handful of candy bars and a package of crackers to stuff in the bag as well. It might be some time before he got a chance to get a meal, and when he found Tisa—well, she was always hungry.

The city office turned out to be small, but was nonetheless a gold mine of information about the area. Soon, with a map and directions to two possible sites which might belong to Bronson, he was back in his car. Neither construction company building the new lodges listed Bronson Enterprises as the funding corporation, but that didn't deter him. By now he had a pretty good idea that the company of record meant little. Bronson could set up a dummy company for the construction phase, then transfer ownership to his known corporation, or he could hide his ownership from Reuben and Artel, as well as the law, by registering under any name he chose.

The first lodge on his map was clearly not the hotel he was looking for. This resort appeared to be along the lines of a basic hikers' hostel. He was looking for something more upscale. A hotel catering to backpackers and hikers wouldn't engage the services of a company like Kurt's Interiors.

Turning back toward Mack's Inn, he crossed the river and headed south. Approaching the area marked on his map he slowed down, watching for a road leading into the densely timbered area that had been described to him. This resort was being built almost a mile from the highway. Spotting a sign warning trespassers away, he noticed a gate across the road. It looked like he might have to hike.

It only took a minute to find a shady spot a short distance away. It was at the entrance to a firebreak that seemed to follow an unused road where he could park his car out of sight. Before leaving the vehicle, he reached for a bottle of water from the pack he'd purchased and took a long cold swallow. He'd take the pack with him as he hiked up the road to get a look at the structure being built. Just as he slipped the straps over his shoulder, his phone rang.

He retrieved the cell phone from the cup holder and fumbled in his eagerness as he pushed Talk.

"Cabe?" Peter's voice reached him. He sounded as though he were out of breath and wasted no time plunging into the problem he faced. "Someone tried to burn my house. I was in my office or with Howie all night, so after checking on Useless I went home to shower and feed Snuff. I found flames pouring from the back of the garage."

"How bad? . . ." Cabe started to ask even while in his mind he was saying a silent prayer of thanks that Peter's family hadn't been in the house.

"It's bad," Peter told him. "The garage and the kids' rooms, which were directly over it, are pretty much gone. There's a lot of smoke and water damage to the rest of the house. I won't really know the extent until the insurance company sends someone to look at it. Lara wisely took her book of remembrance with her so we didn't lose everything. Her mother insisted she take a few pieces of family heirloom jewelry too, and I don't know yet whether any of the furniture or clothes can be salvaged. I'm just so thankful my family is safe."

"I assume we're talking arson." It was almost a question.

"It looks that way, but again we have to wait for the fire marshal to finish investigating." Peter sounded exhausted and discouraged. Cabe's heart went out to him.

"Cabe, you have to find Tisa." There was a note of fear in Peter's voice.

"I will," Cabe promised himself as much as Peter. Briefly he explained where he was and that he planned to hike in to where a lodge was being built.

"You better get started," Peter said. "Oh, just one more thing. It looks as though the arsonist may have tangled with Snuffy. Jamie's cat came crawling out of the bushes when I arrived, and his front paws were covered with blood. He didn't have any injuries that I could see, and he may have only caught his own breakfast, but I had the lab take samples for DNA testing before dropping him off at a pet boarding place."

"Speaking of vets, how is old Useless doing?" Cabe asked after assimilating the information.

"He's at the same place I took Snuffy, and he seems to be recovering. Dr. Hastings is quite optimistic that he'll recover."

"And Howie?" Cabe asked.

"The doctor says he's holding his own, but there hasn't been any significant change." Peter continued to talk about Howie for several minutes, then mentioned that Dave Woods had contacted him and that he was cooperating with the Bureau's investigation since his own had been compromised.

"Woods is a good man. You can trust him," Cabe said.

"We're so close now, if only I could be sure Tisa isn't in danger . . ."

"I'll find her," Cabe promised. Clicking the phone off and locking the car, he set off into the trees. It was a beautiful day and he'd always enjoyed the outdoors, but he couldn't help wishing that instead of searching for Tisa, she was hiking alongside him.

* * *

Tisa changed her clothes in the cabin's spacious bedroom, selecting tan jeans and a pale green-and-cream tunic for her tour of the construction project. Since beginning her decorating career she'd clambered around enough uncompleted buildings to know she'd have to exchange the pretty shoes she loved for heavy, high-topped hiking boots.

A path led directly from the cabin to the hotel. She thought *lodge* would be a more accurate term for the stone-and-log structure with its steeply pitched roof rising over the trees. It was beautiful and appeared to be perched on a stone ledge, providing future guests with a commanding view from all sides.

Scrambling over concrete forms, she approached a framed doorway that had yet to have an actual door hung, and peeked inside. The lounge area was large and boasted a fireplace she could easily stand inside. The stonework matched the exterior river rock and met her approval. Ideas began to form in her mind as she moved eagerly inside.

After circling the main reception area, she moved into a large room with two walls of floor-to-ceiling windows. At once she began visualizing table-placement and ways to ensure guests an outdoorlike experience as they dined. Slowly she drifted to the next room, clearly intended to be a bar, and next to it another lounge, this one appearing more exclusive than the open lounge where guests would enter the hotel. It reminded her of the exclusive areas set aside for high-stakes gamblers in some of the Nevada casinos. The ceiling appeared lower than the ceilings in the other rooms, which would lend a more intimate ambiance she decided—or accommodate security cameras. A closer look revealed several holes in the unfinished ceiling which were filled with an unusually large amount of electrical wires. As far as she knew, gambling wasn't legal in Idaho other than the state lottery, but she couldn't think of another explanation for the room. The room disturbed her and she made a mental note to ask Daman its purpose.

Backtracking to the main lounge, she discovered a short hall leading to an area intended to be used as an exercise room and a sauna. Beyond these was a glass-enclosed pool. Even winter sport enthusiasts would find the pool a relaxing diversion.

Ending her first-floor tour without viewing the kitchen or service rooms, she moved toward the stairs, anxious to visit the suites she would also be decorating. She could visit the other first-floor rooms later. A carpenter knelt partway up the stairs, installing the railing, and she paused to watch, running her hand over the smooth wood and admiring its rich grain, glad that Daman had followed her suggestion during their preliminary meeting to use light pines and ash woods.

"Hi!" she kept her voice low, not wanting to startle the man perched on the stairs. He turned and smiled, his acknowledgment of her natural charm showing in his eyes.

"Hello," he responded. "I hope you're the new assistant I requested."

She laughed and introduced herself. "All right if I go upstairs?" she asked.

"Sure. Just stay close to the wall. The rails aren't secured yet." She passed him and continued up the stairs, but couldn't help feeling a little self-conscious knowing the man's eyes were following her.

The view from each suite was different, and she found ideas for decorating and furnishing each one coming to her mind faster than she could make notes. Several times she paused to make hasty sketches, humming tunelessly as she worked. As hotels go, this one wasn't large. Three stories high, it would have eight two-bedroom sets of rooms on the second floor and four larger suites on the third floor.

She laughed in delight when she reached the last suite. It reminded her of her own condo, but was many times larger. With fireplaces framed in, whole walls of windows, and interesting alcoves, she could do something exciting with this apartment. She wondered if Daman planned to keep this suite for his own use or if it was scheduled to become the honeymoon or grand suite for the exclusive use of rich and famous people. She would need to find out before she went too far with ordering furnishings.

She stepped inside the bathroom that connected to the largest bedroom, noticing at once the gigantic spa tub already in place. The tinted windows surrounding the tub would provide both privacy and an unhindered view of the mountain. As much as she loved windows and light, she wasn't sure she would be comfortable bathing in front of a glass wall even if the glass was specially treated. She could see, too, that the plumbing called for two wash basins, and a shower that would have six spray heads.

"Like it?" She dropped her pencil and turned slowly around. Daman stood framed in the doorway, a teasing smile on his face, almost as if he had read her thoughts. She knew the light streaming through the window would do nothing to hide the blush creeping across her face.

"I didn't know women still did that," he chuckled, and she decided to pretend she didn't know what he was talking about.

"You startled me." Her poise returned as she found her voice and discovered it wasn't going to betray her sudden nervousness. "Is it lunchtime already?"

"Almost." He took a couple of steps toward her. "I would have come right over as soon as I learned you'd arrived, but I got tied up on a call. I hope you don't think I was neglecting you."

"No, not at all. I like exploring on my own," she hastened to assure him. She opened the French door she'd been standing beside and stepped out onto a deck overlooking the valley beyond the hotel.

"Like it?" Daman asked again without moving toward the open door, and she had the uncomfortable feeling he implied more than whether or not she liked the hotel or the view.

"It's beautiful," she answered, deliberately interpreting his question as pertaining to the hotel. She spread her arms as if encompassing the lodge and the mountain it sat on. "I can hardly wait to get started, and I have a few questions already."

"You can ask me over lunch." He smiled and held out his hand. "The chef who will be taking over the kitchen here has prepared lunch at my cabin."

As Tisa turned, a small movement through the window caught her attention. Focusing on the spot, she saw nothing else, but even as she placed her hand in Daman's she wondered why she felt reluctant to tell him what she'd seen—a man carrying a rifle and moving furtively through the trees toward one of the cabins. The figure had been dressed in camouflage like the guard she'd encountered on the road leading to the lodge, and was probably another security guard, but his presence didn't make her feel more secure. If anything, she felt just the opposite.

* * *

Cabe looked around in dismay. Judging from the large cross imbedded in the stained glass at the front of the building he faced, the numerous ball courts, the boat dock along the river, and a row of stables behind the lodge, he guessed he was looking at a soon-to-be church youth camp. It promised to be a fine place for young people to enjoy the outdoors, but again it wasn't the kind of place that would hire Tisa.

Retracing his steps along the rutted road to the highway, he noticed a rough track that might have been a logging road a long time ago. It appeared to be a shorter, more direct route to the place where he'd left his car. He remembered the old road where he'd parked and impulsively began jogging along the faint trail.

On a small rise he stopped to get his bearings and make certain he was still traveling in the right direction. Turning his head slowly, he caught a glimpse of a steeply pitched roof, barely visible between two pine-covered hills. Pallets of shingles sat on the roof, telling him the building was either under construction or being reroofed. Was it possible he'd picked the wrong turn-off? For a moment he considered hurrying on to his car and using it to search for the road leading to the large building he'd discovered, but some instinct warned it might be better if he arrived unannounced.

CHAPTER 13

Cabe's shirt was soaked and his breath was coming faster than normal by the time he topped a mound of rocks and trees and saw the structure beyond a small meadow, half a mile farther up the mountainside. In the distance he caught glimpses of a road weaving through the trees. As he watched, a vehicle looking like a toy Jeep appeared on the road, moving slowly. It stopped and a figure stepped out of the trees. Minutes later the Jeep turned around and left the way it had come.

Cabe wondered if what he had seen was an indication that visitors weren't welcome, or simply a message delivery. He decided not to take chances. He needed to get close enough to see if Tisa was here, but experience warned he'd need to remain unseen.

When the track he was following veered away from the building, he left it and began working his way through the trees. The route he was following made for a more difficult hike and slowed him down, but he caught enough glimpses of the imposing structure ahead to keep him moving in its direction. Thick shrubs made walking difficult on the steep slope, and several times he had to backtrack to work his way around impenetrable thickets. He was so intent on working his way to the large building that he almost stumbled into a clearing where he saw a cabin.

Drawing back into the tree line, he studied the small log structure. A beat-up Ford pickup and a small tractor of some sort were parked in front of it. From the accumulation of toolboxes and building supplies scattered about, he figured it was occupied by some of the construction workers for the larger building.

Carefully skirting the cabin, he moved with greater caution, staying in the trees as he went. He found two more cabins, one of which didn't seem to be occupied. They both appeared to be much more upscale than the first cabin had been. The second one had an SUV parked in front of it that looked just like the Navigator he'd leased in Salt Lake. As he drew closer he could see the dealer's symbol that marked it as a rental. A tingle of excitement went through him. This could be what he was looking for.

Leaving the trees, he approached the cabin. The stillness of the small clearing was an indication there was no one in the cabin now, but perhaps he could determine whether or not Tisa was staying here. Deciding to take the direct approach, he stepped onto the porch and knocked at the door. Silence met his knock and he waited a few moments before knocking again. When there was still no response, he cupped his hands near his eyes and peered through the front window.

There wasn't much to see. The room was nicely furnished, but there were no personal items sitting around giving away clues to its occupant. Working his way around the cabin, he peered into several more windows, but thick screens prevented him from seeing anything. After a few minutes he returned to the Navigator. It didn't give any clues as to who had driven it here, either. Or did it? He noticed a small plastic bag hanging from the dash. It was filled with empty snack wrappers, and a nearly empty doughnut box sat on the passenger seat.

Drawing back into the trees to think, he looked around carefully. Trees blocked his view of the large building, but he could hear the drone of a generator and the sharp tapping of a nail gun coming from the direction he'd been heading, and he recalled seeing men working on the roof. He wondered if he would be able to approach the building without being challenged by the construction workers. He decided to take that chance. Tisa was probably there.

Once more he began walking, this time following the sound of the power hammers, and again avoiding the road. He also kept a watch out for other cabins. If Tisa and the workers were staying in the cabins, there was a good possibility Bronson was making use of a cabin as well.

In all, he found three more cabins which all seemed to be occupied, judging from the vehicles parked in front of them. The largest cabin was closest to the building under construction and had two expensive vehicles parked in front of it. From a slight elevation behind the cabin, Cabe waited in the trees keeping his eyes on the place. If this was Bronson's project site, it would be best to remain out of sight.

At first he thought the cabin was empty, then the back door opened and a short, heavyset man stepped out. Cabe had a good view of the man, and he could see he wasn't any known associate of any of the Dempskys Cabe was familiar with. It was possible he'd erred again in his search.

He continued to watch as the little man, dressed in white, seated himself on a tree stump and shook out a cigarette, then returned the pack to his shirt pocket. Guessing the man would be occupied for several minutes, Cabe began taking careful steps around to the front of the cabin. Checking the clearing with great care and seeing no one, Cabe slipped stealthily from the trees onto the porch. Peering through the front window he saw a table set for lunch—for two.

Cabe wrestled with whether to stay and approach the couple who would soon be sitting down to lunch, or retreat to the trees and wait to discover if Tisa and Bronson were that couple. If it was Bronson, Cabe might endanger Tisa by approaching her directly. Removing himself from the porch, he found a position concealed by shrubs where he could wait.

He didn't have to wait long. He heard Tisa's laughter before he saw the pair coming along the path that led from the hotel. A man's deeper laughter followed, and Cabe felt a stab of jealousy. When they entered the clearing he couldn't clearly see the face of the man walking beside Tisa. His head was lowered attentively toward her and distance prevented a close examination of his face, but Cabe could tell the man he presumed was Daman Bronson was just under six feet tall, with white-blond hair, and muscular. His crisp walking shorts and polo shirt definitely didn't come from K-Mart. He was holding Tisa's hand and as he said something Cabe couldn't hear, Cabe heard Tisa laugh. Only his desire to keep Tisa from a threatening situation prevented him from confronting the man.

Cabe watched as the pair stepped onto the wide veranda-style porch where he had been moments before. Bronson released Tisa's hand to hold the door for her and the two disappeared inside. Now Cabe faced a dilemma. Did he knock on the door and ask to speak to Tisa, or wait to see if after lunch she returned to the other cabin where he might be able to speak with her alone? He settled down to wait.

A mosquito made a nuisance of itself buzzing around Cabe's ear, and he swatted ineffectually at it several times. He wondered if he dared peek in the window again, then decided not to risk it. Feeling a cramp in one leg, he stretched out his foot and felt his shoe catch against some sort of vine. Taking his eyes from the cabin he reached down to disentangle his foot and found a length of wire protruding from the ground. He froze in place while his eyes followed a line where the ground had been disturbed to allow the laying of cable. Near where he crouched, it appeared an animal had scratched at the ground, disturbing the shallowly placed wire.

There was only one reason a length of wire would be buried here. It certainly wasn't for television reception. Bronson had installed an intruder alarm. The only question was, was it operational yet? The hotel wasn't completed and Bronson might not consider the alarm necessary until operation began, but what kind of hotel would need a perimeter security alarm in a peaceful mountain glen? Were there cameras too? Sweat poured down Cabe's back as he visually scanned the trees and searched the eaves of the nearly completed hotel. He didn't see anything, but well-hidden cameras would be hard to spot. He'd been within the area for close to half an hour and had even approached several of the cabins. He'd seen no signs of anyone being aware of his presence or searching for him yet. Still it was possible he was being watched right now.

The sound of a motor racing toward him warned him his luck was about to change. A small, off-road vehicle raced into the clearing carrying the man that Cabe had earlier seen stop the vehicle on the road. Dressed in military fatigues with a rifle slung over one shoulder, the man leaped from his ATV and rushed toward the cabin. Bronson met him at the cabin door. Cabe lingered only long enough to hear Bronson say, ". . . probably just another deer, but get Deke and Bill and do a thorough search. You should be able to deal with it. I have a guest for lunch and don't wish to be disturbed."

That answered his question! The perimeter cable was operational and he'd tripped the alarm. Cabe lost no time backing away from the tattletale wire. Having no idea how good Bronson's security people might be at tracking, he headed for a rocky ridge where he could move quickly but leave no tracks. He hadn't seen any indication of dogs at any of the cabins, so he hoped that staying out of sight would be sufficient.

He was scarcely settled in a cluster of rocks, well screened by trees and shrubs from the cabins below and the workers on the hotel roof, when a commotion broke out on the opposite side of the property. Three ATVs roared toward a spot where a troop of boys in jeans and Scout shirts were clambering down a hill, headed straight for the hotel. Their leader straggled behind, appearing winded as he followed his charges.

Cabe held his breath, wondering if the security men were about to threaten the kids and if the boys were in any danger. The Scouts halted when they saw the armed men. The roar of machines died away, leaving only the rapid pounding of the roofer's nail gun. Cabe's hand instinctively went to the service revolver hidden under his shirt.

From across the small valley the sound of angry voices reached his ears. The words were unintelligible, but there was no mistaking the confrontational anger they were spoken with. At last the Scoutmaster's movements gave clear indication that he was ordering his troop back up the hill. With apparent reluctance, the boys fell into line, and with varying degrees of speed, began retracing their steps. Their leader was the last to disappear over the hill. Cabe felt sorry for them. Wherever the troop was headed, they'd have a much longer walk now.

The ATVs roared to life once more, and Cabe watched to see if the guards would continue their search, or if they would consider the Scout troop the culprits who had tripped the alarm. In a few minutes he saw one of the noisy machines turn onto the road that led to the highway, one park behind the partially completed hotel, and the third one return to the cabin where Cabe had seen one of the sport vehicles parked earlier. Slowly he let out his breath.

Cabe felt safe for the moment, but he wondered how he was going to be able to reach Tisa without arousing Bronson's suspicions. Now that he knew about the perimeter wire, he could avoid stepping on it by watching where the ground had been disturbed, but how could he be sure there weren't any cameras?

* * *

"Your chef will delight your guests." Tisa set her napkin back on the table with a small sigh. Lunch had been exceptional.

"You've had enough?" Daman patted his mouth with the corner of his napkin before dropping it on his empty dessert plate.

"Something I don't say often, but yes, I'm full."

"Something we have in common." Daman reached across the table to take her hand. "I meet few women who aren't dieting. I like to eat, and it's a pleasure to have a dinner companion who enjoys eating."

"Oh, I've eaten with a few other men who enjoy food as much as I do. Of course, they were all well over three hundred pounds." She grinned at Daman, knowing he wouldn't take offense. For a man who had just finished a huge steak, a half gallon of fancy creamed potatoes, nearly a dozen croissants, and a cherry flambé, he was remarkably thin. In fact, if she were in the habit of noticing men's physiques, she'd have to say Daman's was one of the best she'd seen in a long time, almost as good as Cabe's. She quickly banished Cabe's image. It wasn't fair to think about one man while with another, even if she didn't think of Daman in a romantic way.

"Thank you for lunch," Tisa withdrew her hand from Daman's. "But now I think I'd better get back to checking measurements and taking notes. I should have some fairly complete sketches to show you within a week."

"You made that long drive with your injured arm, then worked the rest of the morning; why don't you relax until tomorrow?" Daman stood and held her chair as she rose to her feet.

"All right," she agreed while struggling to hide a yawn. She hadn't gotten much sleep last night between her late arrival in Idaho Falls and her early start on the day. "But my arm really does feel much better today."

"Good. There's plenty of ice in your cabin if you need it. You can rest and let your injury continue to heal. While you pamper that arm, I have some business to take care of this afternoon. If it's not too late when I return, perhaps you'd join me for dinner and a stroll down to the lake." He retrieved her notebook for her and ushered her ahead of him as he reached for the door handle.

"There's a lake?"

"Well, not much of one." He smiled and opened the door. "It's little more than a pond, but I intend to enlarge it and stock it with trout."

"You could add a few benches and create observation points." Tisa stepped ahead of Daman onto the porch.

It didn't take long to reach the cabin she had been assigned. Daman followed her to her door, where he paused. "If I'm not back by six, Chef Bono will deliver dinner to your door tonight. There will be no reason for you to stir from your cabin before I get back. You can just relax and let that arm heal."

"You sound like my brother," Tisa joked. "He seems to think I should do nothing but lie around being bored until the doctor removes the stitches."

"When will that be?"

"Sometime next week," she answered while reaching for her notebook. "I really did enjoy lunch, but now I'm keeping you from your business."

"I wish . . ." Daman paused. "We'll talk later." His voice dropped to a whisper before he leaned forward and touched his lips to her forehead. Seeing her startled expression he murmured, "Next time I'll aim a little lower." Before she could think of anything to say, he turned and walked away.

* * *

Cabe was nervously checking his watch when Tisa and Daman emerged from the cabin where he presumed they'd eaten lunch. "It took long enough!" he grumbled. His disposition didn't improve as he watched them walk much too companionably toward the cabin where the blue Navigator was parked. He wished he was close enough to get a good look at Bronson's face. They disappeared behind trees, and he continued to fume until he saw Daman return to the large cabin without Tisa. At once he began plotting a route to her cabin that would bypass the buried wires. He also needed to know if cameras or any other type of security system was in use.

By staying high above the cabins and keeping an eye on the workmen on the hotel roof, he edged his way around the resort to a spot directly opposite the cabin he suspected housed the guards and their equipment. Keeping watch for signs of buried cable, he stepped gingerly from one hidden spot to the next, working his way down the incline. With his heart pounding so hard he feared it could be heard by anyone in the cabin, he at last eased his way along a log wall until he reached a window. After checking every angle for sight lines or possible hidden cameras, he risked a peek.

The window he'd chosen was directly over a double sink and provided a view straight across a kitchenette into an open area filled with sofas and chairs. He didn't see any screens or electronic monitoring equipment, but littering the floor were a lot of boxes with the names of computer and electronics companies printed on their sides. No one seemed to be inside the cabin, but he carefully checked the view from the cabin's other windows. Two doors opened off the living area, one of which was closed. He needed to get a look inside both bedrooms. While contemplating the best route to gain access to the cabin, he heard a car engine start up. Dropping to his stomach, he lay still, hoping he hadn't been spotted. As the vehicle drew closer, he recognized it as one of the cars he'd seen parked in front of Bronson's cabin.

Lifting his head a small amount, he watched the car come closer. He breathed more normally when it passed the short lane leading to Tisa's cabin. Tisa wasn't in danger, but he still was. Settling as low as possible into the grass next to the cabin, he continued to lie still, and as it passed in front of him, he got a good look at the two men seated on the front seat. Behind the wheel sat Jorge Ortega. The man on the right he recognized from the photo Peter had shown him. He was Tracy Roberts—and his clothes were the same as those of the man he'd seen holding Tisa's hand less than an hour ago. Roberts and the illusive Bronson were the same man.

* * *

Tisa wasn't sure what awakened her or why she was afraid. She couldn't remember what she'd been dreaming, but whatever it was, it had left her feeling anxious and a little guilty. The guilt wasn't anything new. She'd always had this sense of having done something wrong. Fear wasn't unusual either, but for some reason, the vague fears she'd experienced at odd moments her entire life had been intensified these past few weeks, almost leading to panic attacks. When she got back to Salt Lake she really should make an appointment with a therapist, but it wouldn't be the psychiatrist she'd disliked so much as a child. She'd never trusted him.

She didn't trust Daman either. There, she'd admitted it. Something about Daman disturbed her, and she knew she'd have to soon make up her mind how far to let their relationship proceed. He hadn't pressured her for a physical relationship, but she knew he found her attractive and that he would eventually want more than to hold her hand or kiss her forehead. How could she tell him that when he'd held her hand she'd felt like a little girl running away to some great adventure and that there had been nothing romantic in the feeling? How could she reconcile her desire to please him with her suspicion that he would somehow betray her?

Her arm ached more than she could stand and she climbed off the bed to find a couple of Tylenol tablets in her bag whether they made her sick or not. Her fingers touched an unfamiliar bottle of pain medication and she remembered Lara's insistence she have the prescription filled. She wouldn't have bothered normally, but Lara warned her over and over that she might need the stronger medication, and then practically commanded Tisa to put it in her purse before Cabe had driven her home yesterday morning. Tisa hated taking any kind of drug, even Tylenol, and she refused to touch the painkillers the doctor at the hospital had prescribed. She passed up the bottle and dug deeper for the Tylenol.

Sitting at the table a few minutes later, sipping a bottle of water, she found that even becoming fully awake had done nothing to ease either the niggling guilt that plagued her or the sense of fear that hovered at the edge of her mind. Intellectually she knew that her guilt and fear were holdovers from that time before she'd been found by a truck driver, and that whatever it was that she had done, no court would hold her responsible for it more than twenty years later. Her parents had assured her that God didn't hold her responsible either, that in His eyes small children are innocent.

As a teenager she'd tried to reconcile the teachings of the Church concerning the innocence of children with the load of guilt she couldn't dismiss. It made perfect sense that a loving, just God would not hold a four- or five-year-old child responsible for any crimes, even one as serious as taking a life—if that were even a possibility. But knowing with her mind and with her heart were two different things. Not even Peter knew that she'd once hired a private detective to find out who she really was. The investigator had found nothing new beyond the fact that the little sweater she'd been wearing had been mass produced for a chain of discount stores, and that it had sold particularly well in California.

Peter had never understood why she couldn't be content with having Norm and Dixie Lewis for her parents and him as her brother. He didn't need any other family and had let her know he considered it far worse to *know* he'd been born to despicable parents than to simply wonder about her parents as she did. Peter claimed he had no warm memories whatsoever of his first parents, but sometimes, especially when she held the small pink sweater Dixie had saved for her, she knew someone had cared. She wanted very much to remember that person and she hoped it was her mother. But when she tried to remember, the fear grew until it became unbearable. Tisa's head began to throb, and she knew she should stop trying to remember.

Finishing the bottle of water, she rose to her feet to carry it to the trash basket she'd seen earlier under the sink. As she straightened from the task, she found herself face-to-face with someone peering in her kitchen window. An involuntary scream rose in her throat, but she choked it back when she realized the face belonged to Cabe.

"Cabe!" Her voice was a strangled cry. He held a finger to his lips, indicating she should be quiet.

"Let me in," he mouthed, and she slowly nodded her assent. As she turned to take the few steps to the door though, she wondered if she was out of her mind.

"What are you doing here?" She stepped back to allow him access. Her heart was still pounding, but she suspected it was for an entirely different reason than her initial fear.

"Are you alone?" his voice was almost a whisper that somehow made her want to giggle. She nodded her head, feeling almost dizzy—

either from the excitement at his unexpected arrival, or the lingering remains of her headache.

"We have to talk." He steered her to the sofa in a darkened corner. She reached for the drape cord to let in some light, but he stopped her hand. "It will be better if no one sees me here."

She stared in astonishment. He was serious. "Has something happened to Peter?" she asked in a low, frightened voice.

"No, Peter is fine." Cabe lost no time assuring her. "There has been a serious threat aimed at your entire family, though. Peter sent Lara and the children to her father's, and Peter's staying at an undisclosed location. He asked me to get you safely to Raymond and Elena too."

"What kind of threat?" She could tell Cabe was disappointed she hadn't jumped right up and grabbed her bag.

"Peter is getting close to an arrest on a big case." She sensed Cabe was going to give her an abbreviated explanation. "The criminals involved know he has evidence that can be used to convict them. They've threatened your whole family if he doesn't turn it over to them."

"Peter's had threats made against him before."

"I know, but this time it isn't just Peter. They've threatened Lara and the children—and maybe you. To show him they're serious they set his house on fire."

Tisa felt tingles of shock. "Was anyone hurt? With Lara and the children gone, does he need me to be with him?" She would have risen to her feet, but Cabe took her arm and pulled her back down beside him. His arm remained around her shoulders and she found she liked it there.

"Peter's fine. He didn't come because his investigation is at a critical point and it's best he stay out of sight. Just a few more days and he can assist the Bureau in arresting the leaders of this organization. He sent me because he thought there was less chance I would be followed, not because he was injured." Then he told her what he knew about the fire.

"Poor old Snuffy." Tisa shook her head picturing her niece's feisty feline playmate.

"From the blood spattered on Snuffy's fur and on the basement stairs, I'd guess he got in a pretty good swipe before he got kicked," Cabe told her.

"Do you think they might have followed you?" Tisa glanced apprehensively toward the kitchen window.

"No, I wasn't followed, but you're in danger. This new contract means a great deal to you, and Mr. Bronson has made an effort to lavish personal attention on you, so I'm sure you want to see him in the best possible light, but you must understand your new client isn't what he presents himself to be." Cabe hesitated, then touched her arm as though he would protect her from his own words if he could. "Daman Bronson is not your client's real name. He goes by several aliases, and he's connected to the crime organization Peter and I have been investigating. He's a dangerous man, the prime suspect in the murder of a young girl, and he's been connected to the disappearance of more than one person he considered an enemy."

Tisa recoiled at the words Cabe was speaking. She wanted to repudiate his words, say they couldn't be true. Daman Bronson had treated her with courtesy and respect all along. Yet there was something about him . . . She'd sensed something dangerous about him, but surely he hadn't killed someone!

She knew Cabe was trying to cause her as little pain as possible, but that he also respected her intelligence enough to be honest. Or could he be making this all up because he was jealous? No, she didn't believe Cabe was capable of that kind of pettiness, but neither did she believe Daman was connected to some sinister crime organization. She felt some invisible connection to Daman each time she was with him. She didn't want to believe she felt a connection with a criminal.

"You need to leave now while Bronson and Ortega are away." Cabe was still talking, urging her to leave with him. "We can slip out the way I came in. It'll take us a little more than an hour to reach my car. We'll leave your car here so that Bronson's security people don't become suspicious."

"No." She didn't know she was going to refuse to go with Cabe until the word popped out of her mouth. "If everything you said is true, then my sudden disappearance will alert Daman that something is wrong. You said yourself that Peter needs only a little more time to complete his case. I can give him that time."

"Peter wants you safe. It's worth risking the case to know you're safe." She wasn't certain he meant it was worth it to him or to her brother, but either way she felt warmed by the care behind his words.

"But will I or Lara and the children ever be really safe if Peter fails to arrest the people threatening us?"

Cabe didn't answer, but his silence said all she needed to know. "Does Daman know I'm Peter's sister?"

"We aren't certain," Cabe admitted. "There's a good chance he doesn't, but neither of us want to take that chance."

"If he doesn't know—and I don't think he does—then I can help you more by staying right here." A surge of adrenalin sent Tisa to her feet where she began to pace in short, tight circles. "Peter can keep on investigating while I keep an eye on his suspect. Daman asked me to go for a walk with him this evening. I can remember everything he says that might be helpful if you tell me what you're looking for."

"No way." Cabe shook his head. "You can't begin to imagine anyone as dangerous as this group. Come on. Just get what we can carry."

"I'm staying." Tisa folded her arms and sat back down. "I'm not in danger as long as Daman doesn't know who I am, but if I disappear, he'll start investigating. When he discovers I'm Peter's sister, Peter and his family could be in greater danger."

"If he discovers you're Peter's sister, he may hold you hostage," Cabe pointed out.

"He won't find out."

Cabe stood beside Tisa and grasped her shoulders. "Tisa, there's more at stake than just giving Peter more time. There's a dirty cop involved, someone on Peter's team. Whoever he is, he knows you're Peter's sister. It's only a matter of time until he tells Bronson."

Cabe couldn't be right. She knew every one of Peter's men. They were good, honest, hardworking cops. None of them would betray Peter—or her. She took a step back and lifted her chin defiantly. "I know you believe that, but I don't. There's been a mistake. I'm staying right here. Later this evening I'll go for a walk with Daman to a small lake that sits on the western edge of the hotel property. After he brings me back to this cabin, I will do my best to get a good night's sleep. Tomorrow morning I will go with him to the Harriman Ranch for a trail ride, then spend the remainder of the day measuring windows and spaces at the hotel. I will not be stampeded into believing the worst about Mr. Bronson or any of Peter's team, at least not at this point," she amended, knowing she *could* be wrong.

Cabe knew he'd lost, but he also knew he couldn't leave Tisa unprotected. "Here," he said, unclipping his phone from his belt. He punched in a few numbers, then handed the small instrument to Tisa. "One is the agent in charge in Idaho Falls, two is Peter, and three is a spare phone I have in the trunk of my car. I've disabled the ringer, but it will still vibrate to let you know if someone's trying to reach you. I'll be close by."

A soft tapping on the door sent daggers of fear racing along her spine. She might not believe all Cabe had said, but she believed enough to be wary. Soundlessly, she pointed to the bathroom and Cabe darted toward it. She only had time to notice he didn't quite close the door behind him before a louder tap on the door sounded. Taking a deep breath, she dropped the small phone in her pocket and went to answer the door.

CHAPTER 14

Cabe kept an eye pressed against the crack he'd left between the wall and the bathroom door. The plump little man he'd seen taking a break behind Bronson's cabin entered carrying a large covered tray. At least Bronson hadn't returned! With an elegant flourish, the man placed the tray on the table and began unloading a dozen dishes. Tisa thanked him profusely and remarked that with his expertise in the kitchen, the hotel would be a flourishing success. That explained who the man was.

The chef beamed at the praise, then before leaving, said, "Stack the dishes in the kitchen when you finish your dinner. Someone will pick them up in the morning while you and Mr. Bronson are riding."

"All right." She lifted the lid from one of the plates. "But for a dinner like this I'd be happy to wash dishes."

"Nonsense," the man said with a chuckle. "It's my pleasure to cook for a lovely lady who appreciates my work."

"Oh, I certainly appreciate it." She smiled warmly. "And thank you."

When the man had gone, Cabe tucked his gun back under his jacket and strolled out to speak with Tisa again.

"I'm not changing my mind . . ." she began.

"I know." He couldn't keep the regret out of his voice. "Be careful, please, Bronson is a dangerous man. I'll be leaving now; I need to get back to my car and check in with Peter and the Bureau, but I'll be back. I'll always be close by."

"Cabe," she looked worried and seemed to want to say something, then changed her mind.

"What is it?" he asked.

"Earlier today," she hesitated, then made up her mind, "I saw a man with a rifle who seemed to be sneaking through the trees."

"Bronson has at least three guards with rifles watching the cabins and the road," Cabe told her.

"Be careful," she repeated his words of caution. "Oh, and take this. You must be starved." She picked up a thick slice of meat and stuck it inside a dinner roll."

He accepted her offering with a smile. He had a hunch that sharing her dinner wasn't something she did easily. Perhaps it meant she cared—just a little—about him.

Returning to his car took longer than Cabe had anticipated. He climbed well beyond the buried cable before circling back toward the road. He stayed in the trees as much as possible, not wanting to discover any booby traps along the trails or encounter Daman Bronson returning to the property.

Upon finally locating his car, he indulged himself with a bottle of water before digging out his spare phone. His voice kept cutting out, and he had to repeat himself several times as he spoke to Peter, filling him in on Tisa's whereabouts and plans. Peter fumed for several minutes about Tisa's stubbornness, then told him a sheriff down in Washington County had called with some interesting news when he heard the Salt Lake department was asking questions about the Dempskys.

"The Washington County sheriff had received a request from a sheriff in Arizona asking for permission to exhume the bodies of two people who had died in a traffic accident more than twenty years ago near Cedar City, Utah. The Arizona sheriff said that he needed the exhumation order because the couple had been identified as a pair of two-bit con artists from the Mesa area, but another set of bodies had just turned up a few months ago in a shallow grave not far from Mesa with bullets in their skulls. They'd been buried for at least twenty years. This pair had *also* been identified as the same con artists Utah authorities claimed to have buried near Cedar City." Peter took a breath before rattling off the rest of the facts. "The sheriff from Arizona received permission, and this time, using more sophisticated testing, it turned out that the Utah accident victims were really Stefan Dempsky and Josie Bronson—not the pair of con artists."

Cabe gave a low whistle. So Stefan and Josie hadn't just disappeared, and they weren't murdered as almost every officer who worked on the Dempsky case had figured. They'd died in a car accident, presumably driving the con artists' stolen vehicle, which made them the number-one suspects in the murder of the couple buried in Arizona.

A thought worried at his mind long after he hung up the phone. The records on the disk labeled different sections of the far-flung Dempsky empire by initials. Both he and Peter had figured the missing family members were still alive and had found a way to drain the family business accounts through Reuben's son, Bronson. Proof that Stefan and Josie were dead changed the picture considerably. But there was something else . . . He didn't have time to concentrate now, but later he'd remember, he told himself.

Shaking off speculation for the practical, he filled the insulated pack he'd bought with water bottles. He took a few minutes to move the barricade blocking the old fire road, drove his vehicle several hundred feet up the broken, overgrown road, then erased as much evidence of his passage as he could before replacing the barricade. Swinging the pack over his shoulder, he started back up the mountain. He wanted to be sure he was well concealed at the lake before Tisa and Bronson arrived.

* * *

Even after the warning about Daman, Tisa found she wasn't nervous walking beside him on the mountain trail. It was almost as though they'd walked together before. He paused at the top of a steep incline and pointed. She stepped closer and breathed a sigh. The tiny body of water sat like a jewel in the small forest clearing of lush new growth. The pool was formed by a natural spring that plunged down rocks on the far side of the clearing. Grass dotted with meadow flowers grew right up to the edge of the pool, and on the farther, rockier side, several large pines shaded the water. A couple of small stands of aspen framed the lake from the near side, and large boulders formed a natural spot to rest beside the crystal-clear water.

"It's beautiful," she said.

"Shh, over there." Daman pointed and her heart slammed against her chest. Cabe said he would be nearby. Had Daman spotted him?

Expecting to see Cabe, her eyes followed Daman's pointing finger. A deer, followed by two fawns who had nearly lost their spots, stepped out of the trees and moved gracefully toward the water. The doe stretched her neck toward the pond as though delicately tasting it, while the babies copied her action. After a few seconds she raised her head, sniffing the air. She flicked her ears several times, and the fawns scampered into the grass where they almost disappeared. The doe lowered her head for another sip of water just as a small rock near Daman's foot slithered down the path, sending the animal, with her young bounding after her, flying toward the trees.

"I wish I'd brought my camera," Tisa said, staring after the animals with regret.

"Another time," Daman laughed. "There are plenty of deer on this hill, and no hunting season. Most of the resorts encourage wildlife to hang around because it's good for business."

"I can see why." Tisa let Daman hold her hand as they descended the last yard or two of the path to the flat area near the pond. "Seeing a wild animal is usually considered a highlight of a mountain vacation. I certainly feel exhilarated by seeing that little family of deer."

"I think you like my mountain hideaway." Daman's eyes sparkled with a hint of laughter as he seated himself on a large flat boulder and tugged her down beside him. The sun was almost below the mountain rim, painting the clouds pink and gold, while deep shadows were filling the hollows.

"It's lovely here . . . oh look!" Sliding off of the rock, Tisa knelt at the water's edge and pointed out a pair of tiny hand prints.

"I don't believe it!" Daman looked stunned. "How did a baby get up here? I know that church group on the other side of the hill keeps hauling busloads of kids up here, but they're teenagers or close to it. They run all over the place making a nuisance of themselves, but I haven't seen any kids this little."

Tisa sat on the damp sand, nearly bent in two with laughter.

"I said something funny?" Daman scowled his displeasure.

"I'm sorry," Tisa nearly choked on the words, trying desperately to control her amusement. "A . . . a baby didn't make these marks. They're raccoon paw prints."

"You're kidding?" Daman grinned sheepishly, then knelt beside her for a closer look at the marks in the sand. "They look like some little kid . . . You're sure they're raccoon prints?"

"Absolutely! My parents used to take my brother and me camping when we were kids. My dad taught us a lot about animals and the kind of tracks they leave."

"You were lucky to have parents who did stuff like that with you," Daman's voice was gruff.

"Didn't you do things with your family when you were a kid?" Tisa leaned against the large rock they had been sitting on a few minutes earlier. Daman settled back beside her and for several minutes he didn't say anything. When he did speak Tisa heard what sounded to her like pain in his voice.

"No, my father worked all of the time. He didn't come home much, but when he did, he brought enough pills to keep my mother quiet for days, and I learned to stay out of his way if I didn't want to be belted in the teeth."

"I'm sorry," Tisa whispered and meant it.

"It was a long time ago," Daman said, and reached in his pocket for a chocolate bar. He broke it in half and handed a piece to her. They leaned back companionably against the rock and began eating the candy.

"You said you had a brother. Older or younger?" Daman asked. Suddenly Tisa felt a flicker of fear, remembering what Cabe had said. She didn't want to talk about Peter.

"Older," she finally admitted.

"Did he like camping too?" It seemed to be an idle question and Tisa decided to treat it that way.

"Yes, he loved camping. He used to tease me because I was afraid of the dark and didn't like sleeping in tents." She laughed, remembering how Peter used to promise to protect her from all the things that scared her at night. "We were awfully close, and I think if a bear or a monster had stuck its nose in our tent, even though he was only five years older than me, my brother would have attacked it bare-handed before he would have let it touch me."

"I used to tease my little sister too." Daman seemed to be remembering the past more than speaking to her in the present, and from what she could see it was a painful past filled with bitterness and regrets. She stayed quiet, hoping he would go on. After a few minutes he did, "I wasn't as good as your brother, and sometimes it was my fault she got in trouble. I was bigger, and I should have shared with her more, but many times I took what was mine and hers too. She was just a little kid, and she was the only one who really cared about me. No matter how mean I was to her, she still followed me around and wanted to play with me. We used to sit like this behind an old abandoned Oldsmobile in our backyard and talk about all the things we were going to do when we grew up and Pa couldn't hit us anymore. I did most of the talking, but she listened and believed I was smart enough to do it all."

As Daman talked, Tisa could see the two children sitting in the dirt behind a rusty car. She could see the little boy with ragged, dirty overalls and no shirt, his feet bare, and a tiny smear of chocolate at the corner of his mouth. She could feel dry tears on her cheeks, the hot metal behind her back, and she could taste the chocolate. Without warning, she knew she was going to be sick. She stood, and the world tipped crazily as she rushed around the rock to kneel in the grass.

When she at last straightened, it was to see Daman looking at her strangely. He offered her a hand and she stood. In his other hand he held a pond-dampened handkerchief which he used to wipe her face. His touch was gentle as he stroked her face. He didn't say anything, and she was glad. She didn't know how she would explain being suddenly ill or the feelings that seemed about to explode in her heart.

"I feel so embarrassed," she tried to apologize.

"It's all right." His words were kind, though, strangely, she had the feeling kindness wasn't his usual mode of dealing with people. "I've kept you out too late when you're still recuperating from that nasty accident."

He didn't speak as he escorted her back the way they'd come. He helped her over the rough spots and hovered protectively when the trail took them through groves of trees where darkness had already penetrated. At her cabin, he opened her door and held it wide. When she would have stepped away from his protective hold, he kissed her cheek. Deep inside she wanted to cry, not from hurt or disappointment, but because something she didn't quite understand was filling her with a sense of wholeness. She couldn't help feeling that something had been wrong, and it had finally been set right. Though Tisa had always been an intuitive person, these feelings went beyond anything she'd ever experienced before.

* * *

Cabe rocked back on his heels in the tight space he'd created for himself in the grove of aspen overlooking Tisa's cabin. Earlier it had taken every ounce of self-control he had to prevent himself from rushing to Tisa's side when she'd suddenly become ill. He'd been hiding in the trees nearby, in a sort of duck blind he'd arranged, so that he could be close to Tisa without being seen. He hadn't been close enough to hear their words, but he'd seen nothing threatening in Bronson's behavior. There had been plenty to stir his jealousy, however, and Tisa had appeared to be enjoying her companion's conversation a little too much. Bronson had appeared as shocked and concerned as Cabe when Tisa suddenly bolted from his side to throw up a few feet away.

Cabe had concluded shortly after meeting Tisa that she possessed the proverbial cast-iron stomach, so it was hard to believe it had been something she'd eaten that had made her ill—unless she'd been poisoned. *No, poison wouldn't be Bronson's style.* He couldn't be sure of that, he argued with himself. But somehow, he knew he was right. If Bronson wanted to eliminate someone, he wouldn't use anything as subtle as poison.

He needed to get closer so he could check on Tisa, make certain she was all right. She'd seemed to be fine after she returned to her cabin earlier, but it wouldn't hurt to be sure. Besides, even in the summertime it got cold in the mountains, and he was freezing. He pulled his jacket closer around his shoulders and shivered. Then he eyed the cabin from which a faint wisp of smoke still wafted in the chill night air. It shouldn't be too hard to get inside where he could check on Tisa and stay warm for a few hours.

Remembering where the sensor wire was buried, he eased his way down the hill. He paused once when he heard an ATV move slowly down the road. He'd observed the security system—set up presumably by Ortega—long enough to discover that guards patrolled the roads around the cabins and the hotel at regular intervals. The system was pretty low-key, but from what he'd seen in the cabin where the guards stayed, plans were in place for an ultrasophisticated system to protect the new hotel once it was completed. The crates of monitors and electronic gadgets he'd seen in one of the bedrooms rivaled the systems he'd seen in some of the newer Las Vegas casinos.

Picking up a handful of pebbles, he tossed them against Tisa's bedroom window. When there was no movement of the curtains that hid the room from closer inspection, he slipped around to the front of the cabin, which was now in deep shadow. It only took a moment's effort to release the lock and ease his way inside. Embers from an earlier fire offered enough light to allow him to pick his way across the room.

The door to the bedroom stood open, but he couldn't see into the room. Taking a step into the darkness, he paused, holding his breath. In the silence he could hear the rhythmic movement of air that only came from someone deeply asleep. His nose picked up the subtle scent, partly soap and shampoo, that he'd already memorized as uniquely Tisa's. He listened a moment longer, assuring himself that she was safe and sleeping naturally.

Deciding not to disturb her, he moved back into the other room. After a moment he felt his way to the sofa and settled into it to keep warm and to watch over Tisa. He lay still for a few minutes, accustoming himself to the sounds of the night, then he slept.

There was no hint yet of morning when Cabe awoke. Catlike, he rose to his feet and stepped to the door of Tisa's room. Once more he listened to her gentle breathing before padding on silent feet to the door, where he let himself out, reaching back to make certain the lock had caught behind him before joining the shadows on the hill.

He found his cache of water bottles where he'd left them. Slinging them over his shoulder again, he began the long trek back to his car. If he intended to get to the Harriman Ranch before Tisa and Bronson he'd have to hurry.

* * *

Daman arrived with the chef and a breakfast tray shortly after dawn. Like her, he wore jeans, but she suspected his boots had cost several hundred dollars, while her shoes came from a discount store. She hadn't brought riding boots with her and would have to wear her high-topped hiking shoes. She just hoped their wide toes would fit into the stirrups.

She couldn't believe she'd slept so soundly. She'd only awakened once. She'd lain still, listening to the night, and remembered dreaming that Cabe was close beside her. She'd felt secure in his closeness. In fact, his nearness had felt so real that she'd drifted back to sleep, imagining she could hear his breathing.

After breakfast Daman escorted her to his Lexus; there he presented her with a wide-brimmed hat with a low, flat crown before beginning their brief ride to the Harriman Ranch. Catching sight of a man in camouflage waiting near a small ATV a mile down the winding road reminded her of Cabe's warning. She couldn't help wondering if the man was the same man she'd seen sneaking through the trees the day before.

When they arrived at the historic cattle ranch, they found a small crowd of people standing around the pole fence near the barnlike stable laughing and getting acquainted. To one side stood a tall man she recognized at once as Cabe. He was wearing a denim jacket instead of his usual sport coat. A baseball cap was pulled low over his eyes, and the stubble on his face made him look dangerous. He was talking to a pretty blond woman about her own age who was holding onto an excited little boy Tisa guessed was about the same age as Peter, Jr.

The child pulled away from his mother to run toward the corral fence that separated the would-be riders from the horses. Cabe never glanced Tisa's way, but she knew he was as aware of her presence as she was of his. She wondered if it was some kind of survival instinct that kept her from acknowledging his presence, or all the years of listening to Peter talk about various undercover jobs that had been blown by greetings from well-intentioned acquaintances who'd stumbled onto surveillance situations.

"Hey, kid!" The shout from one of the cowboys in the corral drew Tisa's attention, just as it did the blond woman's. The child was leaning through the corral poles jabbing a long stick at the horses.

Cabe reached for the boy, swinging him high in the air with a gentle admonition about scaring the horses while adroitly confiscating the stick.

The woman reached for her son, speaking apologetically to the cowboy and thanking Cabe. She kissed the boy's cheek and warned him to be a "good boy."

Tisa couldn't help thinking of the swift bottom swat she would have been given by Dixie had she ever been caught teasing an animal. Dixie Lewis had been an expert horsewoman with a soft spot for all four-legged creatures.

A man who reminded Tisa of the father who'd raised her lifted his voice to get their attention, introducing himself as Tom. He would be their trail guide. After explaining the rudiments of riding a horse to the mostly novice group, he and an assistant matched riders to horses. Tisa spotted Cabe as a greenhorn at once, but was surprised at the smooth way Daman took immediate control of the spirited horse he was given. Her own horse was a sweetheart; spirited enough to be fun, but gentle enough to inspire confidence in a rider who hadn't sat on a horse since her parents retired from the farm seven years ago.

The line of riders strung out across a wide meadow, moving slowly to allow horses and riders to accustom themselves to each other. Daman urged his horse closer so they could ride two abreast. Tisa noticed several others leaving the single-file line to also ride beside a chosen partner. She didn't miss the fact that Cabe was beside the blond who rode with the child perched in front of her. The boy twisted and bounced so much Tisa suspected the woman would be exhausted before the ride was half over.

Tom pointed out and identified plants and shrubs they passed, with the various riders passing the information back to those behind who were too far from the guide to hear. Tisa mostly shut out the voices around her as she basked in the beautiful morning. She already knew the names of most of the plants they passed. Norm and Dixie had raised her and Peter on mountain lore. She raised her eyes to the high mountain in front of them, remembering the many times the four of them had hiked or ridden in the mountains on days like this with the sun shining and the sky a brilliant blue. She breathed in deeply and wished her family was riding beside her.

"Patricia," Daman spoke her name and she became conscious of the fact that he never shortened her name as others did. Perhaps he'd never heard the shortened version and she should tell him she only used Patricia as a professional name.

"Over to the right, near the trees, there's a moose and calf," Tom's voice interrupted whatever Daman had been about to say. With the same eagerness as those who had never seen a moose before, Tisa turned her attention to the direction the trail guide pointed.

After admiring the pair, Tisa turned back to her riding companion. As she turned her head, she noticed Cabe's struggle with a headstrong mare that assumed they'd paused to graze. Hiding a smile, she wondered why Daman, who also had an obviously urban background, was so at ease on horseback while Cabe was so inexperienced.

"You've ridden before." She smiled at the man beside her, inviting him to share more of his background.

"I spent a few years on a South American ranch when I was a teenager." She suspected the admission made Daman uncomfortable, but she pursued the question anyway.

"You have family in South America?"

"No, they were business associates of my father." His horse side-stepped and he busied himself calming the animal. Tisa smiled to herself; it was a tactic she'd used herself years ago when she'd wanted to divert a young riding companion's attention from a particular line of conversation.

The trail became steeper and Daman dropped back behind her to resume the single-file line the trail guide said was necessary for the narrower path. She noticed that Cabe, too, had dropped behind the woman he seemed to be partnering. As she watched, the little boy grabbed the reins from his mother's hands and began to jerk them up and down. The docile horse ignored the child's actions and plodded on, following the horse in front of it.

She'd always found riding a pleasure and now experienced a sense of oneness with the animal beneath her. She took pleasure in the warmth of the sun on her face, and the sweet pine-scented air mixed with the earthier smells of horses and trail dust. She looked around, enjoying the view, and marveled at how rapidly they'd climbed. Far below she could see a ribbon of river, but the obvious signs of civiliza-tion—roads and roofs—had disappeared.

Suddenly, a loose rock, kicked up by the horse in front of her, spooked her mare, catching Tisa off guard. Her horse reared, then pranced dangerously close to the edge of the narrow path. Even while concentrating on controlling her mount, she could hear a child's scream and was aware of Daman maneuvering to get between her and the steep drop-off at the side of the trail. Her horse objected to his animal's close-ness and kicked out at it with both rear hoofs. Tisa's irritation flared. She didn't need Daman to rescue her like some B-grade movie hero. He should be able to see that what she needed most was room; crowding her was panicking her mount forcing them closer to the edge.

Cabe's earlier words echoed in her mind, and for a fleeting moment she wondered if Daman was deliberately trying to frighten her horse. Leaning forward, she murmured comforting words to the frightened mare, who responded almost magically to Tisa's soothing words and tight control of the reins. Once the horse settled down, she urged it forward again.

As soon as the trail widened both Daman and Tom rode up beside her. Daman's face was flushed, showing his anger.

"You handled that well," Tom complimented her, speaking first.

"No thanks to you. That horse is too jumpy for this kind of thing." Daman's voice held a harsh tone Tisa hadn't heard him use before, and she felt renewed irritation that he didn't trust her to be able to handle her mount. "She could have been killed!" Daman continued to storm at Tom.

"I was fine." Tisa attempted to restrain her irritation in having to reassure Daman by leaning forward to pat her mount's neck. Her horse was the one who needed comfort, not her. "Prancer is a sweet-heart. It wasn't her fault the horse ahead of her kicked up a stone that struck her." She kept her voice pitched low. Daman didn't appear convinced, but he didn't say anything more, and Tom returned to his position at the front of the line. Prancer appeared ready to move forward.

From across the small clearing, she caught a glimpse of Cabe's face and understood he'd been concerned. She could read frustration there, but pride, too. As if she could read his mind, she knew he hadn't tried to rescue her because he knew she could handle a horse better than he could, but the incident had made him feel helpless. She risked a quick smile in his direction. His being there filled her with a warm glow. A newcomer to horseback riding, he really was going beyond the call of duty to endure a three-hour ride for her sake, especially one that would leave him barely able to walk for the next couple of days. He was there to protect her if she needed him, but it was obvious he wouldn't interfere where she could take care of herself. His quiet support meant a great deal more to her than all of Daman's fiery words, though she supposed she should be grateful for Daman's attempted rescue and concern for her.

As the line of horses began moving forward again, she found her thoughts drifting from Cabe to Daman. She had only Cabe's word that Daman was involved with some kind of crime syndicate. She'd accepted Cabe's sincerity almost without question, though she really didn't know him much better than she did Daman. Of course, his friendship with Peter weighed heavily in his favor. Honesty compelled her to admit Daman hadn't done anything to cause her distrust. Thinking back, though, she admitted that right from the start she hadn't fully trusted him. Why did trusting Cabe come so easily, while Daman aroused a vague sense of suspicion?

Peter and their parents had often spoken of the quiet promptings of the Holy Ghost. Was it possible that the Spirit was talking to her, telling her not to place her trust in Daman? The idea was intriguing and she played it back and forth in her mind. There had been a time when she'd thought a lot about the various gifts of the Spirit. She'd even wondered if the gift of discernment could help her know who she really was, and as she'd read more about it, she'd prayed for this gift. Now she wondered if she'd misunderstood the meaning of the gift of discernment. A quiet calm in her heart told her that she had stumbled on the answer to her prayer, but it hadn't been answered as she'd hoped.

Could recognizing good and evil be more important than knowing her real identity? But then again, wasn't she being rather extreme in assigning Daman to the evil category? She glanced over her shoulder, seeing a puzzled expression on his face. He saw her, and his expression immediately changed to one of warmth and pleasure.

She smiled back, then quickly turned to face forward again. If all Cabe had said about Daman was true, and if something inside her was urging her to be cautious around him, why did she still feel so drawn to him?

* * *

Once he adjusted to the rhythm of his horse, Cabe found himself enjoying the ride. He'd done quite a bit of hiking and was familiar with this type of country. As a kid he hadn't particularly enjoyed the pony rides he'd experienced during some of his friends' birthday parties, but he had to admit this was a far cry from sedately going around in circles. Fortunately his horse wasn't as excitable as Tisa's or Daman's mounts, and seemed content to follow the horse in front of it.

As if his thoughts had somehow reached the rider in front of him, Grace turned to smile at him. He knew he'd given the pretty divorcée more reason to think he was interested in her than he should have, but from the moment she'd arrived at the ranch he'd recognized her friendliness as the means to stay with the group without drawing Daman's attention. Fortunately, her son Justin had taken a liking to him as well. He was a cute kid, though more than a little spoiled. A man with a woman and child would appear more normal and attract less attention on a vacation trail-ride than a man alone.

He couldn't hear all of the guide's spiel, but enough was passed back to him from the riders ahead to get the gist of the vast ranch's history. As they followed a steep trail to Thurman Ridge he was surprised to learn the ranch sat inside the largest inactive volcano in the Western Hemisphere and that from the ridge he had a magnificent view of the Grand Tetons.

Their guide Tom gathered the riders around him before starting back down to point out the Continental Divide. Cabe managed to nudge his horse closer to Tisa. He'd been badly frightened when her horse had acted up a short time ago, but he was relieved to see she didn't seem upset or concerned at all over the incident. She laughed at something Daman said and he figured she was fine—since she was eating. From a pocket in her shirt he'd seen her pull two packets of trail mix which she'd shared with Daman. If it weren't for all he knew about Daman Bronson, and his own interest in Tisa, he'd think she'd met her perfect match; the guy was as bad as she in being able to eat nonstop.

A commotion behind him had him turning back to the rest of the group. Justin was hanging half off Grace's horse. He was screaming and flailing about while Grace was pulling at his arms, crying and trying to pull her son upright. The horse shied, sidestepping with quick, nervous steps. Several other horses shook their heads and shifted their feet in anticipation of fleeing. Bolting from his saddle, Cabe leaped toward the dangling child, stumbling on legs cramped from riding. Just as he grasped Justin, Tom clasped the startled horse's bridle.

In seconds Cabe had pulled the child clear and held him while Tom soothed the horse.

He didn't know if Tom helped Grace dismount or if she tumbled off on her own, but she was soon beside him hugging him and her son while scolding the boy and telling him she loved him at the same time.

"Keep the boy with you on the way down," Tom said, and Cabe realized the guide was speaking to him. He also realized that the trail guide was assuming Cabe was the child's father.

"I'm not much of a rider," Cabe attempted to protest. It wouldn't be a good idea to disabuse Tom of his assumption that he had a right to exert some kind of parental authority over the child.

"I've watched you, you're doing fine." Tom was friendly, but his voice conveyed a refusal to be swayed. "Your horse is steady, and other than trying to snatch a mouthful of grass now and then, she moves along without much direction. She doesn't need much of a rider, but the boy needs a firm hand."

Cabe knew the guide was right. Grace was unable to keep the child safe. His eyes scanned the group for Tisa. Her back was to him and she seemed to be arguing with Bronson. A cold sweat trickled down his back. While babysitting a spoiled two-year-old, he'd be of no use to Tisa if Bronson turned on her.

CHAPTER 15

At first holding onto a squirming Justin tried Cabe's patience, but eventually the little boy fell asleep, and Cabe discovered there was something satisfying about the feel of a small child in his arms. Grace didn't say much beyond looking back frequently to check on her son. She seemed in deep thought, and Cabe hoped she was giving serious consideration to how catering to her child's every whim had played in the mishap that might have seriously injured the boy. Thinking of Tom's assumption that Cabe was Justin's father, Cabe thought of his own father and wondered if Justin's father was like his was, so absorbed in satisfying his own desires he didn't have time for his son. In his heart, Cabe renewed a vow he'd made as a disillusioned ten-year-old pressing his face against a window in his mother's house, waiting for a father to come—who never did. *I'll never leave my children and I'll never give them cause to doubt my love for them.*

Tisa and Daman were ahead of him on the descent, which gave him ample opportunity to watch them. With Bronson's reputation, Cabe was surprised by his solicitous concern for Tisa's comfort. He couldn't help wondering if it was all an act, or if the high-flying crook had really fallen for Lieutenant Lewis's sister. If anyone other than Tisa were involved, he'd find something almost amusing in it.

He kept expecting Bronson to make some move, but the rest of the ride passed without incident other than catching a glimpse of a small elk herd and a couple of blue heron as they approached the river. Shortly before they reached the corral, Justin awoke and began crying for his mother. Cabe tried to soothe him, but only his mother would do, and there was no way to return him to her until they reached the end of the ride. Cabe was glad Tom's estimation of his horse was correct. She plodded along, placidly ignoring the screaming child Cabe struggled to hang onto.

Once inside the corral, Tom dismounted and helped Grace. Tom then reached for Justin, and Cabe relinquished him gladly to the older man before trying to duplicate the smooth way Tom had thrown a leg over his animal and stepped to the ground. Dismounting was harder than it looked, and when Cabe at last swung to the ground he could barely stand. With a few strides, Tom placed the child in Grace's arms, then steadied her as she staggered from the corral.

Cabe felt a sensation much like stepping off a boat onto a dock when he tried to step away from his horse. He suspected he looked drunk as he stumbled after Grace to help her get Justin strapped into his car seat. He was glad she hadn't parked as far away as he had.

"Thanks, Cabe," Grace smiled over the fussy child's head after he caught up to her. "I'd like to treat you to lunch by way of thanks for all your help," she offered.

Cabe looked across the parking area to where Daman Bronson was helping Tisa into his Lexus. "No, thanks," he told Grace. "I enjoyed being around you and your son this morning, but I have an appointment I'm almost late for now. If it's not too much trouble, I would appreciate a lift to the parking area where I left my car, though." He hoped she would understand without being offended that he didn't wish to pursue their brief friendship.

"Hop in," Grace invited, and Cabe hurried around to the passenger seat.

* * *

"It's been too long since I've been riding," Tisa laughed as she relaxed into the smooth leather seats. "I'm going to be stiff tomorrow."

"I keep a few horses at my place in California," Daman said, and Tisa suspected he was bragging. "I ride quite often, and I've been thinking of having a couple of my horses shipped out here." His smile changed to a scowl when he noticed the blond woman backing out of a parking spot a short distance away. "Children shouldn't be allowed on these trail rides. That brat spoiled the ride for everyone."

Tisa didn't respond. She didn't think the little boy had spoiled anyone's enjoyment of the trip. Perhaps the child's mother hadn't exhibited the best judgement, taking the child when she wasn't an experienced rider herself, but thanks to Tom and Cabe no harm had come to the boy—or anyone else.

Daman backed out sharply, pulling abruptly in front of the woman. Seeing Cabe sitting beside the pretty young mother, Tisa felt a stab of jealousy. She knew Cabe had only participated in the ride to keep an eye on Daman and to protect her if necessary. Still, he seemed on much too friendly terms with the other woman. Cabe was probably taking the woman to lunch, she thought wistfully, and wished it were Cabe instead of Daman sitting beside her, and who would soon be sitting across a table from her.

Daman drove a little fast for the rough road, but Tisa was anxious to return to the resort, so she didn't say anything. She was hungry and she knew the chef would have lunch waiting for them. After that she intended to spend the afternoon at the hotel measuring and sketching in spite of what Cabe had said about Daman. If she had any suspicion that she was in danger, she'd get in the Navigator she'd leased and leave. Also, the first time she had a few minutes alone, she would call Peter.

She didn't know why she hadn't called her brother when she first awoke this morning. She supposed it was because she'd slept far more soundly than usual and had barely gotten dressed before Daman arrived with breakfast. And maybe because Cabe's gift of the cell phone was a reminder that she was looking forward to spending time with a man she knew Peter considered a dangerous criminal.

* * *

When Grace parked beside his rental, Cabe told Grace and Justin good-bye and hurried to his car. Leaving the door open to allow the cool mountain air to circulate through his vehicle, he picked up his phone to dial Peter.

"Do you have her? Is she safe?" Peter immediately demanded to know the whereabouts of his sister.

"She's gone back to the hotel Bronson's having built." He told Peter about the trail ride and Tisa's stubborn refusal to leave the project she was working on. He also mentioned her concern for Peter's case.

"We're ready to move on the warehouse," Peter said. "We have a warrant and are only waiting for word from the Bureau to synchronize our move."

"That's good, especially if we can bring both state and federal charges."

"I'm worried about that," Peter admitted. "There hasn't been much activity around the warehouse. I suspect it's just a front and that the real base is somewhere else. I've got people tracking every car that stops there in hopes it will lead us to the real distribution point."

"Bronson is driving the white Lexus Carmichael and Jones identified." Cabe remembered something else Peter needed to know. "Ortega's here. He seems to be in charge of security."

"Avendale's dropped out of sight at this end," Peter warned Cabe. "I don't have a good feeling about this. Indications are he left in a hurry early this morning."

"You think he's headed here?"

"I do. The man I've had watching him said Avendale tried repeatedly to call someone. He gave up on the phone in his garage and tried the pay phone several times, then drove to the warehouse. He only stayed a few minutes before returning to the garage. He left minutes later with a small bag."

"I assume your man followed him but lost him," Cabe shortened the story.

"Yes, at a Trax crossing. We found his car in the UTA parking lot at the station, but we have no idea whether he caught the train, boarded a bus, or had another car waiting there." There was no mistaking Peter's frustration.

"If Bronson and Tisa have been on a trail ride without any of his support people or even a phone, Avendale may have been trying to reach him with some information," Peter continued.

"Such as the news that Bronson is entertaining your sister," Cabe concluded. "I think I'd better get back to Bronson's property, fill Tisa in, and hope she'll leave willingly."

"Willing or not, get her out of there."

Cabe ended the call and followed the dust clouds the other departing trail riders were stirring up on their way back to the highway. As he pulled onto the pavement, he reached once more for his phone to dial Dave Woods's direct line.

After sharing the information Peter had given him he asked about the progress the Bureau was making.

"The disks are all you claimed and all we need to take our case to court. Warrants are being prepared right now to pick up Reuben and Artel. We'll have them in custody within twenty-four hours." There was a jubilant note in his voice. He went on almost conversationally, "It's funny though, we got word yesterday that Stefan's and Josie's remains were discovered in Utah. They were buried there more than twenty years ago, yet we've discovered quite a bit of activity lately in an offshore account those disks identify as belonging to Stefan. It took a lot of digging, and we might never have figured it out without the disks.

"Our computer investigators confirmed something else rather strange. Someone is depositing large amounts of money in accounts belonging to two other presumed-deceased people in that family."

"Stefan has an active account?" Cabe didn't try to hide his surprise. "And the other two accounts? Do they belong to Josie and Delray?" Cabe slowed for the firebreak road, checking his mirrors as he did so. He didn't want anyone to see him pull into the nearly hidden turnout.

"No," Woods said. "Remember there was talk of Reuben and Loretta having another child?"

"Yes." Cabe drove into the shaded area behind a stand of willows where he'd parked the first time. He didn't want to take the time to move the barrier. Besides, he and Tisa might be in a hurry when they returned.

"Well, we've found they did have a little girl," Dave was saying. "She was born early, just after Reuben started injecting Loretta with drugs. Reuben always suspected she was Delray's daughter, not his, and from what we've learned he was pretty rough on her. A former neighbor said she was never seen again after one particularly severe beating. She's convinced Reuben killed the girl and hid her body. "

"She's 'TBD' on the disks," Cabe concluded.

"Yes," Dave confirmed. "Loretta named the child Teresa, and she disappeared about the same time as Josie and Stefan. There's a possibility they took the little girl with them."

"I remember reading about that accident." Cabe felt a sick sensation growing in his stomach. "I don't recall any mention of a child being found in the wreckage."

"There wasn't one. If Stefan and Josie took the child, they got rid of her before their car accident. Stefan was suspected of involvement with a black-market baby ring, and chances are if he had the child, he sold her for some quick cash."

"She could still be alive then," Cabe mused aloud. Suddenly a thought filled his mind: *She might have been abandoned along the freeway leading from Arizona into Utah. In shock, he realized Tisa could be the girl—"Tisa" could be a child's lisping pronunciation of "Teresa."*

"She could be alive," Woods agreed without conviction, "but I suspect the neighbor is right, and Bronson is just using his sister's name along with Stefan's and Josie's to hide assets."

"I'm going now," Cabe said. "If I don't report back in by four, send someone in after me." He explained how to find the resort and warned Dave about the buried cable. He didn't mention the feeling about Tisa that had come over him.

Moving as rapidly as the heavy brush allowed, Cabe set a course for the cabins. While his body functioned almost on automatic, his mind played over Dave Woods's words. What he was thinking was too much of a coincidence. Still, a little girl disappeared in California and one suddenly appeared in Utah at about the same time. Could the two little girls be the same child? His heart wanted to protest.

She could be Teresa, his mind stubbornly pursued the possibility. The child found clinging to a wire fence had called herself Tisa. She was only four or five; she might have been trying to say "Teresa"; *Tisa* could as easily be a shortened version of *Teresa* as of *Patricia*. And she might not be a Dempsky; she could be Wallace Delray's illegitimate daughter. That would make her Annie's sister. Annie had been small and blond, and she'd resembled her father more than Dakota.

Daman Bronson was also blond he remembered. Recalling Tisa riding beside Daman, and the times Daman had used any excuse to lightly touch her, Cabe felt sick once more. Tisa could be Daman's

sister. Their coloring was the same and they shared a similar compact-
ness about their builds, and they both sure liked to eat. There was
something about seeing the two of them together . . .

Creeping into the duck blind he'd constructed the day before, he
noticed that Tisa's cabin appeared unoccupied. Farther away, at the
cabin he assumed was Daman's, he could see the white Lexus. They
were probably eating lunch together as they had the day before. He
pictured Bronson sitting across the table from Tisa, smiling into her
eyes, taking her hand . . . Cabe shook off the image forming in his
mind. He had to keep his mind on business.

Through the trees he caught a glimpse of a pickup truck traveling
fast up the rutted mountain road. Ortega himself stepped out of the
trees, then seeming to recognize the driver, waved him on. Cabe had a
hunch Avendale had arrived. Tisa could be Reuben Dempsky's
daughter and Daman's sister; or she could be Annie's sister—it didn't
really matter who she was, except that she was the woman he was
falling more in love with every minute, and she was in danger. He
only cared that she was safe. Leaving the duck blind, he began
working his way closer to Daman's cabin.

* * *

Tisa set down her glass with a sigh. No matter what else Daman
might be involved in, she had to appreciate his devotion to good
food. "That was wonderful," she voiced her appreciation for the
hearty lunch Daman's chef had prepared.

Daman reached across the table to take her hand. "It's a pleasure to
dine with someone who truly appreciates eating. I know women who
adore the ambiance of the right setting, the excuse to dress glam-
orously and wear expensive jewelry, the chance to be seen with a
wealthy or famous escort, but you're different. I believe you enjoy the
food."

"I do." She didn't feel self-conscious at the admission.

"I hope you enjoy the company too." Daman's voice took on a
smooth texture that sent warning signals down her spine.

"You're a remarkable man," she hedged, freeing her hand to reach
once more for her glass.

Daman gently removed the glass from her hand, then laced his fingers through hers. For a moment he stared at her hand as though deep in thought. When he spoke, his words set off a small panic attack inside her. "Emeralds, I think. Your hand is too small for a large diamond. Yes, small diamonds surrounding a triad of half-karat emeralds will suit you perfectly."

Jerking her hand back, she buried it in her lap. She couldn't raise her head to meet Daman's eyes. He couldn't be building up to a proposal! They didn't know each other that well. Even though she felt a strong connection to him, she didn't love him.

"Do I make you nervous? Surely you've guessed I care a great deal about you," Daman followed his question with a vague declaration. She didn't like the knowing smile on his face, one she had a sudden urge to wipe off. Something about that almost speculative smile brought her too close to the black edge of memory. It also made her wonder if he had something much different from a marriage proposal in mind.

A sharp knock on the door saved her from responding. Daman glanced at the door, making no pretense of hiding his irritation. When the knock sounded again, he called to his chef to send whoever was at the door away.

"I have a rule," he told Tisa, picking up her hand again. "All of my people know I am not to be interrupted while dining."

"What if it's important?" she asked. She found herself wishing he'd go deal with business rather than pursue the subject the knocking at the door had interrupted.

"It's probably just that numskull Mr. Harmon you work with. Mr. Ortega informed me he was here earlier to see me."

"Howard was here?" Tisa stared at Daman. "Why was he here?"

Daman laughed. "It seems he's quite convinced you used underhanded tactics to keep me from seeing his superior proposal for my hotels."

"I need to speak with him right now!" an angry voice came from the doorway. "I have information he needs to know about that woman!" Tisa didn't recognize the voice, but it definitely wasn't Howard Harmon. She began to visually search for an escape route.

"It will have to wait. The boss hasn't had dessert yet." The chef's words preceded the slamming of the door. Tisa attempted to appear calm when she expected to be exposed at any minute.

Moments later the rotund little man, looking completely unruffled, appeared in the dining room with two servings of a culinary master-piece featuring peaches floating in a thin sauce and topped by a mountain of whipped cream. A swirl of nutmeg completed the concoction.

Ignoring the hammering and shouting which had resumed, Daman refused to be rushed, and Tisa took her cue from him—at least she tried to. From where she sat she had a perfect view of the road leading to the cabin, and it wasn't long before one of the ATVs arrived, carrying two men; both held rifles and wore camouflage suits. A man wearing an ordinary T-shirt and jeans stepped toward the lead vehicle. The driver clearly knew the man well as they were soon absorbed in an animated conversation. The man turned once to gesture toward the cabin, and Tisa noticed a network of slashes across the man's face. He looked as though he'd recently lost a fight.

Turning her attention back to her lunch partner, she forced herself to remain calm and to appear completely at ease. She patted her napkin against her lips and willed a sparkle to her eyes, while battling a strong premonition that she was the topic of the angry conversation going on just beyond the front porch.

When she'd swallowed the last spoonful of her dessert, she asked permission to go to the kitchen to compliment the chef. One of the men outside was speaking into a radio while the other one reached for the rifle he had left in his vehicle. A voice inside her head was screaming for her to get out of there.

"Go ahead," Daman gestured magnanimously toward the kitchen. "While you do that, I'll see what that idiot finds so impor-tant he thinks he can be excused for disturbing my lunch with a beau-tiful woman. After I let Ortega deal with him, you and I have unfinished business." He smiled suggestively as he lifted her hand to his lips before releasing it, allowing her to stand.

Tisa lost no time retreating toward the kitchen. She paused only when her ears caught her brother's name through the tumult of voices. "I'm telling you the dame is Lieutenant Lewis's sister," someone's voice carried above the tumult. "She's using you to get inside your organization. There's an FBI agent snooping around here too."

It took a moment to realize the man was talking about her, and half a second more to start looking for an escape route. Pushing the door to the kitchen open, she stepped inside in time to see the chef standing in an open doorway on the opposite side of the room, holding a pack of cigarettes in one hand.

"Mind if I join you?" she asked as she hurried across the room.

"No, not at all." He gestured for her to pass through the door ahead of him. "Do you smoke?" He extended his pack toward her.

"Thank you, but no. That dinner was so delicious, I just wanted to compliment you before I go up to the hotel to start sketching." She tried to appear at ease, but her eyes kept darting toward the trees at the edge of the clearing, and she wondered if she could find her way back to the highway. When Daman missed her he'd have her cabin searched first thing, so she didn't dare return there for the Navigator.

"It's a pleasure cooking for people like you and Mr. Bronson," the chef said, looking pleased at her words.

"The pleasure was definitely mine," she told him while her mind was still searching for an escape route. Someone had said something about a federal agent. She wondered if he was close enough to help her.

"Well, I'd better be going." She waved before moving briskly up the trail leading to the hotel. As soon as she was out of sight of the chef, she ducked into the trees and began to run.

"No, don't run." An arm snaked around her waist and a hand covered her mouth. Thankful for the heavy hiking shoes, she kicked at her captor's shins and struggled to free herself, as her heart slammed against her ribs.

"Tisa, it's me, Cabe." The familiar voice registered at last, bringing her struggle to a stop. When she ceased fighting, Cabe slowly removed his hand from her mouth.

"A man came . . . he told Daman . . ."

"I know. I heard him." Cabe spoke matter-of-factly, already leading Tisa deeper into the trees. "I expect they'll start a search any minute now."

"He said an FBI agent . . ." she stopped, reading the expression on Cabe's face correctly. "You . . ."

He nodded his head, and she didn't find the admission as shocking as she might have only a few days earlier. It seemed she'd misread Cabe too.

"I told the chef I was on my way to the hotel." She glanced over her shoulder, hoping to see no one.

"Good, maybe they'll look for you there first. Watch your step here," Cabe whispered. "There's a buried alarm cable just under the soil."

"What!" She stopped, staring in horror at the faint trace of recent digging.

"It's all right, just be careful when you cross it. It's fairly easy to spot now, but by next spring, it will be completely hidden." He took her hand to guide her steps, but didn't relinquish it once they were past the buried line.

Shouts and the pounding of running feet reached them. Cabe paused and pulled her into the shelter of a thick tangle of shrubs. Kneeling, she discovered she had an excellent view of the cabin where she had stayed, and a little farther away was the large cabin where she had dined with Daman. She could see Daman, flanked by half a dozen men, including the man who had insistently pounded on his door. Standing directly in front of Daman was Chef Bono.

As she watched, Daman lifted his arm as though pointing at the little man, who crumbled to the ground in exaggerated slow motion. It took several seconds for the reality of what she had seen to sink in. Horror rose in her throat in waves. She wanted to scream or cry. Instead she found herself bending forward to lose the wonderful lunch the chubby chef had so recently lavished on her.

Without saying a word, Cabe wiped her face and offered her a bottle of water. Once she lifted her eyes to meet his, she saw the sympathy there. Whatever he saw in her eyes caused him to reach for her. He held her close, patting her back as though consoling a child. After what was probably only a minute, he whispered, "We've got to get out of here. Do you think you can hike as far as the highway?"

She nodded her head. She could hike that far, she would run if necessary—she needed to move, to run, to escape. Physical exercise was the panacea she needed to wipe away the guilt and fear, and a pain that went beyond anything she remembered experiencing before in her life.

Cabe set a blistering pace, but she didn't mind. An urgency to get away from Daman's property and the men with guns added wings to her feet. She soon realized that though Cabe had seemed insecure on horseback, he was no stranger to making his way across mountainous terrain. She considered herself in good shape and she'd practically grown up hiking mountain trails, but she was soon out of breath even though they were moving downhill.

After what seemed only minutes, Cabe left the trail, scrambling across rocks to much rougher terrain. He seemed to be choosing the worst route possible as he climbed over dead falls and scrambled down narrow chimneys in the rocks. Once he slipped into a thick grove of aspen that barely left room for them to squeeze between tree trunks.

At one point a sound to their left brought Cabe to a halt. He dived into a thick stand of brush, thrusting Tisa to the ground as well. Small pebbles and dirt bit into her hands and sharp branches clawed at her face, but she was too frightened to object. The roar of an ATV was closer than she liked.

A blur of movement caught her eye as one of the four-wheel ATVs streaked along the side of the mountain no more than fifty yards away. Her breath caught in her throat. That was the trail they had been on minutes ago!

She wasn't aware she was trembling until Cabe placed his arm around her shoulders and whispered, "We're safe. They can't see us here." There was something comforting about his strong shoulder to lean on, but she wasn't the leaning type, she reminded herself. She straightened her shoulders, but she didn't move away.

"How did they know I came this way?" Tisa asked.

"I don't think they do know for sure which way you've gone. But it makes sense that they would assume you'd try to make it to the highway. There's probably another guard on the road, or Ortega could be driving one of the larger vehicles that direction right now." He stood and assisted Tisa to her feet.

"We've got to move quickly." He pointed toward a dead tree that appeared red in the bright light. "Head for that," he said. "Just beyond it is an old logging road. We'll follow it right to my car. If we don't reach it first we'll have a long walk ahead of us."

For a big man he moved with little wasted motion, and Tisa, now past her initial fright, kept pace. Once they reached the old road they moved faster, and she was glad for all the years she'd trailed her big brother around the high school track and hiked the back country with her family.

Suddenly stopping, Cabe crouched behind a thicket of willows, pulling Tisa down beside him. She was already concealed by the time voices drifted toward her. She only caught an occasional word, but that was enough to know someone had found Cabe's car. They couldn't use her car, and now it seemed they wouldn't dare approach Cabe's either.

CHAPTER 16

Cabe and Tisa remained concealed for some time, listening to vehicles move up and down the highway, while the ATVs explored the logging road and every path they crossed. Cabe was grateful Tisa seemed every bit as aware as he was of their precarious position. She never moved or asked a question. They seemed to communicate on some silent level, and he knew he didn't have to explain that they couldn't make their way to the highway. They couldn't risk being seen near it, or attempt to hitch a ride with someone who might turn out to be one of Bronson's people.

They couldn't stay where they were much longer either. Ortega would soon order a foot search of the immediate area. Now that Bronson's right-hand man knew it wasn't just a rumor that an agent was in the area, he would assume Cabe had teamed up with Tisa and stop at nothing to find them.

Taking advantage of the sound created by the noisy ATVs, Cabe motioned for Tisa to remain low but begin moving deeper into the trees. Retreating step by careful step, they eased their way farther into the forest. When they could no longer hear sounds of the search, Cabe headed toward the steepest point he could remember. He had to get them to a place that was too rough for the ATVs to follow.

Tisa had a pretty good idea why Cabe was climbing through patches of deadfall, squeezing between boulders, and generally moving through the thickest stands of timber as they worked their way higher. When she thought she couldn't take another step, he suddenly picked her up and swung her to a ledge above her head. She was impressed when he managed to pull himself up beside her. They sat still, catching their breath for several minutes before he pointed to a break in the jumble of rocks at her back, and urged her behind the largest one.

Once behind the massive rock, she sank to the hard ground and rested her back against the boulder. Cabe joined her, and at first he didn't say anything as together they listened to the sounds of the forest, then he asked if she was all right.

"Fine," she told him.

"We may have to stay here all night," he said.

"I wish we'd remembered to bring dinner with us," was her only comment.

He laughed. "No dinner. But I do have one more bottle of water we can share." He dug in the small shoulder pack he carried and handed her the bottle. She drank deeply, then sighed as she handed it back to him.

"Now what?" she asked. "I take it we can't risk going anywhere near the highway."

"And it would be safer for everyone if we avoid contact with any campers or hikers. We just have to stay out of sight tonight. By morning there will be agents here to rescue us," Cabe told her.

Tisa looked around, noticing that they didn't have long to wait until night. She shivered. "Couldn't you call them and tell them to come now?" she asked. "You told me you always carry a cell phone."

"I do, but I don't think it would be wise to use it now. Jorge Ortega is Bronson's head of security. He knows a great deal about electronics, and he's got a cabin full of snoop gadgets, including a device that picks up cell phone conversations. Most of his equipment is boxed up—obviously they weren't planning to install it until the hotel was closer to completion—but I wouldn't want to bet against him having that item set up by now." He lowered his voice as he continued to explain, "I turned my phone off as soon as I realized you'd left your purse behind with the cell phone I gave you presumably in it. Ortega has probably found it, discovered it isn't locked, and has attempted to call my programmed number by now."

"I'm sorry. I thought taking my purse would make my intentions too obvious," Tisa said.

"You did the right thing. Getting yourself out of there, without appearing to run, was the smart thing to do," Cabe assured her.

"It was strange," she felt as if she were thinking aloud, trying to explain to herself what had happened. "I don't know how I knew I had to get away before that man got a chance to speak to Daman. It was almost like someone was telling me I was in danger and that I had to leave. My request to thank the chef came out of my mouth without me even thinking about it."

"I'm glad you listened to that voice. It took me a long time to learn to act when the Spirit whispered to me, but with practice I've gotten better." Cabe smiled wryly and placed one of his big hands over hers.

"Do you really think it was the Holy Ghost that prompted me to sneak out the kitchen door?" The thought troubled her. As long as she could remember she'd heard phrases like "the still small voice," "listen to the Spirit," and "the prompting of the Holy Ghost," but she'd never experienced that kind of communication. She wasn't sure she really believed in it.

"Yes," Cabe answered the question she barely remembered she'd asked aloud. "I do believe you were guided to take the action you did."

"But I thought—I'm sure someone told me that the Holy Ghost is something like my conscience that tells me whether I'm doing something good or bad."

"Most Primary children are first taught to think of the Holy Ghost that way. The discernment of good and evil is a function of the Spirit, but you know there's more to it than that." Cabe spoke with quiet assurance and she wished she had the kind of faith he and Mark and Peter seemed to have.

"I'm not sure I do know much about the Holy Ghost," she admitted. "I don't even know for certain how to tell whether or not God has answered a prayer."

Cabe looked at her with a puzzled expression on his face, and she knew he was wondering why she knew so little while Peter knew so much about the Church's teachings.

"I think you're more sensitive to spiritual communication than you think." Cabe drew her closer as though he would comfort her.

Resisting the slight pressure he exerted, she turned to look into his face.

"If that's true, why didn't I know Daman is a murderer? Even though I saw him shoot his chef, I still find it hard to believe he's involved in anything as terrible as you said. I know he surrounds himself with men who carry guns, and that he's selfish and egotistical, still there's something about him I can't explain. I like to be with him . . ." Her voice dropped. "You can't know what it's like to not know who you are, to suspect that you did something so terrible that your own parents abandoned you; but the time I've spent with Daman is the only time in my life that I haven't cared who I might really be."

"Does not knowing who you were the first few years of your life bother you so much?" Cabe asked.

"Yes," she admitted. "As long as I can remember I've believed that if I knew where I came from, and why I was left alone miles from any town, I wouldn't be afraid anymore. I need to know if I have loving parents somewhere who are hoping and praying I will return to them."

"And what if you learn your parents were terrible people who hurt and abused you?" Cabe asked softly. "Wouldn't it be better not to know that?"

"I've always suspected that was the case." There was a hint of little-girl sadness in her voice.

Cabe was silent so long she began to fear she'd hurt him in some way. Perhaps telling him about her feelings for Daman had been a mistake. Did he think there was something lacking in her that she could still feel something for a man she'd seen take another man's life? How could she explain the connection she felt with Daman and still make it clear the feelings she had for him were nothing like the way she felt about Cabe? Cabe had never said he cared about her, but she knew he did. A smile twisted her lips. Was that another still-small-voice message?

"I don't care who you were before you became Tisa Lewis." Cabe broke his silence with a fierce declaration. His voice seemed to carry a message that went deeper than his words, leaving her unable to respond. A fleeting memory of Daman's almost-proposal came to mind, then left, leaving her more puzzled. Cabe wasn't making that kind of declaration. "We are all children of Heavenly Father, He loves us. That is the only real truth of identity that should concern us."

Tisa sighed. The only mother she'd ever known had repeatedly told her she was a child of God, but she'd still wanted to know who her earthly parents were.

"In a sense, we're all adopted children of our earthly parents." Cabe's voice told her it was important to him that she believe him. "They're really our older brothers and sisters to whom our heavenly parents entrusted our care. Sometimes mortal parents fail for some reason or another to carry out the charge they've been given. A child who's given a second chance to be cared for by a different set of earthly parents has a rare blessing other children unfortunately miss out on," Cabe finished.

"If that's true, why was I given a second chance and someone like Daman wasn't?"

"I don't know," Cabe admitted. "But I do know he's a child of God too, and will only be held responsible for his actions to the extent he has been given the opportunity to knowingly choose between right and wrong. His parents will have to answer for the way they raised him. No one is all bad." Cabe said the words as though he'd spent some time trying to convince himself of that fact and hadn't yet quite succeeded.

"You may have touched a part of Daman Bronson that I know nothing about," Cabe spoke, trying to comfort her. "From what I could see, I suspect he cares about you. From all I knew about him prior to coming here, I would have bet he cared about no one but himself. Now I wonder if he might have become a different man if he'd been given a second chance to have parents who faithfully carried out the responsibility God entrusted to them."

Tisa sat still, thinking about Cabe's words. Cabe was the last person she'd expected to hear defend Daman in any way. Yesterday, when he'd told her of Daman's crime involvement, she'd sensed a personal loathing for the man. Today she recognized a reluctance to paint the man entirely black, not because Cabe's view of Daman had changed, but because he didn't wish to hurt her.

Shadows began to deepen and the last rays of the sun turned the opposing mountain tops a brilliant gold, then the light was gone.

How could she still feel a sense of connection with a man she'd watched take an innocent life? He'd killed a man for nothing more than not stopping her from escaping when he hadn't even known she was attempting an escape. She felt a wave of grief, tinged with guilt, for the death of the little man who had treated her with deferential respect.

"Do you think they're still looking for us?" Tisa asked.

"Yes, I think they'll search a little longer, but Bronson himself will leave soon. He won't risk being here when federal agents arrive. Ortega will probably go with him. I think we're pretty safe now if we stay put until morning and do nothing to attract attention."

"You're sure we have to stay here?" Tisa's voice sounded small and timid, reminding Cabe of Peter's description of Tisa's fear of the dark.

"Come here." He turned her so her back was against his chest and his arms encircled her. "This spot is sheltered from the wind and we'll be fine."

"I might not make it to morning without something to eat." Tisa pretended to bite his hand, and he responded with a chuckle before snuggling her closer. He recognized her teasing as an attempt to think of something other than the darkness or danger. For a moment he wondered if the frightened little girl, abandoned all those years ago, had also used thoughts of food to chase away her fears.

"Perhaps I can find something better than my arm to eat," he teased in return, attempting to keep the mood light. With one hand he pulled the pack from his shoulder and fumbled inside it before holding up an almost empty package of crackers.

"It seems you started without me," she grumbled, reaching for the package.

"I'm not the one who had a five-course lunch." Cabe reached for a handful of the crackers.

"I'm sorry." Hastily thrusting the package back into his hands, she looked chagrined.

"It's okay," he reassured her, dividing the stack of crackers in two and returning half to her. "I'm not starving, and there's enough here for both of us. I think I can even find a bit of dessert." Cabe stuck his hand in his pack again and pulled out a candy bar. Removing the blue-and-gold wrapper, he picked up one of the small bars and offered it to Tisa.

Tisa paled. No, Cabe thought, he had to be mistaken. The light was nearly gone and he had only imagined the flicker of terror in her eyes.

"No, you keep it." She thrust out her hand to halt his offering. "There aren't many kinds of food or snacks I dislike, but I've never liked that kind of candy bar."

He couldn't believe his ears. Tisa loved chocolate, and he'd seen the way she relished peanut butter; she couldn't be serious.

"There really is plenty for both of us." He tried again to persuade her to eat the candy, clearly not understanding her refusal to share the treat.

"I don't understand it either." She gave a self-deprecating laugh. "Peter always refers to my stomach as being of the cast-iron variety, but one bite of that candy, and you'll swear you gave me syrup of ipecac, not candy. I've already had one embarrassing episode of that type today, I don't need another."

"All right then. You eat the crackers." He dropped his share of the crackers back into her hands. "And I'll hog all of the candy."

"Deal." She bit into a cracker.

It seemed they talked for hours, and Tisa never expected to sleep, but eventually she drifted off. When she awoke, it was to find she'd been sleeping for a long time. In spite of the stars overhead, she knew morning was near. She'd lain awake too many nights on camping trips with her family to mistake that moment when black turns to gray before the first pink hints of morning appear over the mountains. She was a little cold, even with Cabe's arms around her and her back absorbing the warmth of his chest, but she wasn't afraid.

The absence of fear surprised her more than the sudden awareness that she was sitting on a mountain in the middle of the night, hiding from people carrying guns. She must have made some small movement or sound because Cabe asked, "Are you all right?"

"Yes," she whispered back. "It's so strange."

"Strange to be sleeping on a pile of rocks, or strange to be with me?" She could hear the smile in his voice.

"That too." She couldn't help smiling, though she knew he couldn't see her face. "I mean it's strange to not be afraid."

"Be not afraid, only believe," Cabe spoke the words in a whisper. He was no longer teasing, and she recognized the words, knowing they came from the New Testament. They brought a kind of comfort. It was odd that she could sleep outdoors on a dark night and not be afraid. Was it Cabe who made the difference, she wondered, or could her newly found spiritual awareness be the reason for her lack of fear? She suspected the answer was both.

"Cabe? . . ."

"Shh." He placed his hand over her mouth and she stiffened. Then she heard it, at first a faint rustling of branches, then the tread of heavy feet.

Maintaining his hold on Tisa, Cabe slid deeper into the shadow of the rocks. When he was sure she understood that someone was approaching, he removed his hand from her mouth and lifted her until she was positioned behind him, then he reached for his service revolver. Scarcely daring to breathe, he waited.

It soon became obvious to him that someone was following a trail cut by deer that passed at the foot of the steep jumble of rocks where he and Tisa crouched. He had seen the trail, but it wasn't the route he had followed to reach this point, which was somewhat reassuring, because it meant they hadn't been followed.

The rustle of movement ceased, and again Cabe tensed for sudden action. A whiff of smoke floated on the air, telling him they were still safe. The men had only paused to catch their breath and rest a moment. He wished he knew how many men were on the trail.

A string of profanities rose to their hidden lair, followed by a hacking cough.

"Quiet!" Cabe recognized the harsh whisper, belonging to Jorge Ortega.

"She's gone, her and the FBI man," an angry voice snarled back. Cabe recognized this voice too. Avendale must be having a difficult time with the hike; being overweight and a heavy smoker, he wasn't in shape for climbing mountains. "There's nothing but a bunch of stupid trees to hear me here. If the boss did his thinking with his head we wouldn't be in this mess." A fit of coughing followed.

"Meaning?" This voice was quiet, and Cabe couldn't positively identify it, but he suspected the speaker was Bronson.

"The feds aren't here yet. We could have taken the cars and been a long way from here by now instead of stumbling over trees and rocks in the dark."

"The fed spy that was here has turned in every one of our plates by now," someone else scoffed. He had, Cabe acknowledged silently and with great satisfaction.

"I told you . . ." Ortega's voice came again and was cut off by Avendale.

"You don't tell me nothing! If you'd been doing your job, Bronson would have known that skirt was the lieutenant's sister."

"The cop knew!" Ortega's temper exploded, and he forgot his own warning to be quiet. "He's dead meat! He gave me pictures of Lewis's family, but he didn't say nothing about a sister."

"Good lookin' dame," another voice laughed. "Your little cop boy probably has his own sights on her."

Avendale made a crude remark about Lewis's sister, and Cabe had to struggle not to charge down the pile of rocks and slug the man in his mouth.

"Enough!" The white-hot fury in Daman Bronson's voice was unmistakable. Cabe felt Tisa stiffen and knew she'd recognized his voice this time too. "You won't have to worry anymore about this arduous journey or how I do my thinking." A spit of sound and a flash of light came from below almost simultaneously, followed by a few grunts which could have been unspoken approval from the remainder of Bronson's men, or Avendale's dying moans.

"He couldn't keep up anyway," someone said. "Too out of shape."

"Move! And keep your mouth shut," Ortega ordered. This time there was silence.

The faint sounds of the passing men were long past before Cabe heard a small whimpering behind him and turned to pull Tisa into his arms. She didn't cry, but her small body shuddered as though she were sobbing her heart out. He brushed his hand across her cheek and found no tears; still he crooned her name and rocked her until she was still.

Together, without speaking, they watched the sky grow lighter. At last Tisa straightened her shoulders and reached for the water bottle that had rolled away during the night. She took a long swallow, then poured some on her hands and scrubbed her face. She shivered at the touch of the cold water on her skin, but when she smiled faintly in his direction, Cabe knew she was ready to face whatever the morning would bring. Taking her hand, he led her from their shelter to begin their descent. Bronson may have left someone to watch his car, but by the time they reached it, the whole mountainside should be swarming with agents.

Reaching the trail, Cabe didn't immediately see any sign of the men who had paused there a few hours earlier. Releasing Tisa's hand, he began looking around. Seeing a fallen log a few feet from the trail that partially protected them from the view of anyone approaching in the direction the men had disappeared, he suggested Tisa wait there for him.

"No, I'm staying with you." She sidled closer.

"Okay, but you know someone was shot here, don't you?"

"Yes." She said nothing more, so he began a careful scrutiny of the trail. It didn't take long to find a cigarette butt and signs of a scuffle and a body being dragged. Ten feet down a grassy slope they spotted the body, lying against a log where it had stopped rolling down the steep incline.

Cabe approached the body carefully, then knelt for a closer examination. There was no doubt Ross Avendale was dead.

"He's the man who came while Daman and I were eating lunch." Tisa's voice didn't sound unduly upset.

"I know." Cabe acknowledged her observation.

"He's the one who set Peter and Lara's house on fire." Tisa was still calmly stating facts.

"How do you know that?" Cabe looked at the badly abused body. He was the trained investigator and he couldn't state his suspicion with that much certainty.

"Snuffy."

Startled, Cabe bent closer. The deep scratches down the side of Avendale's face had not been caused by his tumble through the brush. They had scabbed over and were spaced just right for the angry claws of a big tomcat protecting his territory. Peter had saved samples from the blood on Snuffy's fur, but Cabe didn't need a lab report to know Tisa's guess was right.

CHAPTER 17

"Tisa!" Peter swept her into his arms and she felt dampness on his cheeks. "Come in." With the heel of his shoe he quickly closed the door behind them before turning to extend a hand to Cabe—without releasing his sister.

"I can't thank you enough," Peter said to Cabe with emotion in his voice.

"Don't thank me," Cabe turned to grin at Tisa. "You're little sister is one tough lady. She got herself out of there." She grinned back at him.

"What's this about her becoming a federally protected witness?" Peter tightened his hold on his sister, but spoke to Cabe. It annoyed her that he chose to address Cabe as though she weren't also present.

"It's nonsense, that's what," Tisa told him. The flight from Idaho Falls hadn't taken long, but she was tired from a night with little sleep and her early morning hike; and irritated by the long wait at the Bureau office before being driven to Dave Woods's summer house halfway between Park City and Heber for this reunion. Her clothes were filthy and she wanted a shower. "If they think they can put me in a cage until Daman is caught and goes to trial they're mistaken. I'm going home, taking a two-hour shower, and putting on some decent clothes. Then I'm going to order a gallon of spaghetti and a loaf of French bread from the Italian restaurant four blocks from my condo. After that I'll sleep the clock around, and tomorrow I plan to go back to work."

Peter grasped her shoulders and pushed her back far enough to inspect her thoroughly. "Yes, I can see that a shower might be a good idea." He sniffed dramatically, then added, "Definitely a good idea."

Freeing an arm she slugged Peter's shoulder. He only laughed and hugged her again.

"There are two huge suitcases full of clothes for you sitting in the spare bedroom, and there's a bathroom between our rooms. Go ahead and clean up. We'll talk later."

"You're staying here?" Tisa asked her brother. "Are you a protected witness too?"

"In a way," Peter hesitated. "I'm still involved in the investigation for the city, and I'm directing my unit mostly by electronic means, but the Justice Department has assigned two marshals to keep an eye on me. Now they'll look after you too."

"I don't want someone following me around or keeping me here," Tisa protested.

"You don't have a lot of choice," Peter's voice turned stern. "You witnessed two murders."

Just the mention of what she had seen and heard made her slightly ill, but she wasn't ready to drop the subject. "What about Cabe? He was a witness too, does he have to stay here?"

"No, I won't be staying," Cabe answered for himself. "My situation is a little different from yours. Bronson doesn't know my name or anything about me, but he knows a great deal about you, including your name and address."

"I heard the man you called Ortega say there was a cop involved. If one of the officers working with Peter is really working for Daman, he knows about you," Tisa persisted.

"Sit down," Peter said with a sigh, pointing toward a cluster of sofas and chairs surrounding a low table. Once they were seated, Peter cleared his throat and looked at Cabe as though seeking reinforcement.

Cabe seated himself beside her and took her hand. "Tisa, no one except Peter and the police chief know I'm a federal agent. Except for the events of the past few days, you wouldn't know either. Since you do know and because your life is at stake if you don't stay hidden, I think it's time you know more. I've been working for several years on a broad case; one where drugs are being moved into the states, illegal gambling casinos for high rollers are being disguised as other businesses, and vast amounts of money are being laundered. Murder, prostitution, and illegal immigration also play a part in a crime syndicate controlled by one family. This isn't a Chicago mafia family, but a West Coast family headed by two brothers, one of which is Daman Bronson's father.

"When Dave Woods met us at the airport this afternoon," he continued, "he took me aside and told me that Daman Bronson has not been picked up. He seems to have vanished completely, along with his right-hand man, Jorge Ortega. He also said that early this morning the Bureau raided the club from which the brothers run their empire. One brother, Artel, was arrested and is awaiting arraignment later today. The Justice Department will try to prevent his being allowed to post bail. The other brother, Reuben, chose to resist arrest and was killed."

Cabe stopped, and Tisa seeing the look that passed between the two men, expected Peter to insist that was all she needed to know, so she was surprised when Cabe tightened his grip on her hand and resumed speaking.

"Reuben is Daman's father," Cabe said with a gentleness that warned her he was saying more than just words. "I told you on Tuesday that Daman Bronson isn't really the name of the man who hired you to decorate his hotel. His real name is Darren Dempsky, and he's in position to take over the entire operation. The only person standing in his way is you." For some reason that name froze her.

The monster was coming! Blackness rushed toward her with eyes that blinded and a rush of wind that sucked and pulled her into its grasp. No! She wasn't afraid. She wouldn't be afraid! It was Cabe, no, Cabe only reminded her of the words; it was the Savior who said, "Be not afraid, I am with you."

Taking a deep breath, Tisa stood. "I think I'll take that shower now."

The two men watched her leave the room. Neither spoke until they heard the shower come on.

"I thought telling her might trigger some memory." Peter's voice held a terrible sadness.

"She knows," Cabe said. "She's just not ready to face it. She might not ever be ready," he added.

"It might not be true. We're only guessing." Peter sounded more optimistic.

"DNA samples would be easy to acquire and would answer the question once and for all. I'll arrange for them." Cabe rose from his chair and walked to the window. He stood with slumped shoulders staring out at a mountain scene, not too different from the one he'd shared with Tisa in Island Park, but here there was no sense of threat or danger in the scene before him. The only threat came from the power he held to end the question that had tormented Tisa for so many years.

"Will you tell her?" Peter asked.

"I don't know." Cabe paced back to the chair where he'd sat earlier, and slumped his body into its soft shape.

"She's changed," Peter observed.

"Who wouldn't change after going through what she's been through?"

"That's not what I mean."

"She's probably still feeling some shock. She witnessed a guy she was developing strong feelings for murder two people in cold blood. She hiked for miles over some really rough terrain and slept on the ground on a cold mountainside last night. All this after a three-hour trail ride and very little to eat." Cabe defended Tisa. "She'll be all right. I learned that about her. She has strong survival instincts and an inner core of faith she's starting to recognize."

"That's what I mean," Peter leaned forward, resting his elbows on his knees. "Tisa's first thought, even before a shower, would normally be food. And this faith you speak of, when did she acquire that? She's always been the questioning, doubting one in the family."

"Questioning and doubting don't necessarily go together." Cabe, too, was earnest. "I don't think Tisa ever doubted God; she merely questioned His means of communication and only doubted her own worthiness to receive His help. In the past few days I believe she's begun to understand how much He's always guided her."

"You seem to have gotten well acquainted with my sister." There was a hint of sarcasm behind Peter's words which Cabe chose to ignore.

"I love your sister." He hadn't meant to tell Peter how he felt before he told Tisa, but the words just came out.

Peter frowned. "Have you considered how you'll feel if Tisa really is Teresa Dempsky?"

"Yes," he admitted. "At first the prospect overwhelmed me, and I questioned whether I could love her enough to block that information from my mind. But then she told me how much she wanted to know who her real parents were, and I found myself telling her that being a daughter of God was all that mattered, and I discovered I really mean that."

The shower turned off and Peter stood. "Will you stay for dinner? It'll be ready by the time Tisa dresses and reaches the kitchen."

"No, tell her good-bye for me and that I'll be back tomorrow." He followed his message with a wide grin. "I'm working out of the Bureau's office now, but you'll still be seeing a lot of me."

"I warned you about her track record for engagements." Peter's words were meant to tease, but they carried a bite. Cabe didn't bother to tell his friend that he had no intention of becoming one of Tisa's discarded fiancés. When the time was right, he meant to become her husband.

* * *

The days dragged as Tisa remained at the summer home with Peter. At first it was pleasant to catch up on her sleep and spend her days talking and playing games with the brother she adored. Cabe's frequent, unexpected arrivals were the highlight of each day. When she got bored with games and television, Cabe brought her books, and even a stack of sketch pads with charcoal, pen and ink, and an array of pastels. He told her he'd talked to Phillip and explained that she wouldn't be returning to work, possibly for a few months, and that he'd explained to her boss that the client she'd gone to see was a criminal wanted by the police. Phillip had expressed his disappointment, then said most of her other clients had already been given to the other designers and that it would be fine for her to take as much time as she needed. And he would welcome her back whenever she was ready to resume work.

One day Cabe arrived with a cat-carrier and bandages on his fingers. She and Peter were both pleased to see Snuffy, but he wasn't the kind of cat that permitted just anyone to lavish attention on him, and they knew better than to attempt to hug the animal. Jamie was the only one who could lug the nasty-tempered cat around or dress him in doll clothes. He quickly established a chair as his territory and she and Peter chose alternative seating.

A short time later Cabe arrived at the house with Useless and the news that Howie was fully conscious now and anxious to begin physical therapy. Tisa was glad the old dog was well enough to leave the veterinarian's care, but she was dubious about allowing the shaggy animal to share quarters with Snuffy. The cat hissed and spit a few times to make certain the dog knew who was in charge, then both animals settled down to a semipeaceful coexistence. All went well as long as Useless steered clear of Snuffy's padded armchair, and Snuffy avoided the braided rug in front of the fireplace.

Occasionally the marshals guarding the house came to the door to speak with Peter. Tisa had learned that their names were Rupert and Lance. Other times Cabe brought tidbits of information about the case. She usually found something else to do in another part of the house when talk turned to the Dempsky family, especially Darren. Her lack of interest seemed to puzzle both Peter and Cabe, but they never commented on it, and she never admitted, even to herself, her own puzzlement over her aversion to hearing more.

Finding a set of scriptures in a drawer in her room, she began reading bits and pieces at random, then one day turned back to the beginning and began to read in earnest. Instead of taking her questions to Peter, she began to pray for understanding. The intensive study seemed to satisfy a hunger within her, not unlike the hunger she'd struggled to satisfy with food since childhood.

By the time the second Sunday rolled around and she had been in hiding for a week and a half, she recognized that she was suffering from a full-scale case of cabin fever. She had to get out or go crazy.

"I'm going to church this morning," she announced as she poured milk over a bowl of cold cereal.

"I wish we could." Peter lifted his cup to his mouth and breathed the chocolate fragrance deeply before sipping the hot liquid. "I miss my ward."

"We don't have to go to our own wards; we could pick a ward at random in any town," she urged. She needed Peter's cooperation because she lacked means of transportation.

"I'm not sure that would be wise." He hesitated, but she could tell he really wanted to attend church. "Let's talk it over with Cabe when he arrives."

To her surprise Cabe agreed that a trip to one of the rural wards, away from the usual tourist centers, wouldn't be too much risk. It didn't take her long to dress, and she arrived back in the front room at almost the same moment as Peter. Catching Peter's smile, she guessed that being cooped up for so long was even harder on her brother than it was on her.

Cabe scrutinized her and she found herself blushing, but all he said was, "You need a hat."

"I don't have one," she told him. She never wore a hat except during the winter.

"Here," Cabe whisked a lace scarf off a small table. "Cover your hair with this."

She wanted to argue, but decided not to risk it. She didn't want Cabe or Peter backing out of this small expedition. She returned to her room with the scarf, folding it several different ways in front of the mirror until she was satisfied that she didn't look too absurd.

One of the marshals sat in the back of the car with her while Peter shared the front seat with Cabe, but when they reached a chapel that sat almost in the middle of a field, it was Cabe who held her door and escorted her inside. The congregation was singing what she hoped was the opening song when they stepped inside and made their way to three empty chairs in the overflow area. She sat between Cabe and Peter. The marshal, the one Peter called Rupert, stayed behind in the foyer with two women, both bouncing screaming infants on their laps.

There was nothing dramatic about that sacrament meeting; it wasn't unlike hundreds she'd attended before, but it felt different. She wanted to smile when the bishop announced Enrichment meeting would be on Wednesday night and the Cub Scouts were to meet at Sister Jones's house on Friday, the Young Women were painting someone's fence, and there would be no correlation meeting next Sunday because of Labor Day weekend. The organist remained a half beat behind the chorister, one of the deacons nearly tripped on his trailing shoelaces, and the youth speaker read his talk word for word.

An older couple, recently returned from a mission to England, spoke knowledgeably of the conversion process and illustrated their points with interesting anecdotes from their mission. It could have been any ward anywhere, but Tisa felt like she'd come home.

During the last verse of the closing song, Cabe touched her elbow and leaned over to say, "We need to leave now." Quietly the three of them filed out a side door. This time Cabe made certain she sat beside him on the ride back.

"I'm glad we went," she said, speaking softly, just for Cabe's ears.

"I am too." Cabe smiled and briefly took one hand from the wheel to squeeze hers. "I'm sorry we couldn't stay for the other meetings."

"I understand. If we'd stayed we would have had to stand and introduce ourselves in Sunday School, priesthood meeting, and Relief Society."

"You say that like you don't mind missing that part." Cabe grinned and Tisa laughed.

"It was different today." She became serious. "Or maybe I should say I felt different today. I don't know if it was because I wanted to get away from the house so badly that I particularly appreciated being in church, or if it was because of all that happened at Island Park and the studying I've done lately, but I was better prepared to listen with my heart today."

"I felt that extra dimension today as well," Cabe told her. "It might have been because it was the first time you sat beside me in church, or it could have been those same things you mentioned. As I took the sacrament I felt almost overwhelmed with gratitude for the blessings the gospel has brought me."

"I felt free," Tisa whispered. "Not just free of the house where Peter and I are staying, but really free. I've never felt that way before."

"Tisa, you . . ." She never heard what he'd been about to say. Her hands flew forward to grasp the dash as Cabe slammed on the breaks. Ahead of them a large tractor-trailer jackknifed in the road behind a boat trailer that had come loose from the RV towing it. No one appeared to be injured, but traffic was brought to a stop and access to Highway 40 was blocked.

"Great!" Cabe looked around and grumbled. "Silver Creek Junction is one of the busiest intersections in the state." He glanced at her and noticed the lace scarf had slipped from her head to her shoulders, revealing the pink stripe in her hair. He reached forward to pull it back over her hair. "You probably should exchange places with the marshal. You'll be less noticeable in the backseat than up here."

Over his shoulder she saw a car stop beside them in the next lane. "Won't that draw more attention to me if we trade places?"

"Probably. Just keep your head down and don't look out the window." He looked worried, and she slouched lower in her seat.

In a few minutes sirens screamed toward them. To Tisa it seemed to take an awfully long time to clear the road enough for traffic to proceed, but at last Cabe shifted gears and turned on his flasher to merge left. The Navigator lurched and Tisa's gaze flew straight into the eyes of the passenger of the next vehicle.

"Stay down," Cabe hissed. Obviously he'd recognized the woman too. Tisa just hoped the woman hadn't recognized her. Gloria DeMott was the worst gossip she knew.

Traffic moved slowly and Cabe did his best to allow as many vehicles as possible between himself and the DeMott woman, but she and the man with her seemed determined to stick as close as possible. There had been a look of triumph on Gloria's face as she'd turned to the man driving that had set Cabe's teeth on edge. When she lifted a cell phone to her ear, he knew they were in trouble. It was pretty safe odds to bet someone had offered the woman an incentive to report any news she discovered concerning Tisa's whereabouts. Howard Harmon had contacted Darren Dempsky once, probably by helping himself to the plot map and Tisa's itinerary from the Bronson's project files at Kurt's Interiors. The man was a logical choice for Dempsky to use in trying to trace Tisa; whatever arrangement Harmon was involved in, he was sure to have Gloria DeMott's support.

"They're too close; I can't risk exiting," Cabe said as he drove past the exit leading to Park City and Highway 40.

"Who's too close?" The marshal and Peter were both instantly on the edge of their seats.

"The woman in that car is the receptionist where I work," Tisa muttered. "Do I still have to stay down? It's too late to hope she didn't see me."

"She called someone as soon as she recognized Tisa," Cabe reported.

"Stay clear of Park City," Peter said. "Whoever she called could be there. There's a rumor that the hub of the drug-smuggling ring has shifted from Salt Lake to Park City."

"Does the man with Gloria have thinning hair, a weasely face, and a pencil mustache?" Tisa asked.

"Yes, and stay down." Cabe suddenly changed lanes, sending the SUV swaying.

"That's Howard Harmon," Tisa reported. "He has a cabin near Park City. Maybe they're headed there."

"I don't think so. They're attempting to keep us in sight and they're watching for something, probably someone."

"We have reinforcements on the way too," Rupert said, and Tisa caught a glimpse of the small phone in his hand. Those highway patrolmen at the accident site aren't far behind us." Seconds later Tisa heard the wail of sirens.

"Hang on," Cabe ordered. "We're heading down the canyon." The Navigator shot forward, throwing Tisa back against the seat, giving her an excellent view of the cars and trucks pulling to the side to make way for the approaching patrolmen. She felt tempted to smile and wave as they flew past Howard's Durango. In the side mirror she caught a glimpse of the patrol cars pulling her nosy co-workers to the side of the road.

Her glee was short-lived. Someone else was out there, hurrying to intercept her, someone who now knew she was in the area and who surely knew the license-plate number, make and model of the car she was riding in.

* * *

Cabe slowed down, feeling confident the patrolmen would detain the DeMott woman and her friend long enough for them to disappear, but the sooner he switched vehicles the safer he'd feel.

"Take my phone, Peter. It's there in the cup holder," Cabe said as Tisa reached for the cell phone and handed it back to Peter. "Call Dave Woods and let him know we're coming and to have another vehicle waiting for us."

CHAPTER 18

Darkness had fallen by the time the four weary church-goers reached the Midway cabin. They had first gone to Dave Woods's Salt Lake office where he met them with a Jeep and a change of clothes for each of them. He'd insisted that Tisa allow an agent to change her hair color too, before instructing them to return to the cabin by way of Provo Canyon. Peter was driving the Jeep with Rupert riding shotgun. Tisa leaned against Cabe's shoulder in the backseat and slept the last few miles. Detouring through Provo and Heber had taken longer, but he'd agreed with the others that it was a safer route. Cabe stroked Tisa's hair, and though he couldn't actually see it, he considered the mousy brown color that covered her gleaming blond hair a necessary change. He'd kind of miss that sassy pink streak, but hair color had nothing to do with the beauty he saw in her.

Peter took advantage of a long stretch of nearly deserted tree-lined pavement to switch off the Jeep's headlights. Two miles later he pulled onto the dirt road that led to the house. Cabe was glad Tisa was asleep. The day had been nerve-wracking enough for her without her being aware they'd driven up the canyon without the benefit of lights.

She mumbled something in her sleep and he settled her more comfortably against his side. She'd blamed herself for exposing them all to danger, but in his opinion she was too quick to assume blame. He was the one who was in charge of this part of the investigation, and he was the one who had approved venturing out to church. And he was the one Dave Woods had lectured for exposing a witness to risk.

He didn't entirely regret the trip. There had been something right and filled with promise during that brief service. Tisa had felt it too, and it encouraged his hope that the two of them had a future together. And he certainly didn't regret the hours he and Tisa had spent tonight snuggled together in the Jeep's small backseat.

Lance stepped onto the porch of the house as they pulled into the clearing and signaled that all was secure. *For now,* Cabe thought, *but how long will it take Bronson to track us down?* He'd wanted both Tisa and Peter to leave for Texas, feeling Peter's father-in-law could provide better protection than they would receive by returning to Dave's summer home. Neither Tisa or Peter wanted to go. Peter felt his presence in his father-in-law's household would increase the danger to his family, and Tisa didn't explain her refusal to leave. Was it vanity to hope being near him had something to do with her desire to remain in Utah?

"We're here." Peter switched off the engine and turned to look at his sister. "No wonder she's been quiet so long."

"Don't wake her," Cabe kept his voice low. "I'll carry her inside." He suited action to words as he released both of their seat belts and stepped down from the Jeep, then reached back inside to lift her into his arms. The walk to the house and down the hall to Tisa's room seemed much too short. It was with reluctance that he placed her on the bed, where he stood beside her watching her sleep for several minutes, then knelt to slip off her shoes. Before leaving her he pulled a quilt over her sleeping form. On an impulse he bent to kiss her cheek.

When he returned to the front room he found Peter waiting for him. "She's sleeping soundly," he answered the unspoken question in Peter's eyes.

"Poor kid, she's exhausted," Peter said. He had dark circles under his eyes and looked nearly as tired as his sister. Being away from his family and his department was taking its toll on him. He stood with his back to the cold fireplace with his hands clasped behind his back.

"We've got to find Dempsky and Ortega," he said. "Tisa won't be safe until they're behind bars. The only alternative is to place Tisa in the witness protection program, create a new identity for her, and help her disappear."

"I'm not sure she could handle that." Cabe stepped to the other end of the fireplace and leaned against the stones. "Tisa already feels she's living under an assumed identity—she's felt that for years. To once again lose touch with everything familiar might be more than she can handle."

"I've thought of that. Perhaps if you went with her . . ." It was the first time Peter had verbally acknowledged that Cabe might be a permanent part of Tisa's future.

"You know I would, but I'm not sure she'd allow it. Family is important to her, and she'd know it would mean that I would never see my mother again. She would be miserable if she thought she was the cause of separating me from my family. I don't think she could face cutting you out of her life either."

"Then let's take what we learned today and push hard before Dempsky locates this place." Peter began to pace. "At first I was sorry we had gone out this morning, but as I've thought about it, I've concluded we may have gained some advantage. That receptionist, the DeMott woman, knows how to get in touch with someone in Darren Dempsky's organization. I suggest someone pay a call on her."

"Dave promised he'd have agents on her doorstep first thing in the morning. He's also checking to see where her friend's cabin is."

"One other thing," Peter added. "While you were taking evasive action on the freeway this morning, I saw a dark green sports car racing from Park City toward the freeway entrance. I've nothing to base my theory on except a hunch, but if that was Darren Dempsky, trying to catch up to us in response to Gloria DeMott's call, we've narrowed the search to the Park City area."

"And don't forget, the Dempsky organization is still functioning. Even with Artel in jail and Reuben dead, the drug shipments are continuing. If your information is correct, then Park City is the new hub for drug distribution. I'll start checking on it immediately."

"You need some sleep as badly as I do," Peter yawned. "There isn't much you can accomplish tonight in Park City. If you sleep here tonight that will put you closer to where you should start searching in the morning. You can have one of the twin beds in the room I'm using."

"All right. I'll just let Dave know we got here, and see if some of his people can start some of the search by computer overnight." He was talking to Peter's back as the lieutenant was already doing a thorough check of the doors and windows before retiring.

* * *

Tisa dressed in jeans and a pink, cotton-knit shirt. She looked at her hiking boots before pulling on a pair of tennis shoes. She didn't often wear tennis shoes, but she wasn't the one who had packed for this extended stay in a mountain cabin, and the boots and tennis shoes were the only choices she had other than the pair of high-heeled shoes she'd worn to church. She didn't want the extra weight of the boots today. She sighed. She knew she should be grateful the secretary sent to purchase a wardrobe for her had guessed her size fairly well from Peter's description. The nondescript jeans, shirts, and dresses she'd selected weren't meant to attract attention. It was just that tennis shoes and low heels made her feel small.

Swiping a brush through her hair, she glared into the mirror. Her hair was awful. It needed a cut, and the brown rinse she'd been given before leaving Salt Lake was boring. At least a good scrub in the shower had almost restored her own pale blond color, though it now lacked the pink streak she'd paid her hairdresser a fortune to add a few weeks ago.

Leaving her room, she walked down the hall to the kitchen. "Good morning," she directed a greeting toward the table and hesitated before sliding onto a chair. Cabe was sitting at the breakfast table with a full plate of pancakes and eggs in front of him.

"Did you stay all night?" He hadn't done that before. A guilt attack struck her. "Are you stuck here now too, because I insisted on going out yesterday?"

"Yes, I stayed all night, and by the way, your brother snores. Next time I want a better roommate." He added a wicked grin before reaching for her plate and piling it with pancakes and three eggs.

"Hey," Peter protested. "I didn't hear a thing."

"If it weren't for his promise of breakfast, I would have headed for the closest motel." Cabe poured syrup over Tisa's pancakes. "As for your second question, no, I'm not stuck here. I'll be leaving right after breakfast, and if all goes well, you won't be stuck here much longer either. When I checked in with Dave he said the Bureau had received a tip from INS concerning a couple of illegals caught carrying drugs. One of them had a scrap of paper with a Park City address on it."

"You aren't going there alone are you?" Her hands shook and she set her fork back down on her plate.

"I'll drive by, but I won't approach the place without backup," he assured her. "If this turns out to be a dead end, I won't be back tonight. I'll have to stay away now that I've been seen with you. I can't risk leading anyone who might recognize me to this place."

"We'll have to leave soon anyway," her brother said. Peter turned off the griddle and joined Cabe and Tisa at the table. "Dempsky will narrow his search to this area just as the Bureau will begin focusing on Park City, which pretty much leaves me out of it. The warehouse in Salt Lake is as clean as a whistle. It was nothing but a decoy set up to keep me busy while Dempsky and Ortega do their business somewhere else. The drugs are still coming in, but I'm convinced the distribution point has moved out of my area." He set the syrup pitcher down with enough force to slop syrup over the side, leaving a dark puddle on the table. His chair made a grating sound as he shoved it back to reach for a paper towel.

Tisa briefly touched her brother's arm as he swiped at the spilled syrup. If only he'd been able to arrest the entire ring in Salt Lake before she'd even met Daman, Peter would be happier and so would she. She wouldn't be straddling a fence as it were, hoping that Daman would soon be caught, freeing her to get back to her life, but feeling a constant aching hurt at the thought of his spending the rest of his life in prison.

Cabe gave her a look of sympathy, almost as though he could read her thoughts. *Cabe is another man tearing me in two. He isn't like the other men I thought I loved; perhaps he's a little like Mark, but stronger. His faith in God is like Mark's, but deeper, more tried. I like him. I trust him. But do I love him? How can I be sure? I want a forever marriage like Peter and Lara, but with my track record, I don't trust myself to make that kind of choice. I don't want to hurt Cabe the way I did Mark . . . I'm being premature,* she attempted to dismiss her thoughts. *Cabe hasn't mentioned marriage—but I don't think I'll survive if he doesn't.*

"Earth to Tisa." She glanced across the table into Cabe's smiling face. She could feel the heat climbing her neck and burning her face. He didn't tease her about her fiery cheeks, but there was no doubt he saw and wasn't entirely displeased.

"I was just saying I'm leaving now." There was a gentleness in his voice. "Will you walk me to the door?"

She rose to her feet, and as soon as they were out of sight, Cabe's arm came around her. At the door he tightened his hold, drawing her against his chest. With exquisite softness, his lips touched hers. When he would have released her, she wrapped her arms around his neck and urged his mouth back to hers. This time they kissed with a fierceness that stunned her.

He was the first to pull back. With a catch in her voice she urged him to stay. "Don't go after Daman. He knows who you are now, and I'm sure he suspects you saw him kill Chef Bono too. "

"I have to go," he said. "Lara and Peter can't be together again, and neither can we, until this threat is ended."

"I can't believe Daman would hurt me," she protested, but she really wasn't sure. She would have sworn a few weeks ago that the last person Daman would attack was the man who cooked and served him such wonderful meals, but she'd seen him do so with her own eyes.

"You know better," Cabe told her, as though he could read her mind, before giving her one more quick kiss. "I'll be in the Park City area, not too far away. You have the phone I gave you; if you feel threatened, or if anything unusual should happen, call me. You have my cell-phone number, and I'll keep it on the vibrator setting, so that you won't have to worry about the wrong people hearing it."

"All right," she agreed. He was gone before she could finish warning him to be careful. From a narrow crack between the door and frame she watched him walk toward the trailer that was partially hidden in the trees, where Rupert and Lance took turns sleeping while the other one kept watch. He spoke with one of the agents for a few minutes, then climbed into the Jeep. In a few minutes the Jeep disappeared from sight down the long winding lane. She closed the door and snapped the locks in place. He was gone, and she hated the hopeless finality that filled her.

Closing her eyes, she leaned back against the door, turning slightly so that her cheek pressed against the smooth wood. If Daman saw Cabe first, he would kill him, just as he had killed Chef Bono and that horrible Avendale man. She had no doubt of that. Daman might spare her, but he wouldn't hesitate to kill Cabe. Desolation swept over her as she contemplated never seeing Cabe again. Squeezing her eyes tighter, she felt as though she were floating high in the air.

She was a little girl, kneeling on slick leather, with her forehead pressed against cool glass. All around her were flashing lights, and just below where she knelt, a man dressed in a uniform bent over a much-too-still form lying on the ground. When the man moved, Tisa could see that the body belonged to a woman. She didn't want to see any more. She didn't want to know that under the blood that streaked her face, the woman was beautiful, but Tisa did know, and she knew, too, that the woman had loved her, had given her the pink sweater she was now gripping. The woman's image disappeared, replaced by Cabe's still form. He lay on the ground. Pain ripped her heart. She wanted to scream, but no sound escaped the crushing darkness weighing her down. Without Cabe, she thought she would die.

"Tisa," Peter knelt beside her. She wasn't sure when she'd sunk to the floor. The last she remembered she'd been standing, leaning her cheek against the door panel. "What happened? Are you all right?" He touched her face, and it was the first she knew her cheeks were wet.

"You're crying." He sounded as astounded by her tears as she was. Her own hand touched her face and she felt the tears with a kind of wonder. She knew what they meant; she loved Cabe, loved him as she'd never dared love anyone before.

"Peter," she spoke her brother's name and leaned her head against his shoulder as sobs racked her slender frame. She cried for Cabe and for herself, for Peter, and Daman. She cried for all the lost, lonely children everywhere. And she cried for the dead woman who might have once loved her. He held her until her tears subsided.

"Can you tell me about it?" he asked as she straightened and pulled herself to her feet. Standing too, he reached for a box of tissues, plucking a handful to give to her. She blew her nose and wiped her eyes before answering.

"I don't know what happened," she admitted. "I watched Cabe leave and an intense sadness seemed to overcome me. Only the sadness wasn't just because Cabe went away and I don't know when

I'll see him again. In my mind I saw a woman who died in a terrible car accident. Do you think I remembered my mother?"

"I don't know." Peter seemed to want to say more, then decided against it. "What I do know is that you care about Cabe and that your feelings are troubling you."

"I do care about Cabe. I love him, but it would be cruel to let him love someone like me." One narrow strip after another, she began shredding the tissue in her hand, unable to look her brother in the face. "Mark deserved someone better than me, so did the other men I almost married. I won't let Cabe think I love him, then panic, ending everything before we're married."

"None of those other men were right for you." Peter took the ball of wet tissue from her and tossed it into a trash basket, then placed his arm around her, leading her to an overstuffed chair before continuing. "You wouldn't have ended those engagements if you'd really loved any of those men."

"I cared about Mark."

The look he gave her was filled with pity. Seating himself in a chair that faced hers, he took his time voicing his thoughts. "Not the same way you care about Cabe." There was no mistaking the conviction in her brother's voice. "I think you've always wanted to love someone and to be loved in return, but those old uncertainties about your past have convinced you you're not worthy of love."

She hung her head, not really disagreeing with her brother, then she said, "I didn't become a different person because Norm and Dixie gave me their name."

"Our parents never tried to change who you are," Peter said. "Mom and Dad loved the little girl they had spent so many years hoping and praying for. They recognized you as the child of their hearts the moment they met you. Cabe doesn't want to change who you are either; he only wants to love you. I think you can't let someone love you until you love yourself, and you won't love yourself until you know who you are."

"But how can I know who I am?" She pounded a fist against the arm of her chair. "I've tried to remember, but I can't."

"I don't think it's a matter of remembering, but one of discovering. Once you understand your relationship to God, when you're spiritually prepared to do whatever He expects of you, then you will know who you are."

Peter's words lingered in Tisa's mind as she washed the dishes and performed the minimal housekeeping chores that needed to be done. By midmorning she'd run out of things to do. Television held little appeal, and she'd already read the few books she'd found in the house. She needed something to do. Noticing Peter's scriptures sitting on a table, she picked them up and began leafing through them, reading verses here and there.

She'd attended seminary, and though she hadn't been the most diligent student, she knew how to use the topical guide. Turning to the back of the Bible she began slowly turning pages, hoping something would catch her eye. Nothing stood out, and she remembered all the times she'd heard someone say they'd opened the Bible or the Book of Mormon and a needed verse had "jumped" to their attention. That had never happened to her. She started to close the book, then words entered her heart that she'd heard Dixie say long ago. "Easy isn't always best. If you'd been born to me, I might not have loved you so much. We value most what we have to work and pray the hardest to get."

Opening the book wider, she ran her fingers down page after page. With painstaking care she read every verse pertaining to daughters or children. In her mind a pattern began to grow, merging with Peter's words and the words Cabe had spoken while they hid in the mountains. She paused after reading in the twenty-fifth section of the Doctrine and Covenants, "all those who receive my gospel are sons and daughters in my kingdom." Could it be that her identity had more to do with her own actions than it did with who her parents might be?

Setting the triple combination aside, she stood and paced about the room. At last she went to her room, closing the door behind her. She approached the bed, then knelt. Resting her clasped hands on the nubby-textured bedspread, she wondered what to say. She knew how to pray, and she'd gained a deeper understanding of prayer this summer than she'd ever known before; she even felt more experienced in knowing how to listen for an answer. But even now, though she wanted to pray, in fact felt a need to pray, the words weren't there.

Bowing her head, she voiced her frustration. "Father, help me, please love me." The plea came from the depths of her soul. Something flickered in the far recesses of her mind and she thought she'd pleaded the same way once before. She braced herself, fighting a terrible dread. Then came a gentle calm that filled her soul. Love, profound and sweet, filled her heart with peace and she knew her Savior loved her. Unaccustomed tears once more flooded her eyes, dampening her cheeks.

She stayed on her knees until her legs began to cramp, then she sat on the edge of the bed and continued to read, this time in Psalms. She suddenly understood so much more. ". . . and all of you are children of the most High." If only she'd known—but perhaps she was like her mother, if her faith had come too easily, before she was spiritually prepared, she wouldn't have understood.

"Tisa, are you okay?" Peter's voice came through the closed door.

"Yes, I'll be out in a minute," she called back. She wiped her eyes and brushed her hair before leaving her room.

"Tisa?" Peter looked uncertain. She knew he sensed something different about her.

"I'm fine." She stood on her toes to kiss his cheek. "For the first time in my life, I'm really fine." And she was. Heavenly Father loved her. No longer did she feel the need to find her first parents. She knew her true identity. She was Heavenly Father's beloved daughter and that's all that mattered.

Settling his hand on her shoulder, he examined her closely, then seeming satisfied with what he saw, he smiled and a light filled his eyes.

* * *

Cabe felt the tingle of his phone vibrating against his thigh. He thought of ignoring it, but remembered it might be Tisa. If it were in its usual spot in the cup holder he could reach it. Frowning in annoyance, he pulled to the side of the road, released his seat belt, and thrust his hand into his pocket. Had someone been watching the house and seen him leave? He pressed Talk.

It wasn't Tisa's voice but Dave's that spoke to him. Without preamble, Dave launched into his message. "The Summit County sheriff got a tip half an hour ago that an abandoned mine south of Park City is being used as a drug warehouse. A couple of Lewis's officers volunteered through the statewide drug unit to assist in searching the place. Their car has stalled along the freeway a couple of miles before the Park City turnoff. You're the closest; pick them up and join the others at the mine." He gave instructions on how to locate the mine and rang off.

Cabe whistled softly as he drove. This might soon be over. He looked forward to telling Tisa she could move back into her apartment. He was looking forward even more to the day when he could discuss with her whether she preferred to give up her job and move to Los Angeles, or if he should request a transfer or consider a job change and join her in her condo.

It wasn't long before he spotted Stone Aldredge's restored '57 Chevy parked alongside the road. Aldredge was behind the wheel, but there was no sign of the other officer Dave had mentioned. The other officer had probably hitched a ride into Park City to look up a towing service.

Pulling in behind the disabled car, he paused, expecting Aldredge to jump from his car and hurry to join him. When the other man didn't move, Cabe opened his door, knocking the phone he'd carelessly left on the seat to the floor. Grabbing it, he shoved it into his pocket, and, leaving his engine running, hurried to the other car.

"Let's go, Aldredge." The man didn't move or respond and Cabe stepped closer, a shiver running down his spine. His eyes zeroed in on a trickle of blood forming a thin line from just in front of Aldredge's ear. He was already reaching for the gun he wore in his shoulder holster when a blow from behind blacked out his world.

* * *

Cabe lay still, absorbing the sounds around him, pretending to still be unconscious. His face burned where it pressed against coarse carpet, and he could hear the sounds of traffic not far away. It wasn't the steady hum of freeway traffic, but the stop and go of a busy street. From the harsh breathing behind him, he could tell someone else, probably one of the officers he'd stopped to help, was still alive, but in a bad way. He was pretty sure it wasn't Aldredge.

Banking back his anger, he blamed himself for being so easily duped. After the way Carmichael and Jones died, he should have been expecting a trick. He opened his eyes until he could see beneath lowered lashes.

Cabe was aware of cuffs on his wrists and that he was lying face-down behind what looked like a long bar or counter of some type. The space was narrow and he was tightly wedged between the body behind him and the wooden counter.

He recognized one of the men he'd seen with Ortega at Island Park. He was sitting balanced on an old wooden chair a few feet away that leaned back on two legs against the wall. A rifle rested across the guard's legs and his attention was focused on something on the other side of the counter, outside Cabe's narrow range of vision.

Cabe's gun was gone, which didn't surprise him any; he could tell from the flat feel of the leather against his chest that the holster was empty. He was lying on something hard, and it took a few minutes to identify the uncomfortable lump in his front pocket as his phone, telling him his unconscious body hadn't been searched too thoroughly. Whoever had hit him had been in a hurry to get him away from the freeway.

He wondered why he was still alive. Aldredge certainly wasn't, which meant the person behind him was either Vasquez or White. He began at once formulating a plan to reach his phone.

Keeping his narrow range of vision focused on the guard in the chair, Cabe slowly twisted his body and shifted his cuffed hands bit by bit. When his shoulders ached and his back burned with pain, his fingers at last touched their objective.

His chance came when an argument erupted on the other side of the counter. While the guard was focused on the disturbance, Cabe used the tips of his fingers to touch his phone through the fabric of his pants. Praying the phone hadn't been switched off, he pressed the button he thought would dial Dave Woods's number. He didn't hear Dave answer, but he knew the agent was in the habit of listening for a couple of seconds before verbally responding to a call on his private line. A wise precaution he'd devised for just this sort of situation. Cabe didn't dare speak to ensure his message was understood, but if he'd punched the right button, Dave would know he was in trouble and send agents to begin searching for him.

"Lewis will be at the mine any minute. I know him. He won't be able to resist rushing to one of his men's rescue. And he'll come when I tell him you have McCabe Evans as well." He'd heard that voice before, but now it was muffled, making identification difficult. The voice said something about hurrying back to the search group before he was missed.

Now there was no doubt, the Judas who was on his way to deliver Peter to Dempsky was one of Peter's own men.

CHAPTER 19

The ringing of the phone interrupted a late lunch. It was a secure phone, installed specifically so Peter could stay in touch with his unit and with Cabe. Tisa couldn't help hoping Cabe was the caller. Sometimes he had called just to let her know he was thinking of her, but after what he had said when he left this morning, she hadn't expected to hear from him again today. They never talked more than a few minutes, but it had always given her day a lift to hear his voice. Peter reached for the instrument, grasping it before it could ring again. She was under strict orders to never answer the phone, and there was something about that single, strident trill that sounded ominous to Tisa. She waited, watching Peter, and silently praying that nothing bad had happened to Cabe.

Peter's side of the conversation wasn't very informative, but when he finished the brief call, he turned to Tisa. "I'll be gone for a few hours," he told her.

"You can't go. It's too dangerous."

"I have to, Tisa." She could see fear in his eyes and she began to tremble. She'd never seen Peter afraid. He was her rock, the big brother who always kept her safe.

"Two of my men and one of Woods's agents failed to check in." He reached to the top of the closet where he'd set his gun. "Their cars have been found abandoned alongside the freeway. Woods received a tip that Darren Dempsky is holding them in a boarded-up mine shaft south of Park City that's rumored to be a drug warehouse. The statewide drug unit, twenty federal agents, and most of Summit County's deputies are already en route to the mine. I'll meet my unit there."

"Can't someone else go?"

"No, this is my case and my men. I have to be there." He hesitated. "I didn't want to tell you, but now I think you need to know. One of my men is working for Dempsky. If he should find this number, he might trick you into revealing your location or try to get information that could endanger the men being held."

"Who?" She grasped his arm.

"I don't know who he is." The anguish in his voice twisted her heart, but she'd given little thought to who the turncoat might be.

"No, I meant which men are being held hostage?"

"Aldredge and Vasquez." His voice was stony. "But one or both of them may be on Dempsky's payroll."

"And . . . the agent?" Her heart pounded with dread, waiting for Peter to answer.

He hesitated, then as if he knew she'd already guessed, in a hoarse whisper he added, "McCabe."

Restless energy kept Tisa moving about the house. She cleaned the refrigerator and thought about the little phone in her pocket. She scrubbed the bathroom and was conscious only of the weight of the device tucked in her jeans. She tried to read and gave up to pace the floor.

Her mind filled with every moment she'd spent with Cabe. She wished she'd told Peter about the cell phone Cabe had given her in Island Park and had returned to her when he brought her here, but she'd been so shocked at hearing that he was missing, it hadn't occurred to her until after Peter had gone. She fingered the small phone, wondering if she dared call Cabe. He said to call him if she was in danger, but nothing had changed here. He was the one in danger.

Besides she was afraid to call. If he didn't answer, that could mean Daman had killed him. No, she wouldn't think about that. Cabe was alive; she had to believe that. She held the telephone in her hand, staring at it, willing it to ring.

This is ridiculous! Cabe said he'd keep it on the vibrator setting. No one but Cabe will even know if I call, and if anyone other than Cabe answers, I'll hang up.

Gingerly she pressed Direct-dial. She held the phone to her ear and listened, hearing only a steady ringing. When the ringing stopped a recorded voice said, "The number you dialed is not available at this time. To leave a message . . ." Clicking off, she tried to think what to do.

The phone, still in her hand, rang, startling her so much she nearly dropped it. With clumsy, shaking fingers she pressed Yes and held the phone to her ear. She tried to say hello, but nothing came out of her mouth.

"I want the other one too." The words, though shouted, were muffled, but she knew the voice—Daman!

"He'll come when I tell him you have McCabe Evans." This voice was farther away, less clear. It too seemed familiar, though she couldn't immediately place it. "Got to get back to the mine . . ." the voice was lost in a flurry of sound. Some instinct warned her not to speak, but to continue to listen. She couldn't make out much of the conversation between the two men, and her mind groped to understand why Daman, or Darren or whatever his real name might be, had called her. The truth dawned slowly. Daman hadn't called her; he didn't even know she could hear him. Someone else, she could only presume Cabe, had pressed Call-back on his phone.

"Not mine . . . street." Cabe mumbled the words, then the connection broke before she could respond. She pressed the code to call him back, but there was no response. Panic made her hands shake and her mind numb. She had to be rational, not succumb to panic, but at first her mind refused to cooperate, then the words she'd heard began to sink in.

What wasn't his? And which street? Cabe was in trouble and he was counting on her to get help for him. Or was it her help he was seeking? He might not have meant to push Call-back; he could have been trying to press the key for any of the programmed numbers in his phone. The conviction grew that Cabe had meant to call Special Agent in Charge Dave Woods—or Peter—and had accidently called her instead. That made more sense.

She didn't know how to contact Woods, but she knew Peter's number. He'd warned her not to answer any calls, but he hadn't said she shouldn't call him. She keyed the number she'd memorized long ago.

"Lewis," her brother answered on the first ring, his voice abrupt.

"Peter, Cabe is in trouble." She told him about the cell phone Cabe had given her and the call she'd received, stumbling over the words in her haste. "At first I thought he was saying something wasn't his, but now I believe he used the word *mine* to tell me the mine tip you're following is a hoax. I'm sure that's what he meant. He was trying to give me an address, but I only understood the word *street.*"

"You don't have any idea which street he meant?"

"No. He wasn't talking directly into the phone and someone else was talking at the same time."

"Think! How many voices were there? Were there background sounds, anything that would give us a clue to where he might be?"

"One of the voices might have had a Spanish accent. Another voice besides Daman's sounded familiar, but I don't know . . . he said something . . . I can't remember. I think there were at least three people, maybe more. I can't be sure."

"Which phone are you on now?" The harshness in Peter's voice frightened her.

"The cell phone . . ."

"I'll find him. Hang up immediately and go find Rupert or Lance. Tell them everything." He hung up on her.

Barely remembering to press Off at her end, she set the phone down. Peter had sounded angry. Had she done the wrong thing by calling him? Had she placed him in danger too?

Hurrying to the door, she remembered to look for any sign of trouble before dashing into the open space between the house and the marshals' trailer. Everything looked normal. She'd only taken a few steps when she saw Rupert running to meet her. He urged her back to the porch, where she explained about Cabe's call, then her own call to Peter.

"Let's go." She hadn't been aware of Lance joining them on the porch. Evidently he'd been there long enough to have heard most of her story.

"Go?"

"Yes, our orders are to move you if security is breached in any way. We can't be sure McCabe Evans placed that call."

"But I heard his voice."

"You heard Dempsky too." Lance was already hustling her toward the two marshals' car which they had parked beside the trailer. Rupert slid into the back beside her, while Lance climbed into the driver's seat.

"Get down," Rupert ordered. "Cover yourself with this." He handed her a plaid car-blanket.

"Aren't you being a little melodramatic?" she protested.

Rupert ignored her question as he pushed her toward the carpeted floor. At least sitting on the floor with the blanket over her head gave her an opportunity to think. She tried to make the best of a situation she definitely didn't like. Over and over in her mind she went over the few words she'd heard during that strange phone call. Each bump and jolt was magnified by her position on the narrow floor space, but her personal discomfort was unimportant compared to the danger facing the two men she loved most. Cabe's call, she felt certain, meant he was either Daman's prisoner or he was close enough to Daman that the smallest sound might give away his position.

And Peter? Where was Peter? Maybe looking for Cabe in an abandoned mine, but Cabe wasn't there! If only she had understood the name of the street.

Please, Father, she began to pray. *Protect Cabe. Help Peter find him in time.*

"We'll be slowing for the freeway entrance," Rupert spoke, his voice low. She felt the reduction in speed and braced herself for the acceleration that would follow.

"No! Wait!" She shoved the blanket back from her face. "I remembered what the other man said. We have to find Peter. He's walking into a trap!" Frantically she searched her pockets, then remembered dropping the cell phone on the desk back at the summer home.

"Stay down." Rupert pushed the blanket back over her head and pressed her toward the floor.

"I've got to call Peter, warn him!" She could hear the timbre of her voice turning to a shriek.

"Don't worry. There's still time," Rupert tried to comfort her.

"I'll call the SAC; Woods will pass on the message," Lance's voice reached her from the front seat, followed by the murmur of his voice, presumably talking to Dave Woods from the car phone.

"Tell him to call Peter," she pleaded. "He's got to warn Peter one of his own men is planning to turn him over to Daman!"

Moments later the car picked up speed and once more Lance's voice floated over where she lay curled on the floor. He was whispering as though he thought she couldn't hear just because she had a blanket over her head! "He said to take her someplace where she won't be seen. He gave me an address. As soon as we get there he wants to talk directly to her."

Silently she urged Lance to drive faster.

* * *

Tisa looked around and hid a feeble smile. She knew exactly where she was. The room she'd been hustled to was one of the suites she'd decorated a few months ago for the Skye Hotel.

"This is the same hotel Daman Bronson was staying in when we first met," she told the two agents as she moved toward the telephone, but she could see she'd startled them.

"Just a minute." Lance blocked her way, then after fiddling with the phone for a few minutes, dialed a number. She heard him repeat to the person on the other end that they were at the same hotel where Daman had been registered when he first met Tisa. He handed the phone to her and soon she was telling Dave Woods about the background voice.

"I'm certain someone is planning to separate my brother from the rest of the men searching the mine and deliver him to wherever Cabe is being held," she finished explaining.

"Put Lance back on the line," Woods told her.

"But Peter . . ." she started to protest, but Woods cut her off with a single word.

"Now!" She handed the phone to Lance, but remained close, hoping to hear what Woods had to say to him. Her efforts were in vain, because after only a few moments of silence, Lance hung up. For what seemed a long time to Tisa, he stood staring at the phone as though lost in thought.

"Well? Where to from here?" Rupert saved her the need to question Lance.

"Woods is pulling in every available agent, and the men assigned to search the mine are pulling back, returning to town. Lewis isn't with them, and he isn't answering his phone or pager."

Tisa felt herself sway and was only vaguely aware of Rupert pushing her down to sit on the edge of the bed. Despising her weak reaction, she forced herself to stay conscious. *In, out,* she thought, breathing deeply.

"Woods wants Rupert and me to search this hotel, starting with a look at the registration books." Lance was kneeling beside her and she could see the worry in his eyes. "If there's any chance Dempsky is still booked here, finding his room could speed up the search."

"Do you think he might be holding Cabe and Peter here?" She felt a surge of hope.

"Probably not," Rupert's face revealed his sympathy, "but if there's any chance at all, we've got to check it out. You'll be all right here until we get back. Just don't let anyone but us into this room."

After the two marshals left her alone, she slipped the chain on the door, then retreated to the bathroom. Hoping the cool water would clear her mind, she turned on the cold faucet full blast, then using her hands splashed the water on her face. After patting her face dry, she wandered back into the bedroom and gave herself a stern talking-to. She couldn't panic or black out. The old monster that hid in the blackness of her mind couldn't be allowed to escape. She had to think.

Was it only this morning that she'd felt the calmness of knowing she had a Heavenly Father? It was almost evening now and soon the sun would set, making the search more difficult. Her joy and serenity were gone. Though perhaps they weren't completely gone. She sank to her knees. *God knows where Cabe and Peter are.*

Words sprang to her mind and she prayed with all the fervency she'd previously used to search for her own identity. This time there was no hesitancy; she knew that Heavenly Father could be with the two men she loved. The hard part was accepting whatever He willed concerning their fate. Though she didn't love Daman, she cared about him. She added a plea on his behalf.

When she whispered "amen," she remained on her knees, head bowed. Her mind filled with the bright summer day when she'd driven her sports car up the canyon. She'd parked in the parking lot of this very hotel and casually wandered down the street, peering into shop windows, happily anticipating her date with Daman.

Daman! He'd been in the alley, then disappeared inside the empty half of the building that housed that strange craft store.

"That's where he's holding Cabe and Peter!" she shouted the words aloud as she scrambled to her feet. She had to find Lance and Rupert. Jumping to her feet she ran to the door, jerked the chain from its holder, and dashed into the hall. Seeing the hall was empty, she ran for the stairwell.

The heavy fire door thumped behind her and her shoes slapped against the stairs. If she ever saw Dave Woods's secretary again she'd thank her for the boring, flat tennis shoes. At each floor she opened the door and glanced down the hall. When she reached the garage level she stared in dismay at the cars parked in neat rows, wondering what to do. She couldn't rescue Cabe and Peter by herself.

The elevator chimed and she barely had time to hide behind a car before the doors slid open. Crouching low, she waited, then nearly sobbed with relief when Rupert stepped out.

"Rupert," she called, just loud enough for him to hear. He turned swiftly and she gasped, seeing a gun appear in his hand.

"It's me," her voice quavered, and she stood with outstretched hands to face him. "I know where Cabe and Peter are being held."

"You're sure?" His eyes never stopped scanning the parking area.

"I think so." She told him about seeing Daman enter the abandoned store that night earlier in the summer. Rupert grasped her arm and practically dragged her to their car where he placed a call to Woods. By the time he finished speaking with the SAC, Lance had joined them.

"We'll accompany you back to your room. Then . . ." Rupert began.

"No, we're wasting time." Tisa shook off any suggestion that she remain behind to wait. "I'm going with you."

"Too much risk," Lance backed his partner.

"It will save time if I show you the building Daman entered that day." She stepped out of the car and began running. Rupert caught her before she left the garage.

"All right. Show us the building. There's no time to argue, but walk—running draws attention we don't need."

"Okay," she agreed. She would have agreed to almost anything other than being sent back to the hotel room.

"This side of the street?"

"No, it's on the other side." Her strides were as long as possible without actually running. Rupert took her arm to slow her down, then matched his steps to hers to give the appearance they were out for an early evening stroll. Lance trailed several paces behind.

"There!" She stopped to point across the street. The craft shop looked the same as it had when she'd visited it earlier in the summer, only now a *CLOSED* sign hung on the door. The *FOR SALE* sign still sat in the corner of the empty shop next door. She tried to remember if the windows of the vacant shop had been covered by dull green blinds before. Staring with all her might, she wished she could see through walls and know if Cabe was somewhere in that building.

Rupert nudged her behind a cement planter box minutes before a car slowed to enter the alley. She could see the silhouettes of two men in the front seat of a small, green sports car. Shadows filled the alley making it impossible to identify the driver or his passenger. Her heart pounded, telling her Peter had arrived. The tall, thin man who stepped from the passenger side of the car was all the confirmation of her brother's identity she needed.

"It's Peter!" She started to rise.

"Stay here and keep down!" Rupert hissed the order.

"Someone's keeping an eye on the street," Lance said. "I saw movement at the craft store window. The blind moved on the abandoned side too. I'd guess Dempsky has guards posted at every entrance and at all of the windows."

"The agents aren't in place," Rupert cut in, speaking to Tisa, "but if Lance and I slip around the corner, we might be able to enter the alley from the next street without being seen."

She hated being left alone, but she didn't protest. Peter needed the two men far more than she did.

* * *

Cabe tried to estimate how long he'd been a prisoner. It seemed to him the light in the room was beginning to dim, which must mean it was nearly sunset. That meant at least eight hours had passed since he left the summer home where Tisa and Peter were hidden. The guard no longer sat on his chair. Dempsky had ordered him and whoever else was with him to watch the windows. Cabe tensed at each sound that reached his ears from outside, fearing Peter would be thrust through the door any minute.

"Evans." Cabe's ears barely registered the faint whisper that came from behind him. He'd tried to make contact with the man earlier and had concluded he was unconscious. Obviously the man was awake now and recognized him. "Key . . . shirt pocket."

Cabe's heart raced. If he could reach that key they might have a chance. No one seemed to be paying much attention to the prisoners. They were hidden behind what he'd decided was an old-fashioned store counter where a clerk in the distant past had stood to ring up sales.

With his cuffed hands, it took a great deal of wiggling and shifting to position himself where he could reach into the other man's pocket. Pinching the slim metal key with his fingertips he carefully drew it out of its hiding place. "Got it!" he whispered, letting the other man know of his success.

But now that he had the key, what could he do with it? There was no way he could twist his hands to a position where he might unlock the metal cuffs that cut into his wrists, and even if the man behind him turned to face the wall, chances of inserting the key in the locks to free him were practically nil.

"Can you turn over?" He hoped the voices coming from some-where behind them were enough to cover the slight sound of his voice.

"No." There was a long pause. "Ribs busted. My teeth." At first he thought the other man was saying his teeth were broken too, then he realized that the officer was telling him to place the key in his teeth.

"Okay." He hoped he understood what his fellow prisoner was suggesting, and that neither of them would drop the key. He eased his body a few feet farther along the ratty carpet, then waited, holding the key between two fingers. While he waited, he prayed. Transferring the key from his fingers to the cop's mouth was risky. If they dropped it . . . He felt a flicker of movement against his fingers, which he held so still he feared they might involuntarily twitch with the tension.

Once the key left his fingers, it was up to Cabe to scoot a little farther along the floor until his wrists were positioned near the other man's mouth. The cop was clearly in too much pain to do any of the moving.

It seemed to take forever, and the soft scrape of metal against metal, along with the strained breathing of the other man, made Cabe want to cringe. What if someone heard and came to see what they were up to? He didn't know how large the room was where they were being held, but from the instructions Dempsky had given earlier he was fairly certain an armed man was positioned inside the room near some kind of window.

He heard a faint click and felt the pressure ease on one wrist, but they were a long way from being out of danger. The first thing he needed to do was free the man who had just set him free, then check out their prison. He sensed time was running out and the turncoat cop would return with Peter any minute.

Cabe moved swiftly to free his other wrist and remove the shackles from the other man. Only when his fellow prisoner's hands were free did he take a good look at him. The hands were brown. Moving his gaze to the man's swollen, bloody face, which was almost unidentifiable, he noted the dark hair that curled around the other man's ears. "Vasquez!" He mouthed the man's name.

Vasquez nodded his head and offered a grimace that passed for a smile. He didn't move beyond slowly flexing his hands to regain circulation. Cabe scooted to the end of the counter which was blocking their view of the room. Reaching the empty chair where a guard had sat earlier, he eased his head and shoulders around the obstruction.

They were in a long narrow room which appeared to be a store of some kind. Display shelves loaded with junk lined the two long sides of the room. and at the far end were large, grimy windows on either side of a door. A sign hung on the door. He could read *OPEN,* which meant that from the street side, it would read *CLOSED.*

Stifling the impulse to make a dash for the door, he took his time studying the clutter that filled low tables between him and the exit. A slight movement caught his eye and had him hastily pulling his head back behind the counter. He'd been correct to think he and Vasquez were not alone in the room. Someone sat in a concealing wingback chair with a perfect view of anyone approaching the door.

Taking care not to make any noise, Cabe crawled to the other end of the counter. At this end he discovered a curtained doorway. By lying flat on the floor he could see under the curtain into what appeared to be an empty storeroom. The door at the back of the storeroom sported a heavy padlock which eliminated it as a means of escape. It most likely led to a loading dock or opened onto an alley, but it was the second door that caught his attention. It stood open, linking the small storage room to another area he couldn't see clearly. From it came the sound of voices.

Shrinking back behind the counter he tried to think of a plan. Vasquez was clearly too seriously injured to help, so it was up to him to find a way to reach the man standing between them and the front door. There were too many voices coming from the unseen room to risk exiting that way, so he would have to devise a plan to incapacitate the guard before Peter arrived.

"Jorge!" The man in the chair suddenly erupted to his feet and came running toward the counter behind which Cabe crouched. Thinking he'd been discovered, he groped for a weapon of any kind with which to defend himself. His hand fell on a heavy tape dispenser and he grasped it. To his surprise the man ran past him without glancing his way, straight into the storeroom.

"Jorge!" the guard yelled. "That girl, the one the boss has been looking for, she's across the street!" Fear poured through Cabe's veins. Did he mean Tisa? She should be safe at the summer home, not here.

"Quiet!" someone else hissed. "The cop just pulled into the alley with Lewis." There was excitement in his voice. Cabe felt only sickness and panic. Peter was walking innocently into a trap, and if he understood the guard right, Tisa was here too, and would also be trapped.

CHAPTER 20

Cabe looked toward the window, then back at the helpless man lying on the floor. This might be their only chance. He reached for Vasquez, who groaned slightly as Cabe picked him up. There was no question Cabe was hurting the injured man, but he couldn't leave him behind. Draping him over his shoulder in a fireman's carry, he charged toward the door. The knowledge that a bullet could strike him in the back any moment lent speed to his feet.

The door yielded to a quick twist of the old-fashioned lock, and Cabe staggered through with his burden. He looked around in a daze, unsure which direction to go. A shout, followed by the whistle of a bullet fired undoubtably from a handgun equipped with a silencer—sent him stumbling toward the cars parked farther down the street.

"Put me down!" Vasquez groaned. "Go after Tisa."

He turned to follow Vasquez's stare in time to see Tisa disappearing into the alley beside the store. The sight galvanized him into action. In a couple of strides he reached a car parked on the street. Placing Vasquez behind the vehicle where he would be out of the line of fire, he dropped his phone in the cop's lap before turning to race toward the alley.

Checking his headlong dash, he stopped at the corner of the building. Flattening himself against the wall, he moved his head until he could catch a quick glimpse down the alley. What he saw filled his veins with ice.

Peter stood before Ortega with his arms wrenched behind his back. Both Darren Dempsky and Bob White stood with guns leveled toward the lieutenant. Peter said something and White laughed.

Dempsky struck the side of Peter's head with his gun grip, causing the lieutenant's knees to buckle and his body to sag against Ortega.

"No one is going to believe Evans and I shot each other," Peter scoffed, still defiant.

"They will when I tell them how you objected to having a PI sharing your office, and the fight you had over Evans coming on to your sister," White mocked Peter.

"My sister will soon contradict that story. You're crazy, both of you, if you think anyone is going to believe that nonsense."

"Ah, but they will. You see, this is Evans's gun. It will be found in his hand, with only his fingerprints on it." Dempsky raised the pistol, aiming it at Peter.

"No!" Tisa's scream reached Cabe's ears, and he saw her leap from the shadows to run toward her brother.

"Tisa!" White turned, gasping her name in a startled cry. He reached for her, capturing her before she could reach Peter. She fought to free herself.

Taking advantage of the attention focused on Tisa, Cabe slipped into the alley, moving into the shadows provided by the disappearing sun. If only he had a weapon. His mind raced, searching for a way to provide Tisa with an opportunity to run. His greatest fear was that even if he created a diversion, she'd refuse to leave Peter. Tisa was the sort who would try to help him rescue her brother; she wasn't likely to abandon either Peter or him to their fate.

White held Tisa with little effort. The words White spoke in her ear didn't carry to where Cabe crouched, watching for a chance to rush the boyish-looking rogue cop. Whatever he said made Tisa angry. She struck out at him, and White pressed his gun against her neck.

"It's always been Peter!" White's voice was an angry snarl. "Ever since Norm and Dixie Lewis adopted you and that half-breed, you've been blind to every other man. With him dead, you would have turned to me, Tisa!" Cabe couldn't believe what the maniac was talking about, but the absurdity of it made it all the more dangerous.

Cabe prepared to leap. A strangled sound momentarily shifted his attention to Dempsky. For a moment Cabe thought Dempsky had been shot; seeing the agony on the crime boss's face, he felt a moment's sympathy for the other man.

"Let her go." There was no emotion in Dempsky's voice as he slowly walked toward Tisa and Bob, the steel barrel of his .45 pointed directly at them. Cabe inched closer, tensed to spring, but now he could see the gun was pointing at White, not Tisa. "Step away from her," Dempsky ordered.

White shifted the gun from Tisa to point it at Dempsky, so fast Cabe almost missed the movement. It was a standoff, but Dempsky's gun didn't waver.

A bullet from either gun could hit Tisa. Cabe began to run.

Shots rang out. White crumbled to the ground and Tisa fell with him. Blinded by indescribable rage, Cabe threw himself at Dempsky, but the man was already down. Grabbing Dempsky's weapon, which was really his, from where it lay in the dust, he turned toward Ortega. Again he was too late, Lance had Ortega by the throat and Rupert knelt at Peter's side. Two more agents with drawn guns materialized out of the darkness of the alley and a flurry of shots came from inside the building. Silence prevailed for several seconds, then a dozen agents crowded into the alley with four prisoners, two of whom were in need of medical attention, though their wounds didn't appear life threatening.

Staggering with sorrow and confusion, Cabe stumbled in the near darkness toward where Tisa had fallen. Tears streamed down his face when he touched her. He couldn't believe he wasn't hearing a ghost when he heard his name.

"Cabe." It was just a whisper of sound, but it brought tears to his eyes again. Tisa was alive! His arms closed around her, and he whispered a prayer of gratitude as it sank in that she wasn't even injured. His mind reviewed the scene that had played out in front of him seconds ago, and he realized that Darren Dempsky had saved Tisa's life. He didn't know how he felt about that, but as long as she was alive, that was all that mattered.

Tisa hugged him back, and he felt her tears against his neck. He remembered Peter saying she was unable to cry, but she was crying now. He felt her pull back against his arm, and he let her go. He watched her walk to where Darren Dempsky lay sprawled on his back in the dirt.

He thought his heart would break when she sat in the dirt, gently cradling Dempsky's head in her lap. He watched her stroke the face of one of the most wanted criminals in the country, and he moved closer, ready to protect her, when he realized Dempsky also was still alive. He tightened his grip on the weapon he still held in his hand.

"Tisa?" Cabe knew what the man was asking. Dempsky, too, may have had suspicions all along about the woman he knew as Patricia, but hearing White shout her name must have gelled all the pieces. Cabe had no doubts that Dempsky had figured out the puzzle of his little sister's disappearance.

"Yes, I'm here." Tisa's voice was like a caress, but Cabe wasn't certain she even knew what she had admitted. He had to steel himself not to feel jealous of the tender way she spoke to the fallen man.

"I couldn't let him kill you. I wasn't strong enough to save you . . . I didn't know Josie . . ." His voice trailed off, and Cabe knew the man was dying.

"Shh, don't talk." Tisa laid her cheek against Darren's. When her body began to shake, Cabe stepped forward to rest a hand on her shoulder, offering her solace.

When the paramedics arrived, Darren's head still rested in Tisa's lap, though he no longer breathed. The ambulance's lights revealed an expression of peace on his face. Tears streaked Tisa's face, but she seemed calm. Cabe helped her to her feet. She hugged him, then turned to hug Peter.

An agent approached them to speak with Cabe briefly. When Cabe turned back to Tisa, she was gone. He searched the dark shadows of the alley, which was now lit by the headlights of several vehicles. Then he saw her sitting against the side of the building with her knees drawn up and her head tilted back against the rough brick wall. Peter was kneeling beside her.

Cabe turned at the feel of a hand on his shoulder. "Good work," Woods said.

"The real credit should go to Peter Lewis," Cabe responded, watching paramedics, assisted by law officers, examine the various prisoners' wounds.

"I offered him a job but he turned me down," Dave said. "He'd rather stay in Salt Lake and sleep in his own bed at night. That sister of his is sharp too. It was from her call that Peter caught on to White's plan to separate him from the rest of the men preparing to search the mine."

"And he alerted you to make certain your people followed him and White to me," Cabe finished the story.

Fifteen minutes later Cabe was aware Peter had moved from his position beside Tisa to stand beside him as the paramedics lifted the bodies of both White and Dempsky into the ambulance. Together they watched the ambulance make its way slowly down the street. There was no need for speed or flashing lights.

"I've known Bob since we were children." Peter stared after the disappearing taillights.

"He shot Carmichael and Jones, Aldredge too, and he had no qualms about killing you."

"I know." Peter's shoulders slumped with the weight of that knowledge.

At last Cabe knelt to tuck his arms beneath Tisa and lift her against his chest. She wrapped her arms around his neck and held on with all her might. With Peter beside him, they walked to the end of the alley where another ambulance waited. With infinite care, Cabe set Tisa on a waiting gurney, then prepared to climb in beside her.

"Stay with her," Peter said.

"You're going to the hospital to be checked out too, aren't you?" Cabe asked.

"No. It's time for me to go get Lara. Tisa's in good hands now." Then Peter turned to walk toward a waiting squad car.

EPILOGUE

Peter paced the floor and looked at his watch.

"No amount of pacing will hurry a woman," Cabe drawled from where he sat sprawled in a gracefully carved chair.

"I don't know how you can just sit there." Peter sighed and looked at his watch again before sinking into the chair next to Cabe. "She's dumped six fiancés! Doesn't that worry you even a little?"

"No." He wasn't just putting up a good front for his friend. He really wasn't worried. Tisa would arrive in plenty of time. "This is why we didn't tell you sooner. It was Tisa's idea to invite you and Lara to accompany me to the temple this morning and tell you after you got here. I figured Lara needed a little more warning than that to get her hair done, buy a dress, and arrange for a sitter for all day. Mother warned me that if I wanted to be on good terms with my sister-in-law for the next fifty or so years, I'd better not spring that kind of surprise on her. That's why we told you last week."

"You're really leaving the Bureau and going to work for the county sheriff's office?" Peter shook his head. "If you'd asked I could have gotten you on with the city."

"The county suits me, especially since we'll be living at the south end of it." He watched Peter pace the length of the room a few more times, then pause in front of him.

"I haven't dared ask before," his soon-to-be brother-in-law started hesitantly. "Is she really all right? Does she know she was born Teresa Dempsky? Did you tell her about the DNA tests?"

Cabe was silent, thinking back six months to the night Darren Dempsky died. He and Tisa had talked about Dempsky's criminal record, and they had both signed statements attesting to all they had witnessed. They had talked, too, about small things she remembered from the distant past. He knew she had been halfway between her fifth and sixth birthdays when that truck driver had found her, and that most adults remember little more than vague impressions of the years prior to that. Tisa was no different, but she no longer cared about the past.

When he'd tried to bring up the subject, she'd made it clear she didn't want to discuss it. He suspected that somewhere deep in her heart she knew Darren was her brother, and that in spite of all the evil in his life, she would always love the good part only she had seen. As for her parents, she had discovered she was a child of God, and that was enough.

"Cabe!" Tisa arrived flushed and laughing, a plastic dress-bag draped over one arm and Cabe's mother and Lara trailing behind carrying small suitcases. "I was afraid you would give up on me. Lara forgot her recommend and we had to go back to the house, then I remembered . . ."

He stood and shifted the dress-bag from her to her brother before kissing her to silence. "I'll never give up on you," he murmured in her ear. Straightening, he offered her his arm. "I think it's time to shed another fiancé. Number seven is tired of this fiancé business and would like to try his hand at being a husband."

Jennie Hansen graduated from Ricks College in Idaho, and Westminster College in Utah. She has been a newspaper reporter, editor, and for the past twenty years has been a librarian for the Salt Lake City library system.

Her Church service has included teaching in all auxiliaries and serving in stake and ward Primary presidencies. She has also served as a den mother, stake public affairs coordinator, ward chorister, education counselor in her ward Relief Society, and teacher improvement coordinator.

Jennie and her husband, Boyd, live in Salt Lake County. Their five children are all married and have so far provided them with six grandchildren.

Abandoned is Jennie's eleventh book for the LDS market.

Jennie enjoys hearing from her readers, who can write to her in care of Covenant Communications, P.O. Box 416, American Fork, UT 84003-0416.